6/24

Omnibu

CAST, IN ORDER OF DISAPPEARANCE
and
SO MUCH BLOOD

Simon Brett

Back-In-Print Books Ltd

Published by Back-In-Print Books Ltd 2001
ISBN 1 903552 32 X
Previously published in Great Britain by
Victor Gollancz under ISBN 0 575 01998 0 and 0 575 02116 0

A CIP catalogue record is available from the British Library.

Printed and bound on demand by
Lightning Source.

Back-In-Print Books Ltd
P O Box 47057
London SW18 1YW
020 8637 0975

BY THE SAME AUTHOR:

STAR TRAP
&
AN AMATEUR CORPSE

A COMEDIAN DIES
&
THE DEAD SIDE OF THE MIKE

SITUATION TRAGEDY
&
MURDER UNPROMPTED

MURDER IN THE TITLE
&
NOT DEAD, ONLY RESTING

DEAD GIVEAWAY
&
WHAT BLOODY MAN IS THAT?

A SERIES OF MURDERS
&
CORPORATE BODIES

A RECONSTRUCTED CORPSE
&
SICKEN AND SO DIE
&
DEAD ROOM FARCE

This is a Back-In-Print Book.

- This title was out of print for some time but Back-In-Print Books has brought it back in to print because of demand from Simon Brett fans.
- This re-print was produced on demand using up-to-date digital printing technology.
- Paper and print quality are higher than most conventionally printed paperback novels.
- Digital printing may cost somewhat more but ensures that book titles need not go out of print as long as there are readers who want them.

What other titles are available from BiP?

Check out our web site at www.backinprint.co.uk for other titles released by Back-In-Print Books Ltd and news about forthcoming titles.

Do you want any other titles?

If you know of a title which is out of print and you think there might be a reasonable demand please contact us.

Back-In-Print Books Ltd
P O Box 47057
London
SW18 1YW
020 8637 0975

e-mail: info@backinprint.co.uk

CAST, IN ORDER OF DISAPPEARANCE

TO LUCY

When Simon Brett studied at Oxford he became President of the OUDS, appeared in cabarets and directed the Oxford Theatre Group at the Edinburgh Festival Fringe in 1967.

Later he worked as a light entertainment producer for BBC radio and TV before taking up writing full time in 1979.

Simon created the Charles Paris and Mrs Pargeter detective series and, to his fans' relief, he is still writing more. He also made a name as the author of the radio and TV series *After Henry*. The radio series *No Commitments*, the best-selling *How to be a Little Sod* and the novel *Shock to the System* filmed starring Michael Caine are other fruits of his imaginative mind. He is married, has three children and lives in a village on the South Downs.

CONTENTS

CHAPTER ONE

Cinderella Alone

'CHARLES, CHARLES LOVE, it's your cue.'

Charles Paris jerked out of his doze. He looked down for the script on his knees, but *The Times* crossword with two completed clues stared blankly up at him. He dropped the paper, opened his script, and looked hopefully at the little actress next to him for the page number.

'Page 27, Line 4,' the producer snapped with all the exasperation of a large mortgage in Pinner and another nineteen years till his BBC pension.

'Sorry ...' said Charles, trying to remember the producer's name. 'Sorry, love,' failing to do so.

He read his lines with leaden incomprehension. A twinge of guilt for having done no preparation soon passed when he heard the lines he was reading. Wasn't anyone writing good radio plays any more? As his scene ground to a halt, he looked across at the spindly raffia-haired youth responsible. The Author sat by the producer in a twisted attitude of intense concentration or bad piles. Every now and then he winced as another nuance of his writing was steamrollered.

The play reached its denouement with all the impact of a wet dish-cloth, and there was a ripple of dejected laughter. 'Well,' said the producer, 'now the real work starts. But first let's send the lovely Sylvia for some tea.'

Charles took the opportunity to go to the Gents and lose lunchtime's excesses of wine. To his annoyance the Author joined him at the adjacent urinal. Charles resolutely pretended he hadn't noticed.

'Um, Charles ...'

'Yes.'

'I hope you don't mind my saying ...'

'No, of course not.'

'Well, I'd seen the Inspector rather Grand Guignol ...'

'And I thought you read him rather ...'

'Yes ...?'

'Well, Petit Guignol.'

'Ah,' said Charles Paris. 'I'll try to do something about it.'

Even Arctic nights end, and so, somehow, did the day in the studio. Charles' performance, however Grand its Guignol, was fixed on tape. It all seemed to matter less as he stood in the BBC Club and the first large Bell's glowed inside him. It was December 3rd and the short walk from Broadcasting House to the Club had been breathtakingly cold after the recycled warmth of the studio.

Sherlock Forster (known to his intimates as Len) was an undemanding companion. A distinguished radio actor and a great piss-artist, he had been playing the murderer in the play and was now slumped against the bar, caressing a large Riesling, his toupee'd head deep into the *Evening Standard*. 'Hoarding outside said "Motorist Shot Dead". Thought it might have pushed the bloody Arabs out of the headlines,' he said to no one in particular.

'Did it?' asked Charles.

'No such luck. Main story's still bloody petrol queues. "Motorist Shot Dead" is way down the column.'

'Where'd it happen?'

'Just off the M4 somewhere. Apparently the bloke'd run out of petrol, got out of the car, and some bugger shot him.'

'Poor sod.'

'Police are treating it as a case of murder.'

'Shrewd of them. Anything else in the paper?'

'Well, the Archbishop of Canterbury's being driven round in a Morris Minor to save petrol. And a couple of Cabinet ministers turned up at the House in a Mini.'

'Chauffeur-driven, no doubt.'

The second large Bell's changed the glow within Charles to a feeling of positive well-being. Forty-seven years old and still attractive to women. The lack of matinee-idol good looks which had kept him from being a star in the Fifties was no longer a disadvantage. He had worn better than a lot of his contemporaries. Hair still grew thick and only lightly silvered at the temples. He looked at Len's theatrical toupee and felt grateful.

Life, Charles reflected, was not too bad. Even financially, for once. He was still flush from a ghastly television series in which he'd minced around some unlikely Tudor monarch in doublet and hose for a couple of months. And when he'd drunk through that money, or when the tax man caught up with him, something else would happen. He cast a professional eye round the bar. A few standard-issue BBC spinsters; one or two attractive younger secretaries, sentried by men; nothing worth chatting up.

'Petrol, bloody petrol,' said Len. 'There's nothing else in the paper. Look at this—"Attractive 9-year-old model Patti Winchester isn't worried. She's been showing a leg and riding her bicycle for months now".'

Charles glanced over. 'Tatty.'

'Hmm. Footballer Bobby Lithgoe has bought a bicycle too.'

'Wow.'

'And Marius Steen has put the Rolls in the garage.'

'Steen? What does it say about him?'

' "Impresario Marius Steen, the man behind such stage successes as *One Thing After Another, Who's Afraid of the Big Bed Wolf?* and, of course, his current smash-hit at the King's Theatre, *Sex of One and Half a Dozen of the Other,* phoned today at his Berkshire home, said, 'We'll leave the Rolls in the garage and use the Datsun.' " '

'He's got a good publicity machine. It's just a straight plug for that bloody *Sex of One* ...'

'Clocked up a thousand performances last week.'

'God. How revolting.'

'Big party on-stage at the King's on Saturday.'

'It'll probably run forever. There's no justice.' Charles picked up Len's empty glass. 'Another one of those?'

'Why not?'

Predictably the BBC Club had led to the George, the George to a small pub off Drury Lane, and at about midnight Charles, having lost Len somewhere along the line, found himself leaning against a banister in the Montrose with a pint in his hand.

The Montrose (a small theatrical drinking club off the Haymarket) was full as usual. A lot of rooms on different levels, shoddy like converted bedsitters, overflowing with actors talking and gesturing loudly.

'... got a *Z-Cars* coming up. Small part, but nice ...'

and he said to William, "You've got as much humour as a crutch!" She was furious ...'

'... working towards a modern commedia format ...'

'... ultimately it's a matter of identity ...'

'Hello, Charles.' A voice detached itself from the rest and Charles focused on a small blonde girl in front of him. 'Jacqui.'

Jacqui had a top-floor flat in Archer Street, opposite a casino, whose lights usually flashed yellow all night. But now with the power restrictions, they were dark. Only the blue glow of a solitary street lamp touched their anaemic neon tubes. But there were still the noises of the casino—the hum and slam of taxis, the shouts of drunkards and the chatter of Chinese gamblers in the street below.

Charles looked at Jacqui with pleasure. She was an actress-cum-dancer-cum-most-things he'd met in pantomime at Worthing. He'd been Baron Hardup, Cinderella's father; and she had been a Villager, White Mouse and Court Lady (for the Finale). They'd had quite a pleasant time in Worthing. It was good to see her again.

But she looked upset. Charles filled his glass from the bottle of Southern Comfort and slumped back on to the white fur of the bed, shaking a small oil-lamp on the bedside table. 'And you can't get in touch with him?'

'No. I've tried both the houses. And the office.'

'I wouldn't worry, Jacqui. He'll call you.'

'Maybe.' She still looked tense and hurt. Strange, how a girl like that, who'd had everyone and done everything, could be so affected by one dirty old man not getting in touch with her. And Marius Steen of all people.

Jacqui stretched out her strong dancer's legs and stared at her toes. 'No. He often doesn't call for weeks on end. He's moody. Sometimes he doesn't want me around. I'm his secret vice. Just a tottie. I mean, if he's going to a do with the Queen Mum, he can't take a tart along.' Charles grunted uncomfortably. 'No, that's what I am. I don't really want to be more than that. He's an old man, he's nice to me, we have a few giggles, that's all. It couldn't possibly last. I know that.' She sounded as if she was bravely repeating a formula she didn't believe.

'When did you last see him?'

'Saturday afternoon.'

'For God's sake, what is it now? Only Monday. Give him a chance.'

'I know, but this time I think it's over.'

'Why?'

'When I rang, there was a message. Said I wasn't to contact him again.'

'Ah.'

Jacqui poured herself a large glass of Southern Comfort and took a savage swallow at it. 'Bugger him. I'm not going to get miserable about an old sod like that.' She rose and flopped down on the bed beside Charles. 'There are other men.'

'Still older men, I'm afraid.'

'You're not old.'

'I'm forty-seven.'

'That's cradle-snatching by my standards,' she said with a wry laugh. Then she stopped short. 'Old sod. It's all because of the knighthood.'

'Hmm?'

'His last ambition. Reckoned he might get one this New Year.'

'Services to the Theatre?'

'I suppose so. And I suppose I let down the image. Well, I don't care about him.' She snuggled up to Charles.

'Jacqui, am I being used merely for revenge? As a sex object?'

'Yes. Any objections?'

'No.'

Charles kissed her gently. He felt protective towards her, as if she might suddenly break down.

Her tongue flickered round the inside of his mouth and they drew apart. 'You smell like a distillery,' she said.

'I am a distillery,' he replied fatuously and hugged her close to him. She had a comforting little body, and the smoky taste of her mouth was familiar. 'Hmm.

We had a good time in Worthing. We were better than the dirty postcards.'

Jacqui smiled closely into his eyes and her hand fumbled for his zip. She couldn't find the little metal pull-tag. An exasperated breath. 'You know, Charles, I always think it's simpler to take your own things off. If you're both in agreement.'

'I'm in agreement,' said Charles. He rolled over to the side of the bed and fumblingly undressed. When he turned round, Jacqui was lying naked on the bed, familiar in the pale street light. 'Charles.'

'Must take my socks off. Otherwise I feel like an obscene photo.'

He lay down beside her and hugged her, warm on the fur. They held each other close, hands gliding over soft flesh.

After a few moments Charles rolled away. 'Not very impressive, am I?'

'Don't worry. It doesn't matter.'

'No.' A pause. 'Sorry. I'm not usually like this.'

'I know,' Jacqui said meaningfully. 'And I know what to do about it.'

He felt her moving, a soft kiss on his stomach, then the warmth of her breath as it strayed downwards. 'Jacqui, don't bother. I'm not in the mood. It's the booze or ...'

'OK. Poor old Baron Hardup.'

'I'm sorry, Jacqui.'

'Don't worry. All I really need is a good cuddle.'

'Tonight I'm afraid that's all I can offer you.' And he hugged her very closely like a teddy bear in his arms. In a moment he had sunk into a heavy, but troubled sleep.

CHAPTER TWO

The Fairy Godmother

AS CHARLES WALKED past the manicured front gardens of Muswell Hill, he tried to piece together his feelings. It was a long time since he had been so churned up inside. For years life had jogged on from hangover to hangover, with the odd affair between drinks, and nothing had affected him much. But now he felt jumpy and panicky.

Impotence is perhaps not unusual in a man of forty-seven. And anyway it probably wasn't impotence, just the dreaded Distiller's Droop. Nothing to worry about.

But that wasn't the important part of his feelings. There was a change in his attitude to Jacqui. He felt an enormous need to protect the girl, as if, by failing in bed, he had suddenly become responsible for her. She seemed desperately vulnerable, like a child in a pram or an old man in a launderette. Perhaps these were paternal feelings, the sort he had somehow never developed for his daughter.

Together with this new warmth came the knowledge that he had to go and see Frances. 'Marriage,' Charles reflected wryly as he clicked open her wrought-iron gate, 'is the last refuge of the impotent.'

She wasn't there. Still at school. Not even six o clock yet. Charles had a key and let himself in. His hand instinctively found the light-switch.

The house hadn't changed. As ever, a pile of books to be marked on the dining table, concert programmes, an old Edinburgh Festival brochure. Earnest paperbacks about psychology and sociology on the book-shelves. Auntie May's old upright piano with the lid up. And on top, that terrible posed photograph of Juliet with pigtails and a grim smile over the brace on her teeth. Next to it, the puzzle jug. Then that windswept snapshot of him, Charles Paris, taken on holiday on Arran. It was a real LP sleeve photograph. Better than any of that expensive rubbish he'd had done for *Spotlight*.

He resisted the temptation to raid the drinks cupboard, switched on the television and slumped into the sofa they'd bought at Harrods when flush from selling the film rights of his one successful play.

He heard the guarded voice of a newscaster, then the picture buzzed and swelled into life. The news was still dominated by petrol and the prospect of rationing. Charles couldn't get very excited about it.

Police had identified the motorist shot off the M4 at Theale. A blurred snapshot was blown up to fill the screen. It had the expression of a man already dead. There had been no petrol in the victim's car; the back right-hand wing was dented; he had been shot through the head and left by the roadside. Police were still trying to find a motive for the killing.

'In the second day of the Sally Nash trial at the Old Bailey, a 17-year-old girl, Miss C., told of sex-parties at London hotels. A lot of show-business people—' Charles switched over to the serious face of Eamonn Andrews talking to someone about petrol rationing. He switched again and got a sizzling snowstorm through which a voice imparted mathematical information.

'Sodding UHF.' He got down on his hands and knees in front of the box and started moving the portable aerial about. The snowstorm varied in intensity. Then he remembered the UHF contrast knob and went round the set to turn it.

'Television repair man.' He'd been too close to the sound to hear Frances come in.

'Hello.' He stood up. 'Look. The picture's perfect.'

'Are you doing an Open University degree?'

'No. I was just getting it right. It's the UHF contrast.'

'Ah.' She looked at him. 'How are you?'

'Bad.'

'I thought so. Do you want something to eat?'

'I don't know.'

'That means yes. Did you have lunch?'

'Pie in a pub.'

'Ugh.' Frances went into the kitchen and started opening cupboards. She continued talking through the serving hatch. It was restfully familiar.

'I went down to see Juliet and Miles at the weekend.'

'Ah.'

'Nice to get out of town.'

'Yes.'

'They said they'd love to see you. You should go down, it's a lovely place.'

'Yes. I will. At some stage. How's Miles?'

'Oh, he's doing very well.'

'Ah.' Charles visualised his son-in-law, Miles Taylerson, the rising executive, neat in his executive house on his executive estate in Pangbourne with his executive car and his executive suits and his executive haircut. 'Do you like Miles, Frances?'

'Juliet's very happy with him.' 'Which I suppose,' Charles reflected, 'is some sort of answer.' Thinking of his daughter made him think of Jacqui again and he felt a flutter of panic in his stomach.

Frances produced the food very quickly. It was a dish with frankfurters and sour cream. Something new. Charles felt jealous at the thought that she was developing, learning new things without him. 'Tell you what,' he said, 'shall I whip down to the off-licence and get a bottle of wine? Make an evening of it.'

'Charles, I can't "make an evening of it". I've got to be at a PTA meeting at 7.30.'

'Parents-Teachers? Oh, but can't you—' He stopped. No, you can't come back to someone you walked out on twelve years ago and expect them to be instantly free. Even if you have kept in touch and had occasional reconciliations. 'Have a drink together later, maybe.'

'Maybe. If you're still here.'

'I will be.'

'What is the matter, Charles?'

'I don't know. Male menopause?' It was a phrase he'd read in a colour supplement somewhere. Didn't really know if it meant anything.

'You think you've got problems,' said Frances.

She was always busy. Two things about Frances—she was always busy and she was never surprised. These, in moments of compatibility, were her great qualities; in moments of annoyance, her most irritating traits.

The next morning she cooked a large breakfast, brought it up to him in bed, and hurried off to school. Charles lay back on the pillows and felt mellow. He saw the familiar gable of the Jenkinses opposite (they'd had the paint work done blue) and felt sentimentality well up inside him.

Each time he came back to Frances, he seemed to feel more sentimental. At first. Then after a few days they'd quarrel or he'd feel claustrophobic and leave again. And go on a blinder.

The impotence panic seemed miles away. It was another person who had felt that nausea of fear in his stomach. Long ago.

They had made love beautifully. Frances' body was like a well-read book, familiar and comforting. Her limbs were thinner, the tendons a bit more prominent and the skin of her stomach loose. But she was still soft and warm. They had made love gently and easily, their bodies remembering each other's rhythms. It's something you never forget, Charles reflected. Like riding a bicycle.

He switched on the radio by the bedside. It was tuned to Capital Radio—pop music and jingles. So that's what Frances listened to. Strange. It was so easy to condemn her as bourgeois and predictable. When you actually came down to it, everything about her was unexpected. What appeared to be passivity was just the great calm that emanated from her.

When he was dressed, he needed human companionship and so rang his agent. 'Maurice Skellern Artistes,' said a voice.

'Maurice.'

'Who wants him?'

'Maurice, I know that's you. It's me, Charles.'

'Oh, hello. How'd the radio go?'

'Ghastly. It was the worst script I've ever seen.'

'It's work, Charles.'

'Yes, just.'

'Were you rude to anybody?'

'Not very. Not as rude as I felt like being.'

'Who to?'

'The producer.'

'Charles, you can't afford it. Already you'll never get another job on *Doctor Who*.'

'I wasn't very rude. Anything coming up?'

'Some vacancies on the permanent company at Hornchurch.'

'Forget it.'

'Chance of a small part in a *Softly, Softly*.'

'Put my name up.'

'New play at one of these new fringe theatres. About transvestites in a prison. Political overtones. Written by a convict.'

'It's not really *me*, is it, Maurice?' in his best theatrical knight voice.

'I don't know what is *you* any more, Charles. I sometimes wonder if you want to work at all.'

'Hmm. So do I.'

'What are you living on at the moment?'

'My second childhood.'

'I don't get ten per cent of that.'

'No. What else is new?'

'Nothing.'

'Come on. Give us the dirt.'

'Isn't any. Well, except for the Sally Nash business ...'

'Oh yes?'

'Well, you know who the disc jockey was, for a start ...' And Maurice started. He was one of London's recognised authorities on theatrical gossip. Malicious rumour had it that he kept a wall-chart with coloured pins on who was sleeping with who. The Sally Nash case gave him good copy. It was the Lambton affair of the theatre, complete with whips, boots, two-way mirrors and unnamed 'show-business personalities'. For half an hour Maurice named them all. Eventually, he rang off. That's why he was such a lousy agent. Spent all his time gossiping.

By the Thursday morning Charles' mellowness felt more fragile. When he woke at nine, Frances had already gone to school. He tottered downstairs and made some coffee to counteract the last night's Beaujolais. The coffee tasted foul. Laced with Scotch, it tasted better. He drank it down, poured a glass of neat Scotch and went upstairs to dress.

The inside of his shirt collar had dark wrinkles of dirt, and his socks made their presence felt. Soon he'd have to get Frances to wash something or go back to Hereford Road and pick up some more clothes.

He sloped back downstairs. Frances' *Guardian* was neatly folded on the hall chest. No time to read it at school. Organised read in the evening. It had to be the *Guardian*.

Charles slumped on to the Harrods sofa and started reading an article on recycling waste paper. It failed to hold his attention. He checked the television times and switched on *Play School*. The picture was muzzy. He started fiddling with the UHF contrast knob. The phone rang.

'Hello.'

'Charles.'

'Jacqui. Where on earth did you get this number?'

'You gave it me ages ago. Said you were contactable there in the last resort.'

'Yes. I suppose it is my last resort. What's up?'

'It's about Marius.'

'Yes?'

'I tried to contact him again. Went to the house in Bayswater. It was a stupid thing to do, I suppose. Should've left him alone. Should be able to take a bloody hint. I don't know.'

'What happened?'

'He wasn't there. But this morning I had a letter.'

'From Marius?'

'Yes. It wasn't signed, but it must be. It's horrid. Charles, I'm shit-scared.'

'Shall I come round?'

'Can you?'

'Yes.' A pause. 'Why did you ring me, Jacqui?'

'Couldn't think of anyone else.'

After he had put the phone down, Charles switched off *Play School*. He took an old envelope from the table and wrote on it in red felt pen, "THANKS. GOODBYE. SEE YOU.' Then he left the house and set out for Highgate tube station.

CHAPTER THREE

Who Was at the Ball

CHARLES LOOKED AT the sheet of paper. It was pale blue with a dark bevelled edge and, on it, scrawled in black biro capitals, was an uncompromising message. Basically, it told Jacqui to get lost when she wasn't wanted. And basically was the way it was done. The language was disgusting and the note anonymous. 'Charming. Are you sure it's from him?'

'No one else had any reason.'

'And is the language in character?'

'Yes, he never was very delicate. Particularly when he was angry. Could be quite frightening.'

'Paper familiar?'

'Yes. He had it on his desk at Orme Gardens. Some headed, some plain like this.'

'Hmm. Well, there's only one way to treat shit of this sort.' Charles screwed the note up into a dark glass ashtray and set it on fire with the table lighter. When the flame had gone, he blew the black ash carefully into the waste-paper basket. 'When did it come?'

'It was on the mat when I got up. About eleven. A bit after.'

'Come by post?'

'No. Plain envelope. On the table.'

Charles leant over and picked it up. Blue, matching the paper. Told him nothing. 'And I suppose you didn't ...'

'See anyone? No.'

'It's a fairly nasty way of breaking something off, isn't it?'

'Yes.' She looked near to tears. 'And I thought it was going so well.'

'Perhaps he's just a nasty man.'

'He could be, I know. But with me he was always kind. When we were in France, he—'

'When was this?'

'We went in August, came back in October. Marius's got a villa down the South. Sainte-Maxime. It's a lovely place. Private beach.'

'Very nice.'

'Anyway, he took me there to recuperate.'

'What from?'

'I'd had an abortion.'

'His baby?'

'Yes. He fixed it up, but it didn't quite go right. I was ill. So he took me out to Sainte-Maxime.

'And he was there all the time?'

'Yes. He'd been ill too—had a minor heart-attack. He was meant to be resting, though, of course, being Marius, he was in touch with the office every day.'

'It was just the two of you out there?'

'Mostly. Some friends of his dropped in, theatre people. And Nigel for a bit.'

'Nigel?'

'His son.'

'Oh yes.' Charles remembered someone once mentioning that Steen had a son. 'I didn't think they got on.'

'That was ages ago. They made it up, more or less. Nigel works in the business.'

'And while you were out in France, it was all OK? Between you and Marius?'

'Yes. We had a marvellous time. He was very silly and childish. And kind.'

'And now he sends you notes like that. You can't think of any reason for the change in his attitude?'

Jacqui hesitated. 'No. Would you like some lunch?'

While she cooked, Charles went down to the off-licence and bought a bottle of wine. It was obvious from Jacqui's manner that she did have an idea why Steen had changed. And that she was going to tell him. It was only a matter of waiting.

The lunch was unremarkable. Jacqui was a frozen food cook. He remembered it from Worthing. Endless beef-burgers and cod steaks with bright peas and diced vegetables. But the wine made it passable. They talked back to Worthing, hedging round the subject of Steen. Eventually, as Charles drained the bottle evenly into their two glasses, he asked, 'What do you want me to do, Jacqui?'

'What do you mean?'

'You've brought me round here for a reason.'

'I was frightened.'

'Yes, but there's something else.'

'Yes.' She looked very vulnerable. Again he felt the sense of debt that had started when he failed her in bed. The contract was unfulfilled. If he could not serve her in one way, he would serve her in another. It's strange, he thought, is this what chivalry's come to?

'I do want you to do something for me, Charles. It's sort of awkward. You see, I think I know ... I think I might know why Marius is behaving like this. He might think ... you see ...' Charles bided his time. Jacqui looked at him directly and said, 'You've heard of all this Sally Nash business?'

'Yes. Is Marius involved in that?'

'Not really. Not with the prostitutes. It's just ... well, she, Sally Nash, used to be at some parties that we went to.'

'Just ordinary parties?'

'Well ...' Jacqui smiled sheepishly. 'No, not ordinary parties really. Things happened.'

'I didn't know that was your scene. I thought you only slept with one man at a time and ...' Charles tailed off, embarrassed.

'No, it's not my sort of thing. But Marius was into all that. Only a bit. Nothing very serious.'

'Hmm.'

'Don't sound so bloody superior. It's easy for a man. If you're a girl you have to get interested in what your bloke's interested in. If he's mad on football, you watch *Match of the Day*. If it's two-way mirrors, well ...'

'Was it like that in the South of France?'

'No. It was only a couple of times we ever did it. Last June. There was a party in Holland Park, and one near Marble Arch.'

'But they were Sally Nash's parties?'

'She was there.'

'And what's the danger? Are you going to be called as a witness?'

'Bloody hell.' She looked very affronted. 'Look, I may be a tart, but I'm not a whore.' Charles tried vaguely to work out the distinction, but fortunately Jacqui clarified. 'All these girls they're calling in the trial do it for money.'

'I'm sorry. Then what's the ...?'

'There are some photographs.'

'Of you and Steen at the party?'

'Yes. With some other people.'

'Naughty photos?'

'A bit naughty. But I think that's why Marius doesn't want to be seen with me.

'Why? Are the photographs going to come up in court?'

'No, they aren't. But Marius must think they will. It's the only explanation.'

'But if you're both in the photos, he could be identified anyway. It doesn't make any difference whether he's seen with you or not.

'No, Charles. The point is, they can't tell it's him. His face is covered.'

'Don't tell me—with a black leather mask.'

'Yes.'

'Really? I was joking.'

'Well it is.'

'But you, on the other hand, are not covered?'

'No. Far from it.'

'Hmm. How do you know they won't come up in court?'

'Because I've got them. I paid a lot of money for them.'

'Did someone blackmail you?'

'No. The Sally Nash trial started on Friday, and I bought them off the bloke who took them on Saturday.'

'How much?'

'Thousand quid.'

Charles looked at her quizzically and she explained. 'Marius had given me some money to buy a car, but it hardly seems worth buying one now, with all this petrol scene.'

Charles reflected momentarily on the difference between a tart and a whore and decided he was being a bit harsh. Particularly as Jacqui continued, 'I wanted to give them to Marius as a present. Set his mind at rest. And now I can't get to see him. I daren't send them through the post or letter-box, because his secretary'll see them ...'

Suddenly Charles' role in the proceedings became very clear to him. 'And so you want me to deliver them?'

Armed with an innocuous-looking brown envelope, Charles Paris returned to his room in Hereford Road, Bayswater. It was a depressing furnished bedsitter, which he'd moved into when he left Frances. Nothing except his clothes and scripts gave it any identity. The furniture had been painted grey by some earlier occupant, but was mostly obscured by drip-dry shirts on wire hangers. A low upholstered chair with wooden arms sat in front of the gas-fire. There was a small table covered with paper and carbons, a rickety kitchen chair, a single bed shrouded in yellow candlewick, and in one corner, inadequately hidden by plastic curtain, a sink and gas-ring.

Whenever Charles entered the room, fumes of depression threatened to choke him. Every now and then, in a surge of confidence, he would consider moving, but he never got round to it. The room was somewhere to sleep and he did his best to ensure that that was all he did there.

He got back about five and, before the atmosphere of the room had time to immobilise him, opened the cupboard, got out a half-full bottle of Bell's and poured himself a healthy measure. After a substantial swallow, he felt he could look at his surroundings. It was more of a mess than usual. Candlewick in disarray on the unmade bed, coffee cup with a white crust on the table. Cold December air was gushing through the open window. He remembered leaving it to air the place on ... when was it? Monday? Yes, Monday, 3rd December. The day he'd done that bloody awful radio play.

He slammed the window and put on the gas-fire. It hissed resentfully but came alight (which was more than it sometimes did). He felt strongly in need of a bath, stripped off his grubby clothes and put on a shapeless towelling dressing-gown. Taking a fivepence from his change, he went down to the bathroom on the first landing, checked that the water wasn't running hot, and fed the meter.

Then he remembered soap and towel. Upstairs again to get them. Inevitably, the bathroom door was locked when he returned. The sound of running water came from inside.

Charles hammered on the door and shouted abuse, but the strange sing-song voice that replied over the sound of water told him it was useless. One of the Swedish girls. There seemed to be hundreds of them in the house. And, he thought as he savagely stumped upstairs, all of them old boots. They really shattered the myth of Scandinavian beauty, that lot. Spotty girls with glasses and ruggerplayers' legs. He slammed the door, picked up the whisky bottle and fell into the chair.

The gas-fire spluttered at him as he sat and thought. There was something odd about the whole business with Jacqui. Her explanation about the photographs seemed unconvincing. In fact, her account of Steen's sudden change of behaviour didn't ring true either. A man in his position who wanted to get rid of a girl-friend needn't go to the length of obscene notes.

For a moment the thought crossed Charles' mind that he was being used in some sort of plot. To carry something. What? Drugs? Or just what Jacqui said it was—dirty pictures? But it seemed ridiculous. A much simpler explanation was that she was telling the truth.

The way to find out, of course, was to look in the envelope. He'd known since he had had the photographs that sooner or later he would. And, he reasoned, Jacqui must have assumed he would. She hadn't asked him not to; the envelope was unsealed. But he still felt slightly guilty as he shuffled them into his hand.

There were six, and they were exactly what Jacqui had said they would be—obscene pictures of her and Marius Steen. Perhaps obscene was the wrong word; they didn't have any erotic effect on Charles; but they intrigued and rather revolted him.

The photographs had the posed quality of amateur dramatics. Steen's body was old, a thin belly and limbs like a chicken's. The tatty little leather mask made him look ridiculous. But, Charles was forced to admit, the old man was rather well endowed.

But it was the sight of Jacqui that affected him. There she was in a series of contrived positions—astride Steen, bending down in front of him, under him on a bed. The sight was a severe shock to Charles; it made him feel almost sick. Not the acts that were going on; he'd seen and done worse, and somehow they seemed very mild and meaningless on these shoddy little snapshots. But it was the fact that it was Jacqui which upset him. He didn't feel jealousy or lust, but pity and again the urgent desire to protect her. It was as if he was seeing the photographs as her father.

A click and silence told him that the gas meter had run out. Blast, he hadn't got a ten p. Brusquely, he shoved the photographs back into the envelope, sealed it and dressed. Then he started his campaign to get to see Marius Steen. It was half past seven. He went to the call box on the landing and rang up Bernard Walton, currently starring in *Virgin on the Ridiculous* at the Dryden Theatre.

CHAPTER FOUR

Prince Charming

GEORGE, THE STAGE doorman at the Dryden Theatre, looked at him suspiciously. 'What's your name?'

'Charles Paris. Mr Walton is expecting me.'

George's face registered total disbelief and he turned to the telephone. Charles wondered vaguely if the old man had recognised him. After all, he'd come in every night for eighteen months during the run of *The Water Nymph* only ten years before. But no, the name Charles Paris meant nothing. So much for the showbiz myth of the cheery old 'never forget a face—I seen 'em all' doorman. George was a bloody-minded old sod and always had been.

'Mr Walton's not back in his dressing-room yet.'

'I'll wait.' Charles leant against the wall. The doorman watched his visitor as if he expected him to steal the light fittings.

There was a big poster of the show stuck up just inside the stage door. It had on it an enormous photo of Bernard in hot pursuit of a cartoon of two bikini-clad girls. That's stardom—a real photo; supports only get cartoons.

Charles thought back to when he'd first met Bernard in Cardiff—a gauche, rather insecure young man with a slight stammer. Even then he'd been pushy, determined to make it. Charles had been directing at the time and cast him as Young Marlowe in *She Stoops to Conquer*. Not a good actor, but Charles made him play himself and it worked. The stammer fitted Marlowe's embarrassment and Bernard got a very good press. A couple of years round the reps playing nervous idiots, then a television series, and now, entering his second year in *Virgin on the Ridiculous*, nauseating the critics and wowing the coach parties.

'Could you try him again?' George acquiesced grudgingly. This time he got through. 'Mr Walton, there's a Mr—what did you say your name was?'

'Charles Paris.'

'A Mr Charles Paris to see you. Oh. Very well.' He put the phone down. 'Mr Walton's expecting you.' In tones of undisguised surprise. 'Dressing-room One. Down the—'

But Charles knew the geography of the theatre and strode along the corridor. He knocked on the door and it was thrown open by Bernard, oozing bonhomie from a silk dressing-gown. 'Charles dear boy. Lovely to see you.'

Dear boy? Charles baulked slightly at that and then he realised that Bernard actually thought himself Nod Coward. The whole star bit. 'Good to see you, Bernard. How's it going?'

'Oh, *comme çi, comme ça*. Audience love it. Doing fantastic business, in spite of all the crisis, or whatever it's called. So I can't complain. I'm just opening a bottle of champagne if you ...'

'Do you have any Scotch?'

'Sure. Help yourself. Cupboard over there.'

'Bernard. I've come to ask you a favour.' May as well leap straight in.

'Certainly. What can I do for you?'

'You know Marius Steen, don't you?'

'Yes, the old sod. He owns half this show. You know, if Marius Steen didn't exist, it would be necessary to invent him.'

Aphorisms too, thought Charles. Noel Coward has a lot to answer for. Generations of actors who, without a modicum of the talent, have pounced on the mannerisms.

'The thing is, I want an introduction to him.' At that moment, the door burst open and Margaret Leslie sparkled into the room, her tiny frame cotton-woolled in a great sheepskin coat. 'Maggie darling!' Bernard enveloped her in his arms. 'Darling, do you know Charles Paris? Charles, have you met Maggie?'

'No, I haven't actually, but I've admired your work for a long time.' Charles could have kicked himself for the cliché. It was true, though. She was a brilliant actress and deserved her phenomenal success.

'Charles Paris?' she mused huskily. 'Didn't you write that awfully clever play *The Rate-payer?'* Charles acknowledged it rather sheepishly. 'Oh, I'm enchanted to meet you, Charles. I did it in rep. once. Played Wanda.'

'Glenda.'

'Yes, that's right.'

'Charles was an incredible help to me at the beginning of my career,' said Bernard with professional earnestness. 'I would have got nowhere without him. But nowhere.'

Charles felt diminished by the compliment. He'd have preferred Bernard to say nothing rather than patronise him. It was the gratitude of the star on *This is Your Life* thanking the village schoolmaster who had first taken him to the theatre.

'Charles was just asking me about Marius.'

'Oh God,' said Maggie dramatically and laughed.

This put Charles on the spot. He didn't mind asking Bernard a favour on his own, but it was awkward with Maggie there.

'You said you wanted an introduction?' Bernard prompted.

Nothing for it. He'd have to go on. 'Yes. I ... er ...' he'd got the story prepared but it was difficult with an audience. 'I've written a new play. Light comedy. Thought it might be Steen's sort of thing.'

'Oh, I see. And you want me to introduce you, so that you can try and sell it to him.'

'Yes.' Charles felt humiliated. He'd never have sunk to this if he was actually trying to sell one of his plays. But it was the only possible approach to Steen he could think of. 'I hope you don't mind my asking ...'

'No. Of course not. Old pals act. Happy to oblige.' And Bernard was. He was the great star and here was an old friend, less successful, wanting to be helped out. Charles winced at the thought of what he was doing. 'Is it urgent, dear boy?'

'It is a bit. There's an American agent nibbling.'

'Ah.' Bernard's tone didn't believe it. 'Well, you leave it with me, old chum. Have I got your number?'

Charles wrote it down. Margaret Leslie, who was wandering restlessly round the room, picked up a script from a table. 'Is this the new telly, Bernard?'

'Yes, it's awful. Not a laugh in it. I do get a bit sick of the way they keep sending me scripts to make funny. Here's a new show—may not be much good—never mind, book Bernard Walton, he'll get a few laughs out of it. I probably could, but I should get a bit of support from the script-writers. You ought to write something for me, Charles,' he added charmingly.

'Not really my style, Bernard.'

'Oh, I don't know.'

'Bernard,' Maggie hinted, 'I think we ought to ...'

'Lord, yes. Is that the time? Charles, we're going out to eat. Why not join us? Going to the Ivy. Miles'll be there, John and Prunella, and Richard, I expect. I'm sure they could make room for another.'

Charles refused politely. He couldn't stomach an evening of bright show-biz back-chat. Outside the theatre he gulped great lungfuls of cold night air, but it didn't cleanse him inside. He still felt sullied by what he'd had to do—to crawl to someone like Bernard Walton.

There was only one solution. He hailed a cab and went to the Montrose. If he couldn't lose the feeling, perhaps he could deaden it.

A tremendous hammering at the door. Charles rolled out of bed and groped his way over to open it. One of the Swedish girls was standing there in a flowered nylon dressing-gown. Charles had time to register that she looked like a dinky toilet-roll cover before his head caught up with him. It felt as if it had been split in two by a cold chisel and someone was grinding the two halves together.

'Telephone.' The Swedish girl flounced off. Charles tried to make it down the stairs with his eyes closed to allay the pain. He felt for the receiver and held it gingerly to his ear. 'Hello?'

'Charles, I've done it!' Bernard's voice sounded insufferably cheerful. Charles grunted uncomprehending. 'I've spoken to Marius.'

'Ah.'

'Well, I haven't actually spoken to him, but I spoke to Joanne—that's his secretary—and I've fixed for you to see him this afternoon at four. That's if he's back. Apparently he's been down at Streatley since the weekend, but Joanne says he should be back today. Got some charity dinner on.'

'Look, Bernard, I ... er ...' Charles' smashed brain tried to put the words together. 'Thanks very ... I ... er ... don't know how—'

'Don't mention it, dear boy.' Bernard's voice sounded as if it was opening a fete, big-hearted and patronising. 'Do you know Marius' office?'

'No. I— '

'Charing Cross Road. Milton Buildings. Just beyond the Garrick.'

'Ah. Look, I ...'

'My dear fellow, not a word. I just hope it does you some good. Always glad to oblige. You helped me in the early days. Eh?'

If anything could have made Charles feel sicker, it was Bernard's bonhomie.

*

By quarter to four the pain in his head had subsided to a dull ache. He found Milton Buildings in Charing Cross Road without too much difficulty, though the entrance was narrow, shuffled between a café and a book-shop.

Inside, however, the buildings were spacious. The board downstairs carried an impressive list of theatrical impresarios, agents and lawyers. 'Marius Steen Productions' was on the second floor. Charles travelled up in the old-fashioned cage lift. The envelope in his inside pocket seemed to bulge enormously. He felt as he had in Oxford, the first time he had taken a girl out with a packet of French letters in his wallet. He remembered the sense of an obscene lump under his blazer, revealing his intentions to the entire university. Didn't know why he'd bothered. Virginal Vera, besotted with phonetics. Middle English and nothing else. The time that one wasted. He felt a twinge of embarrassment for the gaucheness of his youth.

'ENQUIRIES' and an arrow in gold leaf on the wall. It pointed to a panelled oak door. Charles knocked. 'Come in.'

A secretary was sitting behind a solid Victorian desk. This must be Joanne. Unmarried, about forty, but not the standard over-made-up spinster secretary. She looked very positive and rather attractive in a forbidding way. Unmarried by choice, not default. She rose to meet him. 'You must be Mr Paris.'

'Yes.'

'I thought I recognised you from the television.'

'Ah!' There's no answer to that, but it's gratifying. 'Mr Paris, I'm so sorry. I would have tried to contact you, but I hadn't a phone number. I'm afraid Mr Steen hasn't come up from the country.'

'Oh dear.'

'Yes, I'm sorry. I thought he'd be back today. It appears that he's reading some scripts and ...'

'Oh, that's all right.'

'There's no one else who could help? Mr Cawley deals with a lot of the management side.'

'No, I don't think so.'

'Or Mr Nigel Steen should be in town later. He'll certainly be here over the weekend.'

'Has he been down at Streatley?'

'He went down yesterday. Perhaps he could ...?' 'No, no thanks, I wanted to see Mr Marius Steen personally.'

'Ah. Well, I'm sorry. I explained to Mr Walton that ...'

'Yes. Don't worry.'

'Perhaps you could let me have your number and then I'll give you a call when Mr Steen is back in town and we could fix another appointment.'

'Yes.'

So that was it. Charles left the office with his pocketful of pornography, feeling flat. He wandered along the Charing Cross Road, trying to think what to do next, Galahad on hearing that someone else had found the Holy Grail, Knight Errant without an errand. He rang Jacqui from Leicester Square tube station and reported his lack of progress.

'You say he's in Streatley now?'

'Yes.'

'And Nigel's coming up to town?'

'Probably, but, Jacqui, don't try to contact him. Leave it to me. I'll get in touch with him after the weekend.'

'Yes ...' Wistful.

'I'll sort it out, Jacqui.'

'Yes ...' Drab.

Charles wandered aimlessly through Leicester Square to Piccadilly. A cartoon cinema was offering Tom and Jerry and Chaplin shorts. He hovered for a moment, but his mind was too full to be side-tracked. He had to find out more about Marius Steen. So he went down the steps to Piccadilly Underground station and bought a ticket for Tower Hill.

CHAPTER FIVE

Speciality Act

THE OLD PEOPLE'S Home was designed for daylight. Plate glass welcomed the sun in to warm the inmates who sat in armchairs, waiting. But now it was dark. The nurse hadn't been round yet to close the curtains and Charles Paris and Harry Chiltern looked out on galvanised frames of blackness. The offices around were empty and dead, street lights in the backwater thought unnecessary in the emergency. The windows seemed more forbidding than walls.

'I saw some programme on the television the other day,' said Harry after a moment's musing. 'All the club comics it was. Just telling gags. Terrible. No technique. Or do I mean all the same technique? I tell you, I've seen more variety in a tin of sardines.

'They don't have variety now. Not even the word. Variety with a big V. Used to mean something. No, I rang a mate in the Variety department at the BBC. Couple of years back, this was. He said, it's not Variety any more, it's Light Entertainment. Light Entertainment—now that's a different thing altogether.

'I mean, when Lennie and I done our act, we worked on it. Worked hard. A few gags, monologue—that was Lennie's bit—a few more gags, I'd do my drunk routine, and finish with a song and a bit of tap. I mean, rehearsed. Not just standing up there telling some joke you heard from a man in a pub. It was an act. People who come to see the Chiltern Brothers knew they'd get a real show. Get their money's worth. No, this television, I don't hold with it. Entertainment in your living-room. That's not the place for entertainment—it's for your knitting and your eating and your bit of slap and tickle. You gotta go out—that's part of the entertaining. Make a night of it, eh?'

'Yes. I suppose the television's on all the time here.'

'From the moment it starts. Some of the old biddies stuck in front all day long, watching—I don't know-how to speak Pakistani, or what kiddies can do with a cotton-reel. All bleeding day long. I tell you, there's one old cripple, ugly old bird—more chins than a Chinese telephone directory—sits there nodding away at the test-card when it's on, doesn't notice. Mind you, it's a lot more interesting than some of the programmes, eh?'

Harry Chiltern cackled with laughter and subsided into silence as the nurse at last arrived to draw the curtains. 'Evening, Mr Chiltern.'

'Evening.'

'I see we've got a visitor. Hello.' The nurse smiled conspiratorially at Charles. Harry contemplated his highly polished shoes until she had left the room. 'Silly old cow. Thinks we're all gaga. "I see we've got a visitor." Who's we, eh? Apart from Georgie Wood, eh?' He laughed again, then stopped suddenly. 'Come on.' He eased himself out of the chair.

'What?'

'She's off now, doing the other curtains. We can whip down to the Bricklayers for a pint.'

'Should you?'

'Bloody hell, Charles. If I'm going to snuff it, I'd rather snuff it with a pint in my fist than one of their bloody mugs of Ovaltine. Come on.'

The Bricklayers' Arms was one of those modem pubs that capture all the atmosphere of an airport lounge. Hanging red lights shone on leatherette couches and framed relief pictures of vintage cars. Pop music pounded from the jukebox.

Still, it was a pub, and a pint. Harry seemed to appreciate it. He took a long swig, put the glass down and wiped his mis-shaven upper lip contentedly. Charles thought it might be the moment. 'Harry, I wanted to ask you about Marius Steen?'

'Oh yeah. Old Flash Steenie. Why?'

'I'm going to see him about a play I have written.' The lie slipped out easily enough. 'What's he like?' Harry didn't seem to react. 'You knew him round the halls, didn't you?'

'Oh yes. Just thinking about him. Steenie. Tough old bugger.'

'Where did he come from?'

'Poland, I think, originally. His parents come over in—I don't know—early twenties, I suppose. When Marius was about fifteen. He done all kinds of things in the business. I mean all kinds. Wrestling promotions, girlie shows, Variety. I think he even been on the boards himself in the early days. Yes, he was. Never saw him, but I heard he was terrible. Even says so himself, I think. He did a whistling act, maybe. Or speciality of some sort. Fire-eating perhaps it was? Hey, d'you hear about the fire-eater who couldn't go anywhere without meeting an old flame? Eh? Made him feel really hot under the collar.' Harry chuckled. 'Made that one up, y'know. Didn't have any of this script-writer nonsense in my day. You did your own act, and it was yours all the way. Yes.' He gazed absently ahead, and raised his glass to his lips with a trembling hand. Charles feared he might have to prompt again. But the old man continued.

'I first met Steenie at ... where? Chiswick Empire, I think it was. Me and Lennie was some way down the bill and Steenie was managing this tap-dance act, as I recall. Think it was that. I don't know. He'd always got so many acts going.'

'All Variety stuff?'

'Oh yes. Didn't do none of your Oh-my-Gawd theayter till after the war—second big job, you know. No, he was going round the halls, picking up the odd act, putting shows on, making money. Making money. Always knew where every penny was. Tight as a bottle-top. You hear him squeak every time he moves.'

'What was he like?'

'I don't know how to answer that. Hard as nails. A real bugger, particularly about money. Made a lot of enemies.'

'What sort of people?'

'People who hadn't read the small print of their contracts. Never missed a trick, old Steenie. I remember, one bloke, mind-reader he was—Steenie booked him for some Variety bill, forget where it was now. Anyway, opens first night—this mind-reader comes on—audience really gives him the bird. Load of savages they were, only come to see the girls. Lots of audiences were like that. Mind you, Lennie and I could usually get them round. Lennie had this thing, when the act was going bad, he'd ... ah, Lennie—God rest his soul. Got them wetting themselves up on the clouds, I daresay ...

'Anyway, this mind-reader act got the real bum's rush, no question. So Steenie sacks him. Fair enough, that's what you'd expect. But Steenie doesn't pay him nothing. Some let-out he'd got in the contract. Bloke may have been able to read minds, but he couldn't read a bleeding contract. Eh? Mind-reader got quite nasty. Tried to do old Steenie over.'

'What happened?'

'Not a lot. Steenie had Frank with him.'

'Frank?'

'Don't know what his real name was. Everyone called him Frank after Frankenstein—you know, the old monster. He was Polish and all, I think. Probably had some unpronounceable name. Ex-wrestler.'

'A sort of body-guard?'

'That's the idea. Steenie needed one of them, the way he done business.'

'Did he ever do anything illegal?'

'Ah, what's illegal? He was no more illegal than most of the fixers in this business. If you mean, could the law have got him, no. He'd never do nothing himself but, you know, things might happen. Frank was a big boy to have lean on you.'

'Is he still around?'

'Frank? No, he must be dead. Or shovelled off into the Old Folks like me. One of those big muscle-bound Johnnies. Go to fat when they stop training. Die of heart failure, most of them.'

'Do you reckon Steen would have found a replacement?'

'I don't know. He'd got a well-developed sense of self-protection, you know, always carried a gun in the glove-pocket of the car. Probably got another bruiser after Frank. But perhaps you don't need that sort of thing in the old lee-gitimate theayter. Only thing you have to look out for is the nancy-boys, eh?'

They laughed. Harry looked into his glass as if he could see for miles and Charles nudged him back on to the subject. 'Do you know Steen's son?'

'Nigel, isn't it?'

'That's right.'

'Yeah, I met him. Nasty bit of work. Oh, nothing criminal. Just a bit slimy. Often happens. Old man does well and the kids don't quite make it. I don't suppose you'd remember old Barney Beattie. Vent act. Dummy called Buckingham. Barney and Buckingham. Great they were. Barney, he had these two sons—tried to set up a song and dance act. Nothing. Nothing there. Hooked off every stage in the British Isles, they was. It happens like that.' The old man drained his pint reflectively.

'Can I get you another one, Harry?'

'No, it's my throw.'

'Oh, but I'll ...'

'I can still pay my way.' And with dignity he took the two glasses over to the bar. He looked small in the crush and it was some time before the order got through. Then he returned, face contorted with concentration as he tried to keep the glasses steady in his blotched hands.

'There.' With triumph. 'Put hairs on your chest, Charlie.'

'Thanks.'

Now, where were we? Yes. Steenie's boy. Ain't got the old man's talent, none of it. Been involved in one or two real disasters. You know, putting on drag shows, that sort of spectacle. But he ain't got the touch. Old Steenie, he'd make money out of a kid's conker match; Nigel'd close *The Mousetrap* within a week.'

'Do they get on?'

'Father and son? God knows. Sometimes they do, sometimes they don't. Great arguments, old man used to keep disowning the boy. Then they'd be as thick as thieves again. He likes all the family bit, Steenie. Wife died—oh, years ago, so the boy matters a lot. Jews are like that aren't they?'

'Yes.'

'You want to know a lot about them, don't you?'

'Just interest.'

'Yes.' A pause. 'You know, Charlie my boy, from the way you says that I can tell what you really want is the dirt. All right then—' he edged closer so that he was whispering rather than shouting over the juke-box '—here's the nastiest rumour I've ever heard about Steenie— really nasty rumour. Dancer he knew—she was on a bill with me and Lennie down the Hackney Empire. Steenie was putting the show on, and he'd got a thing going with this bint Veronica. Always put it about a bit, Steenie. Had a lot of lead in his pencil, that boy'—the image of the photographs flashed across Charles' mind—'Anyway, this girl gets knocked up, and when Steenie finds out about it, he don't want to know. Won't talk to her, doesn't know her, gives her the boot. Out of the show.

'Well, this Veronica won't put up with this—comes round the theatre between shows one night—really drunk—really—I don't like that in a woman—and she's swearing and effing and blinding—big shout-up with Steenie—going to tell his wife, all that. Next morning she's found floating face-down in the Thames.

'All right. Could have fallen in. Could have decided to do away with herself. But nasty rumours at the time said she could have been helped in. Certainly her being off the scene was handy for Steenie. And Frank wasn't round the theatre the night she disappeared. It's a long time ago, though. Just rumours.'

'Do you think Steen would be capable of that sort of thing, Harry?'

'If someone was in his way, Charlie, he'd be capable of anything.'

'I see, a real bastard.'

There was a long pause. 'Yes, a real bastard.' Harry chuckled. 'But you can't help liking him. One of the most likeable lumps of shit I ever come across.'

They talked a bit more, but Harry was tiring quickly. He seemed to be having difficulty with the second pint, and had only drunk a third of it when he looked at his watch. 'Better be on my way, you know, Charlie. Not as young as I was.'

'Will there be trouble when you get back?'

'No. I'll pretend I've had a turn or something. Ah, you know, I don't like that place. Still, not for long.'

'Are you moving somewhere else?'

Harry smiled. 'Join Lennie. Won't be long now. Still, can't complain.'

'A whole life-time in the business.'

'Yes. Did our first show when we was four. And our last one three years ago on some stupid television thing about the music-hall. Seventy-four years in the business, that was, Charlie. Seventy-four.'

'And you wouldn't have had it any other way.

'Good God, yes. It was Lennie who wanted all that. I wanted to be a professional footballer.'

CHAPTER SIX

Transformation Scene

CHARLES TRIED TO think it all out on the Saturday morning. He'd woken without a hangover and even done a token tidying-up of his room. Then out for a newspaper and some rolls, and he was sitting in front of the gas fire with a cup of coffee. Glance at the paper; no particular interest in petrol queues or Ireland without Whitelaw, so he settled down to think about Jacqui and Steen.

What he had heard from Harry Chiltern was disturbing. True, the business about the dancer in the Thames sounded a bit too melodramatic—the kind of story that gets embroidered over the years—and probably started out just as an unfortunate coincidence. Charles discounted the facts of it; but it was significant that Marius Steen attracted that sort of accusation. It didn't bode well for Jacqui.

Then there were the photographs and her own story. Something didn't ring true there. He pieced it together. In June, Jacqui and Steen went to a party, which was attended by Sally Nash, now on trial at the Old Bailey on charges of controlling prostitutes. At this party a fairly insipid orgy took place. Some pictures were taken by a nameless photographer. All through this period (according to Jacqui) things were swinging between her and Steen. She even got pregnant by him. He arranged an abortion which went wrong and they went off to the South of France to recuperate. And there, apparently, had an idyllic time. This idyll had continued up until the previous Saturday, 1st December, when they last met. That was the day after the Sally Nash trial started, and the day that Marius Steen's terrible show, *Sex of One and Half a Dozen of the Other* celebrated a thousand performances. And from that day on Jacqui had been unable to contact Steen. He had very deliberately told her to get lost, and when she didn't take the hint, he'd sent her an obscene note. And according to Jacqui, the reason for this must be Steen's fear of her being associated with him in the Sally Nash case because it might affect his chances of a knighthood. It was preposterous. Nobody would behave like that.

Charles wasn't sure whether Jacqui believed she was telling the truth or not. She might have her own reasons for obscuring the issue. But, leaving that aside for a moment, he tried to make some sense of Steen's behaviour.

The simplest explanation was that he had just got tired of Jacqui. That was quite possible, however well she thought the affair was going. He was a man who had always put it about a bit, as Harry Chiltern said. Jacqui was an attractive enough bit of stuff, but there were hundreds more like her and why should he stick to one? He'd be very unlikely to stay with her or marry her, particularly with a knighthood in the offing. As Jacqui herself admitted, she wasn't the sort of consort for a 'do with the Queen Mum'.

And, Charles' mind raced on, Steen could have picked up a new tottie at the *Sex of One* ... party on the Saturday night. That would explain the sudden change in his affections.

But as he thought of it, Charles knew the explanation was inadequate. Even if that had happened, it didn't justify the violence of Steen's attempts to get Jacqui off his back. No, Steen's behaviour certainly suggested that he regarded her as a threat in some way. Perhaps she had tried to blackmail him ...? Yes, that made sense. She had actually tried to use the photographs ... perhaps to blackmail him into marrying her. (That would tie in with the pregnancy in the summer—an earlier attempt to force Steen's hand.) She could have tried the blackmail approach on the Saturday afternoon; then, when Steen cut up rough, she realised she'd overstepped the mark and brought in Charles as a go-between to patch things up. That would even explain why she took him back to Archer Street from the Montrose. She'd just gone down there to look for any good-natured sucker.

But the new explanation wasn't much more satisfactory than the first. For a start. Charles didn't like to think of Jacqui in that light. And also he doubted whether she had the intelligence to be so devious. The only convincing bit was the thought of Steen as a frightened man. What was it he was afraid of?

Charles marshalled his knowledge of blackmailers' habits. It was limited, all gleaned from detective novels. He got out the brown envelope and spread the photographs on his lap. His reaction to them had numbed. They just seemed slightly unwholesome now, like used tissues. Just photographs. What would Sherlock Holmes, Lord Peter Wimsey, Hercule Poirot and the rest have made of that lot? Charles made a cursory check for blood-stained fingerprints, the thread of a sports jacket made from tweed only available in a small tailor's shop in Aberdeen, the scratch marks of an artificial hand or the faint but unmistakable aroma of orange blossom. The investigation, he concluded without surprise, yielded negative results. They were just photographs.

Just photographs. The phrase caught in his mind. Negative results. Yes, of course. Where were the bloody negatives? Jacqui had paid out a thousand pounds for something that could be reproduced at will. A very rudimentary knowledge of detective fiction tells you that any photographic blackmailer worth his salt keeps producing copies of the incriminating material until he's blue in the face. It would be typical of Jacqui's naivety to believe that she was dealing with an honest man who had given her the only copies in existence.

If this were so, and the photographer was putting pressure on him, then Steen's reactions were consistent. He had reason to be frightened. But why should he be frightened of Jacqui? Charles shuffled through his pockets for a two p piece and went down to the phone.

'Jacqui?'

'Yes.' She sounded very low.

'All right?'

'Not too good.'

'Listen, Jacqui, I think I may be on to something about the way

Steen's behaving.'

'What?' She sounded perkier instantly.

'Jacqui, you've got to tell me the truth. When you bought those photographs ...'

'Yes?'

'Did you buy the negatives too?'

'No. I didn't. But he'd destroyed them. He said so.'

'I see. And did you mention to Steen that you'd got the photographs at any time?'

'No. I wanted it to be a surprise—a present. He had mentioned them vaguely, said he was a bit worried. So I fixed to get them.'

'When were they actually handed over to you?'

'Last Saturday evening.'

'And you never mentioned them even when you tried to ring Steen?'

'I started to. On the Sunday evening when I first rang him. I spoke to Nigel. I said it was about the photographs, but even before I'd finished talking, he gave me this message from Marius to ... you know ... to get lost.'

'Right. Give me the name and address of the bloke you got the photos from.'

As Charles limped along Praed Street, he began to regret dressing up for the encounter, but when he reflected on the exceptional violence of blackmailers in all detective fiction, he decided it was as well to conceal his identity. The disguise was good and added ten years to him. He'd greyed his temples and eyebrows with a spray, and parted his hair on the other side. He was wearing the démodé pinstriped suit he'd got from a junk-shop for a production of Arturo Ui ('grossly overplayed'—Glasgow Herald) and the tie he'd worn as Harry in Marching Song ('adequate if uninspiring'—Oxford Mail). He walked with the limp he'd used in Richard III ('nicely understated'—Yorkshire Post). He wasn't sure whether to speak in the accent he'd used in Look Back in Anger ('a splendid Blimp'—Worcester Gazette) or the one for When We are Married ('made a meal of the part'—Croydon Advertiser).

'Imago Studios', the address Jacqui had given him, proved to be in a tatty mews near St Mary's Hospital in Paddington. The downstairs stable-garage part had apparently been converted into a studio. On the windows of the upper part the curtains were drawn. Charles rang the bell. Nothing. He rang again and heard movement.

The door was opened by a woman in a pale pink nylon housecoat and pink fur slippers. She had prominent teeth and dyed black hair swept back in the style of a souvenir Greek goddess. Her face was heavily made up and eye-lashed. Charles couldn't help thinking of a hard pink meringue full of artificial cream.

She looked at him hard. 'Yes?'

'Ah, good afternoon.' Charles plumped for the *When We are Married* accent. 'I wondered if Bill was in.' Jacqui had only given him the Christian name. It was all she knew.

'Who are you? What do you want with him?'

'My name's Holroyd. Bill Holroyd.' On the spur of the moment he couldn't think of another Christian name. He grinned weakly. 'Both called Bill, eh?'

'What's it about?'

'Some photographs.'

'What is it—wedding or portrait? Because my husband—'

'No, no, it's a more ... personal sort of thing.'

'Ah.' She knew what he meant. 'You better come in.'

She led the way up the very steep stairs. The large nylon-clad bottom swished close to Charles' face as he limped up after her. 'Can you manage?'

'Yes. It's just my gammy leg.'

'How did you do it, Mr Holroyd?'

'In the war.'

'Jumping out of some tart's bedroom window, I suppose. That's where most war wounds came from.'

'No. Mine was a genuine piece of shrapnel.'

'Huh.' She ushered him into a stuffy little room lit by bright spotlights. It was decorated in orange and yellow, with a leopardette three-piece suite covering most of the carpet. Every available surface was crowded with small brass souvenirs. Lincoln imps, windjammer bells, lighthouses, anchor thermometers, knights in armour, wishing wells, everything. On the dresser two posed and tinted photographs rose from the undergrowth of brass. One was the woman, younger, but still with her Grecian hair and heavy make-up. The other was of a man, plumpish and vaguely familiar.

The woman pointed to an armchair. 'Sit down. Rest your shrapnel.'

'Thank you.'

She slumped back on to the sofa, revealing quite a lot of bare thigh. 'Right, Mr Holroyd, what's it about?'

'I was hoping to see your husband.'

'He's ... er ... he's not here at the moment, but I know about the business.'

'I see. When are you expecting him back?'

'You can deal with me,' she said. Hard.

'Right, Mrs ... er?'

'Sweet.'

'Mrs Sweet.' Charles was tempted to make a quaint Yorkshire pleasantry about the name, but looked at Mrs Sweet and decided against it. 'This is, you understand, a rather delicate matter ...'

'I understand.'

'It's ... er ... the fact is ... Last summer I was down in London on business and ... er ... it happened that, by chance ... through some friends, I ended up at a party given by ... er ... well, some people in Holland Park. Near Holland Park, that is ...'

'Yes.' She didn't give anything.

'Yes ... Yes ... Well, I believe that ... er ... your husband was at this particular party ...

'Maybe.'

'In fact, I believe he took some photographs at the party.

'Look here, are you from the police? I've had enough of them round this week.'

'What?' Charles blustered and looked affronted for a moment while he took this in. Obviously the police had been making enquiries about the Sally Nash case. Marius Steen's anxiety was justified. 'No, of course I'm not from the police. I'm the director of a man-made fibres company,' he said, with a flash of inspiration.

'Thank God. I couldn't take any more of that lot.'

'No, no. The fact is, Mrs Sweet, that ... er ... I am, you see, a married man. I have two lovely daughters at boarding school and ... er ... well, I have become rather anxious about these ... er ... photographs.'

'Yes.' She didn't volunteer anything.

'I have come to the right place, have I? I mean, your husband was at this party in ...?'

'Yes. He was there.' She paused and looked at him, assessing. 'Well, Mr Holroyd, I think I know which photographs you are referring to. Of course, photography's an expensive business.'

'I understand that, Mrs Sweet. How much do you think your husband would part with the ... er ... photographs for?'

'Two thousand pounds.'

'That's a lot of money.' The price has gone up, thought Charles. 'And would that be for the negatives as well?'

'Ah, Mr Holroyd. How shrewd you are. No, I'm afraid not. The photographs *and* the negatives would cost you five thousand pounds.'

So, as he suspected, Jacqui had been done. A thousand pounds for one set of photographs; there might be any number of others about. Bill Holroyd blustered. 'Oh, I don't think I could possibly raise that.'

'That's the price. Mind you, when things start moving in a certain court case, they might get even more expensive.

'Oh dear.' Charles let a note of panic creep into Bill Holroyd's voice and looked anxiously around the room.

'No point in looking for them, love.' It was 'love', now she knew she had the whip hand. 'You won't find them here.'

'How do I know you've got them?'

'I'll show you.' She opened a drawer in the dresser, pulled out a folder and handed it to him. 'Only copies, love. You'll never find the negatives, so don't try.'

'No.' Charles opened the folder and looked at all the photographs. There were a lot and they included some identical to the set still bulging in his pocket. His hunch about the morals of blackmailing photographers was right. He handed them back. 'You don't think there's any possibility that the price might be—'

'Five thousand pounds.'

'Hmm.' (A pause, while Charles tried, according to the best Stanislavskian method, to give the impression of a man torn between the two great motives of his life—love of money and fear of scandal.) 'Of course, it would take me some time to put my hands on that amount of money. Some days.'

'I can wait.' She smiled like a Venus fly-trap. 'I'm not so sure that you can. Once they start getting deeper into this trial, I'm sure the interest in photographs of this sort will—'

'Yes, yes. I'm sure it won't take too long. It's unfortunate not having my bank in London. It's in Leeds. But ... er ... perhaps by Wednesday ... Would Wednesday ...?'

'I'll be here. With the negatives.'

'Oh good.' Although he was only acting the part, Charles felt Bill Holroyd's relief. And in his own character he'd found out what he wanted to know. If there were other copies of the photographs, there was no doubt that Bill Sweet was blackmailing Steen. Steen had assumed from Jacqui's message to Nigel that she was involved too. Charles was relieved that the information put her in the clear; she had been telling the truth. All he had to do now was what she had asked—get to see Steen, give him the photographs and explain that Jacqui was nothing to do with Bill Sweet. If Sweet himself continued his blackmail, that wasn't Charles' concern.

Mrs Sweet rose from the sofa. 'That's our business concluded. I'm glad we reached agreement in such a reasonable way. Would you like a drink?'

'Oh, thank you very much.' Perhaps a little too readily for Bill Holroyd. 'That is to say, I don't make a habit of it, but perhaps a small one.'

'Gin?' She went to the door.

'That'd be ... very nice.' Charles just stopped himself from saying 'Reet nice'. Would have been too much.

After a few moments, Mrs Sweet returned with a bottle, poured two substantial gins, added tonic and proffered a glass. Charles rose to take it. They were close. She didn't move back. 'Cheers, Mr Holroyd.'

'Cheers.'

She looked at him, hard. 'You like all that, do you, Mr Holroyd?'

'All what?'

'Parties. Like the one in Holland Park.'

'Oh ... well. Not habitually, no. I'm a respectable man, but, you know, one works very hard and ... er ... needs to relax, eh?'

'Yes.' She sat back on the sofa and motioned him beside her. 'Yes, I find I need to relax too, Mr Holroyd.'

'Ah.' Charles sat gingerly on the mock leopard. He couldn't quite believe the way things appeared to be going, and couldn't think of anything else to say.

But Mrs Sweet continued, softly. 'Yes, and relaxation becomes increasingly difficult.' Her hand rested gently on top of his. The scene was getting distinctly sultry.

Charles decided to play it for light comedy. 'I go in for a certain amount of golf, you know. That's good for relaxation.'

'Oh really.' Her hand was moving gently over his. Charles stole a sidelong glance. The mouth was parted and thickened lashes low over her eyes. He recognised that she was trying to look seductive, and, while he didn't find her attractive (rather the reverse), he was intrigued by the sudden change in her behaviour.

Mrs Sweet leant against him, so that he could feel the lacquered crispness of her hair on his ear. Her hand drew his to rest casually on her thigh. 'I've never played golf.'

'Oh, it's a grand game,' said Charles fatuously. In spite of himself, he could feel that he was becoming interested. Her perfume was strong and acrid in his nostrils. 'Champion game.'

'But I'm sure you play others.' Quite suddenly the grip hardened on his hand and he felt it forced into the warm cleft between her legs. Instinctively he clutched at the nylon-clad mound.

But his mind was moving quickly. Mrs Sweet and her husband were blackmailers. This must be a plot of some sort. 'Where's your husband?'

'A long way away.'

'But wouldn't he mind if—'

'We lead separate lives. Very separate lives now.' Her face was close to his and he kissed her. After all, he reflected, I am one of the few people in the world who isn't worth blackmailing. And Bill Holroyd was already showing himself to be pretty gullible, so it's in character.

Mrs Sweet reached her free hand down to his flies. No impotence problem this time. Charles began to consider the irony of life—that with Jacqui, whom he found very attractive, there was nothing, and yet with this nymphomaniac, who almost repelled him ... but it wasn't the moment for philosophy.

Mrs Sweet stood up and stripped off the housecoat. There was a crackle of static electricity. Her underwear was lacy red and black, brief and garish, the kind of stuff he'd seen in Soho shops and assumed was the monopoly of prostitutes. Perhaps she was a prostitute. The thought of another dose of clap flashed across his mind. But he was by now too aroused to be side-tracked.

He hastily pulled off his clothes and stood facing Mrs Sweet.

'It doesn't show,' she said.

'What?'

'Your war wound. The shrapnel.'

'Ah. No. Well, they do wonders with plastic surgery. He advanced and put his arms round her, fumbled with the back of her brassiere. 'The front,' she murmured. It unclipped.

They sank down on to the leopardette sofa and he slipped off the crisp lacy briefs. Underneath he'd expected her to be hard and dry, but she was very soft and moist. Again he thought of meringues. And as he had her, he emitted grunts which he hoped were in character for the director of a man-made fibres company.

CHAPTER SEVEN

Cinderella by the Fireside

CHARLES FELT DISTINCTLY jaded as he walked along Hereford Road. Mrs Sweet had kept him at it some time. He ached all over, and felt the revulsion that sex without affection always left like a hangover inside him. It was half-past four and dark. No pubs open yet. He felt in need of a bath to wash away Mrs Sweet's stale perfume.

As he entered the hall of the house, he heard a door open upstairs. 'He is here,' said a flat Swedish voice. There was the sound of footsteps running downstairs and Jacqui rushed into his arms. She was quivering like an animal. He held her to him and she started to weep hysterically. A podgy Swedish face peered over the banisters at them. 'You are an old dirty man,' it said and disappeared.

Charles was too concerned with Jacqui even to yell the usual obscenities at the Swede. He led the trembling girl into his room. She was as cold as ice. He sat her in the armchair and lit the gas-fire, poured a large Scotch and held it out to her. 'No. It'd make me sick.' And she burst out crying again.

Charles knelt by the chair and put his arm round her shoulders. She was still shivering convulsively. 'What's happened, Jacqui?'

The question prompted another great surge of weeping. Charles stayed crouching by her side and drank the Scotch while he tried to think how to calm her.

Eventually the convulsions subsided to some extent and he could hear what she was saying. 'My flat—they broke into my flat.'

'Who did?'

'I don't know. This morning I came back from doing the weekend shopping and it was—it had all been done over. My oil lamp—and the curtains pulled down and all my glasses smashed and my clothes torn in shreds and—' She broke down again into incoherence.

'Jacqui, who did it?'

'I don't know. It must have been someone who Marius—who Marius—' she sobbed.

'Why should he—'

'I ... I tried to ring him again.'

'Jacqui, I told you not to do that.'

'I know, but I ... I couldn't help it ... I had to ring him, because of the baby.'

'Baby?'

'Yes, I'm pregnant again and ...'

'Does Steen know?'

'Yes. We knew a month ago, and he said we'd keep this one and he wanted a child and ...' Again she was shaken by uncontrollable spasms.

'Jacqui, listen. Calm down. Listen, it'll be all right. Steen's only acting this way because he's frightened. There's been a misunderstanding about those photographs.' And Charles gave an edited version of his findings at Imago Studios.

By the end of his narrative she was calmer. 'So that's all. Marius thinks I'm involved with this Bill Sweet?'

'That's it. Jacqui, you might have known he'd keep the negatives.'

'I never thought. I hope you tore him off a strip when—'

'I didn't see him. I saw his wife.'

'What was she like?'

'Oh.' He shrugged non-committally. 'Listen, Jacqui, it'll be all right now. You can stay here. You'll be quite safe. And go ahead as planned. I'll somehow get to see Steen, deliver the photographs and explain the position. Then at least he'll take the heat off you. And turn it on Sweet, where it belongs.' He laughed. 'I must say, Jacqui, I don't care for your boy-friend's methods.'

Jacqui laughed too, a weak giggle of relief. 'Yes, he can be a bastard. You think it'll be all right?'

'Just as soon as I can get to see him. I mean, I don't know about the emotional thing—that's between the two of you—but I'm sure he'll stop the rough stuff.'

There was a pause. Jacqui breathed deeply. 'Oh, it really hurts. My throat, from all that crying.'

'Yes, of course it does. You're exhausted. Tell you what, I'll get you pleasantly drunk, tuck you up in bed, you'll sleep the sleep of the dead. And in the morning nothing'll seem so bad.'

'But my flat ...'

'I'll help you tidy it up, when we've got this sorted out.

'Oh, Charles, you are great. I don't know what I'd do without you, honest.'

'S'all right.' He took her hand and gripped it, embarrassed, like a father with his grown-up daughter. Then suddenly, brisk. 'Right, I'm hungry. Have you had anything to eat?'

'No, I ... I've felt sick. I—'

'Haven't got anything here, but—'

'I couldn't go out.'

'Don't you worry. It was for just such occasions that fish and chips were invented.'

'Oh no. I'd be sick.'

'Don't you believe it. Nice bit of rock salmon, bag of chips, lots of vinegar, you'll feel on top of the world.'

'Ugh.'

It's strange how fish and chip newspapers, out of date and greasy, are always much more interesting than current ones. It's like other people's papers in crowded tubes. You can't wait to buy a copy and read some intriguing article you glimpse over a strap-hanging shoulder. It's always disappointing.

In the fish and chip shop Charles noticed that his order was wrapped in a copy of the *Sun*. On the front page was the tantalizing headline, 'Virginity Auction—see page 11'. The fascination of page 11 grew as he walked home. Who was auctioning whose virginity to whom? And where?

This thought preoccupied him as he entered his room. Jacqui was lying on the bed, fast asleep. Curled up in a ball on the candlewick, she looked about three years old.

He made no attempt to wake her. In her state sleep was more important than food. The Virginity Auction—he settled down in front of the fire to find out all about it. He slipped a hot crumbling piece of fish into his mouth, placed the warm bag of chips on his knees and turned to page 11.

Bugger. He'd only got pages 1 to 8, and the corresponding ones at the back. He'd never know where virginities were knocked down, or how one bidded. A pleasant thought of nubile young girls being displayed at Sotheby's crossed his mind.

There wasn't much else in the paper. It was the last Wednesday's—all bloody petrol crisis. The titty girl on page 3's midriff was stained and transparent with grease from the fish and chips. It looked rather obscene, particularly as the word 'Come' showed through backwards from the other side of the page.

Charles turned over and stopped dead. There was a photograph on the page that was ominously familiar. He had last seen it on a dresser, surrounded by brass souvenirs.

Fiercely calm, he read the accompanying article.

M4 MURDER VICTIM IDENTIFIED

The man whose body was found early on Monday morning by the M4 exit road at Theale, Berks, has been identified as 44-year-old William Sweet, a photographer from Paddington, London. Sweet was found shot through the head at the roadside beside his grey Ford Escort, which appeared to have run out of petrol.

Interviewed at his Paddington studios, Sweet's wife, Audrey, could suggest no motive for the killing. Police believe Sweet may have been the victim of a gangland revenge killing, and that he may have been mistaken for someone else.

Charles put down the fish and chips and poured a large Scotch. He could feel his thoughts beginning to stampede and furiously tried to hold them in check.

Certain points were clear. He ordered them with grim concentration.

Marius Steen must have killed Sweet: Sweet had put the pressure on about the photographs, Steen had fixed to meet him and shot him. Charles grabbed an old AA book that was lying around. Yes, the Theale turn-off was the one you'd take going to Streatley. Sweet was shot Sunday night or Monday morning. Marius Steen was in London certainly on the Saturday night, because he was at the *Sex of One* ... party. And in Streatley during the week. He was therefore likely to have been driving through Theale late on Sunday. As Harry Chiltern had said, there was always a gun in the glove compartment. A glance at the map made Charles pretty sure that that gun was now in the Thames.

Other facts followed too. Mrs Sweet was holding out on the police. It was nonsense for her to say no one had a motive for murdering her husband. As Charles had discovered, she knew about the Sally Nash party photographs. All she had to do was to tell the police about her husband's blackmailing activities and very soon the finger would point at Steen. For reasons of her own, she wasn't doing that. Probably just didn't want to lose a profitable business.

But the most chilling deduction from the fact of Bill Sweet's murder was the immediate danger to Jacqui. If he'd shoot one person who challenged him, Marius Steen would do the same to anyone else he thought represented the same threat. He'd tried to frighten Jacqui off with the telephone messages and vicious note, but if she persisted ... Charles shivered as he thought what might have happened if Jacqui had been in the flat when her 'visitors' called that morning. He looked over to the child-like form on his bed and felt a protective instinct so strong he almost wept.

Confrontation with Marius Steen couldn't wait. Charles must get down to Streatley straight away. If the man was down there ... Better ring the Bayswater house to check. But he hadn't got the number. It seemed a pity to wake Jacqui. He opened her handbag, but the address book revealed nothing.

No help for it. 'Jacqui.' He shook her gently. She started like a frightened cat, and looked up at him wide-eyed. 'Sorry. Listen, I've been thinking. I want to get this sorted out, like as soon as possible. There's no point in your being in this state of terror. I am going to try and see Steen tonight. Get it over with.'

'But if he's in Streatley—'

'That's all right. I don't mind.' He tried to sound casual, as if the new urgency was only a whim. 'My daughter lives down that way. I wanted to go and visit her anyway.'

'I didn't know you'd got a daughter.'

'Oh yes.'

'How old?'

'Twenty-one.'

'Nearly as old as me.'

'Yes.'

'Like me?'

'Hardly. Safely married at nineteen to a whizz-kid of the insurance world—if that's not a contradiction in terms. Anyway, the reason I woke you was not just bloody-mindedness. I want to ring Steen's Bayswater place and check he's not there. It's a long way to go if he's just round the corner.'

Both the phone numbers Jacqui gave were ex-directory. Charles paused for a moment before dialling the Bayswater one, while he decided what character to take on. It had to be someone anonymous, but somebody who would be allowed to speak to the man if he was there, and someone who might conceivably be ringing on a Saturday night.

The phone was picked up at the other end and Charles pressed his two p into the coin box. A discreet, educated voice identified the number—nothing more.

'Ah, good evening.' He plumped for the Glaswegian accent he'd used in a Thirty-Minute Theatre ('Pointless'— *The Times*). 'Is that Mr Marius Steen's residence?'

'He does live here, yes, but—'

'It's Detective-Sergeant McWhirter from Scotland Yard. I'm sorry to bother you at this time of night. Is it possible to speak to Mr Steen?'

'I'm afraid not. Mr Steen is at his home in the country. Can I help at all?'

Charles hadn't planned beyond finding out what he wanted to know and had to think quickly. 'Ah yes, perhaps you can. It's only a small thing. Um.' Playing for time. Then a sudden flash of inspiration. 'We're just checking on various Rolls-Royce owners. There's a number-plate racket going on at the moment. I wonder if you could give me Mr Steen's registration.'

The discreet voice did so. 'Thank you very much. That's all I wanted to know. I'm so sorry to have troubled you. Goodbye.'

As Charles put the phone down, he tried to work out what on earth a number-plate racket might be. It was quite meaningless, but at least he'd got the required information.

He tried the Berkshire number. The phone rang for about thirty seconds, then after a click, a voice gave the number and said, 'This is Marius Steen speaking on one of these recorded answering contraptions. I am either out at the moment or busy working on some scripts and don't want to talk right now. If your message is business ring the office—' he gave the number '—on Monday, if it's really urgent, you can leave a message on this machine, and if you want money, get lost.' A pause. 'Hello. Are you still there? Right then, after this whiney noise, tell me what it is.' Then the tone, then silence.

The voice was striking. Charles felt he must have heard Steen being interviewed at some stage on radio or television, because it was very familiar. And distinctive. The Polish origins had been almost eroded, but not quite; they had been overlaid with heavy Cockney, which, in turn, had been flattened into a classier accent as Steen climbed the social ladder. As an actor, Charles could feel all the elements in the voice and begin to feel something of the man. He dialled the number again, just to hear the voice and find out what else it could tell him.

The message itself was odd. The first reaction to 'if you want money, get lost' was that Steen must be referring to potential blackmailers, but then Charles realised how unlikely that was. Any of Steen's friends might ring him, so the message had to have a more general application. Most likely it was just a joke. After all, Steen was notorious for his success with money. And notoriously tight-fisted. Tight as a bottle-top, as Harry Chiltern had said. For him to make that sort of joke on the recording was in keeping with the impression Charles was beginning to form of his character.

And in spite of everything, that impression was good. Somehow Steen's voice seemed to confirm Jacqui's view. It was rich with character and humour. The whole tone of the recording was of a man who was alive in the sense that mattered, the sort of man Charles felt he would like when he met him. And yet this was also the man who had recently shot a blackmailer through the head.

Somehow even that seemed suddenly consistent. A man as big as Steen shouldn't have to be involved with little second-rate crooks like Bill Sweet. Charles felt more hopeful about his mission, certain that when he actually got to Steen, he'd be able to talk to him and clear Jacqui from his suspicions.

He tried Juliet and Miles' phone-number in Pangbourne, but there was no reply. No doubt out for the evening talking insurance at some scampi supper. Marius Steen might be out too, but he was bound to return at some stage, and the more Charles thought about the urgency of the situation, the more he was determined to meet the man. He said good-bye to Jacqui. She refused the cold remains of the fish and chips, so he took the whole package out to the dustbin at the front of the house (no need to worry her about the Sweet murder if she didn't know—and it appeared she didn't). He caught a train from Paddington to Reading, arrived there to find the last train to Goring and Streatley had gone, and, after a considerable wait, got a minicab.

It was only when he was sitting in the back of the car that he actually thought of the risk he was taking. Because of a mild affection for a tart he now seemed unable even to make love to, he was going to confront a man he knew to be a murderer with copies of the photographs for which a man had been killed. Put like that, it did sound rather silly. Fortunately, there had been time to buy a half bottle of Bell's on the way to Paddington. Charles took a long pull. And another one.

The car drew up outside a pair of high white gates. The driver charged an enormous amount of money 'on account of the petrol crisis' and swore when he wasn't given a tip to match. As the car's lights disappeared round the corner, it occurred to Charles that he should perhaps have asked the man to wait. If Steen turned nasty, he'd be glad of a quick getaway. But the thought was too late.

It was now very cold, the night air sharp and clear. The moon was nearly full and shed a watery light on the scene. It gleamed dully from a puddle outside the gates, which were high and solid, made of interlocking vertical planks. A fluorescent bell-push shone on the stone post to the right. Charles pressed it for a long time. It was now after midnight, Steen might well be in bed.

He pressed the button at intervals for about five minutes, but there was no reaction. His quarry might not be back yet, or perhaps the bell wasn't working. Charles tried the latch of the gate; he had to push hard but eventually it yielded.

He stood on a gravel path, looking at the house. It was an enormous bungalow, with a central block roofed in green tiles which shone in the moonlight. From this main part smaller wings spread off like the suburbs of a city. To the right there was a ramp down to a double garage on basement level. The whole building was painted the frost white of cake icing and its shine echoed the gleam of the silent Thames behind. No lights showed.

The main door was sheltered by a portico with tall columns, an incongruous touch of Ancient Greece grafted on to the sprawling modern bungalow. The door itself was of dark panelled wood with a brass knocker. Since there was no sign of a bell, Charles raised the enormous ring and let it fall.

The noise shocked him. It boomed as if the whole house was a resonating chamber for the brass instrument on the door. Charles waited, then knocked again. Soon he was hammering on the door, thud after thud, a noise fit to wake the dead. But there was nothing. The rush to Berkshire had been pointless. The photographs still bulged in his inside pocket. Marius Steen was not at home.

CHAPTER EIGHT

Inside the Giant's Castle

'IT WOULD HAVE all been easier, Daddy,' said Juliet, 'if you'd had some sort of regular job. I mean, acting's so unpredictable.'

'No, no, darling,' said Miles Taylerson, judiciously, 'not all acting. I mean there are regular jobs in acting—you know, directors of repertory companies, or in serials like *Coronation Street* or *Crossroads*.'

Charles, seated in Miles' karate-style dressing-gown, gritted his teeth and buttered, or rather battered, a piece of toast.

'No, but, quite honestly, Daddy, I do worry about you. I mean, you haven't set anything aside for your old age.'

'This is my old age, so it's too late now,' Charles pronounced with facetious finality.

But unfortunately that was not a conversation-stopper for Miles; it was a cue. 'Oh I wouldn't say that, Pop'— Charles winced—'I mean, there are insurance plans and pension plans for people of any age. In fact in my company we have rather a good scheme. I know of a fellow of over sixty who took out a policy. Of course, the premiums are high, but it's linked to a unit trust, so it's with profits.'

'I thought unit trusts were doing rather badly,' Charles tried maliciously, but Miles was unruffled.

'Oh yes, there haven't been the spectacular rises of the first few years, but we could guarantee a growth figure which more than copes with inflation. I know a case of a fellow who—'

Charles couldn't stand the prospect of another text-book example. 'Miles, I didn't come down here to talk about insurance.'

'Sorry, Pop. It's only because we're concerned about you. Isn't that so, darling?'

'Yes. You see, Daddy, Miles and I do worry. You don't seem to have any sense of direction since you left Mummy. We'd just feel happier if we'd thought you'd made some provisions for the future.'

'Exactly, darling. And, Pop, now you've got the advantage of someone in insurance actually in the family, it makes it so much easier.'

'What? You mean it's easier than having some creep loaded with policies pestering me at my digs—'

'Yes.'

'—to have a creep in the family doing exactly the same thing.'

A pause ensued. Miles went very red, muttered something about 'things to get on with' and left the room. Charles munched his toast.

'Daddy, there's no need to be rude to Miles.'

'I'm sorry, but it is tempting.'

'Look, he's been jolly tolerant. You arriving completely unannounced in the middle of the night, using our house as a hotel. We might have had people staying. As it is, he's put off his fishing so as to entertain you—'

'That was entertainment? My God, what's he like when he's not making an effort?'

Juliet ignored him. 'And I think you might show a bit of gratitude. Daddy, I do wish you'd just get yourself sorted out.'

Oh, sharper than the serpent's tooth it is, to have an ungrateful father. But, Charles reflected, even sharper to have a middle-aged daughter of twenty-one. Where had he gone wrong, as a parent? There must have been a moment when Juliet had shown some spark of individuality which he failed to foster. Some moment when she, as a child, was on the verge of doing something wrong, and he could have fulfilled a father's role and made her do it. But no, his daughter had always been a model of sobriety, good works and even chastity (a virgin when she married at nineteen. In 1973. So much for the permissive society.) It's disappointing for a father.

Miles reappeared, incongruously dressed in brand-new green waders, a brand-new camouflage jacket and brand-new shapeless hat. 'Look, Pop, sorry we got heated.'

'No one got heated. I was just rather rude to you.

Miles laughed in man-of-the-world style. 'Jolly good, Pop. That's what I like. Straight talking. Eh? Look, what I wondered was, would you like to come fishing with me? Got time for a couple of hours, then a quick pint at the local, while Juliet gets the lunch. What do you say?'

'Well, I should be—' Charles remembered his mission.

'We could go into Streatley, there's a nice pub there.'

'Oh, all right.' It was important to get there and a lift in Miles' odious yellow Cortina was as good a way as any other. He graciously accepted the olive branch.

*

Charles persuaded a rather grudging Miles that he had time for a quick bath before they left. It was still only half-past nine. Apparently it was Miles' fishing that got them up so early. Charles wondered. To him, getting up early on a Sunday seemed sacrilegious, particularly if you had a woman around. Some of the best times of his life had been Sunday mornings. Toast, newspapers and a warm body. Not for the first time, he tried to visualise his daughter's sex-life. It defied imagination. Perhaps a regular weekly deposit with a family protective policy and a bonus of an extra screw at age twenty-five.

As he lay in the marine blue bath (matching the marine blue wash-basin and separate lavatory), laced with Juliet's bubble bath, Charles thought about the Steen situation. It seemed a long way away and he focused his mind with an effort. Assuming he could see Steen and hand over the photographs, it would soon be over. Now Bill Sweet was dead, there was no one else to put on the pressure. Charles conveniently put the circumstances of Sweet's death to the back of his mind. He didn't feel any obligation to see justice done in that matter. If Steen was a murderer, that wasn't his business. Let the police deal with it. If they really wanted to find a motive for the murder, they should grill Mrs Sweet. She could supply them with a few answers.

But did Mrs Sweet know about Steen? Had she realised who was responsible for her husband's death? In fact, did she know all the details of his blackmailing activities or was she just cashing in as much as possible? If Mrs Sweet was in the picture, she might continue the pressure on Steen, and that could have unpleasant repercussions for Jacqui. It suddenly became rather urgent to find out how much Mrs Sweet knew.

The trouble with modern architect-designed houses on estates (what's the alternative to an architect-designed house—a milkman-designed house? a footballer-designed house?) is that there's no privacy. The telephone in the Taylersons' executive home was situated in the middle of the open-plan living area, which had unimpeded access to the kitchen area, the sitting area and the upstairs area. In other words, Juliet and Miles were bound to hear every word of any telephone conversation. But there was no alternative.

The ringing tone stopped. 'Hello.'

'Ah, Mrs Sweet. It's ... er ... Bill Holroyd.' The old *When We are Married* voice.

'Ah, Mr Holroyd.' Interest.

'Yes ... er, the reason I'm ringing is ... er ... I've just heard about your husband ...'

'Yes.' No emotion.

'I wondered if ... er ... this changed the situation?'

'No. You deal with me.'

'Yes. Er ... nasty business.' No reaction. 'This doesn't mean that the ... er ... police ... would ... er ...'

'Don't worry. I haven't told them a thing.'

'Oh good.'

'Yes. You just give me what you owe and you'll never hear about that particular business again.'

'Fine. There was ... er ... something else. One or two of my friends were also at the party ...'

'Yes.'

'A Mr Phillips, a Mr Cuthbertson, a Mr—' he tried desperately to think of a name '—Taylerson. They... er ... wondered if they featured in the photographs.'

'Yes, I rather think they did. You'd better put them in touch with me.'

'Yes.' Charles was getting the information he wanted. Obviously Mrs Sweet hadn't a clue who any of the people in the photographs were. But best to be sure. 'Mr Taylerson in particular was anxious. He seemed to think he might feature in some pictures with a blonde girl. And a mask.' The Steen and Jacqui photographs were the only ones that fitted the description.

'That's Mr Taylerson, ah.' She didn't know. 'Perhaps I'd better get in touch with him. Do you know his address?' Charles resisted the temptation to give Miles' address, funny though the image of his son-in-law being blackmailed with dirty photographs was. 'No, I think I'd better put him in touch with you.'

'Yes, do that. And I'll see you Wednesday.'

'Yes.'

'With the money.'

'Yes.'

'And ...' the voice continued with studied casualness, 'perhaps you'd better double the money ...'

'What?'

'Mr Holroyd, you remember yesterday afternoon?'

'Yes.'

'Well, would you believe it, Mr Hoyroyd, there's a camera trained on that sofa.'

'Oh.'

'I'm sure you wouldn't want your wife and two lovely daughters to—'

'No.'

'Ten thousand then, Mr Holroyd, and you'll have the whole album.'

'But I—' The line went dead. Charles felt enormous relief that he wasn't Bill Holroyd. Bill Holroyd was a man with problems. Still, it explained Mrs Sweet's sudden change of behaviour. Oh dear, and he'd thought it was his own animal magnetism.

Charles turned to see Miles and Juliet standing open-mouthed in the kitchen doorway. 'Sorry about that. Talking to an actress friend. Always fool about like that. Putting on voices.

'Yes,' said Miles in a very old-fashioned voice. 'I suppose a lot of that sort of thing goes on with actors and ... you know. Perhaps we can go fishing now.'

'Just one more call. Will be quick, I promise. What's the code for Streatley from here?'

Again it was a recorded answer. Steen's voice gave the number. 'Marius Steen speaking. Not available at the moment. Ring later, or leave a message after this noise.'

Miles had the complete kit. Not only the shining new camouflage clothes, but various shining new containers of tackle. A waterproof khaki bag to hang from one shoulder, a long black leather rod-case to hang from the other, and an assortment of neatly dangling nets, stools and bait-boxes. As he laid out his instruments on squares of cloth like a surgeon, he said, 'You know, Pop, fishing's a very good relaxant. Relaxation is important to anyone in an executive position.'

They were sitting on the bank opposite Steen's house, Miles on a new folding chair of shining chromium tubes, Charles on a relegated wooden stool. He had chosen the location deliberately, assuring Miles that it was a very promising swim, that the swirlings of the current denoted barbel pits and that the overhanging trees were a good lie for large pike. It was all nonsense, but it was in the right language and Miles was impressed.

So Charles had a good view. The bungalow didn't look so large from the back, just discreetly expensive, a low white outline from which the lawn sloped gently down to a neat concreted waterside. To the left there was a small boat-house whose locked doors gave on to the river.

The bungalow showed no sign of life, and there had not been any when they had driven past on the road. Charles had persuaded Miles to stop and tried ringing the bell on the gate. No reply.

But somebody had been there overnight. Not only was there the evidence of the changed recording on the telephone. The puddles outside the bungalow gates showed fresh tyre-marks. Steen was certainly around somewhere; it was just a question of waiting; and, in the meantime, fishing.

'I think the thing for these sort of conditions,' said Miles, 'is a swimfeeder.'

'Ah.'

'Yes. Quite definitely. Filled with a gentle and bread-paste mixture, with a couple of gentles on a number twelve hook, I think it'd be a cert for bream.'

'Maybe.'

'Yes. Or roach.'

'Hm.'

'Well, that's what it recommended in this angling magazine I was reading. I reckon these are the sort of conditions it described. More or less.'

'Yes.' Charles flipped his line out into the water. He'd been lent an old relegated rod with two mottled bamboo sections and a greenheart tip, a plastic centre-pin reel and a yellowed quill float. He'd put a couple of maggots on a small hook. He sat and watched the quill being borne along by the current and then leaning over as it tugged at the end of the swim.

'Have you plumbed?' asked Miles.

'I beg your pardon?'

'Plumbed the depth of the swim. You'll never catch anything if you don't do that. You see, what the angler has to do with his bait is to make it imitate as nearly as possible the conditions of nature. In nature things don't dangle awkwardly in the water. They flow, carried along by the current, a few inches above the bottom. Depending on the season, of course.'

'Of course.'

'Would you like a plummet? I've got one.'

'No thanks. I'm trying to give them up.'

Miles was silent, preoccupied with opening his latest piece of equipment. Proudly he stripped off the packaging and screwed a limp length of fibreglass to the end of his sleek fibreglass rod. Charles looked on with an expression of distaste which Miles took for admiration. 'Swingtip.'

'Ah.'

'Best sort of bite-detector for bottom-fishing.'

'Ah.' Charles reflected how Miles always talked out of books. His son in-law was the least spontaneous person he'd ever met. Nothing came naturally; it all had to be worked at. Whatever interest he took up, he would begin by a painstaking study of the language and then buy all the correct equipment, before he actually did anything practical. Fishing was the latest accomplishment which Miles thought the young executive should not be without.

Again Charles found himself wondering about Miles and Juliet's sex-life. Had that been approached in the same meticulous way? 'Well, here we are on our honeymoon, Juliet darling. What I will do, when we are in bed and an atmosphere of mutual trust and relaxation has been established, is to practise a certain amount of foreplay. This is likely to begin with a kneading or massaging of the breasts in an accelerating stroking motion. This will be followed by manual clitoral stimulation ...' The idea was intriguing. Charles wondered if he was becoming a dirty old man. But it *was* intriguing. Guiltily, he disguised his interest in a standard father-in-law question. 'Miles, have you and Juliet thought of having a family?'

Miles sat up with irritation. He'd just been trying to squeeze a split-shot on to his line and it had popped out of his fingers. 'Yes, Pop, we have. We reckon in about four and a half years I should have gone up at least a grade, so, allowing for the usual increments, and assuming that the mortgage rate doesn't rise above the present eleven per cent, I should think we could afford to let Juliet stop work then.'

There was no answer to that, so Charles sat and looked out over the water to Steen's bungalow. Nothing. It was very cold. The air stung his face and he felt the ground's iciness creep into his feet through the soles of Miles' relegated gum-boots. His body was stiff and uncomfortable. Always got like that when he sat still for a long time. He felt his years. A sure sign he needed a drink.

Miles had now completed the cat's cradle at the end of his line, and had loaded the perspex tube of his swim-feeder with a porridgy mash of bread and maggots. Two favoured maggots squirmed on the end of his size twelve hook (hooked, no doubt, as the books recommend, through the small vent in the thick end). Miles rose to his feet and fiddled with the knobs of his gleaming fixed-spool reel. 'The important thing,' he quoted almost to himself, 'is to remember it's not brute force with a fixed-spool reel; just a controlled flick.'

He made a controlled flick. The line jerked and maypoled itself around the rod. The contents of the swim-feeder sprayed from their case like shotgun pellets and landed with a scattering plop in the middle of the river.

Charles didn't say anything, but controlled his lips and looked at his float.

As he did so, it submerged. He struck, and reeled in rather a good perch.

Four hasty pints before the pub closed at two saw Charles through lunch, and there was a bit of wine too. 'Le Piat Beaujolais Primeur,' said Miles '— young, robust and slightly petillant, ideal with meat dishes.' (Obviously he had read a book on wine too.) The combination of alcohols anaesthetised Charles so that he could even watch the holiday slides of Tenerife without excessive pain.

They were not very varied—'Juliet in front of a shop ... and here's Juliet in this bar place ... and this one's of Juliet sitting on a rock ... and here's Juliet in a boat—that was the day we went for a boat trip ...' Obviously Miles did not trust her with his camera or there might have been a matching sequence of 'Miles in front of a shop ... Miles in this bar place ...' etc. References in the commentary to shutter speeds, and exposures and lenses demonstrated that Miles had read a book on photography too. Charles let it all flow over him. Time was suspended, and he was too fuddled for darker thoughts.

The peaceful mood lasted until he stood alone on Goring Bridge. Miles and Juliet had offered him a lift to Pangbourne Station, but they'd got some people coming and were very relieved when he said he'd get a minicab to Reading. Miles had been dropping heavy hints about how difficult it was to get petrol and how he intended to use the Cortina 'for emergency uses only'. (By moving up from the level of salesman in his insurance company, he'd sacrificed a firm's car and was rather careful about using his own.)

When the cab came, Charles left in a surge of family effusiveness, and then, feeling like the hero of some of the terrible thriller films he'd been in during the fifties, he told the driver to go to Steen's home instead. As they approached Streatley, he lost his nerve and asked to be dropped by the bridge. The driver, with the predictability of all motorists over the last few weeks, commented on the petrol crisis, overcharged grossly, and drove off into the night.

The bridge at Goring is long and narrow; there are two spans to an island in the middle; one side is Streatley, the other Goring. Charles stood on the narrow pavement, leaning on the wooden parapet, and looked down into the water, which seemed infinitely deep in the darkness. Somewhere the church bells rang in the distance, calling the faithful to evensong. Their old-fashioned domesticity seemed incongruous as his thoughts darkened.

The pressure which had been building up all weekend was nearing some sort of explosion. The Steen business had to be sorted out that evening. Charles felt an uncomfortable sense of urgency. It was now nearly a week since Bill Sweet's death on Sunday 2nd December, and Jacqui was still in great danger. Charles had known the full implications of the situation for only twenty-four hours, but he had a sick feeling that time was running out. A sense of gloom blanketed his thought as he looked down to the dark water and heard the hiss of it rushing over the invisible weir ahead of him. Somewhere down in the depths, he felt certain, lay Marius Steen's gun, thrown away after the murder was committed.

He'd wasted the day. The fishing, the slides of Tenerife were all irrelevant; he should have been dealing with Steen. It was one of the most important responsibilities of his life. And this was one he couldn't shirk. It must be done straight away. He looked at his watch. Nearly seven. The pubs would soon be open. Just a quick drink for a bracer and then it must be done.

It was twenty past nine when he left the cosy fireside of the Bull. He was braced to the point of recklessness. Two hours of sipping Bell's and listening to the quacks of the local Scampi and Mateus Rosé crowd made the whole issue seem much simpler. If Steen was there, Charles had only to tell him the truth; if he wasn't, then he could leave the photographs with an anonymous note explaining Jacqui's innocence. He couldn't think why it hadn't occurred to him earlier, as he marched briskly (after a bit of trouble with the door latch) out of the pub.

The moon was fuller than the night before, but its light was diffused by cloud. He could see quite clearly as he climbed the hill out of the village. It didn't feel as cold as it had done earlier in the day. He stopped to relieve himself into the roadside bushes and almost lost his balance as a car screeched round the corner in a clatter of gravel. He zipped himself up and strode onwards. A strange sense of purpose filled him, even a sense of honour. Sir Galahad nearing the end of his quest. Marius Steen, the giant who seemed to have been looming over his life now for a week was about to be confronted. A fragment repeated itself inappropriately like a mantra in Charles' mind. 'My strength is as the strength of ten, because my heart is pure.'

He was almost disappointed when he reached the gates. He'd expected a great brazen trumpet hanging, with a legend in outlandish characters—'Who dares to brave the giant's wrath, let him sound this trump.' And in the trees, clattering sadly, the armour of those who had dared, and failed in the combat. He turned to look at the trees, but they were bare. And the only sound was the wind breathing on their branches.

Charles leant unsteadily against the gate-post and pressed the fluorescent button. He didn't wait for any response, but pushed open the heavy white gates with a scrunch of gravel. The bungalow again seemed to have grown in the moonlight, and was now a Moorish temple, where the infidel foe lurked. A light shone through a chink in the curtains of a window above the garage door.

No one appeared as Charles approached the front door, but he felt as if he was being watched. Suddenly the night had become very silent. He beat a tattoo with the door-knocker, and again its reverberations filled the whole world. But no one came. The quarry was lying low.

Charles pushed the door but it was very solid. He backed away and looked along the front of the house. The windows appeared to be shut firm. Garage? He walked heavily down the ramp and grasped the handle that should lift the door up and over. Locked.

But he had reached a pitch where he couldn't give up. He stumbled round the side of the house, through the flower beds, feeling the windows. All were tightly locked.

Round the back of the bungalow he was suddenly aware of the slow wash of water at the end of the lawn. There was no other sound and no light was visible on this elevation. But he knew Marius Steen was inside.

There was a small door which corresponded with the back of the garage. He walked up a crazy-paving path and tried the handle. Braced for a shove he nearly overbalanced when the door gave inwards.

It was very dark. He blinked, trying to accustom his eyes to the change, but still couldn't see much. There were no windows and only a trickle of light came in through the door behind him. From what he could see, it illuminated a pile of boxes. Perhaps he was in some sort of store-room rather than the garage. He moved slowly forward, groping ahead with a breast-stroke motion.

But discretion was difficult in his alcoholic state. There was some thing in the way of his foot, then an object with a sharp edge fell agonisingly on to his ankle. Whatever it was precipitated an avalanche of other objects which thundered down around him as Charles fell sprawling to the ground.

He lay frozen, waiting for some reaction, but there was nothing. It was only his tense state that made the crash sound so loud. Gingerly he reached forward, found a wall and levered himself up against it. Then he felt along to a door frame and followed its outline until he found a light-switch.

The sudden glare was blinding, but when he unscrewed his eyes, he could see he was in a kind of windowless utility room. There was a washing machine, a spin dryer, a washing-up machine, a deep-freeze and rows of neatly hanging brooms and mops. Above these was a cluster of meters, fuse-boxes and power-switches. Deep shelves on the opposite wall contained boxes of tinned food and crates of spirits. There was a spreading honeycomb of a wine-rack, full and expensive-looking.

And on the floor Charles could see what had caused his fall. A pile of boxes lay scattered like a demolished chimney. He knelt down and re-piled them. They were heavy, as he knew from the numbing pain in his shin. He looked at the writing on the boxes. 'Salmon', 'Trout', 'Strawberries.' 'Do not refreeze.' Marius Steen certainly knew how to live.

When he had finished piling the boxes up, Charles looked once more round the room and his eyes lighted on the very thing he needed at that moment—a torch. It was a long, black, rubber-encased one, hanging from a hook by the back door. He took it down, switched on, turned off the light and opened the door into the rest of the house.

He was in the garage. It was large, but dominated by the huge form of a dark blue Rolls-Royce. Remembering a detail with sudden clarity, Charles knelt down and looked at the left-hand side of the front bumper. There was a little dent, which he'd lay any money corresponded to the dent in the back right-hand wing of Bill Sweet's Ford Escort. The door of the Rolls was not locked. Key in the ignition, nothing in the glove compartment and the petrol gauge read empty.

Charles moved round the great car, looking for any other clues it might give. He felt his foot slip under him and sat down with a jarring shock, landing uncomfortably on a spanner and a piece of plastic tubing. Fate seemed determined to translate his dramatic mission into slapstick.

He found the door which led to the body of the house. Along a corridor and into the large hall. All the walls were hung with hunting prints which were anonymously expensive, bought on advice by a man without natural taste. Two enormous china Dalmatians stood guarding the front door. They seemed to reflect more of their owner's personality. They were Steen the showman; the prints were Steen the man who wanted to gatecrash high society, the man who wanted a knighthood.

There were no lights in evidence, except for a slight glow from the top of a short flight of steps, which must lead to a room above the garage. The room whose light Charles had seen from the front.

He moved purposefully up the stairs and began to feel faint. The drink was telling; he felt his energy wane. He had to get the interview over quickly.

The first room he came to was a kind of study, equipped with telephones, typewriters, and copying machines. The walls were covered with framed photographs of stars from Marius Steen's shows, scribbled with effusive messages. It was a sentimental showbiz touch that again didn't fit the man's character. What he felt was wanted, rather than what he wanted. Bernard Walton's face grinned patronisingly down from the wall.

The study was empty; the light came from the adjacent room. Charles switched off his torch with a dull click and moved towards the half-open door. Through its crack he could see a plush bedroom, dominated by a large four-poster bed. Curtains obscured his view, but the shape of the covers told him that the bed was occupied.

As he entered the room, exhaustion threatened to swamp him, but still he moved forward. Now, in the light of a bedside lamp, he could see Marius Steen lying back on the pillows asleep. The great beak of a nose, familiar from countless press photographs, rose out of the sheets like the dorsal fin of a shark. One large hand lay, palm upward, on the cover.

'Wake him, tell him and go.' Charles formulated his thoughts very simply with desperate concentration. He staggered forward to the bedside and stood there, swaying. As he reached for Steen's hand, he heard a car drawing up outside the gates. He clutched at the hand in panic, and felt the coldness of death.

CHAPTER NINE

Interval

CHARLES WOKE AS if his body was being dragged out of a deep pit, and memory returned slowly to his pounding head. He didn't like it when it came. He could see Steen's face in its pained repose, and felt certain that he was up against a case of murder.

He was lying in bed in Miles and Juliet's spare room. Vague memories of getting there. The rush from Steen's bedroom out through the garage and utility room, as he heard a car stopping on the gravel and footsteps approaching the garage door. Then he remembered skulking breathless behind the bungalow until the car was safely garaged, a rush through the gates, staggering along the road till a police car stopped, warnings—'Had a few too many, haven't you, sir? Still, won't charge you this time. But watch it'—and ignominious delivery on Miles and Juliet's doorstep.

He heaved himself out of bed and limped downstairs. The bruise on his ankle was cripplingly painful and he felt his forty-seven years. Too old to be involved in this escalating round of violence.

Juliet stood staring at him as he made it to the kitchen chair. She appeared not to have inherited Frances' forgiving nature. 'Really, Daddy, what a state to come home in.'

'I'm sorry, love.'

'Miles was furious.'

'Oh well.' There were more important things than Miles' sensibilities.

'I mean, the police coming here. What will other people on the estate think?'

'You can tell them the police weren't coming for you or Miles.'

'They wouldn't think that!'

'Miles can tell them it's just his drunken father-in-law.'

'I don't think they'd find that very amusing.' She turned away to make coffee. 'Honestly, Daddy, I don't think you have any concept of human dignity.'

That hurt. 'Listen, Juliet *darling*. I think I probably have more knowledge of the really important things that give a person dignity than ...' But it wasn't worth explaining; she wouldn't understand. 'Oh, forget it. Shouldn't you be at work?'

'I'm not going in till after lunch. There's not much to do and ... well, I was worried about you.'

It was the first softening Charles could ever remember hearing from Juliet. It warmed him. 'Thank you.'

'Honestly, Daddy, I don't know what you're up to half the time. That peculiar phone-call yesterday morning, and now all this. What on earth were you doing in Streatley anyway? I thought you had taken the cab to Reading.'

'Yes, I know. The thing is, I had to change my plans. It's all rather involved, but ...' He paused, and all the boiling thoughts inside him strained for an outlet. He had to tell someone. Why not Juliet? 'Marius Steen is dead.'

'Yes, I know.' Her answer was cool and unconcerned.

'How do you know?'

'It was on the radio this morning. On the *Today* programme.'

'What? How did it say he died?'

'Heart attack, I think it was. Here's your coffee.' As she placed the cup in front of him, Charles looked at his daughter, wondering if she could be involved in this grotesque business. But in her face, as easily read as her mother's, there was nothing devious; she was telling the truth. 'Anyway, Daddy, why do you tell me that? Was it Steen you went to see last night?'

'No.'

'I didn't know you knew him.'

'I didn't.' He sipped the coffee. It wasn't what he needed. His body felt dangerously unstable and bilious. 'Juliet, could you get me a drop of whisky?'

'At this time in the morning? Daddy'—with all the awe of a television documentary— are you an alcoholic?'

'I don't know. I've never thought about it. Where does liking a drink stop and being an alcoholic start?'

'I should think it starts when you need a *hair of the dog* the next morning.' Juliet italicised the unfamiliar phrase.

'Well, I do need one now.'

'I don't know whether I should—'

'Oh, get it!' he snapped impatiently. As Juliet scurried shocked to the cocktail cabinet, Charles asked himself whether he was in fact an alcoholic. On balance, he decided he probably wasn't. He could do without drink. But he wouldn't like to have to. It was an old joke—a teetotaller knows every morning when he wakes up that that's the best he's going to feel all day. Drink at least offers some prospect of things improving.

He felt Juliet's shocked eyes on him as he poured whisky into his coffee and drank it gratefully. It made him feel more stable, but desperately tired. Waves of relief washed over him. Steen had died of a heart attack. Thoughts of murder had been prompted only by the events of the previous week and the melodramatic circumstances of the discovery of the body. All the contradictory details evaporated. Charles believed what he wanted to believe. The pressure was off. 'Juliet love, what's the time?'

'Twenty past ten.'

'Look, I think I'll go back to bed for a bit.'

'But you must have something to eat.' Frances' eternal cry.

'When have you got to go to work?'

'Have to leave quarter to two.'

'Wake me at half-past twelve. Then I'll have something to eat. I promise.'

*

It wasn't until after lunch and Juliet's departure that Charles remembered about Jacqui, still lying low at Hereford Road. The public announcement of Steen's death had sapped the urgency out of him and yesterday's imperatives no longer mattered. Jacqui was just the frayed end of an otherwise completed pattern and it was with reluctance that he dialled his own number.

Jacqui answered. All of the Swedish girls must be out at their various Swedish employments. Her voice was guarded, but not panic-stricken. 'Charles? I wondered when you were going to ring. I was just about to leave.'

'Jacqui, I've got some bad news ...'

'It's all right. I heard. On *Open House*.'

'What?'

'The radio.'

'Ah. Well, I'm sorry.'

'Thank you.' There was a pause, and Charles could feel how fiercely she was controlling her emotions.

'Jacqui, I'm afraid I never got the photos to him.'

'That hardly matters now, does it? Nothing much matters now.'

'Jacqui ...'

'I'll be all right.'

'Yes. I suppose that's the end of it, isn't it?'

'I wouldn't count on that.'

'What do you mean?' Charles had an unpleasant feeling he was about to sacrifice his recently-won calm.

'Do you think he died of a heart attack, Charles?'

'Yes.'

There was a grunt from the other end of the line, a sound between exasperation and despair. 'Charles, I can't talk about it now. I'm too ... I'll talk when—'

'Tomorrow?'

'Yes, if I feel OK. Come round when you ... Evening. Eight or ...'

'OK. I'll be there. Archer Street. You'll be all right now?'

'Like hell.' The phone went dead.

Before Charles left the house in Pangbourne, he took the envelope of photographs out of his inside pocket and looked at them. With Steen's death they had changed. Already they had the air of curios or souvenirs—oddities from another age. The erotic quality had drained from them and they seemed like sepia prints in an album of someone else's relations. Mildly interesting, but ultimately irrelevant.

He looked around for somewhere to destroy them. The trouble with architect-designed houses on estates is that they have nothing like an open fire. The central heating was fired by oil. (Miles had already spoken gloomily of the inevitable price rises which the Middle East situation must precipitate. As he said portentously, 'You know, Pop, the days of cheap fuel are over.') The cooker was electric. There was no convenient stove to consume the evidence.

Charles took a giant box of matches from the kitchen and went out into the garden. The forty-foot long area was neatly organised. A potting shed of conspicuous new timber, a patio area protected by a screen of lattice-work bricks, a path of very sane crazy paving winding diagonally across the lawn, a meticulous row of cloches. Only the winter shagginess of the grass gave any hint of rampant nature or humanity.

It had started to rain. Big heavy drops that were cold as they fell, penetrating, on his head and shoulders. In the far corner of the garden Charles saw what he was looking for. Neatly screened by another low wall of lattice-work bricks were a compost heap, bound in by wooden slats, and an empty metal incinerator. He lit the photographs one by one and let the flimsy black rectangles of ash drop into the bin. Finally he burnt the envelope, then stirred the dampening fragments into a black unrecognisable mash.

CHAPTER TEN

Second Act Beginners

THE OBITUARY APPEARED in *The Times* the next day, Tuesday 11th December.

MR MARIUS STEEN
Impresario and Showman

Mr Marius Steen, CBE. the impresario, died on Sunday. He was 68. Born in Warsaw in 1905, his full name was Marius Ladislas Steniatowski, but he shortened it for convenience when his parents came to England in 1921. His father was a tailor and for some years the young Steen helped him in his business. But already the attraction of entertainment was strong; Steen spent most of his limited pocket-money on tickets for the music hall and in 1923 launched himself as Mario, the Melodic Whistler. In spite of changes in name and act, he was never a success as a performer, but became increasingly interested in the business of promotion and management. The first act he managed was Herbert and his Horrible Dogs in 1924.

Soon he was progressing from individual acts to the presentation of complete shows. Though he started with wrestling and all-girl revues, by 1930 he was presenting variety bills at music halls all over the country. Through the Thirties he centralised his activities on London and, in 1935, had his first major success with the spectacular revue *Go With The Girls*. None of these early productions had a great deal to recommend them artistically, but Steen always maintained that success must be measured by public reaction alone. And by that criterion his shows were highly successful.

Steen continued presenting revues, with an increasing reliance on scripted comedy rather than just dancing girls, until the outbreak of war. Then he moved into the cinema and, with his customary unflagging energy, set up a series of films in keeping with the jingoistic spirit of the times. Of these the most memorable was *Brothers in Battledress*, directed by William Hankin.

After the war Marius Steen continued to put on shows and gradually he forsook revue for musicals and light comedies. *What's in the Box?* was one of the greatest successes of 1953, and in 1960 Steen's purchase of the King's Theatre off Shaftesbury Avenue heralded a string of commercial triumphs, including *One Thing After Another,* which ran for three years, and, currently, *Sex of One and Half a Dozen of the Other.*

Steen maintained his interest in the cinema and put money into many ventures including the highly successful Steenway Productions, which make horror films. He was also a major shareholder in three commercial television companies, and was at the time of his death interesting himself in the production of programmes for network on the new commercial radio station.

Marius Steen was often criticised for his healthy disrespect for 'Art' and there are many stories of this supposed philistinism which he loved to tell against himself. (On first hearing of Michelangelo, he is reputed to have asked 'Michael who?' His alleged description of opera as 'fat gits singing' is probably apocryphal.) He was a forthright man who made enemies, but was loved and respected by his friends. He had no hobbies, maintaining that if a person needed hobbies, then there was something wrong with his work. He divided his time between his houses in London and Streatley and a villa in the South of France. In 1969 he was awarded the CBE for services to the theatre.

Marius Steen married Rose Whittle in 1934. She died in 1949 and he never remarried. He leaves a son.

Charles was impressed. It was quite an achievement for anyone in the theatre to command that many column inches in The Times. The obituary seemed like a washing of the body. It cleaned Steen up. The existence of the photographs, all the sordid aspects of the man's life were rinsed away by the formalised prose. The Western ritual of death was observed—the obligation to remember the most dignified image of the deceased. Like those ghastly American mausoleums where the embalmed corpse is presented at its best, dressed and smiling, prior to burial. But Charles had a nagging feeling that, however Marius Steen was tarted up in death, his corpse would not lie down.

Charles arrived at the Archer Street flat with a two-litre bottle of Valpolicella from Oddbins and a determination to be very slow on the uptake in any discussion of Steen's death. Jacqui looked ghastly when she opened the door. Her face was pale and her eyes were puffy red slits.

'Are you all right?'

'I will be, Charles. I'll just sit down for a moment.'

'Can I get you a drink?'

'No. It'd make me sick. But help yourself.'

The events of the last few days had made Charles forget about Jacqui's flat being done over, but inside it the evidence was all too clear. She had obviously made some attempt to tidy up. There were two cardboard boxes in the middle of the room full of bits of glass and torn clothes. But the curtains were still hanging shredded from their rails, and the bed smelt of oil from the smashed lamp. The little room looked sad and crippled.

He didn't make any comment, but found an unbroken glass and filled it with Valpolicella. 'Do you want to go out to eat, Jacqui?'

'No, I couldn't.'

'Hmm.' The silence was obtrusive. Feebly he repeated himself. 'Do you feel all right?'

'Charles, the bloke I loved and whose kid I've got has just been murdered.'

'I'm sorry.' He stolidly avoided reacting to the word 'murdered'. Jacqui softened. 'I'll get you some food later. When I can face it.'

'Don't worry about that. Not particularly hungry.'

'No.' Again they were conscious of the silence. Then Jacqui burst out. 'He always was a little sod.'

Charles was genuinely amazed. 'Who?'

'Nigel.'

'Nigel Steen?'

'Well, who else?'

'Why do you suddenly bring him in?'

'Because he killed Marius, that's why.'

This new direction of thought was too sudden for Charles to take in. Deliberately, he slowed down. 'What on earth do you mean? You haven't got any reason for saying that.'

'Of course I have. Who else stood to get anything out of Marius' death?'

'I don't know. I would have thought Nigel was doing all right anyway. He didn't need to murder anyone. Presumably he'd have got everything when his father went. He only had to wait.'

'He's greedy. Anyway, things may have changed. Maybe he had to move fast.'

'What do you mean?' Charles asked patiently, determined to humour her through this crazy new idea.

'Marius was thinking of changing his will in favour of me and the baby.'

'Oh yes.' Charles tried to sound believing, but failed.

'Yes, he bloody was. He was even talking about us getting married.'

'When was this?'

'First in the South of France. Then when I told him about the baby he was more definite. He said he'd felt awful about the abortion last time, and he wanted to keep this one and marry me and start again.'

'And cut Nigel out of the will?'

'I suppose so.'

It didn't sound very plausible. Even if Steen had ever had such intentions, the events of the last week made it clear that he had changed his mind. And the whole idea of remarriage and disowning Nigel was the sort of novelette situation that would appeal to Jacqui. Still, he couldn't be completely brutal with her. 'Why didn't you mention this before?'

'It was a secret. Between Marius and me. It was all going to be secret. Even when we married it was going to be a secret for a bit. But now he's dead ...' She broke down.

Charles calmed her and forced her to drink a little wine. But when she was composed again, he felt he had to be cruel. If Steen had been murdered (and he had no cause to believe that that was the case), then it was something to do with the Sweets and the blackmailing business. It was dangerous for Jacqui to go around blaming his son. She was quite capable of going to the police and making accusations which, since she hadn't a shred of evidence, could only lead to trouble. This nonsense had to be stopped.

'If what you say is true, how do you explain Steen's behaviour during the past week? Hardly the actions of a devoted husband-to-be.'

He could see from her face that that really hurt, and also that it was something she hadn't been able to work out satisfactorily for herself. 'Well, Nigel kept him from me. Marius went off to Berkshire—where he didn't want to be disturbed. He'd often do that,' she added defensively, 'go off with a great pile of scripts, looking for his next show. And then Nigel left all those messages for me.'

'And he sent the note?'

'Yes.'

'Pity I burnt it. We could have got the handwriting analysed,' he said sceptically.

'That note's just the sort of thing the little sod would do.'

'Jacqui, why, if Nigel had decided to kill his father anyway, did he bother to give the impression you were out of favour?'

'So that, when he'd done it, nobody would believe me when I said about us getting married. They'd think we'd had a quarrel.'

It was ingenious, but Charles didn't feel very inclined to accept the reasoning. 'All right then, when did Nigel do the murder?'

'Sunday evening. When he says he found the body.'

'How do you know he found the body? It wasn't in the papers.'

'I rang Morrison. He told me.'

'Who's Morrison?'

'Sort of odd-job man at Orme Gardens. He was meant to be the chauffeur, but Marius liked driving himself. I rang Morrison and he told me Nigel had driven down to Streatley and found the body dead in bed at about quarter past eleven on Sunday night. Well, Marius never went to bed before one, so I don't believe that for a start.'

'I think you may have to believe it.' Charles told her about his movements on the Sunday night, concluding, '... so it must have been the arrival of Nigel's car that made me run out of the place.'

'And you are sure Marius was dead?'

'Quite sure. He was cold. He had been dead some time.'

'Perhaps Nigel had come earlier and killed him and then arranged to come back and find the body.'

'I hate to sound like a detective, but there was a puddle outside the front gate and only one new set of tyre-marks between the Saturday night and the Sunday night. They must have been Steen coming back on the Saturday. I know he did come back because of the new tape on the Ansaphone.'

'Perhaps Nigel killed him on the Saturday night.' Jacqui was desperate to hang on to her theory, but she could feel it slipping away. Charles shook his head. 'I'm sorry, Jacqui, but you must face the facts. Marius had a history of heart trouble—you say he'd had a minor attack before you went to France in the summer. He was a man of 68— worked hard all his life—never made any concessions to age. Is it surprising that he should die a natural death from a heart attack? Apart from anything else, if there were suspicious circumstances, the doctor wouldn't have signed a certificate. So far as we know there's been no suspicion of foul play.'

'The doctor must have been in league with Nigel,' Jacqui insisted truculently.

'If there was any mark on the body, the undertaker would notice.'

'There are poisons which don't leave any trace.'

'Jacqui, my love'—he deliberately sounded patronising. Having chosen the role of the infinitely reasonable older man, he was determined to stick to it—you have read too many detective stories.'

That finally silenced her. She sat still for a full five minutes, then stood up brusquely. 'I'll get you some food.'

It was another of Jacqui's frozen meals. This time fish steaks with still-frozen centres and bright slivers of French beans. Charles consumed most of the Valpolicella and tried to steer the conversation away from anything to do with Marius Steen. It was difficult. Small talk kept erupting into some new accusation or burst of crying from Jacqui. Charles found it a strain and was relieved when the meal was over and he felt he could decently leave. 'You get to bed, Jacqui. You look absolutely knackered. I'd better be off.'

'Yes. Charles.'

'Yes.'

'Do you mind staying?'

'No. OK.' He lied. She obviously needed him, and so the awkwardness must be prolonged.

'I don't mean ... you know ...' she said feebly, and the waif-like expression on her strained face made it difficult to grasp immediately what she did mean. Then he realised she was referring to sex. It seemed incongruous in relation to the events of the last week.

'Of course not. No, I'll stay. As long as you need someone around.'

'Just for the night. I didn't sleep at all last night. It was awful. I kept hearing things and imagining. Just tonight. I'll be all right tomorrow. Got to be. Sort out what I'm going to do about the baby. I'll have to get rid of it.'

'Jacqui, you must keep the baby.' Charles had long since ceased to delude himself that he had any immovable principles on anything, but he felt something approaching that on the subject of abortion. Without having a particular reason, like Catholicism, he found it unjustifiable. He tried to argue in his mind against this conviction, because he was frightened by feelings of such strength. Granted, he'd say to himself, I've never been in a situation where an abortion has been necessary. Natural caution has prevented me from getting anyone into trouble. If it happened, no doubt that principle would crumble like any other. But the instinct remained strong.

And as Jacqui's suffering face looked up at him, he knew he had said the right thing. There was relief and determination there, in spite of her words. 'But I can't look after a baby on my own. I can hardly look after myself.'

She sounded so plaintive that Charles laughed and Jacqui even managed a brief grin. 'Don't worry'—at his most avuncular—'something'll happen.'

'What? Nothing can, now Marius is dead.'

'Something will happen,' he repeated with a confidence whose basis he didn't like to investigate. 'Now, where am I going to sleep?'

'Oh, with me. It's daft for you to get a stiff neck on the sofa when there's room in my bed.'

So they settled down, Charles in shirt and underpants, Jacqui in silk pyjamas, cradled in his arms. It was eight days since they had last lain on the bed together, and sex seemed as far away now as then. But this time Charles' feelings were mellower. It seemed all right that this sad and trembling body should lie in his arms. There was a lot to be said for cuddling. Now he seemed to find it even more attractive than screwing. Perhaps it was the approach of old age, sliding into impotent fumblings. As he fell asleep, Byron's lines floated through his fuddled mind.

We'll go no more a-screwing
So late into the night,
Though the heart is still as loving
And the moon is still as bright.

When he woke, he was alone in the bed. He could hear Jacqui being sick in the bathroom. It was a nostalgic sound, taking him back to the flat in Notting Hill where he and Frances had started their married life; and started Juliet; and, in a way, started living apart. Nappies boiling on the gas-stove, the sweet smell of breast milk—it all came back. 'I am degenerating into a sentimental old fool,' he thought as he rolled out of bed.

Jacqui came in as he was pulling on his trousers, and sat down, looking drained. 'OK?' he asked.

'I will be. I hope I will. It's ghastly. Look.' She closed her eyes grimly and pointed at the table. There was a letter which had been opened and shoved back into the envelope.

'Can I read it?' Jacqui nodded. Charles pulled the papers out. There was a short letter and a smaller envelope, which had also been opened. The letter was on paper headed 'Cohn, Jarvis, Cohn and Stickley—Solicitors and Commissioners for Oaths.'

Dear Miss Mitchell,

On the instructions of my client, Mr Marius Steen, I am sending you the enclosed letter. I have no knowledge of its contents, but was instructed to send it to you as soon as I heard news of Mr Steen's death.

Yours sincerely,
Harold Cohn.

'Can I read the other one?'

'Go ahead.'

He opened the envelope. The letter was written in a sprawling hand, writing that had once undergone the discipline of copperplate, but long ago broken loose from its restrictions and now spread, thick and unguarded, over the page.

2nd November

Dear Titty ...

Jacqui was studying Charles' face and anticipating his reaction. 'Marius always called me that.' Charles continued reading.

If you get this letter, I am dead. So I'm sorry. The old heart or some other bit of my body has given out and fouled the system and I've gone. So that's a pity. Not because I haven't had a good run, just that I'd like the run to continue. I'm a winner and I want to go on winning. And when you came on the scene, I started enjoying my winning even more.

As you know, I wanted to marry you. Depending on when you get this letter, I may already have married you. If not, believe me, it's all I want to do. I only care about you and the little bastard in your belly. I'm sure he'll turn out better than the other one.

And the main purpose of this letter is to tell you and your beautiful body not to worry. If Marius is dead, Marius will still look after you. There'll be money for you and the baby. Call him Marius.

Love,
Marius

Charles looked up at Jacqui. In her face was discomfort and sadness, but also an unmistakable gleam of triumph.

CHAPTER ELEVEN

Enter the Funny Policeman

HE THOUGHT HE must be going soft in the head. To have tried to help Jacqui in the matter of the photographs was illogical, but at least generous, getting her out of an awkward situation. But assisting her investigations into a perfectly natural death as if it were murder was little short of lunacy.

She had read so much into Steen's letter. Channelling all the pain of her loss into arguments to support her theory, she leapt on to the promise of provision for her and the baby, and to the sentence, 'I'm sure he'll turn out better than the other one.' To her mind, these proved conclusively that Marius had decided to change his will in her favour, and that Nigel had got wind of this and forestalled his father's plans by killing him. Charles put up all the arguments scepticism could muster, but somehow ended up agreeing with Jacqui that it was at least worth further investigation.

Which was why, on Thursday 13th December, he was taking Gerald Venables out to lunch. Gerald had been a contemporary at Oxford, who had read Law and acted a little. He had been elected Treasurer of the Oxford University Dramatic Society and, as such, demonstrated the prime motive of his life—an unashamed love of money. This motive led him after university away from the Theatre and into the Law. He joined a firm of solicitors specialising in show-business contract work, became a partner within five years and thereafter just made more and more money. The subject fascinated him; he always talked about money; but did it with such an ingenuous enthusiasm that the effect was not alienating. At worst he was boring, in the same way that a golfer or a photographer or a dinghy-sailor or any other person obsessed by a hobby is boring.

When the Stilton was produced, Gerald undid another button of his exquisitely cut tweed waistcoat and patted his paunch beneficently. 'What is it, Charles? Are you putting some work my way? I'd better warn you, my rates, which were always pretty high, are now almost beyond belief.'

'I anticipated as much. It's not exactly work. I don't know how you'd define it ...'

'Ah, if it isn't readily defined, it's automatically at double the rate.'

'Yes. It's a matter of investigation—or do I mean snooping?'

'That's what solicitors are for.'

'Exactly. The point is, I know solicitors individually are totally immoral'—Gerald nodded assent as if accepting a compliment '—and I suppose, as with any other bunch of thieves, there is honour among you.' Again Gerald graciously inclined his head. 'So no doubt you scratch each other's backs.' The third nod was very positive. 'What I want you to do is to find out some information from another solicitor.'

'Officially?'

'Unofficially.'

'Ah. Comes more expensive.'

'I thought it might.'

'What do you want to know, Charles?'

'You've heard of Marius Steen, bloke who's just died?'

'Of course. Been involved in a lot of contracts with him. He was a real shark, totally immoral.' Gerald's voice carried a hint of respect as he made this tribute.

'So you know his solicitor?'

'Harold Cohn. Of course. He's the hardest bargainer in the business.' A diffident smile. 'Present company, of course, excepted.'

'Of course.'

'And you want to know about the old man's will?'

'How the hell did you know that?'

'Because there's nothing else anyone could possibly want to know about a man three days dead. There has been quite a lot of speculation on the matter in professional circles.'

'Any conclusions?'

'Rumours, but nothing definite.'

'Do you think you could find out?'

Gerald smiled blandly. 'I wouldn't have thought it was beyond the realms of possibility.' A waiter was hovering at his shoulder. 'We'll have coffee, won't we, Charles? And a Cognac, perhaps. Yes, two Cognacs.' He looked thoughtfully over the table. 'Now I wonder why you would be interested in Steen's will, Charles. You're hardly expecting to be a beneficiary, are you?'

'No. Hardly.'

Gerald looked at him, puzzled. He didn't like being in a position of ignorance on any subject, and started probing. 'Whoever it goes to, there's a lot.'

'Yes.'

'Steen did all right. Even with estate duty, it'll be worth having.'

Charles nodded, determined not to give anything away.

Gerald tried another tack. 'You want to find this out for yourself?'

'Yes.'

'It'll be public knowledge soon. If you can only wait a few—'

'I want to know as soon as possible.'

'Well, Charles, you are a dark horse.' Gerald sat back in his chair and sipped his Cognac. It was amusing for Charles to see him in this state, his usual poise unbalanced by childlike curiosity. 'Charles, is it a crime?'

'What do you mean?'

'Are there any suspicions about the will? Surprise heirs in Australia, forgery, skulduggery with birth certificates, secret codicils?' Gerald threw out the ideas like baits, hoping to catch some reaction. Charles smiled in a way that he knew was infuriating.

Gerald was suitably infuriated. 'Oh, for God's sake, Charles. You can tell me. Look, if I know the circumstances, it'll make my enquiries much easier.' Charles continued to smile. Gerald was reduced to infantile tactics. 'Listen, if you don't tell me why you want to know, then I won't find out for you.

'Oh dear. Then I'll have to ask someone else.'

Gerald looked rattled, but controlled himself, smiled and said, 'Charles, if there's anything suspicious, I want to know. Look, I'm a sucker for that sort of thing. Always reading detective stories. I don't know, it's a fascination. It's my hobby, if you like.'

'I thought your hobby was money.'

'That's my main one, but I can't resist suspicious circumstances. It's been a life-long ambition of mine to be involved in something mysterious, a crime. I don't mean the sort of official crime I deal with as a solicitor. I mean real cloak-and-dagger investigation stuff.' Charles remained silent. 'Listen, if you are involved in crime, from whatever side of the law, you need a solicitor. Oh, Charles, do tell me!' he burst out petulantly, but still got no reaction. 'Listen, if you are investigating a crime—'

'And what on earth makes you think I am?'

'I don't know. Something about the way you're behaving. Listen, if you are, I won't charge you anything.'

'You what?'

'I will undertake any investigations free ...'

'Gerald, are you feeling all right?'

'... so long as you let me in on all the details.'

'Hmm.' Charles was circumspect. It was a very good offer, an amazing offer, considering who it came from. But he himself felt so far from convinced there was any crime to investigate, that he had no desire to spread ill-founded suspicions. 'Gerald,' he began slowly, 'if there were something fishy, and I were to tell you, could I trust your discretion?'

'Of course.' Gerald was affronted. 'I am a solicitor.'

'That's what I mean. All right, I accept your offer.'

'So there is a crime?'

'Maybe.'

'All right, give me the dirt.' Gerald made no pretence of maturity now. He was an eager child. Charles remembered that Gerald had always been like that. It was the same quality that made his fascination with money so inoffensive. Not for the first time Charles reflected that growing-up is a myth; getting older is just an intenser form of childhood. 'I'll give you the dirt,' he said, denying the child his treat, 'when you tell me about the will.'

'You bugger,' said Gerald. But he agreed to the deal.

When the bill was brought to Charles, it was enormous. It was a long time since he'd eaten out in this style and he was shocked by the escalation of prices and VAT.

'Think yourself lucky,' said Gerald, as Charles counted out the notes. 'If we hadn't come to an agreement, you d be paying for my time as well.'

Charles didn't tell Jacqui about their new ally in investigation when they met up that evening to report progress. He just said he'd met his solicitor friend who reckoned he could find out the details of the will.

Jacqui was in quite a state. She'd been down to Goring for Marius' funeral, (having found out the time by ringing Morrison at Orme Gardens). At the church she'd ended up in the cliché situation of being frozen out by Marius' relatives. It was the stereotyped picture beloved of cartoonists—the family (Nigel and a few cousins), trim in their black on one side of the grave, and the floosie (Jacqui), in an unsuitable black cocktail dress and purple fur-collared coat, weeping on the other. The burial had been a small affair. Marius was against cremation; he wanted to lie in an English grave with a marble headstone. A memorial service in St George's, Hanover Square, was to follow, for Steen's theatrical and business acquaintances. No one spoke to Jacqui or even acknowledged her, except for Morrison. By the end of the ceremony she was so upset that she hadn't the nerve to go to the house with the small party of mourners, and caught a train straight back to London.

However, she had managed to have a few brief words with Morrison and questioned him about Nigel's movements over the weekend of his father's death. (She assured Charles she had been subtle in her questioning, but he dreaded to think what she meant by subtlety. If there were any alarms to start, he had no doubt she'd set them jangling.) From Morrison she had found out a significant fact, which would have deterred anyone less prejudiced in their conviction of Nigel Steen's guilt. The young man's car, a Jensen Interceptor was out of action at the relevant time. It had had brake trouble and Morrison, who was an expert mechanic, had offered to mend it over the weekend. He'd attended to the brakes on the Saturday, but then, feeling unhappy with the alignment of the wheels, had started work on them. He was a perfectionist, and the job took a long time. When he left the vehicle on the Saturday evening, all four wheels were off, and they were in that state when he returned to the job on the Sunday morning. He didn't finish work until the evening, and it was then that Nigel drove off down to Berkshire, and found his father dead. In reply to the question as to whether Nigel could have used the Datsun, Morrison couldn't say. Miss Menzies had filled it with petrol on the Friday afternoon and used it on the Monday morning. No doubt she would have noticed if it had been used in the interim.

'Who's Miss Menzies?' asked Charles.

'Joanne. Marius' secretary.'

'Oh yes. I've met her. Hmm. And you actually managed to get all that information without Morrison getting at all suspicious?'

'Yes. Anyway, what if he did get suspicious? He doesn't like Nigel any more than anyone else.'

It seemed to be a feature of the case that no one had a good word to say for Nigel Steen. Not having met the man, and basing his conclusions on other people's prejudices, Charles decided that young Steen's main offence was that he was not his father. From all accounts he didn't sound as if he had the spunk to be a murderer.

'Where does Nigel live?'

'I think he's got a flat near Knightsbridge, but he's never there. Spends all his time in Orme Gardens or at Streatley.'

'Father's boy?'

'I wouldn't say that.'

'How did they get on, Jacqui?'

'I don't know. I hardly ever saw them together, and Marius never talked about Nigel. But you've seen the letter.'

'Yes. And did Joanne like him?'

'Did she like who? She liked Marius.' Was there a hint of jealousy there?

'No. Nigel.'

'I don't think she liked him.'

'Hmm. Then I think perhaps she's due for a visitation.'

Charles was making-up next morning in Hereford Road when the phone rang.

'Hello. Oh, Maurice, I was just making-up.'

'What for? You working and not telling me?'

'No, just for fun. Practice.'

'Well, I think it's about time you did some work. You seem to have taken the three-day week to heart too quickly.'

'Three-day week?'

'Don't you read the papers?'

'I haven't yet this morning.'

'Heath's going to put the whole country on a three-day week. Save power. And stop television at half-past ten in the evening.'

'Really.'

'Yes. Think of all the ten per cents of all those series I won't be getting. Johnny Wilson had a repeat scheduled for late evening. That'll be off.'

'I'm afraid I'm not very in touch.'

'I'll say. Look, you know that *Softly Softly* I said might be coming up?'

'Yes.'

'Well, it hasn't.'

'Oh. Thanks.'

'But there is something. Had a call from the casting director of a new horror film yesterday. They're looking for someone to play this sort of deformed hunchback, part werewolf, part vampire. I told them you were made for the part.'

'Thank you very much.'

Silence punctuated with gasps from the other end of the line showed that Maurice was roaring with laughter at his own witticism. He always laughed noiselessly, his jaw snapping up and down as he took in great gulps of air. Charles waited until he'd recovered sufficiently to continue.

'Sorry, just a little joke. But really, it is that sort of part. They seemed quite keen when I mentioned you. Said "Yes, we like using the old fifties stars everyone's forgotten." '

'Thank you again. What would it involve?'

'Two weeks' filming early January—if this three-day week nonsense doesn't interfere. At some stately home. Forget where exactly, but within reach of London.'

'Hmm. What's the film called?'

'*The Zombie Walks!*'

'Oh God. Who's directing?'

'Never heard of him. Some name like Rissole. It's being set up by Steenway Productions.'

'Oh really. I'll take it. Check the dates.'

'Your diary's not exactly crowded, is it?'

'Money good?'

'Goodish. I'll ask for double.'

'Good lad. Thanks for that.'

'My pleasure. If I don't do things for you, you're clearly not going to do anything for yourself.'

'Cheerio, Maurice. Keep smiling.'

'What, with my worries? Cheerio.'

Work, too. And dressing-up. Charles was beginning to feel unaccountably cheerful. He rather relished the idea of secret investigations. With a jaunty step he went upstairs to his room to continue making-up.

Disguise is a matter of presenting oneself to the person deceived in an unexpected context. Then come tricks of stance and movement. Actual changing of colouring and features are less important. And Charles was quite pleased with his disguise. Certainly Joanne Menzies appeared not to recognise him, although he'd rather regretted choosing the character of Detective-Sergeant McWhirter of Scotland Yard when she revealed that she'd been brought up near the Kyles of Bute. But she seemed to accept the Glaswegian accent and his story of having left Scotland for London in his teens.

He had phoned her at Milton Buildings, saying that he had a routine enquiry to make about the Datsun, would have asked for Mr Marius Steen but, owing to the recent regrettable happening, wondered if she could help. She was efficiently affable, and invited him to come round straight away. So there he was, on the Friday morning, sitting opposite her, in the same chair that, only a week before, Charles Paris had occupied.

Detective-Sergeant McWhirter wore a nondescript brown and green suit, a Marks and Spencer pale yellow shirt and brown knitted tie. His shoes were stout brown brogues, suitable for the tramping from place to place which takes up most of a detective's time. When he entered the room he had hung up a pale mackintosh and a trilby hat. His hair was dark brown and slicked back with Brylcreem. He had thick horn-rimmed glasses, a heavy shadow and rather bad teeth. On his wedding finger was a worn gold band. He was the sort of man nobody would look at twice. No doubt a conscientious worker; no doubt a good husband and father; but totally unremarkable.

Miss Menzies couldn't be very helpful about the Datsun, though she answered all his questions very readily. Detective-Sergeant McWhirter explained that he was investigating a robbery in Pangbourne on Saturday night. An eye-witness claimed to have seen a yellow Datsun in the area at the relevant time, and McWhirter was painstakingly investigating all of the local Datsun-owners. The local police had told him that Mr Steen possessed such a vehicle, and he was just making a routine check on the whereabouts of the car at that time.

Miss Menzies felt certain it was in the garage at Mr Steen's Orme Gardens house all over the weekend. When Mr Steen rang on Friday afternoon to say he wasn't certain whether or not he was returning to London at the weekend, she had checked the petrol in the car in case he might want it.

'This was Mr Marius Steen who rang?'

'No. This was his son Nigel. He rang to say that he was coming up to town that evening ...'

'The Friday?'

'Yes. But that his father was still deep in his scripts, and wasn't sure of his movements. So I thought I'd better get some petrol in case Mr Marius Steen did come up to town over the weekend. You know what it's like getting petrol at the moment.'

Detective-Sergeant McWhirter nodded sagely, imagining his eleven-year-old Morris Traveller and the increasing difficulties of driving the wife and kids around. The foam rubber pads in Charles Paris' cheeks were beginning to feel acutely uncomfortable.

'I was lucky,' Miss Menzies continued. 'I managed to get a full tank. It's the garage I always go to.'

'And the tank still registered full on the Monday?'

'Yes.'

'And it wouldn't have done that if it had been driven down to Streatley and back?'

'Good heavens, no.' Miss Menzies looked at him as if he was mad.

'I'm sorry,' said Detective-Sergeant McWhirter stolidly. 'I do have to check all the details. Some cars have a petrol gauge that stays on full for a long time. If it's not properly adjusted.'

'Yes, of course. I'm sorry. The Datsun's does actually. It stays on "full" for quite a while and then drops rather fast.'

'But it wouldn't stay on full all the way to Streatley and back?'

'No. It's pretty good on petrol, but not that good. Might just about make it one way without registering, but certainly not both. Anyway, nobody could have got into the garage at Orme Gardens. It's always locked.'

'Of course. Sorry about all this. We have to check. I'm afraid a detective's life is mostly spent chasing up blind alleys and wasting people's time.'

'That's quite all right.'

'Good.' Detective-Sergeant McWhirter rose to leave and then paused. 'That was very good of you, to look after the petrol. Part of your normal secretarial duties?'

'I am more of a personal assistant to Mr Steen than a secretary. I mean, I was.'

There was just a slight chink in her armour and he pressed a little further. 'Yes. A sad loss.'

'Yes.' He noticed how strained she was looking, much older than a week before. Though she was still immaculately groomed, there seemed somehow less poise about her, as if appearances remained, but the will had gone.

'So I suppose it's all up to the son now.'

'I suppose so.' She couldn't disguise the contempt she felt.

'Always sad for the family, this sort of thing. Is his wife still ... er ...'

'She died years ago.'

'Ah. And he never thought of remarrying?'

'No, he didn't.' She pronounced the words with sudden emphasis, and Charles saw clearly the situation which Jacqui's words—'She liked Marius'—had hinted at. Joanne Menzies had loved Marius Steen. Whether the love had ever been reciprocated or consummated he didn't know—though Steen's reputation made it likely—but the new fact opened interesting avenues of thought. She loved Steen, and she was passionately against his remarriage. The controlled force of her emotion when speaking of it had been frightening. A woman with feelings of that intensity might be capable of any action if she thought the man she loved was seriously in love with someone else. It added a new dimension to the picture.

CHAPTER TWELVE

The Ugly Sisters

WHEN CHARLES GOT back to Hereford Road, there was a Swedish scrawl on the note pad—JERRY VENERAL RING. After a few moments' deciphering he rang Gerald Venables' number.

'Charles, look, we can't talk on the phone.' Gerald was obviously taking all the detective bit to heart, and entering into it with the spirit of a child's game of Cops and Robbers. 'Listen, I've found out about the "you-know-what". We must meet somewhere and talk.'

'OK. Where and when?'

'Two o'clock. The back bar of the Red Lion in Waverton Street.'

'Why? Is it quiet there?'

'No, but you can be overheard in quiet places. The Red Lion's so noisy, nobody'll hear a word,' said Gerald with complete seriousness.

'All right, Peewit.'

'What do you mean—Peewit?'

'Code-name. I'll be wearing a carnation. What's the password?' Charles put the phone down, imagining the expression on Gerald's face.

He was out of costume and looked like Charles Paris when he arrived in the back bar of the Red Lion. Squeezing past the milling lunch time crowds he found himself pressed closely between Gerald and a rather busty Australian. 'Who's she?' he hissed.

'No idea. Where's your carnation?'

'That was a joke.'

'Oh.' Gerald sounded genuinely disappointed.

'Well, you recognise me, don't you?' Gerald was forced to admit he did. 'So, what gives?' Charles shouted above the din.

'Ssh.'

'What gives?' Softer.

'I beg your pardon.'

'Oh, for God's sake.'

Eventually, as the lunch time crowds subsided officewards and the pub was left to a few loud tourists, they found a quiet corner and sat down with their drinks. Charles had a pint and Gerald a dry martini (Charles almost expected him to ask for it 'shaken not stirred'). The solicitor looked round with conspicuous caution.

'The will is very interesting,' he hissed. 'Well, not so much the will as the whole situation. Basically, Nigel gets everything, but he's got a lot of it already.

'Marius Steen made over his three houses and about 75 per cent of his other assets to his son some years ago. You know, the old gift *inter vivos* dodge, to avoid estate duty.'

'I'm sorry. I don't know the old gift *inter vivos* dodge. I'm very stupid about the law.'

'So's everyone. That's what lawyers thrive on. What it basically means is that if someone makes a gift during his lifetime and doesn't die for a given period, that gift is free of estate duty, or partly free. There's a sliding scale. If the donor dies more than seven years after the gift, there's no duty at all payable. If he dies in the seventh year the whole duty is reduced by 6o per cent, if in the sixth by 30 per cent, and in the fifth 15 per cent.' Gerald was talking very fast and fluently, as he always did on the subject of money, but Charles reckoned he had got the gist. 'When was the gift made, Gerald?'

'Nearly six years ago.'

'So Nigel had absolutely no motive to kill his father. In fact, it was in his interests that the old man stayed alive.'

'Ah. That's it, is it?' Gerald's eyes narrowed in the manner of a thousand television thrillers. 'I think you'd better tell me the whole story, Charles.'

So he got the whole story, and when it was spelled out, the catalogue of suspicions and circumstantial evidence did sound pretty feeble. Gerald was clearly disappointed. 'That all hinges on Nigel Steen having a financial motive to kill his father, and, as you just observed, he very positively didn't have such a motive.'

'And it wouldn't have made any difference even if Marius Steen remarried?'

'It would have made a difference in the disposition of that part of the estate which hadn't been given away. But the gift of the rest couldn't be revoked. He had given away all rights in the property. You know, the freeholds were made over by deeds of gift by way of conveyance, and the— '

'Please talk English.'

'All right. Basically, all of the property is Nigel's— exclusively. Marius could not have any beneficial interest in any part of it. In other words, he couldn't benefit from the property or the dividends on the shares, or any part of the gift.'

'So what did he live on?'

'Interest from the remaining shares. Still quite a substantial amount, but only a tiny part of the whole.'

'And how could he still live in the houses?'

'He actually paid rent.'

'So if Nigel had wanted to, he could have turfed his father out of his own houses.'

'Yes. Because they weren't his own houses. They were Nigel's.'

'And what about the business? He still seemed in charge there.'

'Only in an advisory capacity. He made no profit from any of it.'

'Good God. So there again Nigel could have ousted him.'

'Could have done, but wasn't daft. He knew the business depended completely on his father's skill and instinct. No, Steen had organised it all very meticulously to avoid death duties. Nigel has been an incredibly wealthy young man for years.'

'How wealthy?'

'Certainly worth more than a million.'

'Shit.' Charles was impressed. 'And if none of this had been done what sort of death duties would have been charged?'

'80 per cent.'

'Blimey. The Government gets its pound of flesh, doesn't it. But Steen didn't go the full seven years.'

'No, he died just before the six came up. So estate duty is only going to be reduced by 30 per cent. Makes a nasty hole in Nigel's assumed possessions.'

'And certainly rules out any motive for murder.'

'Yes. The only motive for killing Marius Steen could he sheer bloody-mindedness on somebody's part—a desire to make things really difficult for Nigel. Is there anyone around who hates him that much?'

Though everyone seemed to despise Nigel, Charles hadn't met anyone whose feeling seemed strong enough to amount to hatred. It was Marius Steen who inspired violent emotions, not his son. 'And there's no mention of any legacy to Jacqui in the will?'

'None at all.'

'Hmm. I wonder what Marius Steen's letter meant.'

Charles felt depressed as he walked through Soho to Archer Street that evening. For a start there was the gloomy news he had to pass on to Jacqui. And then London itself was depressing. It was cold and dark. Display lighting was out, as Edward Heath began his schoolmasterish campaign of mass deprivation, keeping the whole country in until the miners owned up that they were in the wrong. Time would show that the campaign had misjudged the reactions of the British public. Shops were dark, cold and uninviting. Familiar landmarks, like the neons of theatres and cinemas, disappeared. It was like the blackout, which Charles could suddenly remember with great clarity. A fifteen-year-old in grey flannel wandering around London in school holidays with an adolescent's apocalyptic vision, praying that he would lose his virginity before the bombs came and blasted him to oblivion.

He took a couple of wrong turnings in the gloom and was angry when he reached Jacqui's flat. He prepared an account of the will situation to break to her brutally. There was no point in kid gloves; she had to know sooner or later.

But he didn't get the chance to drop his thunderbolt. Jacqui opened the door in a state of high excitement, more colour and animation in her face than he had seen since the Steen affair started. 'Charles, come in. Bartlemas and

O'Rourke are here!'

William Bartlemas and Kevin O'Rourke were a legend in the world of British theatre. They were a middle-aged couple, whose main activity was the collection of memorabilia of the two great actors, Edmund Kean and William Macready. Bartlemas had an enormous private income, and the pair of them lived in a tall Victorian house in Islington, which was filled to the brim with play-bills, prints, prompt copies, figurines and other souvenirs of their two heroes. They identified with them totally. Bartlemas was Kean, and O'Rourke Macready. In theory they were writing a book on the actors, but long since the fascination of collection for its own sake had taken over and work on the collation of evidence ceased. They spent all their time travelling round the British Isles, visiting auctions and antique shops, following hints and rumours, searching for more and more relics of their idols. But they always rushed back to London for the first night of every West End show. It was a point of honour that, if they were in the country, they'd be there, sitting in the middle of the fifth row of the stalls, both resplendent in Victorian evening dress, clutching shiny top hats and silver-topped canes. Quite what their role in British theatre was, was hard to define, but they knew everyone, everyone knew them and managements even came to regard their presence on a first night as an essential good luck charm. In the camper and more superstitious regions of the theatre world you'd often hear the sentence, 'My dear, Bartlemas and O'Rourke weren't there. The notices'll be up within the week'.

In appearance they fell rather short of their ideals. William Bartlemas was not tall, probably only about five foot seven, but his angular body gave the illusion of height and his knobbly limbs moved with adolescent awkwardness. His head was crowned with an astonished crest of dyed hair. It had that brittle crinkly texture born of much hairdressing, and was ginger, of a brightness to which nature has always been too shy to aspire. Kevin O'Rourke was tiny, with the pugnacious stance of a jockey and all the aggression of a butterfly. He was balding, and had countered the problem by combing what remained forward in a Royal Shakespeare Company Roman Plays style. The dyed black hair was as tight as skin over his head, except at the front where there was a curly fringe like the edge of a pie-crust. The two always dressed identically—a grotesque pair of Beverley sisters. Today they were in oyster grey velvet. Meeting Bartlemas and O'Rourke was an unforgettable experience, and a fairly exhausting one. They talked non-stop in an elaborate relay race, one picking up the thread as soon as the other paused for breath.

They were delighted to see Charles. He had only met them once briefly at a party, but they remembered him effusively. 'Charles Paris,' said Bartlemas, 'lovely to see you. Haven't talked since that marvellous Bassanio you did at the Vic'—that had been fifteen years before—'lovely performance.'

'Yes,' said O'Rourke, 'you always were such a clever actor ...'

'Sensational,' said Bartlemas. 'What are you up to now? My dear, we've just been on the most shattering binge in North Africa.'

'For months and months and months ...'

'In Morocco, of course. O'Rourke disgraced himself continually. So much to drink, my dear, it wasn't true ...'

'And Bartlemas almost got arrested more than once ...'

'Oh, I didn't. Not really ...'

'You did, dear, you did. I saw it all. This Moroccan policeman was watching you with a distinctly beady eye. And I don't think it was your perfection of form that intrigued him ...'

'Well, be that as it may. We go off, we leave the collection and everything, miss all those divine first nights, just simply to have a holiday, to get away from everything ...'

'But everything ...'

'And we come back to hear this shattering news about Marius. Oh, it's too sad.'

'Too sad. We were just telling Jacqui here, we are absolutely desolated ...'

'I mean he was so strong. And such a chum too ...'

'I don't know how we'll survive without him, I really don't.'

'It's terrifying. If someone like Marius who was so robust ...'

'So full of living ...'

'If he can just pop off like that ...'

'Then what chance is there for the rest of us?'

They both sat back, momentarily exhausted. Charles opened his mouth to speak, but missed the chance. 'So of course,' said Bartlemas, 'as soon as we heard the ghastly news about Marius, we just had to rush round here ...'

'Immediately,' said O'Rourke. 'Because of *our secret*.'

They paused dramatically and gave Jacqui time to say, 'Charles, they've got a new will. Marius made another will.'

Charles looked round at Bartlemas and O'Rourke. They were glowing with importance. 'Yes,' said Bartlemas, 'we witnessed the will and he gave it to us to look after it ...'

'Which is a pity,' said O'Rourke, 'because that means we can't inherit anything ...'

'Not that he had anything we'd really like to inherit. I mean, nothing to do with Edmund and William ...'

'No, but it would have been nice to have a little memento, wouldn't it, Bartlemas?'

'Oh yes. Yes, it would. You see, what happened was, we were in the South of France in the summer, when Jacqui and Marius were out there ...'

'At Sainte-Maxime ...'

'Yes. Marius' villa. Lovely spot ...'

'Oh, lovely ...'

'And suddenly, one night, after Jacqui had gone to bed, Marius suddenly said he was going to make a new will, and there was someone on holiday down there who was a solicitor—'

'Not his usual one?' Charles managed to slip in.

'Oh no, not dear Harold,' said Bartlemas.

'No, not Harold,' echoed O'Rourke. 'This was a rather sweet young man Marius found in a casino ...'

'And anyway, Marius said this boy was coming over and he was going to draw up a new will, and would we witness it? ...'

'So of course we said yes ...'

'Well, we were so *intrigued*. It was so *exciting* ...'

'And we've got it with us, and we were just about to show it to Jacqui when you arrived.'

'Look,' said Bartlemas, and, with a flourish, produced a sealed envelope from his inside pocket. At this gesture both he and O'Rourke burst out into riotous giggles. 'I'm sorry,' said O'Rourke when they had calmed down, 'it's just that that was the gesture Edmund Kean is supposed to have used on the "Is this a dagger?" speech in *Macbeth* at the New Theatre Royal, Drury Lane, in 1823.'

'Oh,' said Charles, as Bartlemas and O'Rourke went into new paroxysms of laughter. Again it took a little while for them to calm down and when they had, Bartlemas, with mock solemnity, handed the envelope to Jacqui. 'Of course,' he said conspiratorially, 'we know what's in it, don't we, O'Rourke?'

'Oh yes, Bartlemas.' They both sat back with smug smiles on their faces and looked at Jacqui, like favourite uncles watching a child unwrap their Christmas present.

Jacqui opened the envelope, pulled out a document and looked at the sheet for some long time. Then she looked up, perplexed. 'It's all in funny English.'

'That's because it's a legal document,' said Charles. 'They are always incomprehensible. It's a point of honour among lawyers never to be understood.'

'You read it, and tell me what it means.' Jacqui handed the document over.

'We could tell you what's in it,' said Bartlemas.

'Yes, but we won't,' said O'Rourke coyly.

Charles read the will.

I, MARIUS LADISLAS STENIATOWSKI, commonly known as MARIUS STEEN, and hereinafter referred to as such, of 173, Orme Gardens, London, W2 and 'Rivalon', Streatley-on-Thames in the County of Berkshire, Theatrical Impresario, HEREBY REVOKE all wills and testamentary documents heretofore made by me AND DECLARE this to be my LAST WILL

1. I APPOINT WILLIAM DOUGLAS D'ABERNON BARTLEMAS and KEVIN CORNELIUS O'ROURKE to be jointly the Executors of this my WILL

2. In the event of my dying before remarriage, I DEVISE and

BEQUEATH all of my real and personal estate whatsoever and wheresoever not already disposed of as to my freeholds in fee simple and as to my personal estate absolutely to the issue of my union with JACQUELINE MYRTLE MITCHELL, the property to be held in trust for the said issue, the trust allowing a monthly sum of not less than FIVE HUNDRED POUNDS to the said JACQUELINE MYRTLE MITCHELL to pay for the upbringing of the said issue, this arrangement to cease on his or her attaining the age of twenty-one years, whereupon a quarter of the remaining estate—whether in freehold property, stocks, shares or chattels shall be granted in perpetuity to the said JACQUELINE MYRTLE MITCHELL, and the remainder to be granted to the said issue. In the event of the said JACQUELINE MYRTLE MITCHELL dying before the child attains twenty-one years, all of the estate shall devolve upon the said child and be held for him or her in trust, as my executors and their appointees shall devise.

IN WITNESS whereof I the said MARIUS STEEN the Testator have to this my LAST WILL set my hand this fifteenth day of October One Thousand Nine Hundred and Seventy-Three.

SIGNED AND ACKNOWLEDGED by the above-named MARIUS STEEN the Testator as and for his LAST WILL in the presence of us both present at the same time who at his request in his presence and in the presence of each other have hereunto subscribed our names as witnesses:

William Bartlemas

17, Ideal Road,
Islington

Keanophile

Kevin O'Rourke

17, Ideal Road,
Islington

Macreadophile

Jacqui was looking at him eagerly. Obviously she had understood the gist of the will and just wanted confirmation. Charles grinned. 'Basically you'll be all right. You can afford to have that baby.'

'What, and the baby'll get everything?'

'Not exactly, no.' And Charles explained briefly about the gift *inter vivos* to Nigel. 'So what we're talking about is only 25 per cent of Marius Steen's assets other than the houses. Mind you, it's still more money than you've ever seen in your life.'

Bartlemas and O'Rourke had been silent too long and burst again into stereo action.

'Ooh,' said Bartlemas, 'fancy all that going to little Arsehole ...'

'Who?'

'Nigel,' said O'Rourke patronisingly. 'Everyone calls him little Arsehole. Why on earth would Marius make all that over to him?'

'It's the family thing, isn't it,' said Bartlemas. 'Marius always wanted to found a dynasty.'

'But I thought he and Nigel didn't get on.' Charles was still rather puzzled by the whole gift business.

'Well, it varied, didn't it, O'Rourke?'

'Oh yes, up and down all the time ...'

'I remember, there was a time when Nigel ran off to America ...'

'With some woman, ghastly actress ...'

'But ghastly. Marius was awfully upset. Nigel stayed away for two, three years ...'

'All of that, Bartlemas, all of that. Then he came crawling back ...'

'Tail between his legs. Woman had left him ...'

'Who could blame her? Marius really did the prodigal son bit ...'

'Oh yes, you couldn't move in Orme Gardens for fatted calf. All the great reconciliation, my son, my son ...'

'It's the Jewish character, you know. Love of the family. Terribly important to them .'

'You're right, O'Rourke. That's what it is.' This was pronounced with finality and followed by a breath pause. Charles, who was beginning to understand the technique of conversation with Bartlemas and O'Rourke, leapt in. 'When was it this reconciliation took place?'

'About five or six years ago,' said Bartlemas.

'Ah, that figures. It must have been then, in a final flush of family feeling, that he made everything over to Nigel.'

'Yes.'

'And, so far as one can tell, he regretted it ever after.'

'Yes,' said O'Rourke. There was a pause. 'Jacqui,' said Charles. 'I didn't know your middle name was Myrtle.'

'It was after an aunt,' said Jacqui.

CHAPTER THIRTEEN

Who Does the Slipper Fit?

THE NEW WILL was passed over to Gerald Venables, who got in touch with Harold Cohn of Cohn, Jarvis, Cohn and Stickley, and the law began the grindingly slow processes on which it thrives. Charles thought that the whole affair was now out of his hands, and, though it was unsatisfactory that so many questions remained unanswered, at least some kind of justice had been done. Nigel got most of the estate, but would be more than a little embarrassed by estate duty; and provision for Jacqui and her baby would be sorted out in time. If the police persevered they were bound to crack Audrey Sweet's defence and find out about the family blackmailing business. Then they had only to check through the photographs and the Sally Nash guest lists (which, as the case at the Old Bailey trickled on inexorably, were becoming public property anyway) to find their murderer. Charles even felt a twinge of pity for Mrs Sweet. She was a desperate woman, her incompetent attempts at blackmail motivated only by a desire to get as much money as possible in her new widowhood. It was now three days since Bill Holroyd had promised to bring her ten thousand pounds and by now she must realise the likelihood of his appearance was decreasing.

It was Saturday 15th December. Christmas was coming, but without much conviction in a darkened Britain. The cold shops with their sad gas-lamps were full of Christmas shoppers feeling sorry for themselves, and shoplifters having a field-day. The ever-present possibility of bombs made buying presents even jollier.

Charles rose late and managed to beat one of the Swedes into the bathroom. He returned to his room wrapped cosily in his towelling dressing-gown and sat in front of the gas-fire with a cup of coffee. Now that the excitements of the last fortnight were over, he would have to think again about getting some work. True, he'd got *The Zombie Walks* coming up, but that wasn't going to make him a millionaire, and the old overdraft was getting rather overblown. Perhaps the answer was to write another television play. But, even if he could write the thing quickly, all the subsequent processes took such a bloody long time. Getting the thing accepted, rewritten, rewritten, rewritten, rehearsed, recorded, edited, scheduled, rescheduled, rescheduled, rescheduled ad infinitum. Not much likelihood of getting a commission either. Charles Paris wasn't a big enough name these days. And no doubt, with the prospects of a three-day week and early closedown, none of the television companies would commit themselves to anything.

But as he tried to think of his work (Charles had long since ceased to grace it with the name of 'his career'), his thoughts kept returning to the Steen situation. There was something fishy about the whole set-up. He tried to think himself into a detective frame of mind. What would Sherlock Holmes do in the circumstances? He would sit puffing on his pipe, Dr Watson goggle-eyed with admiration at his side, and suddenly, by a simple process of deduction, arrive at the complete solution. Somehow Charles Paris, sitting on his own in a towelling dressing-gown, hadn't quite the same charisma. Or the same powers of deduction.

Reflecting sadly on his inadequacy, Charles rose to get dressed. He opened the dull grey wardrobe and pulled a pair of trousers off a hanger. As he did so, he noticed that there was a dark smudge on the seat. It smelled of petrol. He was about to put his trousers back and take out another pair, when a sudden thought stopped him in his tracks.

The trousers he was holding were the ones he'd been wearing at Streatley the previous weekend. And he must have got the mark on them when he slipped over in Steen's garage. The scene came back to him with immediate clarity of detail. The enormous bulk of the blue Rolls illuminated by his torch, then suddenly his feet going from under him, slipping in a pool of petrol, landing on a spanner and a piece of tubing.

A piece of tubing. And the Rolls petrol gauge registered empty. Joanne Menzies' words about the Datsun came back to him—'It's pretty good on petrol, but not that good. Might just about make it one way without registering, but certainly not both.' But what was simpler than to drive the car to Streatley, siphon petrol out of the Rolls into it (possibly even siphon some into a can as well, to top it up near London) and then drive back? Charles decided that a visit should be paid to Mr Nigel Steen.

Joanne Menzies still looked drawn and strained when she ushered Detective-Sergeant McWhirter into Mr Steen's office on the Monday afternoon. The policeman thanked her and stood deferentially until he was invited to sit down.

The man who made the invitation was very like his father, but without the vitality that had distinguished Marius Steen. Nigel had the same beak of a nose, but, without the dark eyes, its effect was comic rather than forceful. His eyes were blue, a legacy from the English rose whom Marius had married; and his hair was light brown rather than the black which his father had kept, only peppered with grey, until his death. The general effect was of a diluted Marius Steen, ineffectual and slightly afraid.

Nigel was ostentatiously smoking a big cigar to give an illusion of poise. He flashed Charles what was meant to be a frank smile. 'Well, what can I do to help?'

'I'm very sorry to bother you,' said Detective-Inspector McWhirter slowly, 'and I do very much appreciate your putting yourself out to see me. Particularly at what must be a very distressing time for you.'

'That's quite all right. What is it?' With a hint of irritation, or was it anxiety?

'I have already spoken to your secretary on the matter and she proved most helpful.' Charles reiterated his lies about the theft in Pangbourne on the Saturday night.

'But you see, since I spoke to her, we have had another witness's account of having seen a yellow Datsun in the Goring area. And they identified your number plate. I mean, you can never trust members of the public; they are extraordinarily inaccurate in what they claim to remember, but I can't discount anything. All I'm trying to do is to establish where your father's Datsun was on that night, and then stop wasting your time.'

'Yes.' Nigel drew on the cigar and coughed slightly. He was clearly rattled. Not a man with a strong nerve, and certainly on the surface not one who could carry out a cold-blooded murder. He capitulated very quickly. 'As a matter of fact, I was in Streatley in the Datsun on that Saturday night.'

Charles felt a great surge of excitement, but Detective-Sergeant McWhirter only said, 'Ah.'

'Yes. I'd phoned my father in the evening, and he didn't sound too well, so I drove down to see how he was.'

'And how was he?'

'Fine, fine. We had a few drinks together, chatted. He seemed in very good form. Then I drove back to London.'

'Still on the Saturday night?'

'Yes. It's not far.'

'No, no, of course not.' Charles was about to ask about the subterfuge of the full petrol tank, but decided that Detective-Sergeant McWhirter might not be in possession of all the relevant facts for that deduction. As it happened, Nigel continued defensively without needing further questions.

'You're probably wondering why I didn't mention this fact before. Well, to tell you the truth, your boys asked me when had I last seen my father alive and I said Friday instinctively, and then by the time I'd realised my mistake, it was all written down, and, you know, I thought if I changed it, that'd only create trouble.'

It sounded pretty implausible to Charles, but Detective-Sergeant McWhirter gave a reassuring nod. 'Yes, of course, sir. And you're quite sure that while the car was down in Streatley, the thieves who I'm after wouldn't have had a chance to take it and use it for their break-in?'

'No, that would be quite impossible. I put the car in the garage and I'm sure I'd have heard it being driven off. Anyway, I wasn't down there very long.'

'No. Oh well, fine, Mr Steen. Thank you very much.' Detective-Sergeant McWhirter rose to leave. 'I think I'd better start looking for another yellow Datsun.'

'Yes. And ... er ... Detective-Sergeant ...'

'Yes?'

'Will you have to mention the discrepancy in my story— you know, my confusion about when I last saw my father—?'

'Good Lord, no. That's quite an understandable mistake in a moment of emotion, sir. So long as an account's written down somewhere, no one's going to fuss about the details. After all, there wasn't anything unusual about your father's death. If there had been any grounds for suspicion, it'd be a different case.' And Detective-Sergeant McWhirter laughed.

Nigel Steen laughed too, Charles thought a bit too heartily. But perhaps he was being hypersensitive and letting his suspicions race like Jacqui's.

'Anyway,' the Detective-Sergeant continued, 'I don't have anything to do with your father's death. Different department, you know.'

'Yes, of course.'

'Well, goodbye, Mr Steen. And thank you again for your help. If only more members of the public were as co-operative as you have been, our life would be a lot easier. They shook hands. Nigel's felt like a damp face cloth.

Detective-Sergeant McWhirter went through into Miss Menzies' anteroom. 'All sorted out now?' she asked brightly.

'Yes, thank you, Miss Menzies.'

'Hmm. We've seen quite a lot of you lately.'

'Yes,' said the Detective-Sergeant casually, unprepared for what happened next.

Miss Menzies suddenly stood up, looked him straight in the eyes and said, 'Do you know it's a very serious offence to impersonate a police officer?'

'Yes,' said Detective-Sergeant McWhirter slowly, waiting to see what came next.

'I rang up Scotland Yard to tell you something this morning, and they'd never heard of you.'

'Ah.'

'And from the start I thought your accent was a bit phoney. I know a lot of people who come from Glasgow.'

'Yes.' There was a pause. Then Charles continued, still in his discredited Glaswegian. 'Well, what was it you rang up the Yard to tell me?'

Joanne Menzies looked at him coolly. 'You've got a nerve. But I think you're probably doing something I'd sympathise with, so I'll tell you. I checked with Morrison, the chauffeur at Orme Gardens, and he was suspicious that the Datsun may have been used on the Saturday night.'

'Yes, I know. I've just got that from Mr Nigel Steen.'

'Ah.' She sounded disappointed that her information was redundant. 'You're suspicious of him too, aren't you?'

'Maybe.'

'No maybe,' she said, 'you are. Incidentally, "Detective Sergeant", what's your real name?'

'Charles Paris.'

'Ah.' Her eyes widened and she nodded slowly. 'Very good.' It was a warming compliment, from someone who knew about the theatre. 'Well, Charles, if there's anything else I can tell you, or I can find out for you, let me know.'

'Thanks.' As he was leaving, he turned and looked at her. 'You hate Nigel Steen, don't you?'

'Yes,' she said simply.

*

Christmas intervened and the business of investigation was suspended. Charles told Jacqui the new information he'd gleaned, but met with little luck in following it up. When he rang Joanne to check Nigel's movements in the week before Steen's death, a strange female voice answered and informed him that Miss Menzies had already gone up to Scotland for her Christmas holidays. Gerald Venables was getting a very slow response from Cohn, Jarvis, Cohn and Stickley on the matter of the new will, and also seemed preoccupied with family arrangements and Christmas drink parties. His enthusiasm for the cloak-and-dagger business of detection seemed to have waned.

Charles felt his own sense of urgency ebbing too. Though he got excited at each new development in his investigations, he soon became disillusioned again. And Joanne's seeing through his disguise made him a bit wary. He had no particular desire to break the law. Detection was a serious business, and perhaps he should leave it alone. The days of the gifted amateur investigator were over. It was better to leave everything to the police, who with superior training and equipment must stand a greater chance of uncovering crime.

And each time Charles looked at his progress it seemed more negative. Though he had enjoyed his little investigations and masquerades, his only real discovery was that Nigel Steen had tried to disguise the fact of driving down to Streatley on the night of Saturday 8th December. And though the visit could have given him an opportunity to kill his father, and then drive down the next day to discover the body, that was the one crime which every logical motive screamed against. By killing Marius then, Nigel would have been sacrificing a great deal of money. Duties at 80 per cent on an estate of a million, only reduced by 30 per cent, because of the donor's death before the end of the sixth year (to borrow Gerald Venables' terminology) would mean that Nigel would be paying more than half a million in estate duty. Whereas if he only waited till the seven years were up, all the given property would be his without any tax. It's a rare character who commits murder in order to lose half a million pounds.

And the only other fact, hanging around in the background, was Bill Sweet's death, which, by some fairly dubious reasoning and some circumstantial evidence, could be laid at Marius Steen's door. But Marius Steen was dead. Why bother him now?

The Montrose was open over Christmas and so, along with a lot of other divorced and debauched actors, Charles Paris spent a week sublimely pissed.

*

He was feeling distinctly drink-sodden when the phone rang on the morning of the 3rd of January, 1974. He wanted to be picked up and wrung out like a floor cloth to get the stuff out of his system. He lay in bed, hoping the phone would go away or someone would answer it. But the Swedish girls were still in Sweden for the holidays and he was alone in the house. The phone went on ringing.

He stumped savagely downstairs and picked up the receiver. 'Hello.' His voice came out as a croak.

'It's Jacqui.' Her voice was excited again, bubbling. 'Charles, I've been to the police.'

'What?'

'About Nigel. I went to Scotland Yard this morning and saw an Inspector and told him all about our suspicions, and about how we knew Nigel had been down at Streatley that Saturday—'

'I hope you didn't tell him how we found out.'

'No, I didn't. I didn't mention you at all.'

'Thank God for that.'

'Anyway, the Inspector said it all sounded very suspicious and he's going to authorise an aupopsy—'

'Autopsy.'

'Yes. Anyway, he's getting an order to have Marius exhumed and check the cause of death. He took everything I said very seriously.' The last sentence was pronounced with pride. There was a pause; she was waiting for him to react. 'Well, what do you think, Charles?'

'I don't know. In a way, I think it's asking for trouble ...'

'Oh, Charles, we've got to know whether or not Marius was murdered.'

'Have we? It's all sorted out. The baby's being looked after ...'

'Charles, do you mean that?'

'No.'

'We've got to know.'

'Yes. When's the exhumation to be?'

'Quite soon. Probably next Monday.'

'And when will the results be known?'

'End of next week. There should be an inquest on Friday.'

'You realise that, by doing this, you have virtually made a public accusation of murder against Nigel?'

'Yes. And that is exactly what 1 meant to do.'

*

Ten days passed. In America, with the tide of Watergate rising around him, President Nixon celebrated his sixty-first birthday. In England wild storms swept the country, and commuters were infuriated and inconvenienced by the ASLEF dispute. Housewives started panic buying of toilet rolls. And in a churchyard in Goring, the body of Marius Steen was moved from its grave after a stay of only four short weeks. Then it was opened up and samples of its organs were taken and analysed.

All of these events, international and domestic, seemed unreal to Charles.

Since sobering up after Christmas he had degenerated into a deep depression. Inactivity and introspection left him lethargic and uninterested in anything. His usual solutions to the problem—drink and sex—were ineffectual. He drank heavily, but it gave him no elation, merely intensified his mood. And his self-despite was so strong that he knew reviving an old flame or chasing some young actress would only aggravate it. He tried to write, but couldn't concentrate. Instead he sat in his room, his mind detached, looking down on his body and despising what it saw. Forty-seven years old, creatively and emotionally sterile. He thought of going to see Frances, but didn't feel worthy of her warmth and eternal forgiveness. She had sent him four stout dependable Marks and Spencer shirts for Christmas, nursing him like a mother who respects her child's independence. He'd sent her Iris Murdoch's latest novel. In hardback, which he knew she'd think an unnecessary extravagance.

His only comfort was that the following Monday he was to start filming *The Zombie Walks*. Though he didn't view the prospect with any sort of enthusiasm (he'd been sent a script, but hadn't bothered to read it) he knew that activity of some sort, something he had to do, was always better than nothing. Eventually, if enough kept happening, the mood would lift without his noticing its departure and he would hardly remember the self-destructive self that went with it.

But as he walked through the dim streets of London to Archer Street on the Friday evening, the mood was still with him. He felt remote, viewing himself as a third person. And he had a sense of gloom about the findings of the inquest.

When Jacqui opened the door of her flat, he knew from her face that his forebodings had been justified. She was silent until he'd sat down. Then she handed him a glass of Southern Comfort and said, 'Well that's that.'

'What?'

'According to the coroner, Marius died of natural causes.'

'A heart attack?'

'They had some fancy medical term for it, but yes, that's what they said.'

'Well.' Charles sighed. He couldn't think of anything else to say. Jacqui looked on the verge of tears, and, as usual, converted her emotion into a violent outburst. 'Little Arsehole's been clever, the sod. He must have given Marius an electric shock, or injected air into his veins, or—'

'Jacqui, you've been watching too much television. That sort of thing just doesn't happen. I'm afraid we have to accept the fact that Marius did die from natural causes, and that all our suspicions of Nigel have been slander, just based on dislike and nothing else.'

'No, I don't believe it.'

'Jacqui, you've got to believe it. There's nothing else you can do.'

'Well, why did he go down to Streatley on the Saturday night, and make such a bloody secret of it?'

'I don't know. Perhaps for the reasons he said. He was worried about his father, so he went down, they had a few drinks, then he came back to London.'

'Oh, for Christ's sake, that won't wash.'

'Why not?'

'He and Marius didn't get on at the time. We know that from the new will and the letter to me and— '

'Perhaps they had another reconciliation.'

'Piss off, Charles. There's something fishy and Nigel's behind it. Marius was murdered.'

'Jacqui, the most sophisticated forensic tests have proved that he wasn't.'

'Well, they're wrong. They're all bloody wrong. Nigel paid them off. He bribed them.'

'Now you're getting childish.'

'I am not getting bloody childish! ' Jacqui stood up and looked as if she was about to hit him. Charles didn't respond and after a frozen pause, she collapsed into a chair and burst out crying. When he had calmed her, she announced very coolly. 'I'm not going to stop, Charles. I'll get him. From now on there's a war between Nigel and me.'

'Well, you certainly nailed your colours to the mast by setting up the post-mortem.'

'Yes. And I'm going to win.' Thereafter she didn't mention anything about either of the Steens for the rest of the evening. She cooked another of her frozen meals (country rissoles) and Charles drank moderately (a rather vinegary Spanish Rioja). Then they watched the television. She had just bought (in anticipation of her legacy) a new Sony portable ('I'll be sitting about a lot when I get very big'). There wasn't much on the box, but that night it was preferable to conversation. At ten-thirty, by Government orders, came the close-down. Charles rose and after a few mumbled words about thanks, and keeping in touch, and being cheerful, and seeing himself out, he left.

Jacqui's flat was on the top floor and the bulb in the light on her landing had long since gone and not been replaced. As Charles moved forward to the familiar step, he felt his ankle caught, and his body, overbalancing, hurtled forward down the flight of stairs.

The noise brought Jacqui to the door and light spilled out over the scene. 'Charles, are you all right? Are you drunk, or what?'

He slowly picked himself up. The flight was only about ten steps down to the next landing, and though he felt bruised all over, and shocked, nothing seemed to be broken. 'No, I'm not drunk. Look.'

And he pointed up to the top step. Muzzily outlined in the light was a wire, tied tightly between the banisters on either side. It was about four inches above the step. Jacqui turned pale, and let out a little gasp of horror. 'Good God. Were they trying to kill me?'

'No! ' said Charles, as he leant, aching, against the wall at the foot of the flight. Suddenly he realised the flaw in the will Marius Steen had so hastily improvised in the South of France. 'I don't think it was you they wanted to kill. Just your baby.'

CHAPTER FOURTEEN

Slapstick Scene

THE ZOMBIE WALKS was one of the worst film scripts ever conceived. The Zombie (played by a well-known Horror Film Specialist) had walked for a thousand years in a subterranean cavern which was broken open by an earthquake in Lisbon. By means not specified, from Portugal he arrived in Victorian England, where he got the idea that Lady Laetitia Winthrop (played by a 'discovery' from the world of modelling, whose acting talent was 36-23-36) was his long-lost love from a world before the subterranean cavern. He therefore determined to seize her from Winthrop Grange where she lived with her father Lord Archibald Winthrop (played by a well-known character actor who did commercials for tea-bags). After the Zombie's travels through Victorian London (where, incidentally, he committed the crimes attributed to Jack the Ripper) he arrived at the Grange and enlisted the help of Tick, a deformed coachman of evil character (played by Charles Paris). As the Zombie progressed, he committed murder after murder, and his victims, rather than dying and lying down, became zombies too, until at the end Winthrop Grange was besieged by a whole army of the walking dead. Had it not been for the activities of Lady Laetitia's lover, bold Sir Rupert Cartland (played by an odious young actor who'd risen to prominence by playing a tough naval lieutenant in a television series) making with the garlic and the wooden stakes (a bit of vampire lore crept into the script), Lady Laetitia and her father would have been turned into zombies and carried back to the subterranean cave, where they would never be heard of again. Which, to Charles' mind, wouldn't have been a bad thing.

They were filming at Bloomwater, a stately home in Berkshire which had been built by Sir Henry Manceville, an eccentric nobleman, in 1780. Manceville had designed it himself as a great Gothic palace and even incorporated the specially-built ruins of an abbey into one wing. It was a monumental folly, which could have been made for horror films. In fact, had the cinema been invented at the time, it probably would have been. Sir Henry Manceville had been obsessed with ghosts and, in later life, when his eccentricity slid into madness, he used to terrify his servants by walking the Long Gallery, dressed in a sheet, dragging a length of chain and wailing piteously.

Bloomwater's present owner was a more prosaic figure, Sir Lionel Newman, the paper magnate. He was a man who, like Marius Steen, had risen from humble origins to immense wealth and had surrounded himself with all the symbols of the established aristocracy. His association with Marius Steen had been the reason why Bloomwater was being used for the filming.

Charles found that, as ever, making a film involved much more hanging around than actual work. The director, a little Cockney who glorified in the name of Jean-Luc Roussel, generated an impression of enormous activity as he buzzed around checking camera angles, getting the lighting changed, demonstrating the special effects and bawling out the continuity girl. But very little actually seemed to get done.

Charles didn't find many sympathetic characters among the cast. The Horror Film Specialist was surrounded by an admiring coterie of lesser horror film specialists and most of their conversation referred back to previous triumphs. ('Do you remember that *Dracula* when your fang got stuck in the girl's bra?'; or 'I'll never forget that girl who had hysterics during that human sacrifice'; or 'Do you remember that take as the Werewolf when you forgot your line and said "Bow-Wow"?') They all sat around, reminding each other of things they all remembered, each waiting his cue for the next reminiscence to be slotted in.

So Charles went off on his own most of the time. He sat in the Library (later to be the scene of the appallingly-written quarrel between Lord Archibald and Sir Rupert) and did the crossword or played patience.

On the Wednesday morning of the first week of the schedule he was sitting with the cards spread before him and feeling fairly secure. The film world still has an outdated generosity in its dealings with actors. The big-spending Hollywood myth retains its influence and the Zombie cast were well looked after by Steenway Productions, with cars organised to get them to and from the set. The early starts were a disadvantage, but Charles had minimised that by staying with Miles and Juliet and having the car pick him up at six. Then he could sleep through the drive and the laborious business of make-up. Quite cosy. And the money was good.

He also felt as secure as he could about Jacqui. The shock of the trip-wire incident had worn off and she was fairly well hidden. He'd wanted to send her off to some relative in the country, but she didn't seem to have any family. In fact, when they went into it, it was amazing how few people Jacqui had to call on. No family, or at least none she kept in touch with, no girl-friends. The centre of her life had always been men, either one at a time or many. A lot of girls end up promiscuous, when all they're looking for is friendship. Jacqui's lack of other resources explained both her desolation when Steen seemed to have dropped her and her reliance on Charles. (Even her leaping into bed with him again. She needed to keep up her continuity of male companionship, and humbly thought she had nothing to offer but sex.)

Charles had considered parking her on Frances in Muswell Hill, but the incongruity of the thought of the two women together was too great. So in the end he had given her his keys to the room in Hereford Road. He felt fairly confident that Nigel Steen, or whoever was mounting the campaign against her, did not know of any tie-up with Charles Paris. Hereford Road was dangerously near Orme Gardens, but it was only a short-term solution while the film lasted. Jacqui was likely to stay in most of the time with her portable television; her pregnancy made her quite content to do so. Obviously she'd have to go out to the shops from time to time, but she'd had her hair dyed black on the Saturday, bought a new winter coat and a large pair of dark glasses. That should keep her safe. Charles could imagine Jacqui quite happy in her enforced confinement. Hers was not a demanding character, and so long as she felt some evidence of a man's care (which living in Charles' room would give her) she would not need more. When the Zombie had finished his walk, a more permanent method of protecting her for the next four months would have to be found.

They'd considered going to the police, but agreed that, after the embarrassing debacle of the inquest, further accusations from Jacqui against Nigel Steen would sound more like the ramblings of a paranoid than anything else. It was safer for her simply to go underground. Charles rang daily to check everything was all right.

So he felt secure as he sat looking over the rolling lawns of Bloomwater. To add to his pleasure, the patience came out. He was just laying the cards down for another game, when he heard the door open behind him. He turned and the girl who had just come in let out a little scream.

For a moment he couldn't think what was worrying her, until he remembered his make-up. His own hair was hidden under a latex cap from which a few grey wisps straggled crazily. His eyes were red-rimmed and sagging, his nose a mass of pustules, and his teeth had been blacked out with enamel. The whole face had the unearthly green tinge of dead flesh, which Jean-Luc Roussel was convinced was the mark of a zombie.

'I'm sorry,' said Charles. 'I'm afraid I do look rather a fright.'

'Oh, that's all right. I just wasn't expecting it.' The girl looked about sixteen and recently aware of her considerable attractions. Her black hair was swept back in the careless style that only the most expensive hairdressing can give. She was wearing check trousers and a red polo-necked sweater that accentuated the perfect roundness of her bra-less small breasts. For the first time in over a month Charles felt certain that he hadn't lost interest in sex.

'I take it you're in the film,' said the girl.

'No, I always look like this. You're making fun of my natural affliction.'

The girl was checked for a moment, then laughed. 'That's not fair. Who are you?'

'I am Tick, the deformed coachman,' he said in his First Witch voice ('Macabre in the extreme'—*Plays and Players*). She laughed again. Obviously she was still at an age to be amused by funny voices. Charles felt distinctly inclined to show off. 'No, who are you really?' she asked.

'Charles Paris.'

'Oh, I think I've heard of you;' she said, polite but uncertain. Ooh, just a minute. Were you ever at the Royal Shakespeare Company at Stratford?'

'Yes, a long time ago.'

'About seven years?'

'Yes.'

'Did you play Cassius in *Julius Caesar?'*

'Yes.'

'Ooh. I thought you were marvellous. We went in a school trip. We all got quite silly about you.'

'Oh,' said Charles, in what stage directions describe as a self-deprecating manner. This was all rather playing into his hands. Seeds sown unknowingly long ago. Cast your bread upon the waters, and it will come back buttered. 'Who are you then?'

'I'm Felicity Newman. I live here. Daddy owns this place.' (The 'Daddy' caught the slight quack of an English girls' public school . It was a sound Charles had always found exciting.) 'I'm fascinated by all this filming. Somebody's going to show me round, a friend of Daddy's. I want to work in films.'

'With your looks I should think you'd stand a very good chance.'

'No, silly.' She was still sufficiently girlish to blush at the formula compliment. 'Not that side of films. The production side. I'm doing a secretarial course and want to get in that way. Daddy knows quite a lot of people in the cinema.

Yes. Charles felt sure that Daddy could pull the odd string on his daughter's behalf. Sir Lionel Newman put a great deal of money into film production. Charles even had a feeling that he was a major shareholder in Steenway Productions. 'And how come you're not doing your secretarial course today?' he asked in the Morningside accent which he had drummed into the cast of his production of *The Prime of Miss Jean Brodie* ('Slow-moving' – *Evening Argus).*

She giggled. 'Oh, I just took the day off. How do you do that Scottish accent?'

She was easily impressed, but Charles felt like indulging himself in a little tour de force. He went through his entire gamut of the accents of Scotland, from his Hebridean fisherman through to the harsh tones of Glasgow. Indeed, he was in full flood in his Detective-Sergeant McWhirter voice, to an accompaniment of giggles from Felicity, when he heard a voice behind him. 'Ah, there you are.'

He stopped in mid-flow and turned to see Nigel Steen standing in the doorway. Steen looked annoyed, but it was difficult to tell whether or not he had recognised the voice. 'Felicity. I'm sorry to have kept you. Shall we start our tour?'

'Yes. Certainly, Nigel.' She was suddenly downcast, obviously sharing the world's lack of enthusiasm for Marius Steen's son. 'Do you know Charles Paris?' she asked.

'No, I don't think we've met,' said Nigel Steen, and he looked at Charles intently.

The scenes to be shot were rescheduled and Charles didn't in fact do anything that day. When this truth, which had been apparent from early morning, was finally recognised by Jean-Luc Roussel and Charles was released, it was about five o'clock. In a state of some exasperation, he was about to organise his car back to Pangbourne, when Felicity appeared round the corner of one of the make-up caravans. 'Hello,' she said brightly, 'do you fancy a drink?'

It was exactly what Charles did fancy (or at least part of what he fancied), so he said so. 'Come on,' said Felicity, and led him round the back of the house and through a herb-garden into a large modern kitchen. 'This is the part of the house we actually use. The rest's just for show.' She led him upstairs to a homely-looking sitting-room, and opened the drinks cupboard. 'What?'

'Scotch, please.'

She took out a bottle of Glenfiddich and poured a wine-glassful. 'Hey. Stop.'

'Why?'

'It's an expensive malt whisky.'

'I know,' she said superciliously, and passed him the glass. He took a long sip. It was very welcome. Felicity still looked rather piqued at his assumption of her ignorance of drink lore. He tried to open out the conversation. 'Still keen on films after seeing them in action for a day?'

'Yes,' she said shortly, and then, to show her sophistication in the matter of alcohol, 'I think I'll have a gin and tonic.

'So it was a good day?' Charles knew he sounded horribly patronising.

'All right. The company could have been better.'

'Nigel Steen, the great impresario.'

'Shit,' she said unexpectedly. 'He's a creep, always has been. I've known him for years. Daddy knew Marius. I think they had plans for match-making. Yeugh.'

'Not your type?'

'God, no. I don't know what my type is really, but it's not that. Ergh. He made a pass at me once. It was horrible, like being groped by liver. Actually, he invited me out tonight, probably with an ulterior motive. I told him I was otherwise engaged.'

'Are you?'

'No. Not unless you'd like me to cook you a meal.'

'Oh well ... I'm sure that you don't want—'

'It's no sweat. I'm doing this Cordon Bleu course as well as the secretarial thing, and I need the practice.'

So they both agreed to show off for the evening. She demonstrated her culinary skills with a splendid Chicken Kiev and Dauphinoise potatoes, and he kept her entertained with a variety of accents and theatrical reminiscences. Felicity raided her father's cellar for a couple of bottles of an excellent Chateau Margaux. 'He'll never notice. Doesn't know a thing about wine. Just takes advice all the time.'

'Where are your parents?'

'Oh, they've gone to Jamaica. As soon as all these lighting restrictions came in, Daddy said he wasn't going to stay in England and they pissed off.' Felicity's lapses into strong language, which were meant to make her sound cool, only made her sound immature. But appealing.

Charles found it very difficult. This girl was plainly throwing herself at him, and he knew that if he took advantage of something so easy, he would really feel shabby. And she looked sixteen. Possibly even under age. There is a point where going around with younger women stops and cradle-snatching begins. And Charles prided himself that he had never knowingly taken advantage of anyone (anyone, that is, who didn't deserve it).

It would have been easier if he hadn't found her attractive. Usually the sort of woman who makes such blatant advances is eminently resistible. But in Felicity's case, she was not impelled by the plain girl's need to take the initiative, but by youthful enthusiasm and social immaturity. Charles was determined to resist her.

But as the alcohol warmed and relaxed him, he could feel lust beginning to take the upper hand. When he had finished her excellent chocolate mousse, he made an immense effort of will, and rose to his feet. 'I think I'd better be off now. I'm doing my big scene tomorrow. Perhaps I can ring for a minicab.'

She didn't move. 'What's your big scene?'

'My death. The death of Tick, the deformed coachman, shot down by Sir Rupert Cartland, as he rushes along the gallery to capture the abysmal Lady Laetitia Winthrop.'

'You needn't go.'

'I must.' Well done, Charles. The Festival of Light would be proud of you.

Felicity rose very deliberately from the table, walked towards him, and pressing her body close to his, kissed his lips. Charles stood like a carved idol receiving the homage of the faithful. He gave nothing. 'I think I had better go.'

'Why?' She used that word disconcertingly often.

'Well, I ... um ... you know ...' It was difficult to think of a good reason at a moment like this.

'If you don't find me attractive, you can say so. I'll survive.

'It's not that. You gotta believe me, it's not that.' He dropped into American to hide his confusion.

'Are you worried about my age?'

'Yes. Amongst other things.'

'Listen, Charles. I am eighteen, which is not only two years above the age of consent, but is also now the age of majority. And I'm on the Pill, so you needn't worry about that.'

Her frankness was very confusing. Charles felt himself blushing. 'Um ... you mean, you're not a virgin?'

Her short derisive laugh made him feel suitably patronised. 'Charles, I lost my virginity when I was twelve, and since then quite a few other things have happened.' The weakness of the ending of her sentence again revealed her youth.

Charles could feel his resolve slackening, but made one last effort. 'I'm too old for you, Felicity.'

'You're not as old as the man who had me first.'

'Oh. Who was he?'

'Marius Steen.'

The next day Charles was feeling elated. He had parted from Felicity on good terms after breakfast; she had returned to continue her courses. He'd rung Jacqui, and she was fine. To crown the day, he was going to film the death of Tick, the deformed coachman, and he enjoyed a bit of ham as much as any other actor.

They rehearsed the scene in the morning. Tick crept in through the window of the dining-room and surprised Lady Laetitia Winthrop playing at her virginals (a likely story). He carried a rope with which to bind her. When she saw him, she let out a little cry (that bit took ages to rehearse: every bit that required Lady Laetitia to do more than flash her tits took ages), then turned and ran to the end of the room. Tick cried out, 'Not so fast, my proud beauty!' (really), and pursued her. She ran up the stairs to the minstrels' gallery with Tick in breathy pursuit. (That was filmed in long-shot from the other end of the room.) Then a quick close-up of Lady Laetitia cowering panic-stricken against the wall. (That took a long time too. 'For Christ's sake,' said Jean-Luc Roussel; 'panic-stricken, not bleeding constipated! Imagine he's going to cut yer tits off!') Then a long-shot from behind Sir Rupert Cartland's shoulder as he forced open the dining-room door, saw the scene of Tick advancing menacingly on his beloved (or 'that silly bitch', as he always called her off the set), raised his pistol, cried, 'No, you monster' and shot the deformed coachman. Tick stopped and staggered. Cut to close-up of blood trickling from his face as he fell against the rail. Cut to shot of stuntman falling backwards over rail to the floor.

When the rehearsal was finally over, they adjourned for lunch in the billiard room, where the covers on the tables had a splendid buffet laid on them. Charles piled up his plate and sat on his own in the corner. To his surprise, two men came over and joined him. They were called Jem and Eric; he recognised them; they'd been around since the filming started. Jem was one of those burly figures who proliferate on film-sets. His role was ill-defined except to himself and other members of his union, but he spent most of his time carting scenery around and moving heavy props into position. Eric was a smaller, colourless man who worked in some clerical capacity in the production office. They never said much on the set except to each other. Nobody took much notice of them or expected them to start up any form of conversation, so Charles was surprised when Eric addressed him by name.

'Yes?'

'There's a bit of a query on your contract,' said Eric in his flat London voice. 'Been a typing error on some of them. Maybe on yours. Anyway, we want to send a duplicate just in case. It doesn't change anything.'

'OK. Fine.'

'Don't seem to have your address. Where should we send it to?'

Charles gave him the address of Maurice Skellern Artistes.

'Oh, we want it signed quickly. Wouldn't it be better if we sent it to your home?'

'No. My agent deals with all that kind of stuff.'

'Oh. Oh well, fine. We'll send it there then.' And Jem and Eric wandered off.

It gave Charles an uncomfortable feeling. True, it might be a genuine enquiry, but it could be Nigel Steen relating him to Jacqui for the first time. If so, a new hiding-place must be found quickly. Yes, it was fishy. If a new contract had to be signed urgently, why hadn't Eric brought it to him there and then, rather than posting it? Still, there was a bit of breathing space. Maurice would never give away the Hereford Road address and very few people knew it. Even friends. Charles hated the place so much he always arranged meetings in pubs, and never took anyone there. But the incident was disquieting.

He soon forgot it as the filming restarted. It was painfully slow. Lady Laetitia had forgotten all she'd been taught in the morning and everything had to be rehearsed again. Charles felt he would scream at another repetition of 'Not so fast, my proud beauty!' But progress was made and, shot by shot, Jean-Luc Roussel was satisfied. ('Not bleeding marvellous, but it'll have to do if we're going to get it all in before the bleeding electricians have their bleeding break.')

Eventually Lady Laetitia and Tick made it to the minstrels' gallery. Then there was a long break as the cameras were set up for the dramatic shot over Sir Rupert Cartland's shoulder. Make-up girls fluttered in and out with powder puffs. Electricians looked at their watches and slowly pushed their arc-lights about. Jem handed Sir Rupert his props. Sir Rupert complained that one of the buckles on his shoes was loose (the shot was only going to reveal his right ear and shoulder). Eventually all was ready. *'The Zombie Walks:* Scene 143, Take One'—the clapper-board clapped shut. Tick advanced on his prey cowering constipated against the wall. The doors of the dining-room burst open. Sir Rupert Cartland cried, 'No, you monster', and a shot rang out.

Charles Paris felt a searing pain as a bullet ripped into his flesh. He crumpled up in agony.

CHAPTER FIFTEEN

Poor Old Baron!

CHARLES REALLY THOUGHT he was dying when he woke up the next morning. Cold tremors of fear kept shaking his whole body. It wasn't the wound that worried him, though his arm still ached as though a steam-hammer had landed on it. Head and body felt disconnected and the foul taste in his mouth seemed to his waking mind a symptom of some terrible decay creeping over him from within.

For once it wasn't alcohol, or at least not just alcohol. The Battle Hospital in Reading had given him a sedative to take if necessary when he was discharged. The wound was clean and dressed; there was no point in keeping him inside with such a shortage of hospital beds. So the film company organised a car to take him from Reading to Pangbourne. Jean-Luc Roussel himself had come to the hospital and fretted and fluttered about like a true Cockney sparrow. Steenway Productions were very anxious about the injury; it is the sort of thing all film companies dread, because it inevitably leads to enormous claims for compensation.

They had tried to find out how the accident had happened. The gun was a genuine late-Victorian revolver (another anachronism in a film so full of them that its period could be any time between 1700 and 1900). How live bullets had got into it no one could imagine. The props people said they hadn't touched it; it had come like that from the place of hiring. The hiring firm were very affronted when rung up, and assured the film company that they only ever supplied blanks. No doubt a further investigation would follow.

The thought of substantial compensation didn't comfort Charles much. It was the taste of death in his mouth that preoccupied him. He staggered out of bed and cleaned his teeth, but the taste was still there. He put his hands on the marine blue wash-basin and his body sagged forward. The face in the mirror of the marine blue bathroom cabinet looked terrified and ill. Partly he knew it was last night's sedative, coupled with a large slug of Miles' Chivas Regal. Coming after the sleepless night spent with Felicity, it was bound to affect him pretty badly. But more than that it was the shock, a feeling that left his body as cold as ice, and sent these involuntary convulsions through him.

He started to dress, but almost passed out with the pain from his arm. To steady himself he sank down on the side of the bed. At that moment, Juliet came into the bedroom. 'Daddy, are you all right? I heard you moving and—'

Charles nodded weakly.

'You look ghastly,' she said.

'I feel it. Here, would you help me get dressed? This bloody arm ... I can't do anything.'

Very gently his daughter started to help him into his clothes. As she bent to pick up his trousers, she looked just like Frances. 'Daughter and wife whom I'll leave when I die'—the phrase came into his maudlin thoughts and he started crying convulsively.

'Daddy, Daddy.'

'It's just the shock,' he managed to get out between sobs.

'Daddy, calm down.' But his body had taken control and he couldn't calm down.

'Daddy, get back to bed. I'll call the doctor.'

'NO ... I can't go back to bed, because I've got to get to London. I've got to get ... to London. I've got to get to London.' Suddenly the repetition seemed very funny and his sobs changed to ripples of high-pitched giggles. The situation became funnier and funnier and he lay back on the bed shaken by deep gasps of laughter.

Juliet talked calmingly to no avail. Suddenly her hand lashed out and slapped his face. Hard. It had the desired effect. The convulsions stopped and Charles lay back exhausted. He still felt ill, but the hysterics seemed to have relaxed him a bit. Juliet helped him back under the bedclothes. 'I'm going to get the doctor,' she said, and left the room.

Charles dropped immediately into a deep sleep where lumbering Thurber cartoon figures with guns in their hands chased him through a landscape of pastel green, dotted with red flowers. There was no menace in their attack. He was running hand in hand with a girl who was Juliet or Felicity, but wearing Frances' old white duffel coat. They stopped at a launderette. The girl, whose face was now Jacqui's, clasped his arm and said 'It's a pity the *Battleship Potemkin* is booked for Easter.' She kept hold of his arm and shook it till it became elastic and extended out of its socket like a conjuror's string of handkerchiefs.

'Mr Paris.' Charles opened his eyes warily, disgruntled at being dragged out of his dream. 'Mr Paris. I am Doctor Lefeuvre.'

'Hello,' said Charles sleepily.

'It's rather difficult you not being one of my regular patients, but since your daughter is, I'm stretching a point. She's told me about your accident yesterday, but I gather that's not what's troubling you?' The voice had a slight Australian twang. Charles looked at Doctor Lefeuvre. A man in his mid-thirties with dull auburn hair and a freckled face behind rectangular metal-rimmed glasses. He had very long hands, which were also covered in freckles and sported three gold rings.

'I don't know, Doctor. I just feel very weak and ill.'

'The arm's all right?'

'It feels bruised, but that's all.'

'Only to be expected. Let's just have a look at the dressing.' He cast his eye expertly over the bandage on Charles' arm. 'It's been very well done. When are you due to go back to the hospital?'

'They'll change the dressing next Monday.'

'That seems fine. I won't meddle with it then. But otherwise you're feeling run down and ill. It's probably just shock.'

'Yes.'

'I'd better have a look at you.' And the doctor began the time-honoured ritual of taking temperature and pulses. In fact, Charles felt better now. His body had regained some warmth and the sleep had relaxed him. He just felt as if he'd run full tilt into a brick wall.

Doctor Lefeuvre looked at the temperature. 'Hmm. That's strange.'

'What?'

'You seem to have a slight temperature. Just over a hundred. That's not really consistent with shock. Let's take your shirt off. There. Not hurting the arm?'

'No.'

'Hmm.' The doctor started probing and tapping. 'Let's have a look at your throat. Open. There. Tongue down. No, down. Yes. Is your throat at all sore?'

'A bit. Sort of foul taste in my mouth.'

'Yes. Hm. That's strange. You haven't been in contact with German measles recently?'

'Not to my knowledge, no.'

'No. Hmmm. Because, on a cursory examination, I would say that is what you've got. There's a slight rash on your chest, hardly visible. The temperature and the sore throat are consistent.

'Oh. Well, what should I do about it?'

'Nothing much. It's not very serious. If you're feeling bad, stay in bed. It'll clear up in a couple of days. You don't have to rush back to work, do you?'

'No, they've reorganised the shooting schedule.'

'Oh.' Doctor Lefeuvre obviously didn't understand what that meant, but equally obviously it didn't interest him much either. 'Look, I'll prescribe some penicillin.' He scribbled on his pad. 'You'd better check with Battle Hospital, tell them you're going to take it. Just in case they want to put you on something else.'

'Fine.'

'Good. Oh. I'd better just have your address and National Health Number for the records.' Charles gave them, digging the number out of a 1972 diary which was so full of useful information he'd never managed to get rid of it.

'Right.' Doctor Lefeuvre gathered his things together and prepared to leave.

'So there's nothing special I should do? Just rest?'

'Yes. You'll feel better in a couple of days. The rest won't do the arm any harm either.'

'OK.'

'Oh, there is one thing of course with German measles.'

'Yes.'

'You mustn't be in contact with anyone who's expecting a baby. If a woman gets German measles while she's pregnant, it can have very bad effects on the unborn child.'

Charles dressed with Juliet's help (he didn't like staying in bed alone) and rang Jacqui as soon as the doctor had left. He didn't mention the 'accident' at Bloomwater because it would only upset her. In fact, she sounded particularly cheerful; it was the first morning she had woken up with no trace of sickness, and was cheered at the thought of entering the 'blooming' phase of pregnancy. No, nothing disturbing had happened. Nobody had rung. She was quite happy in her little prison.

Charles felt fairly confident of her safety for the time being. Though the shooting on the film set, if it wasn't accidental implied that Nigel Steen knew of his involvement, he still might not have realised the direct connection with Jacqui, and certainly was no nearer getting the Hereford Road address. But she would have to be moved soon. Charles determined to ring Frances and ask her to take the girl in. It would be a strange coupling, but Frances wouldn't refuse. He explained to Jacqui about the German measles.

'Oh no, for God's sake keep away from me,' she said. 'The child is born blind or something terrible.'

'Don't worry. I'll stay away.'

'How long are you infectious?'

'I should be better in two or three days. But I don't know how long the quarantine period is. It's probably just as well I haven't been near you for the last week. Don't worry though. I won't come back till I'm quite clear of it. I'll ring Doctor Lefeuvre and check.'

'Who?'

'Doctor Lefeuvre.'

'Australian?'

'Yes.'

'Good God.'

'Why. Do you know him?'

'Yes. He was the one who did my abortion in the summer.'

'What? But it wasn't a legal one, was it?'

'No. Marius got Nigel to fix it up.'

'Was Lefeuvre the family doctor?'

'I suppose so. Marius didn't talk about doctors. He kept saying he was never ill.'

'So it was probably Lefeuvre who was called in when Marius died.'

'Yes, it was. He was at the inquest.'

'He was? Jacqui, for Christ's sake. Why didn't you tell me this before?'

'I didn't think it was important. Is it?'

'Jesus! But there was no time to explain. And no point in worrying her. 'Jacqui, just sit tight. Don't worry about anything.' He slammed the phone down. 'Juliet, can I have your car keys? I've got to go up to London immediately.'

Juliet emerged dazed from the kitchen area. 'But you can't take the Cortina. Miles'll be furious.'

'I haven't got time to worry about Miles. Give me the keys.'

'Juliet was amazed by the sudden force of his personality and held out the keys, as if hypnotised. 'But, Daddy, you can't drive with that arm.'

'I bloody can.'

CHAPTER SIXTEEN

Back at the Fireside

BEING BACK IN London was a disappointment. The mad drive up the M4 with pain like barbed hooks turning in his arm had all been for nothing. He had screeched to a halt in the residents' parking bay in an unimpressed Hereford Road, let himself in, banged on his own door and, keeping his distance, ordered Jacqui to go off to the pictures for the afternoon. Then he'd driven round to the surgery of Drs Singh and Gupta, with whom he was registered, only to find that both were out on their rounds. He rushed to St Mary's Hospital, Paddington, and, after the hours of waiting that are statutory in hospitals, finally persuaded a callow houseman to examine him and pronounce him clear of German measles. It was evident from the young man's circumspect excitement that he thought he'd got his first genuine schizophrenic hypochondriac. Charles ended up with a clean bill of health and a parking ticket.

As he sat in his drab room in Hereford Road, it all seemed a bit futile. The dark fears of the morning had subsided into childish fantasies. He felt he should be watching the road from behind the curtains, waiting for the badmen to arrive at High Noon, while in the background a voice intoned 'Do not forsake me, o my darling'. But since his windows faced the back of the house, it was impossible. And in the familiar banality of his room thoughts of approaching badmen seemed ridiculous. He just felt tired and ill again. The excitements of the day had put him back considerably. Pain throbbed in his arm with agonising regularity. He felt himself drifting asleep.

Suddenly the phone rang. Swedish feet in wooden sandals clumped down the stairs past his door, then up again, paused, knocked, said 'Telephone' and continued back to their room.

He went down and picked up the dangling receiver. 'Hello.'

'Hello. It's Joanne Menzies.'

'Oh. Hi.'

'Charles, can we meet and talk? About Marius' death.'

'Yes, sure. Have you got anything new?'

'Not really. But I'm just convinced there was something fishy going on.'

'Yes. There are a lot of things that don't fit. When do you want to meet? After work?'

'I'm not at work.'

'Oh.'

'I came back after Christmas to the news that my services were no longer required by Mr Nigel Steen. A year's salary in lieu of notice.'

'That's a substantial pay-off.'

'Yes. Hush-money, no doubt. Where shall we meet?'

'Do you mind coming round here? I'm not very well.'

'Fine. What's the address?' Charles gave it. 'I'll be round straight away.' He put the phone down and had a moment's doubt. Was he wise to give Joanne Menzies his address? She seemed straight enough, but her motives weren't absolutely clear. Oh well, if she told Nigel Steen, fair enough. Charles' suspicions of Dr Lefeuvre made him think his address was already common knowledge. At least he was here now, and could supervise moving Jacqui to another hide-away. He rang Frances' number to make his strange request, but there was no reply. It was only five o'clock. No doubt she was supervising the school debating society or another of her public-spirited activities.

Joanne Menzies arrived quickly and they started talking over a glass of whisky. Charles gave the shortest possible explanation of his sling—'an accident on the film set'. He didn't want to voice any suspicions until he felt a bit surer of Joanne's allegiances. 'So. What do you think is fishy?'

'No one big thing, Charles. Just a lot of dubious details.'

'Like ...?'

'Like the way Nigel lied over that Saturday night, all the subterfuge over the petrol in the Datsun. Like the way he's been behaving since his father's death—and the week before, come to that—'

'How's he been behaving?'

'Very twitchy. Jumps whenever the phone rings. As if there's something he's frightened of.'

'What else?'

'The way I've been dismissed. All right, I was Marius' personal assistant and there's no reason to assume that Nigel would want to take me over in the same role. But it was rather sudden. And a year's salary is excessive—out of character too for someone as mean as Nigel.'

'Hmm. So you think that Nigel murdered Marius?'

'That's the obvious thing to think.'

'Except for the findings of the inquest.'

'Yes.' Joanne spoke with the same contempt Jacqui had shown for the high achievements of forensic science.

'And the fact that Nigel had no motive. It was in his interests that his father should live at least until the seven years were up.' Joanne's face revealed that she didn't know about the gift, so Charles gave a brief résumé of the legal position. He finished up, 'You know, we are not the only people who are suspicious of Nigel and would attribute any crime to him. But the fact remains that, in the matter of Marius Steen's death, we have not a solitary shred of evidence to go on. Just prejudice and dislike.'

'Yes. I'm sure he's done something, though.' Her conviction was reminiscent of Jacqui's, overriding little details like facts.

'All right, Joanne, let's talk through it all again. Actually, one thing you said interested me. You said Nigel was twitchy the week before the murder—I mean, the death.'

'Yes.'

'I thought he was in Streatley that week.'

'Only part of it. He went down on the Thursday to go through some business things with Marius, then came back on the Friday late afternoon—just after you came round about your play. Was that another blind, by the way?'

''Fraid so.'

'Why?'

'Too complicated to explain.' He didn't want to bring in the Sweets and the implied charge of murder against the dead man. 'So look, let's trace through the movements of the two of them. Where were they on the Sunday, that'd be what ...?'

'The 2nd of December.'

'Right.'

'I think they were both in Orme Gardens. Then Marius drove to Streatley that night to read the scripts on his own.'

'Was that unexpected?'

'No, he'd been talking about it. He'd noticed a slight waning in the receipts on *Sex of One* ... though I think it was just the power crisis and the railways. Anyway, he felt he had to make a decision on the next show for the Kings.'

'And when he did one of these script-reading sessions, he used to cut himself off completely?'

'Yes. Just switch on the Ansaphone.'

'I see. So when did you last speak to him?'

'Small hours of Sunday morning. At the *Sex of One* ... party.'

'Oh yes. A thousand performances. Ugh. Let's continue their movements. Marius is in Streatley. Where's Nigel, say on the Monday morning? Milton Buildings?'

'No, he came in after lunch.'

'Was that unusual?'

'No. Particularly considering the late night we'd all had on the Saturday.'

'Right. Incidentally, how was Marius at the party?'

'In marvellous form—leaping around like a boy of twenty. Dancing with all the girls.' The pride was evident in her voice.

'Including you.'

'Yes.'

'You loved him, didn't you?'

'Yes.'

'Did you know he was contemplating remarriage?'

'I knew.'

'Did you mind?'

'Yes, but if it made him happy ... If Marius wanted something there was no point in trying to stop his getting it.'

'No.' Her answers sounded perfectly honest. 'Let's continue our tracing movements. Which car did Nigel go down in on the Thursday?'

'His own. The Interceptor. It was after that that he complained about the brakes to Morrison.'

'Right. And then he goes down again in secret on the Saturday in the Datsun. The Datsun, the Datsun. You know there's something at the back of my mind about that Datsun and I can't think what it is.' He looked round the room for inspiration. It was an untidy mess. Jacqui's occupation hadn't improved it; she wasn't the sort of girl who immediately revolutionised a place and gave it a woman's touch; she just spread her belongings over the widest possible area. A flouncy negligee and a pair of tights lay over one chair; the tiny television was perched on another; a soggy packet of frozen spinach lay beside the gas-ring; on the crumpled candlewick of the bed an *Evening Standard* was open at the entertainments' page so she could decide which film to go and see.

A thought suddenly illuminated Charles' brain like a flash of lightning. 'That's it. The *Evening Standard*.'

'What?' Joanne was left floundering as his mind raced on. Very clearly he saw himself standing in the BBC Club with Sherlock Forster and hearing the name of Marius Steen, the name that had come to dominate his life. When was that? It was a Monday. Yes, Monday the 3rd of December. After that terrible play. And what had the paper said? Something about Marius not using the Rolls, but sticking to the Datsun. Oh, if only he could remember the details.

There was one person who could help. Johnny Smart, who'd been at Oxford with him and edited one of the university magazines, landed what seemed then an amazing job on the *Evening Standard*. In the years since he'd sunk into alcoholic indifference in the same job, which at his present age was less amazing. With a murmured excuse to Joanne, Charles rushed to the telephone and rang the paper. Fortunately Johnny was still there—a stroke of luck considering that the pubs were open. In rather breathless fashion, Charles explained that he wanted to find out who researched and wrote an article about the petrol crisis in a late edition on Monday 3rd of December.

Johnny thought he could probably find out. It was bound to be one of the young reporters. Why didn't Charles come down and join them at Mother Bunch's? A lot would be down there at this time of night. He'd be there himself except that the newsroom was on sodding tenterhooks waiting to see if Heath would call a sodding snap election and they'd have to bring out a sodding slip edition. He'd be down in half an hour though.

Just as Charles put the phone down, Jacqui returned. She had been to see *Enter the Dragon* and started to tell him all about the code of *kung fu* as he hurried her upstairs. Joanne recognised Jacqui the moment the dark glasses came off and Charles felt the room temperature drop as the two women faced each other. Still, he hadn't time to worry about that. Leaving strict instructions to Joanne to stay there at all costs and to both of them under no account to let anyone in, he hurried to the Cortina and set off for Fleet Street.

Reporters are proverbially heavy drinkers, and it took a few bottles of bonhomie with Johnny Smart before Charles could actually get down to the business for which he had come. He sat in the broad circle of young journalists in Mother Bunch's Wine House and, with the rest of them, sank glass after glass of red wine. Eventually Johnny drew him to one side with a shock-haired young reporter who sported horn-rimmed glasses and a velvet bow-tie. His name was Keith Battrick-Jones. Charles explained his mission.

'Bloody hell,' said Keith Battrick-Jones. 'Done a lot of stories since then. I don't know if I can remember that far back. When was it?'

'Monday 3rd December. Six, seven weeks ago. It was a sort of round-up of people's reactions to the petrol crisis. Pictures and comments. There was Steen ...' The boy looked blank. '... and some footballer ...' Still blank. '... and a leggy girl on a bike—'

'Oh shit. I remember. Yes. Crappy idea, wasn't it? Somebody thought of it at an editorial conference, and Muggins here had to ring round all these celebrities to get comments. As usual, the interesting people told me to piss off, and I ended up with the same old circle of publicity seekers.'

'Can you remember phoning Marius Steen?'

'No, I don't think I can. If it was Monday morning, I must have had a skinful the night before. No, I ... oh, just a minute though. I remember. I rang through and I got some old berk being facetious on an Ansaphone. So I told the machine what it was about, and moved on to a golfer and one of the Black and White minstrels.'

'But Steen did phone back?'

'Yes. Made some fatuous comment about using the smaller car. Well, we'd got a library picture of him, so we put it in.'

'And you are sure it was Marius Steen himself who spoke to you?'

'I don't know. I've never met the bloke.'

'Was it the same voice as the one on the Ansaphone?'

'Oh no. It was much more cultured. And younger.'

CHAPTER SEVENTEEN

The Broker's Men

CHARLES HAD A lot of wine inside him as he drove along the Strand on his way back, but he was thinking with extraordinary clarity. Suddenly Nigel had two secret trips to Streatley to explain, not one. If he had been at the Sex of One ... party, he must have driven down some time between the small hours of the Sunday morning and when he rang Keith Battrick-Jones on the Monday morning. That was, of course, assuming that he had gone down on his own. It was possible that he had been in the Rolls with his father on the Sunday night.

If that were the case, and Charles' other conjecture was correct, he must have witnessed Marius shooting Bill Sweet on the roadside at Theale. That might well explain the twitchiness which Joanne had noticed during the ensuing week. Possibly Nigel had shot Bill Sweet himself? But no, that was nonsense. He had nothing to do with the Sally Nash affair, and the Sweets represented no threat to him. If anyone had committed murder on the lonely turnoff from the M4, it must have been Marius.

At Hyde Park Corner, a taxi travelling from Knightsbridge suddenly cut across the front of the Cortina and Charles had to slam on all his brakes. The shock jarred every bone in his body and he felt as if he was about to pass out. There was nothing else coming. He swung the car across the yellow line and stopped by the marble colonnade at the roadside. His body was in agony. Slowly the total blinding pain broke down into individual centres of hurt. First there was his arm, with its bone bruised by the bullet. That pain seemed to swell and swamp the others. Then there were the bruises on his knees and elbows that he'd received from the fall over the trip-wire at Jacqui's. And then, lower down the league of pain, there was the dull ache of an old bruise on his ankle.

Suddenly, he saw in his mind the utility room at Streatley and a scattered pile of boxes. Some words of Gerald Venables reverberated in his head. Dr Lefeuvre's role came clearly defined into focus, and Charles Paris knew what Nigel Steen's crime was.

As he walked up the stairs at Hereford Road, he was glowing with the intellectual perfection of it. Not the intellectual perfection of the crime—that was a shabby affair—but the intellectual perfection of his conclusion. Suddenly, given one fact, all the others clicked neatly into position. As he drove back, he had tried each element individually, and none of them broke the pattern. He was looking forward to spelling it all out to Jacqui and

Joanne. Actual evidence was still a bit short on the ground (burning the vicious letter to Jacqui and the Sweet photographs had shown a regrettable lack of detective instinct). But he felt sure facts would come, now the basic riddle was solved.

The door of his room was open, the lock plate hanging loose. A cold feeling trickled into his stomach as he went inside. It was dark. He switched on the light. A body lay tied, gagged and struggling on the floor by the bed. Joanne. There was no sign of Jacqui.

He fumbled with the knots of Jacqui's tights which had been tied cruelly round Joanne's mouth. She gave a little gasp of pain as he tightened to release them, and then she was free to talk. 'Two men ... someone must have let them in the front door ... they took Jacqui ...'

'Did you see them?'

'They had stockings over their heads. One was big and burly, the other was smaller ...'

'Yes. I know who they are.' He cut her other bonds free with a kitchen knife. 'Come on. We must follow them.'

'Where to? How do we know where they've gone?'

'I think it's Streatley. And I pray to God I'm right. For the sake of Jacqui's baby.'

CHAPTER EIGHTEEN

King Rat

THEY ROARED DOWN the M4, fifty miles an hour limits contemptuously ignored. They swung off the motor way at Theale, past the scene of Bill Sweet's death, and on, through the dark roads, past Tidmarsh, Pangbourne, Lower Basildon, towards Streatley. About a mile outside the town, the Cortina suddenly lost power and pop-popped to a stop at the roadside. 'Sod it. Bloody petrol. The whole case hinges on it, and I forget to fill up.'

'He might have a spare can,' said Joanne. But there was nothing in the boot. Miles' odious efficiency was absent when actually needed. 'I'll have to walk the rest.' Charles started off into the gloom.

'What shall I do?' Joanne's voice floated after him.

'Get the police.' He stumbled on, occasionally trying a little jogging run. His body ached all over and the wounded arm felt as if it were dropping off. The strain of the last few days was beginning to tell, and he knew he hadn't got much energy left. If it came to violence, he wasn't going to do too well. He didn't relish facing Jem and Eric (he felt sure it was they who'd carried Jacqui off).

Sweat trickled down his sides in spite of the cold. His clothes were heavy and awkward. Still the road seemed to stretch onwards endlessly, darkness replacing darkness, as he staggered forward. Occasionally a car would pass, fix him like a moth in its headlights, and then vanish.

Eventually he was at the top of the slope that led down to the little towns of Streatley and Goring, separated, like their respective counties of Berkshire and Oxfordshire, by the River Thames. Revived by the proximity of his goal, Charles hurried painfully onwards along the road to the familiar white gates. It occurred to him that being on foot was probably an advantage; a car drawing up on the gravel would be heard from the house. And in his position he needed advantages.

He opened one gate slowly, trying not to let it scrape on the gravel. Then he moved round on to the flower-bed at the side of the path, to muffle his footsteps. The house looked quiet and the same, except for a strange car parked by the front door. Again, as on the previous occasion, there was a chink of light from Marius Steen's bedroom. Was it possible that Charles' previous luck could be repeated and he'd find the door to the utility room open? Keeping to the lawn, he crept silently to the back of the garage. Moved in close to the door, and felt for the handle.

He closed his eyes, uttered a silent prayer and turned the knob. For a moment the door seemed firm, but then, blissfully, it gave.

He sidled into the utility room, treading with remembered caution, and reached for the light switch. The room had been tidied since his last visit. All the tins and boxes were neatly on their shelves, and, thank God, the torch was still in its place. He took it and started to put into action a plan that had half-formed in his mind during the run from the stranded Cortina.

He locked the door by which he had entered and put the key in his pocket. Then he turned his attention to the door that opened into the garage. There was no lock on that one. For a moment he stood, defeated, but then, memory working overtime, he moved into the garage, opened the door of the Rolls, and shone his torch over the dashboard. With a small grim smile of satisfaction, he went back to the utility room and looked at the power switches. He closed his eyes and memorised their positions. Then one by one, with a series of quick movements, he switched them all off. He scurried into the safety of the great car.

There was a murmur of voices from the room above, then the slow sound of people feeling their way downstairs and towards the garage. The faint glow of a match shone through the door from the house. Charles shrank into the deep upholstery of the Rolls' front seat.

There were two voices, a deep slow one, and a higher London whine. Jem and Eric, as he'd thought. They went into the utility room. Charles heard the scrape of a match, then a muttered curse. With another prayer, he turned the key in the ignition of the Rolls. It started immediately. He found first gear and eased the great machine slowly forward until it hit the utility room door, closed it, and pinned it fast. Then he pulled on the hand-brake and leapt out.

The hammering of Jem and Eric followed him, as he rushed upstairs with the torch to Marius Steen's bedroom. As he entered it, one of the prisoners found the switches, and the lights came on again.

The scene which they revealed was an ugly one. On the bed, Jacqui lay unconscious. She was on a sheet, naked with her legs spread apart. Another sheet was crumpled over her thighs. On either side of her, blinking in the sudden light, were Nigel Steen and Dr Lefeuvre. Laid out on a cloth on a stool were a row of bright instruments. A scalpel gleamed in the doctor's long freckled hand.

Nigel was the first to speak. 'Charles Paris ... You are taking a very great risk.'

'Nothing to some of the risks you've taken, Steen.'

There was a silence. Nobody moved. Then came the sound of renewed battering from downstairs. Dr Lefeuvre dropped his scalpel with the other instruments, gathered them up in the cloth and put them in his bag. 'I'm leaving, Steen.'

Panic flashed into Nigel's face. 'You can't do that. I need your help.'

'No, Steen. Get out of this one on your own.'

'You've got to help me.'

'No.'

'You did the other things for me.'

'Not for you. For money.'

'I'll tell the police what you've done.'

'I think that unlikely. It might involve too much explanation of your own activities. Anyway, I will have left the country by then. I'd planned to go back to Australia when I'd made enough. And, thanks to you'—he tapped the case—'that time's come.'

'But—'

'Goodbye, Steen.' Dr Lefeuvre left the room. Neither Charles nor Nigel spoke as they heard his footsteps on the stairs, the slam of the front door, the gates being opened, and his car departing in a scurry of gravel.

'What do you want, Paris? Money?' said Nigel Steen suddenly.

'No.'

'I could give you a lot. I'll pay for silence.'

'And then set your thugs on me the first time my back's turned. No, thank you.'

'Then what do you want?'

'Just to talk. See if what I think is correct—until the police come.'

'I see. Come through here.'

Nigel Steen led Charles, with what was meant to be a lordly gesture, into the study next door. He sat behind the desk and offered the older man a plush leather seat. 'Well now,' in deliberately even tones, 'what is all this about the police? Shouldn't I be calling them to get you, as a common house-breaker?'

'You could try, but I think they'd find your case more interesting.'

'Do you? Why? What are you accusing me of? The inquest has already proved I didn't murder my father.'

'I know. That's not what I am accusing you of.'

Nigel's face went pale. 'What are you accusing me of then?'

'I'll tell you. Stop me if I'm wrong. This is the story as I see it. On Saturday 1st December, your father Marius Steen went to the party on stage at the King's Theatre to celebrate the one thousandth performance of *Sex of One and Half a Dozen of the Other.* He enjoyed the party, danced, drank and generally had a whale of a time.

'The following day, Sunday 2nd December, your father, because of his exertions, suffered a second heart attack, and died. You, with a shrewd sense of your own advantage, realised that you were now liable to pay one hell of a lot of estate duty on your father's gift to you because of his inconvenient death; but that if he had died a fortnight later it would be six and not five years since the property was made over to you. If you could maintain the illusion that your father was still alive for another fortnight you would be saving—say the property was worth one million—about £240,000. A quarter of a million pounds has been the motive for far worse crimes than the one you contemplated.

'Obviously you needed help. And it was to hand. Dear Dr Lefeuvre, who had already arranged at least one abortion for you, was always susceptible to bribery, or, if not that, to blackmail. All he had to do was to come round when you called and sign the death certificate with all particulars correct. Except the date.

'Now there was a problem, of course. The police might want to see the body; the undertaker certainly would. How to preserve it? Why not the good old deep-freeze? Keep the old man in there, get him out in good time to defrost, maybe even put him in a hot bath to remove any traces of his preservation. And there you are.

'So, late on the Sunday night, with your father's body propped up in the Rolls, you drive to Streatley, move a few boxes out of the deep-freeze and put your father in. On the Monday, after making one mistake by phoning the *Evening Standard*—and I can sympathise with your reasons for that mistake; after all, it was a heaven-sent opportunity to assert your father's continued existence— anyway, after that you get a train back to London ... I'm guessing there, but it's not important.

'So it was all set up, and your father's known habit of shutting himself up with his scripts made the deception all the easier. The only fly in the ointment was Jacqui. If she kept on trying to contact your father, it could be awkward. Still, she was on her own, and not very brave. A little intimidation should keep her quiet. An anonymous letter, and, when that didn't work, Jem and Eric doing her flat over. Easy.

'On the Thursday you return to Streatley, to maintain the myth of your father's continuing business interests; and perhaps to check a few details with Dr Lefeuvre. Or even to put the pressure on him, maybe?

'Then on the Saturday, something rattles you. You lose your nerve, drive down to Streatley in secret, change the tape in your father's Ansaphone, prepare the body and move your whole schedule forward a week. That, I must confess, is the bit I don't understand. By doing that you made the whole crime worthless. You were losing money. No doubt you had your reasons.

'But when the new will came to light, you were liable to lose even more money. So, seeing the flaw in its hastily drawn up provisions, you started your vendetta against Jacqui's child, a vendetta that Dr Lefeuvre was about to complete when I arrived. No doubt, before that you used the cruder talents of Jem and Eric. Certainly, when you realised my connection with the case at Bloomwater, they were the bully-boys you turned on to me.

'Well, I think that sums up most of my conclusions. How am I doing?'

He looked up at Nigel Steen. The man's face was white and mean and he was pointing an automatic pistol at Charles' chest. But he still tried to maintain some shreds of panache. 'Very good,' he said slowly. 'How did you know about the boxes in the freezer?'

'Ah, I must confess I have been in this house before. Just before your dramatic "discovery" of your father's corpse, I ... er ... fell over the boxes. They were heavy and had the words "Do not refreeze" written on them, but I didn't immediately realise the significance of that. Sorry. I was a bit slow on the uptake.'

'I see. Well, since I am going to kill you anyway—an intruder in my house, I met you, drew my gun; you attacked me and in the ensuing fight the gun went off, unfortunately killing you—I—'

'If that's as successful as your other crimes, I think I'm fairly safe.'

'Quiet !' Nigel waved the gun. 'Let me fill in the details. One thing you were wrong about is the extent of my crime. The things you describe could be classed as fraud and harassment maybe, but in fact there is a murder involved.'

'Yes, I know.' Steen looked at him open-mouthed, robbed of the drama of his pronouncement, as Charles continued, 'Bill Sweet's murder.'

'Whose?'

'Bill Sweet, the man who was found shot dead at Theale.'

'Oh, was that his name? I didn't know.'

'You mean you didn't know his connection with your father?'

'No. Was there one?'

'What happened, Steen?'

'We came off the M4 and suddenly there was this maniac in the middle of the road, flagging us down. I swerved to avoid him and hit his silly little car. I tried to drive on, but he came at me with some story of having run out of petrol. Then he looked in the car, saw my father crumpled up and started to speak. I panicked and shot him. I went through his pockets—for some reason they were full of dirty pictures. I took them and his wallet and threw the lot, with the gun, into the river.'

'Why his wallet?'

'To disguise his identity. I don't know. I panicked. I wanted to forget all about him—pretend it hadn't happened.'

'And that's why you haven't moved the Rolls since that night. You even left your father's keys in it. You seem to do rather a lot of panicking, don't you? Not a very impressive criminal.'

'If my plan had worked, it would have been a master-stroke. To save a quarter of a million—that's the sort of thing my father used to do.' The envy in his voice was almost pathetic.

'But you could never do what your father did, could you, Nigel? Business, women, even crime. You just never made it.' Nigel Steen's knuckles whitened around the gun and Charles uttered another silent prayer. He seemed to be getting very religious all of a sudden. 'Because you never had the guts to carry anything through,' he continued. 'Why didn't you carry this one through?'

'Because of you, you little sod.' Nigel spat the words out.

'Me?'

'Yes, you and your bloody Detective-Sergeant McWhirter business. When you rang up that Saturday and checked the registration of the Rolls, I thought the police were on to the Theale murder.'

'Good Lord.' Charles had completely forgotten about the first entrance of McWhirter. It came back to him vaguely. And that had actually ruined Nigel's crime. Charles could have chosen any excuse for the phone call and it was pure chance that he had lighted on the meaningless 'number plate racket'! 'So that's what made you drive down in the Datsun, and move the plan forward, and lose a quarter of a million pounds?'

'Yes.'

'Good Lord.' Charles was absolutely flabbergasted, but he hadn't really got time to analyse his reactions. Nigel was still pointing a rather businesslike gun at him. 'Nigel, I'd put that thing away. The police are coming. You stand a chance as things stand at the minute. They need never find out about Sweet's murder. Just get you on the other charges.'

'I don't believe you, Paris. You're bluffing. There aren't any police coming.'

'There are.' Charles prayed that he was speaking the truth. 'Joanne Menzies is getting them.'

'So, she was involved with you. The bitch.'

'I think you'd better hand that gun over, Nigel.' Charles rose to his feet.

'Don't move! I'll shoot you ! ' Nigel held the gun away from him, as if he was afraid of the bang it would make. Charles felt himself sweating.

He tried desperately to control his voice. 'No, Nigel, you won't shoot me. This is cold blood, Nigel. Something you've got to think about. Not like shooting Sweet in a moment of blind panic. Not like doing it by remote control, having Jem set up a trip-wire. This is you committing a crime, Nigel.'

The two men faced each other. Their eyes were interlocked and the gun pointed directly at Charles' heart. The pause seemed endless.

Suddenly the doorbell rang. Nigel tensed as if to fire, and Charles closed his eyes. Then he heard the clatter of the gun falling on to the desk. He looked at Nigel Steen and saw the glint of tears in his eyes as the young man rushed out of the door.

Charles collapsed like a glove puppet with the hand withdrawn, and stood for a long moment, sagging. The doorbell was still ringing. But before he went downstairs, he crept into Marius Steen's bedroom.

Jacqui was still unconscious, breathing heavily under the anaesthetic. Gingerly Charles raised the sheet that lay over her thighs. There was no blood, no sign that she had been touched. As he looked down at the body he used to love, he thanked God for letting him arrive in time.

When he opened the door downstairs, he heard the roar of a motorboat leaving from the boathouse at the back. On the doorstep in front of him stood Joanne Menzies, alone. She was breathless. 'I couldn't get the police. Didn't see a phone. I've just walked from the car.'

So it had been a bluff. Charles started laughing, clear ripples of relief shaking his body. He clasped Joanne in his arms, not for love or lust, just sheer joy at being alive.

*

The speedboat was found splintered against Goring Bridge. It had missed the lock and been driven full-tilt down the hard steps of the weir. Nigel Steen's body was found in some weeds nearly a mile downstream. Whether the death was suicide, or a result of his natural aptitude for failure, was never established.

CHAPTER NINETEEN

Finale and Curtain-Call

BARTLEMAS AND O'ROURKE'S tall Victorian house in Ideal Road, Islington, was like a chaotic museum. Every available wall surface was covered with memories of Kean and Macready; even in the lavatory the twin deities looked down beneficently on lesser mortals.

A battered life-size carving of Kean as Shylock greeted Charles as he entered the front door. The beak of a nose seemed strangely reminiscent of Marius Steen. O'Rourke took his coat. 'You know, people keep saying we ought to hang coats on Shylock's arm ...'

'But we're sure Edmund wouldn't like it,' said Bartlemas, appearing from nowhere in a shiny apron with an advertisement for 'Camp Coffee' on it.

'No, he wouldn't. The party was really Bartlemas' idea ...'

'Oh, I wouldn't say that, O'Rourke. Let's say we arrived at the idea mutually ...'

'Yes, let's. Nearly everyone's here. Do go through. Bartlemas, do you want a little succour with your vinaigrette?'

'Wouldn't say no, O'Rourke. Excuse us. Titivating the goodies. Do go through ...'

'Just toddle through ...' They vanished in a shimmer of saxe-blue silk shirts.

The sitting-room had two walls devoted to prints of Edmund in all his greatest roles, and the other two to William. Between them, sitting with drinks, were Joanne Menzies and Gerald Venables. Gerald rose to greet Charles in typical style. 'Hello, old boy. What's the budget going to do to your savings then?'

'I haven't got any.'

'Wise feller.' Charles greeted Joanne and helped himself to a large Scotch. Gerald continued. 'Do you realise, Charles, that if these Labour Johnnies go and slap on this gift tax they're talking about, crimes like young Nigel Steen's won't be worth committing.'

'His wasn't worth committing anyway, as it turned out.'

'No. Fascinating, though, from the legal point of view. Do let me in on any more of your detective work, won't you, Charles?'

'There won't be any more, Sherlock Holmes.'

'Oh, I'm sure there will. How's the arm?'

'Healed up long ago. A nice scar though.'

'And a good story to go with it.'

The conversation drifted. Joanne talked about her new job in a concert agency. Bartlemas and O'Rourke came in and talked about the first night of Gielgud's Prospero ('Doing it again, dear') at the National. Charles felt detached and rather sad. A little parcel had arrived through the post that morning from the old people's home at Tower Hamlets. Harry Chiltern had died, and asked that all his possessions be sent to Charles. It was depressing to think that he was the closest friend that the old man had, and it stirred all the usual guilt feelings—should have gone to see him more often, and so on. The package contained a watch, a silver cigarette case, a Ronson lighter and *Stanley Matthews' Book of Football*.

It suited Charles' melancholy mood well. Nothing much seemed to be happening. He had finished shooting the rescheduled scenes of *The Zombie Walks* without meeting Felicity again. (However, the episode was not without profit, since the film company had paid very substantial compensation for his 'accident'.) He was now involved in a dreary radio serial, which was driving him slowly mad with boredom. Life went on, at its usual alcoholic level.

A ring at the doorbell announced the late arrival of Jacqui, blonde again and resplendently pregnant in a long red and white flowered dress. It was so far from her usual style that Charles thought she must have undergone some violent change of personality. She greeted him slightly gushingly, and that again struck a false note.

The reason for the change soon became apparent. Given Jacqui's simple character, it could only be a man. Her escort followed her into the sitting-room. It was Bernard Walton.

'Hello, Charles. Dear boy. Joanne. darling. Hello, all you lovely people. Haven't met you, have I, sir, but I'm sure we'll get on. Tell you what, Jacqui and I were thinking of tootling on to the midnight matinee at the Parthenon after this lot. It's a charity thing—something to do with April Fools' Day. Perhaps that means it's raising money for a looney bin. Whole thing will probably be a ghastly no-no, but everyone will be there. What do you all say to the idea?'

Bartlemas and O'Rourke were terribly enthusiastic, and the others mumbled politely. Charles didn't even mumble. He knew what wasn't his scene.

The dinner was very good, though the conversation tended to be dominated by Bernard's stories of his new television series and the director who was disastrous, but disastrous. At one point, however, they did get around to Marius Steen and the circumstances of his death.

'What I never could understand,' said Gerald, 'was why Steen, who was so good with money, made such a cock-up of that final will. I mean, just leaving it to the baby, or making it dependent on the baby's survival. It's insane.'

'But you see, dear,' said Bartlemas, 'he only got that one together in a hurry ...'

'Yes,' said O'Rourke, 'he was going to sort it all out properly when he got back to England. I mean, the so-called solicitor he found out at Saint-Maxime was a boy, hardly even qualified. Just got his articles—I always think that sounds rude.' A snigger. 'So the will was only a stop-gap. But when Marius felt better, he forgot about it ...'

'Yes. He was intending to get married you see. '

Gerald nodded. 'Of course. Remarriage would revoke all previous wills.'

But Charles was intrigued by something O'Rourke had said. 'When Marius felt better? What did you mean by that?'

'Oh no! Didn't we tell you?' O'Rourke's eyes opened wide.

'I don't think we did, O'Rourke ...'

'Oh well, you see, Marius had this heart attack while we were out there. Not a bad one, but it frightened him. That's why he was in such a rush about the will ...'

'That's right. And that's why he made us witnesses and executors ...'

'Doesn't that sound grand ...'

'Yes, because we were the only people there ...'

'And then he gave us the will and the other papers and he said to us, just before we toddled off to Morocco— '

'Just a minute, O'Rourke,' Charles interposed. 'What other papers?'

O'Rourke looked at Bartlemas and both of them opened their eyes wide and put their hands over their mouths in mock horror. 'Oh no, Bartlemas, we haven't ...'

'We have, O'Rourke ...'

'Forgotten all about them ...'

'Oh no!'

'Where did we have them last?'

'Well, we certainly had them when you were cleaning that playbill of William as Lear at the Theatre Royal, Covent Garden ...'

'And then we ...'

'Ooh. Do you know, I think I left them in my dinki-doodi-den ...'

'Oh no, Bartlemas !'

'I'll scurry up and get them straight away.'

There was a brief pause. Nobody quite liked to ask what Bartlemas' dinki-doodi-den was. Fortunately he scurried back before the silence became awkward.

'Here it is, acres of bills and things.'

Gerald assumed control and looked through the papers while the others watched. Then he chuckled. 'The old sod.'

'Who?' asked Jacqui.

'Marius Steen. He'd really got it in for Nigel. He must have regretted that gift business.'

'Why? What did he do?' asked Charles.

'Marius wrote a letter to his son last November—this is a copy of it—complaining in humble terms about how he'd left himself short by the gift and not taken inflation into account, and would Nigel let him have a small income from various shares and properties? And here's the agreement duly signed by Nigel.'

'And what does it mean?'

'It means that Marius was retaining a beneficial interest in the gift.'

'What?' asked Jacqui blankly, which saved the embarrassment of someone else's asking.

'It means that the whole gift thing was invalid. Nigel would have had to pay duty on the whole estate without reduction.'

'Good God,' said Charles. 'You can't help admiring the old bugger. Making his own son sign away his fortune.'

'Yes. He was an amazing character. He understood money,' said Gerald with respect, 'and, having made one mistake, determined that most of it would die with him.'

'Will it affect my inheritance?' Jacqui asked anxiously. 'Ah, who knows?' Gerald smiled. 'That all has to be sorted out by solicitors and accountants.'

Charles gave a mock yawn. 'I know. Endless meetings, confabulations, discussions and mumblings about the law. Where does all that get you?'

'Rich,' said Gerald smugly.

At half past eleven, they all left the house to go to the April Fools' Midnight Matinee at the Parthenon. Bartlemas and O'Rourke had dressed in their Victorian first-night gear specially. They looked like a pair of Dickensian undertakers.

The bright young theatrical crowd (including Gerald, who had decided he would go after all) piled into Bernard Walton's Bentley, leaving Charles and Joanne on the pavement outside the house. 'See you,' yelled Jacqui out of the window as the great car roared off.

'How've you been?' Charles asked Joanne.

'All right.'

'You still miss Marius?'

'Yes, but the new job's very busy, so it's not too bad.'

'Good. Do you fancy a drink somewhere?'

'Thanks very much, but no, I don't think so. I've got to be up early in the morning.'

Charles found a cruising taxi to take Joanne Menzies home. Then he hailed another for himself and gave the driver the address of the Montrose.

SO MUCH BLOOD

TO THE CITY OF EDINBURGH

Chapter headings by Thomas Hood
(1799–1845)

CHAPTER ONE

My brain is dull my sight is foul,
 I cannot write a verse, or read—
Then, Pallas, take away thine Owl,
 And let us have a Lark instead.

TO MINERVA—FROM THE GREEK

'MAURICE SKELLERN ARTISTES,' said the voice that answered the telephone.

'Maurice—'

'Who wants him?'

'Maurice, for God's sake. I know it's you. Why you always have to go through this rigmarole of pretending you've got a staff of thousands, I don't know. It's me—Charles.'

'Ah, hello. Pity about the telly series.'

'Yes, it would have been nice.'

'And good money, Charles.'

'Yes. Still, in theory it's only been postponed. Till this P.A.s' strike is over.'

'When will that be, though?'

'Don't know.'

'What is a P.A. anyway? I can never understand all that B.B.C. hierarchy. Do you know what a P.A. is?'

'Vaguely.' Charles Paris had a feeling that a P.A. was either a Production Assistant or a Producer's Assistant, but his knowledge of the breed was limited to an erotic night in Fulham with a girl called Angela after recording an episode of *Dr Who*. And they had not discussed the anomalies of the P.A.s' conditions of service that led to the strike which in August 1974 was crippling B.B.C. Television's Drama and Light Entertainment Departments. 'Anything else on the horizon, Maurice?'

'Had an enquiry from the Haymarket, Leicester. Might want you to direct a production of ...' he paused, '... the Head Gabbler?'

'*Hedda Gabler*?'

'That's it.'

'Could be fun. When?'

'Not till the spring.'

'Great.' Heavy sarcasm.

'Might be a small part in a film. Playing a German football manager.'

'Oh yes?'

'But that's very vague.'

'Terrific. Listen, Maurice, I've got something.'

'Getting your own work, eh?'

'Somebody's got to.'

'Ooh, that hurt, Charles. I try, you know, I try.'

'Yes. My heart bleeds, an agent's lot is not a happy one, mournful violin plays *Hearts and Flowers*. No, it's for *So Much Comic, So Much Blood*.'

'What?'

'You know, my one-man show on Thomas Hood. Thing I did for the York Festival and the British Council recitals.'

'Oh yes.' The tone of Maurice's voice recalled the tiny fees of which he had got ten per cent.

'A friend of mine, guy I knew in Oxford who now lectures in the Drama Department at Derby University, has offered me a week at the Edinburgh Festival. Some show's fallen through, one the students were doing, and they're desperate for something cheap to fill the lunch time slot. Just for a week.'

'Charles, how many times do I have to tell you, you mustn't ever take something cheap? It's not official Festival, is it?'

'No, on the Fringe. I get fifty per cent of box office.'

'Fifty per cent of box office on a lunch time show on the Fringe of the Edinburgh Festival won't buy you a pair of socks. There's no point in doing it, Charles. You're better off down here. A voice-over for a commercial might come up, or a radio. Edinburgh'll cost you, anyway. Fares, accommodation.'

'I get accommodation.'

'But, Charles, you've got to ask yourself, is it the right thing for you to be doing, artistically?' Maurice made this moving appeal every time Charles suggested something unprofitable.

'I don't know. It's a long time since I've been to Edinburgh.'

'Charles, take my advice. Don't do it.'

As he emerged from Waverley Station, Charles Paris sniffed the caramel hint of breweries in the air and felt the elation which Edinburgh always inspired in him. It is, he thought, a theatrical city. The great giant's castle looms stark against the cyclorama, and from it the roofs of the Royal Mile tumble down a long diagonal. There are so many levels, like a brilliant designer's stage set. Plenty of opportunities for the inventive director. The valley of Princes Street, with a railway instead of a river and the Victorian kitsch of the Scott Memorial instead of an imposing centrepiece, is ideal for ceremonial entrances. From there, according to the play, the director can turn to the New Town or the Old. The New Town is designed for comedy of manners. Sedate, right-angled, formal, George Street and Queen Street, regularly intersected and supported by the tasteful bookends of Charlotte and Saint Andrew Squares, stand as Augustan witnesses to the Age of Reason.

The director should use the Old Town for earthier drama, scenes of low life. It is a tangle of interweaving streets, wynds and steps, ideal settings for murder and mystery, with a thousand dark corners to hide stage thugs. This is the city of Burke and Hare, of crime and passion.

The Old Town made Charles think of Melissa, an actress who had been in a show with him at the Lyceum fifteen years before. After a disastrous three months he had returned to London and his wife Frances, but Melissa had made Edinburgh seem sexy, like a prim nanny shedding her grey uniform behind the bushes in the park.

On Sunday 11th August 1974 the city still felt sexy. And this time Charles Paris was free. He had left Frances in 1962.

Everything smelt fresh after recent rain. Charles felt vigorous, younger than his forty-seven years. He decided to walk. Frances would have caught a bus; she had an uncanny ability for comprehending any bus system within seconds of arrival in a town. Charles would walk. He set off, swinging his holdall like a schoolboy. The only shadow on his sunny mood was the fact that Scottish pubs are closed on Sundays.

He couldn't miss the house in Coates Gardens. Among the self-effacing homes and hotels of the Edinbourgeois there was one whose pillars and front door were plastered with posters.

D.U.D.S. ON THE FRINGE!
Derby University Dramatic Society presents
*FOUR WORLD PREMIERES!
ONE GREAT CLASSIC!
A Midsummer Night's Dream—Shakespeare's Immortal Comedy Revisualised by Stella Galpin-Lord.
**Mary, Queen of Sots*—a Mixed-Media Satire of Disintegration by Sam Wasserman.
**Isadora's Lovers*—Lesley Petter's Examination of a Myth in Dance and Song.
**Who Now?*—a Disturbing New Play by Martin Warburton.
**Brown Derby*—Simply the Funniest Late-Night Revue on the Fringe.

There followed lists of dates, times and prices for this complicated repertoire, from which Charles deduced that the show he was replacing was Isadora's Lovers. For some reason Lesley Petter was unable to Examine the Myth in Dance and Song. He felt annoyed that the poster had not been amended to advertise *So Much Comic, So Much Blood*. They had known he was coming for more than a week. And publicity is enormously important when you're competing with about two hundred and fifty other shows.

The doorbell immediately produced a plain, roly-poly girl in irrevocably paint-spattered jeans.

'Hello, I'm Charles Paris.'

'Oh Lord, how exciting, yes. I'm Pam Northcliffe, Props. Just zooming down to the hall to make the axe for *Mary*. Going to build it round this.' She waved a squeezy washing-up liquid bottle. 'So the blood spurts properly.'

'Ah.'

'Brian's in the office. Through there.' She scurried off down the road, bouncing like a beach-ball.

The shining paint on the partitions of the hall was evidence that the house had only recently been converted into flats. The door marked 'Office' in efficient Letraset was ajar. Inside it was tiny, the stub-end of a room unaccounted for in the conversion plans. A young man in a check shirt and elaborate tie was busy on the telephone. He airily indicated a seat.

'Look, I know it's the weekend, I know you're working every hour there is. So are we. It's just got to be ready. Well, what time tomorrow? No, earlier than that. Midday ...'

The wrangle continued. Charles looked at a large baize covered board with the optimistic Letraset heading, 'What the Press says about D.U.D.S.' So far the Press had not said much, which was hardly surprising, because the Festival did not begin for another week. In the middle of the board was one cutting. A photograph of a girl, and underneath it:

UNDERSTUDY STEPS IN

> It's an ill wind, they say, and it's certainly blown some good the way of Derby University Dramatic Society's Anna Duncan. When one of the group's actresses Lesley Petter broke her leg in an accident last week, suddenly 20-year-old Anna found she was playing two leading roles—in a play and a revue, both to be seen at the Masonic Hall in Lauriston Street when the Festival starts. Says Anna, 'I'm really upset for poor Lesley's sake, but it's a wonderful chance for me. I'm very excited.' And with lovely Anna on stage, Fringe-goers may get pretty excited too!

The reporter, whatever his shortcomings in style, was right about one thing. Even in the blurred photograph the girl really was lovely. She was pictured against the decorative railings of Coates Gardens. Slender body, long legs in well-cut jeans, a firm chin and expertly cropped blonde hair.

The telephone conversation finished and Charles received a busy professional handshake. 'I'm Brian Cassells, Company Manager.'

'Charles Paris.'

'I recognised you. So glad you could step in at such short notice. Nice spread, that.' He indicated the cutting. 'Helps having a pretty girl in the group. Important, publicity.'

'Yes,' said Charles.

The edge in his voice was not lost on Brian Cassells. 'Sorry about yours. That's what I was on to the printer about. Posters and handouts ready tomorrow.'

'Good. Did you get the stuff I sent up? The cuttings and so on.'

'Yes. Incorporated some in the poster. They were very good.'

Yes, thought Charles, they were good. He particularly cherished the one from the *Yorkshire Post*. 'There are many pleasures to be had at the York Festival, and the greatest of these is Charles Paris' *So Much Comic, So Much Blood*.'

The Company Manager moved hastily on, as if any pause or small talk might threaten his image of efficiency. 'Look, I'll show you the sleeping arrangements and so on.'

'Thanks. When will I be able to get into the hall to do some rehearsal?'

'It's pretty tied up tomorrow. Stella's having a D.R. of the *Dream*. Then Mike's in with *Mary*. That's Tuesday morning. Tuesday afternoon should be O.K. Just a photo-call for *Mary*. A few dramatic shots of Rizzio's murder, that sort of thing, good publicity. Shouldn't take long.

The sleeping arrangements were spartan. The ground-floor rooms were filled with rows of ex-army camp-beds for the men, with the same upstairs for the girls. No prospects of fraternisation. 'It's not on moral grounds,' said Brian, 'just logistical. Kitchen and dining-room in the basement if you want a cup of coffee or something. I'd better get back. Got to do some Letrasetting.'

Charles dumped his case on a vacant camp-bed which wobbled ominously. The room had the stuffy smell of male bodies. It brought back National Service, the first dreary barracks he'd been sent to in 1945 to train for a war that was over before he was trained. He opened a window and enjoyed the relief of damp-scented air.

He felt much more than forty-seven as he sat over skinny coffee in the basement, surrounded by blue denim. An epicene couple were wrapped round each other on the sofa. A plump girl was relaxing dramatically on the floor. Three young men with ringlets were hunched over the table discussing The Theatre.

'What it's got to do is reflect society, and if you've got a violent society, then it's got to reflect that.'

The reply came back in a slightly foreign accent. German? Dutch? 'Bullshit, Martin. It's more complex than that. The Theatre interprets events. Like when I'm directing something, I don't just want to reflect reality. Not ordinary reality. I try to produce a new reality.'

Charles winced as the other took up the argument. 'What is reality, though? I reckon if people are getting their legs blown off in Northern Ireland, if they're starving in Ethiopia, you've got to show that. Even if it means physically assaulting the audience to get them to react.'

'So where is the violence, Martin? On stage? In the audience?'

'It's everywhere. It's part of twentieth-century living. And we've got to be aware of that. Even, if necessary, be prepared to be violent ourselves, in a violent society. That's what my play's about.'

'That, Martin, is so much crap.'

The youth called Martin flushed, stood up and looked as if he was about to strike his opponent. Then the spasm passed and, sulkily, he left the room. Charles deduced he must be Martin Warburton, author of *Who Now?* a Disturbing New Play.

The other ringletted youth looked round for someone else to argue with. 'You're Charles Paris, aren't you?'

'Yes.'

'What do you think about violence in the theatre?'

'There's a place for it. It can make a point.' Charles knew he sounded irretrievably middle-aged.

The youth snorted. 'Yes, hinted at and glossed over in West End comedies.'

Charles was riled. He did not like being identified exclusively with the safe commercial theatre. His irritant continued. 'I'm directing *Mary, Queen of Sots*. That's got violence in perspective. Lots of blood.' He turned on Charles suddenly. 'You ever directed anything?'

'Yes.' With some warmth. 'In the West End and most of the major reps in the country.'

'Oh.' *Mary, Queen of Sots*' director was unimpressed. 'What, long time ago?'

'No, quite recently.' Charles' anger pushed him on. 'In fact I'm currently considering a production of *Hedda Gabler* at the new Haymarket Theatre in Leicester.'

'Big deal.' The ringletted head drooped forward over a Sunday newspaper.

Without making too much of a gesture of it, Charles left the room. In the hall he checked with a D.U.D.S. programme for details of his antagonist.

MICHAEL VANDERZEE—After work in experimental theatre in Amsterdam and in Munich under Kostbach, he made his directorial debut in this country with *Abusage* by Dokke at the Dark Brown Theatre. He has been responsible for introducing into this country the works of Schmiss and Turzinski, and recently directed the latter's *Ideas Towards a Revolution of the Audience* at the Theatre Upstairs. Drawing inspiration from the physical disciplines and philosophies of East and West, he creates a theatre indissolubly integrated with working life.

*

'Huh,' said Charles to himself. As he started towards his dormitory, a key turned in the front door lock and a middle-aged man in a sandy tweed suit appeared. He smiled and extended his hand. 'Hello, you must be Charles Paris.'

'Yes.'

'I'm James Milne, known to the students as the Laird. I live in the flat on the top floor. Would you like to come up for a drink?'

It was the most welcome sentence Charles had heard since he arrived. Edinburgh regained its charm.

'Yes, I agree. I am an unlikely person to be involved with Derby University Dramatic Society. It's a coincidence. I've only moved into this house recently and I sold my previous one in Meadow Lane to a lad called Willy Mariello. Have you met him yet?'

'No.'

'No doubt you will. He's with this lot. Well, the conversion here was more or less finished, but the summer's not a good time to get permanent tenants—holidays, the Festival and so on. So when Willy said this crowd was looking for somewhere, I offered it for the six weeks.'

'Brave.'

'I don't know. They pay rent. There's no furniture, not much they can break. And they've sworn they'll clean everything up before they go. I just hurry in and out and don't dare look at the mess.'

'What about noise?'

'This flat's pretty well insulated.'

'Largely by books, I should imagine. And this has only just been converted too? I can't believe it.'

The Laird glowed. Obviously Charles had said the right thing. But the flat did seem as if it had been there for centuries. Brown velvet upholstery and the leather spines of books gave the quality of an old sepia photograph. A library, an eyrie at the top of the building, it reminded Charles of his tutorials at Oxford. Dry sherry and dry donnish jokes. True, the sherry was malt whisky, but there was something of the don about James Milne.

'You like books?' He half-rose from his chair, eager, waiting for the slightest encouragement.

Charles gave it. 'Yes.'

'They're not first editions or anything like that. Well, not many of them. Just good editions. I do hate this paperback business. Some of the Dickens are quite good. And that *Vanity Fair* is valuable ...'

Charles wondered if he was about to receive a lecture on antiquarian books, but the danger passed. '... and this edition of Scott might be worth something. Though not to the modern reader. Nobody reads him nowadays. I wonder why. Could it be because he's a dreary old bore? I think it must be. Even we Scots find him a bit of a penance.' He laughed. A cosy-looking man; probably mid-fifties, with a fuzz of white hair and bushy black eyebrows.

Charles laughed, too. 'I've read half of *Ivanhoe*. About seven times. Like *Ulysses* and the first volume of Proust. Never get any further.' He relaxed into his chair. 'It's very comforting, all those books.'

'Yes. "No furniture is so charming as books, even if you never open them or read a single word." The Reverend Sydney Smith. Not a Scot himself, but for some time a significant luminary of Edinburgh society. Yes, my books are my life.'

Charles smiled. 'Wasn't it another Edinburgh luminary, Robert Louis Stevenson, who said, "Books are all very well in their way, but they're a mighty bloodless substitute for real life"?'

James Milne chuckled with relish, which was a relief to Charles, who was not sure that he had got the quotation right. 'Excellent, Charles, excellent, though the point is arguable. Let me give you a refill.'

It turned out that the Laird had been a schoolmaster at Kilbruce, a large public school just outside Edinburgh. 'I retired from there some five years ago. No, no, I'm not as old as all that. But when my mother died I came into some money and property—this house, an estate called Glenloan on the West coast, a terrace of cottages. For the first time in my life I didn't have to work. And I thought, why should I put up with the adolescent vagaries of inky boys when I much prefer books?'

'And inky boys presumably don't appreciate books?'

'No. Some seemed to—appeared to be interested, but ...' He rose abruptly. 'A bite to eat perhaps?'

Half a Stilton and Bath Olivers were produced. The evening passed pleasantly. They munched and drank, swapped quotations and examined the books. Their crossword minds clicked, and allusion and anecdote circled round each other. It was the sort of mild intellectual exercise that Charles had not indulged in since his undergraduate days. Very pleasant, floating on a cloud of malt whisky above everyday life. The book-lined room promised to be a welcome sanctuary from the earnest denim below.

Eventually Charles looked at his watch. Nearly one o'clock. 'I must go down to the bear-pit.'

'Don't bother. I'll make up the sofa for you here.'

'No, no. Downstairs is the bed I have chosen, and I must lie on it.'

The bed he had chosen had been left vacant for good reason. At half-past three he woke to discover it had come adrift in the middle and was trying to fold him up like a book. He wrestled with it in the sweaty breathing dorm and then tottered along to the lavatory.

It was locked and a strange sound came from inside. As Charles took advantage of the washbasin in the adjacent bathroom, he identified the noise through a haze of malt. It was a man crying.

CHAPTER TWO

The very sky turns pale above;
  The earth grows dark beneath;
The human Terror thrills with cold,
  And draws a shorter breath—
An universal panic owns
  The dread approach of DEATH!
THE ELM TREE

THE EDINBURGH FREEMASONS' revenue must shoot up during the Festival, because they seem to own practically every strange little hail in the city. Each year the gilded columns of these painted rooms witness the latest excesses of Fringe drama, and the gold-leaf names of Grand Masters gaze unmoved at satire, light-shows, nudity or God-rock, according to theatrical fashion.

On the Monday morning the Temple of the Masonic Hall, Lauriston Place, was undergoing *A Midsummer Night's Dream*, Shakespeare's Immortal Comedy Revisualised by Stella Galpin-Lord. As Charles Paris slipped in, it was clear that the process of revisualisation had hit a snag. The snag was that Stella Galpin-Lord was having a directorial tantrum.

'Where are those bloody fairies? Didn't you hear your bloody cue? For Christ's sake, concentrate! Bottom, get up off your backside ...'

As she fulminated, it was clear to Charles that Stella Galpin-Lord was not a student. Far from it. The over-dramatic name fitted the over-dramatic figure. She was wearing rehearsal black, a polo-necked pullover tight over her presentable bosom, and clinging flared trousers less kind to her less presentable bottom. Honey-blonded hair was scraped back into a broad knotted scarf. The efforts of make-up—skilful pancake, elaborate eyes and a hard line of lipstick—drew attention to what they aimed to disguise. The slack skin of her face gave the impression of a badly erected tent, here and there pulled tight by misplaced guy-ropes. The tantrum and her twitchy manner with a cigarette spelt trouble to Charles. Neurotic middle-aged actresses are a hazard of the profession.

'Well, don't just amble on. You're meant to be fairies, not navvies. For God's sake! Amateurs! This show opens in less than a week and we don't get in the hall again till Thursday. Good God, if you don't know the lines now ... Where is the prompter? Where is the bloody prompter!'

Charles, who had only come down to check the details of staging in the hall, decided it could wait and sidled out.

Back in Coates Gardens he looked for somewhere to work. In the men's dormitory a youth was strumming a guitar with all the versatility of a metronome. Sounds from upstairs indicated a revue rehearsal in the girls' room. Charles felt tempted to seek sanctuary with James Milne again, but decided it might be an imposition. He went down to the dining-room.

Mercifully it was empty.

With a tattered script of *So Much Comic, So Much Blood* open on the table, he started thumbing through an ancient copy of Jerrold's edition of Hood, looking for *The Dundee Guide,* an early poem which might add a little local interest for an Edinburgh audience. It was not there. He was perplexed for a moment, until he remembered that only a fragment of the work survived and was in the *Memorials of Thomas Hood*. He started thumbing through that.

So Much Comic, So Much Blood had begun life as a half-hour radio programme. Then Charles had added to the compilation and done the show for a British Council audience. Over the years he had inserted different poems, played up the comic element and dramatised some of the letters. The result was a good hour's show and he was proud of it. He was also proud that its evolution predated the success of Roy Dotrice in John Aubrey's *Brief Lives*, which had set every actor in the country ransacking literary history for one-man shows.

'I'm going to make some coffee. Would you like some?' Charles looked up at the girl in the photograph, Anna Duncan.

'Please.' She disappeared into the kitchen. He stared with less interest at the extant fragments of *The Dundee Guide*.

'Here's the coffee. Do carry on.'

'Don't worry. I like being disturbed. I'm Charles Paris.'

'I know. Recognise you from the box. It's very good of you to step into the breach.'

'I gather you did more or less the same thing.'

'Yes. Poor Lesley.' A brief pause. 'What is your show about?'

'Thomas Hood.'

She did not recognise the name. 'Why's it called what it is?'

'Because he once wrote "No gentleman alive has written so much Comic and spitten so much blood within six consecutive years". In a letter to *The Athenaeum* actually.'

'Oh. I don't think I've even heard of Thomas Hood.'

'I'm sure you know his poems.'

'Do I?'

'Yes. "I remember, I remember ...'

' "... the house where I was born"? That one? I didn't know that was Hood.'

'It was. And *November*. *Faithless Sally Brown*. Lots of stuff.'

'Oh.'

Her eyes were unusual. Very dark, almost navy blue. Her bare arm on the table was sunburned, its haze of tiny hairs bleached golden.

'What are you reading at Derby?'

'French and Drama in theory. Drama in practice.'

'Last year?'

'One more. If I bother.' The navy eyes stared at him evenly. It was pleasantly disconcerting.

'I've just been down to the hall. Saw the lovely Stella Galpin-Lord. A mature student, I thought.'

Anna laughed. 'She lectures in Drama.'

'Ah. She seemed rather to have lost her temper this morning.'

'That's unusual. She's always uptight, but doesn't often actually explode.'

'She was exploding this morning.'

'Everyone's getting on each other's nerves. Living like sardines in this place. I'm glad I'm in a flat up here.' (On reflection, Charles was glad she was too.) 'And people keep arguing about who's rehearsing what when, and who's in the hall. It's purgatory.'

'You're rehearsing the revue at the moment?'

'Yes, but I've got a break. They're doing a new number—about Nixon's resignation and Ford coming in. Trying to be topical.'

'Is the revue going to be good?'

'Bits.'

'Bits?' Charles smiled. Anna smiled back.

At that moment Pam Northcliffe bounced into the room, her arms clutching two carrier bags which she spilled out on the table. 'Hello. Oh Lord, I must write my expenses. I'm spending so much on props.'

'What have you been buying?' asked Charles.

'Oh Lord, lots of stuff for *Mary*.'

'Did you get the cardboard for my ruff?'

'No, Anna, will do, promise. No, I was getting black crepe for the execution. And all these knives that I've got to make retractable. And some make-up and stuff.'

'Good old Leichner's,' said Charles, picking up a bottle which had rolled out of one of the carriers. It was labelled 'Arterial Blood'.

'What other sort is there?'

'There's a brighter one, for surface cuts. It's called ...' Pam paused for a moment. '...oh, I forget.' And she bustled on. 'Look, I'm not going to be in your way, am I? I've got to do these knives. I was going to do them on the table, if you ...'

'No, it's O.K. I've finished.' Charles resigned himself to the inevitable. Anna returned to her rehearsal and he went to see **if** the men's dormitory was still being serenaded.

Passing the office, he heard sounds of argument, Michael Vanderzee's voice, more Dutch in anger, struggling against Brian Cassells' diplomatic tones. '... and the whole rehearsal was ruined yesterday because that bloody fool Willy wasn't there. Look, I need more time in the hall.'

'So does everyone.'

'But I've lost a day.'

'That's not my fault, Mike. Look, I've worked out a schedule that's fair to everyone.

'Bugger your schedule.'

'It's there on the wall-chart—'

'Oh, bugger your wall-chart!' Michael Vanderzee flung himself out of the office, past Charles, to the front door. The windows shook as it slammed behind him.

Brian Cassells appeared in the hall looking flushed. When he saw Charles, he smoothed down his pin-striped suit as if nothing had happened. 'Ah, morning.' The efficient young executive was reborn. 'I've ... er ... I've got your posters. Just picked them up.'

'Oh, great.'

'In the office.'

On the desk were two rectangular brown paper parcels. 'A thousand in each,' said Brian smugly. 'Did the Letrasetting myself. Do have a look.'

Charles tore the paper and slid one of the printed sheets out. As he looked at it, Brian Cassells grinned. 'O.K.?'

Charles passed the paper over. It was headed:

DUDS ON THE FRINGE
... and the greatest of these is Charles Paris'
So Much Comic, So Much Blood.

'Oh,' said Brian, 'I am sorry.'

Undisturbed rehearsal in the Coates Gardens house was clearly impossible. Charles decided a jaunt to one of his Edinburgh favourites, the Museum of Childhood in the Royal Mile, might not come amiss. It was only Monday and there was a whole week till he had to face an audience. And with Brian Cassells in charge of publicity, the chances were against there being an audience anyway.

Back at the house late afternoon, he found Martin Warburton hovering in the hail, as if waiting for him. 'You're Charles Paris, aren't you?'

'Yes.'

'I've written this play. *Who Now?* We're doing it. I want you to read it.' A fifth carbon copy was thrust forward.

'Oh, thank you. I'd like to.'

'You don't know. You might like to; you might think it was a waste of time.'

'I'm sure you wouldn't have written it if you thought it was a waste of time.'

The boy looked at Charles fiercely for a moment, then burst into loud laughter. 'Yes, I might. That's exactly what I might have done.'

'Why?'

'Everything we do is just random. I happened to write this. It's just chance. I might have written anything else. It's nothing.'

'I know sometimes it seems like that, but very few things are random—'

'Don't patronise me!' Martin's shout was suddenly loud, as if the volume control on his voice had broken. He reached out to snatch the play back, then changed his mind, rushed out of the house and slammed the door.

In spite of Brian Cassells' assurances, the Masonic Hall was not free for Charles to rehearse in on the Tuesday afternoon. When he arrived at two o'clock Michael Vanderzee had just started a workshop session with the Mary cast and most of the Dream lot too. Brian was not there to appeal to (he'd apparently gone down to London for a Civil Service interview), so Charles sat at the back of the hall and waited.

Everyone except Michael was lying stretched out on the floor. '... and relax. Feel each part of your body go. From the extremities. Right, your fingers and toes, now your hands and feet. Now the forearms and your calves—feel them go ...'

Charles' attitude to this sort of theatre was ambivalent. He had no objection to movement classes and workshop techniques. They were useful exercises for actors, and kept them from getting over-analytical about their 'art'. All good stuff. Until there was a show to put on. At that point they became irrelevant and the expediency of getting everything ready for the opening left no time for self-indulgence.

Michael Vanderzee (who drew inspiration from the physical disciplines of East and West and created a theatre indissolubly integrated with working life) obviously did not share these views. 'Right. O.K. Now I want you to sit in pairs, and when I clap, you start to tell each other fairy stories. And you've got to concentrate so hard, you tell your story and you don't listen to the other guy. Really concentrate. O.K. I clap my hands.'

While the assembly shouted out a cacophony of Red Riding Hood and Goldilocks, Charles looked down at Anna. Squatting on the floor, mouthing nonsense, she still appeared supremely self-possessed. Her T-shirt did nothing to hide her contours and the interest she had started in him was strengthened.

The door of the hall opened noisily. An enormously tall young man in blue denim with a Jesus Christ hairstyle strolled purposefully up the aisle. 'Willy!' roared Michael. 'Where the hell have you been? Why weren't you at rehearsal this morning?'

'I had things to do.' The voice was sharp and the accent Scottish.

'You've got things to do here as well. I had to drag you in yesterday.'

'Piss off.' Willy collapsed into a chair in the front row, ungainly as a stick insect.

'Look, do you want to be in this show or not? You've got to rehearse.'

'I don't mind rehearsing, but I don't see why I should waste time poncing about with relaxation and pretending I'm a pineapple and all that. I'm only meant to be doing the music.'

'You're playing Rizzio in the show, and you're meant to be part of an ensemble.'

Willy gave a peculiarly Scottish dismissive snort. 'All right, all right. What do you want me to do?'

'I want you to shout, all of you. Scream your heads off. Really uninhibited screams. Let everything go. Right. When I clap.'

The noise was appalling. Charles sunk into his chair with hands over his ears. It was going to be a long time before he got the stage to himself.

When the baying mouths onstage had finally closed, he uncovered his ears and heard another sound close behind him. A sniff. He turned to see the shipwrecked face of Stella Galpin-Lord, who had just slipped into the hall. She saw him and blew her nose.

At that moment Pam Northcliffe bustled in, her arms as ever full of parcels and packages. 'Hello, Charles,' she hissed loudly. He grinned at her.

'Just brought down the props for the *Mary* photo-call.'

'All O.K.?' he whispered.

'Oh Lord, I suppose so. Just about. I was up till two last night doing the daggers.'

'Work all right?'

'Yes.' She showed him her artefacts proudly. Charles picked up one of the knives. Its metal blade had been replaced by silver-painted plastic which slid neatly back into the handle. He pressed it into his hand. 'Very good.'

'Oh. I'm afraid the paint's not quite dry.'

Charles looked down at the silver smudge on his palm. 'Never mind.'

'What's Mike up to now?'

'God knows.'

'All right. Now we're relaxed, all uninhibited. Now an ensemble is people who know each other. Love each other, hate each other. We try hate. Right, as we've done it before. Somebody stands in the middle and the others shout hatred at him. Doesn't matter what you say, any lies, anything. Hate, hate. We purge the emotions.

'O.K., Willy, you first. Stand in the middle. We form a circle round. And we shout. Ah, hello, Stella, you join our workshop?'

'Might learn something,' she said patronisingly.

'You might, you might. Hey, Charles Paris. You want to learn something too?'

Charles choked back his first instinctive rejoinder and meekly said, 'Yes, O.K.' Enter into the spirit of the thing. Don't be a middle-aged fuddy-duddy.

The large circle around Willy Mariello waited for the signal. Michael clapped his hands and they shouted. Abuse poured out. Young faces swelled with obscenities. Stella Galpin-Lord screamed, 'Bastard! Bastard!' her mouth twisting and pulling a whole map of new lines on her face. Anna s expression was cold and white. Martin Warburton almost gibbered with excitement. And Charles himself found it distressingly easy to succumb, to scream with them. It was frightening.

Another clap. They subsided, panting. 'Good. Catharsis. Good. O.K. Now someone else. Charles.'

It was not pleasant. As the mob howled, he concentrated on Sydney Carton, borne on his tumbril to the scaffold. 'It is a far, far better thing that I do now ...' It still was not pleasant.

But a clap ended it and another victim was chosen. Then another and another. The repetition took the edge off the discomfort of being abused. Just an exercise. They finished, breathless.

'O.K. Another concentration exercise. Truth Game. You sit on the ground in pairs and ask each other questions. You have to answer with the truth instantly. If you hesitate, you start asking the questions. And don't cheat. It's more difficult than you think.'

They started forming pairs. Charles saw Willy Mariello speak to Anna. She turned away and sat down opposite a colourless girl in faded denim. Willy and Charles were the only ones left standing. They squatted opposite each other.

The Scotsman sat awkwardly, his long legs bent under him like pipe-cleaners. Stuck to his denim shirt was a purple badge with white lettering: *It's Scotland's Oil*. The long messianic hair was full of white powder and the hands were flecked with white paint. His expression was aggressive and he had the hard mouth of a spoilt child. But the brown eyes were troubled.

Charles tried to think of something to ask. 'What do you make of all these exercises?'

'I think they're a bloody waste of time.' The answer was instant, no question about the truth there. Voices started up around and made concentration difficult.

'Um. Are you happy?'

'No.'

'Why not?'

'A lot of hassles.'

'Anything specific?'

'Yes.'

The concentration of talking and listening over the other voices was intense. Everything seemed focused in this one conversation. Charles pressed further. 'What's worrying you?'

Willy hesitated. Then, 'I've found out something I'd rather not know, something that might be dangerous.'

'Something about a person?'

'Yes.'

'Someone connected with this group?'

A slight pause. 'Yes.' There was fear in the brown eyes.

Charles pushed on, mesmerised by the direction of the conversation. 'Who?'

Willy opened his mouth, but paused for a moment. Stella Galpin-Lord's piercing voice was suddenly isolated. '...and lost my virginity when I was fourteen...' The spell was broken. 'No, I didn't come in quick enough,' said Willy. 'I ask. How old are you?'

The exercise continued, but Charles felt a vague unease.

The Truth Game was followed by a Contact Game. 'O.K.? We close our eyes and move around. When you touch somebody, you make contact. Feel, explore, encounter. Get to know them with your hands. This will increase your perceptions. O.K.?'

Perhaps it was by chance that the first person Charles touched was Anna. In accord with his director's instructions, he made contact, felt, explored, encountered and got to know her with his hands. Her eyes opened to a slit of navy blue. He smiled. She smiled.

'Are you rehearsing tonight?'

'No.'

'Fancy dinner?'

'O.K.'

Charles moved away to feel, explore and encounter someone else. His probing hand felt the arm of a tweed jacket, then up, over a chest criss-crossed with leather straps to the bristly wool of a beard.

'What the hell do you think you're doin'?' The voice had the broken-bottle edge of Glasgow in it. 'I'm the photographer. Who's Michael Vanderzee?'

Getting people into costume took some time. The photographer fretted and cursed. Then Michael announced he did not want posed shots; he wanted natural action shots. That involved rehearsing whole chunks of the play. The photographer cursed more.

'Right, come on. Let's do the scene of Rizzio's murder. O.K.? You'll get some good shots from this. Action stuff. Violence.'

'How long's the bloody scene?'

'We'll only do the end. Three, four minutes.'

'Why you can't just pose them ... I've got some fashion pictures to do later this afternoon.'

'I don't want them to look like amateur theatricals.'

'Why not? That's what they bloody are.'

The scene started and Charles sat under a light at the back of the hall to watch. *Mary, Queen of Sots* was written in a blank verse that was meant to sound archaic but only sounded twee. Since Willy needed a prompt every other line, it was heavy going.

'Willy, for God's sake!'

'Shut up, Michael!' The tall figure looked incongruous in doublet and hose.

'Look, for Christ's sake, can't we get these bloody photos taken? My time's expensive and these models are waiting.'

'I say, we haven't got the daggers,' said Martin Warburton suddenly from the recesses of a dramatic conspirator's cloak.

'Oh, Pam, where the hell are they? Here, quick. Look, the blades retract on the spring like this. O.K.? Now come on, let's get it right first time.' Charles started to scan his *So much Comic* ... script.

Suddenly his eyes were jerked off the page by a scream. Not a theatrical workshop scream, but an authentic spine-tingling cry of horror from Stella Galpin-Lord.

Onstage the scene was frozen. Anna stood white-faced in her black Tudor costume, looking down at Willy Mariello, whose great length had shrunk into a little heap on the stage. Around him were a circle of cloaked conspirators clutching daggers with retracted blades. In the centre Martin Warburton gazed fascinated at the weapon in his hand. Its blade was metal and the Arterial Blood which dripped from it was not made by Leichner's.

CHAPTER THREE

The BLOODY HAND significant of crime,
That glaring on the old heraldic banner,
Had kept its crimson unimpaired by time,
In such a wondrous manner.
THE HAUNTED HOUSE

THE POLICE ARRIVED promptly and were very efficient. An ambulance took Willy to hospital, but he was dead on arrival. Everyone gave statements and was told to expect further enquiries. Pam Northcliffe and Martin Warburton were taken away for extended questioning. A distraught Pam was returned to Coates Gardens in the early hours of the Wednesday morning and treated in the girls' dormitory with sleeping-pills and inquisitive sympathy.

The atmosphere in the house throughout the Wednesday was charged with tension. The accumulated pressures of living together and building up to the shows' openings were aggravated by the shock of Willy's death. Rehearsal schedules were thrown out and the continual reappearance of policemen at the house and hall got on everyone's nerves. All day Coates Gardens was full of uneasy jokes, sudden flares of temper and bursts of weeping.

Charles escaped the worst of it. Fortunately James Milne had suggested that he might be glad of a little seclusion from the community hysterics and offered the sanctuary of his flat. It was a great relief to be with someone who did not want to discuss the death. Milne dismissed the subject. 'I didn't know the boy well and I wasn't there at the time, so I don't feel too involved. It's an unpleasant business. And the best thing to do about unpleasant things is to put them out of your mind.'

But Charles did not find it so easy. He felt he was involved and, as he tried to concentrate on revising *So Much Comic* ..., his mind kept returning to the scene in the Masonic Hall. He suffered from the communal shock. And another uncomfortable feeling which he did not want to investigate.

By the Thursday morning the atmosphere among the D.U.D.S. was more settled. The Procurator-Fiscal's enquiry (which is held instead of a public inquest in Scotland) was no doubt following its private course, but the students were unaffected by it. Only Martin Warburton remained hysterical, which was hardly surprising after his long ordeal of questioning.

The police were not making any charges against him and, though the investigation was far from complete, the general impression was that they considered the death to have been a ghastly accident. The real knife had been put in one of Pam's carrier bags with the treated ones by mistake and foul play was apparently not suspected.

On the Thursday afternoon rehearsals restarted in earnest. More than in earnest, in panic. Everyone realised at the same time that a day and a half had been lost and there were still three shows opening on the following Monday.

Brian Cassells' rehearsal schedule was ignored. (Since its originator was still in London he could not argue.) Stella Galpin-Lord commandeered the Masonic Hall for the rest of the day as her right and Michael Vanderzee demanded it for the Friday. Charles began to think he would be lucky to get onstage there for his actual performances. Rehearsal in the house was equally impossible. In the basement Pam and a couple of A.S.M.s were building a wall for Pyramus and Thisbe. Three smelly technicians lay over a greasy lighting plot in the men's dormitory. The Laird's flat was locked and silent. In fact Charles was relieved; his mind was too full for serious rehearsal.

Still, as a gesture of good faith, he tucked his script and Hood's *Collected Poems* under his arm before he set off into the city. It was a warm afternoon and only five o'clock. There were lots of places to sit and study in Edinburgh—Princes Street Gardens, the Castle, or it might even be worth a stroll down to Arthur's Seat. He weighed the possibilities, but was not surprised when he went straight into the nearest pub and ordered a large whisky.

He sat hunched at the bar and realised that he could not put off thinking any longer. And the one thought which he had been holding back for nearly two days resolved itself clearly in his mind.

Whatever the police thought, Willy Mariello had been murdered.

Charles could not forget the expression in those brown eyes during the Truth Game, when Willy had spoken of finding out something about someone that he would rather not know. There had been pain in that look, but also there had been fear, even horror. Whatever it was that he had found out it was nasty. Nasty enough for someone to commit murder to keep it quiet.

Charles had tried to express this suspicion to the detective who took his statement, but he knew the man did not take it seriously. Somehow the words had not come out right. 'It was a moment of such concentration ... I could see such fear in his eyes ... It made me feel a sense of danger ...' The further he got into it, the more tenuous the idea seemed and the more Charles knew he sounded like an effete actor emoting. In spite of polite assurances about complete investigations, that was obviously what the detective took him for. By the time he got to Charles, he had probably had a bellyful of the 'vague feelings' and 'premonitions' of self-dramatising students.

And, objectively, it did sound pretty nonsensical. Charles, whose normal thought processes involved reducing everything he did to the absurd and seeing if there was anything left, was surprised that the conviction remained so strong. But it did. It was an instinct he could not deny.

Facing the fact that Willy had been murdered led automatically to the question of what should be done about it. Charles had done his duty as a citizen by voicing his suspicions, and it was quite possible that the police were already way ahead of him, working on investigations of their own. He was no longer involved.

But involvement does not cease like that. It was easy enough for James Milne to say he wanted to forget about it; he had not sat opposite Willy in the

Truth Game, he had not been present at the killing.

Charles knew he had to get to the bottom of it. He recalled an earlier occasion when he had come up against crime, in the case of Marius Steen. Then he had been forced into involvement by circumstance; this time he was making a positive decision. He was not driven by any crusading fervour for the cause of justice, but he knew he would not feel at peace until he had found out all the facts.

And the only facts he had were that Willy Mariello had found out something unpleasant about one of the people involved with the Derby University Dramatic Society in Edinburgh. And that he had subsequently been killed by a dagger in the hand of Martin Warburton.

No more facts. Now on to feelings. Charles had a strong feeling that the one person who did not kill Willy was Martin Warburton. Unless he were a lunatic or playing some incredibly devious game of his own, no one would commit a premeditated murder in front of thirty people, under stage lights, with a photographer on hand. And unless Charles' suspicions about the motive were wrong, the murder was premeditated.

The elimination of Martin still left about forty suspects. Any of the students themselves or of the hangers-on who surrounded the D.U.D.S. could have switched one of the treated knives for a real one, and so stood a reasonable, though not infallible, chance of killing Willy Mariello.

Charles ordered another large whisky. A little mild investigation was called for.

Things could not have worked out better when he returned to Coates Gardens. Pam Northcliffe was in the dining-room alone mixing porridge to roughcast Pyramus and Thisbe's wall. The cooks of the day were clattering about in the kitchen preparing a dinner whose main ingredient smelled like cabbage.

Pam looked up, red-eyed and guilty when he entered. 'Hello.'

'Hi. Feeling better?'

'Yes.' Spoken with determination.

'I was going down to the pub for a drink and looking for someone to join me. Do you fancy it?'

'What? Me?'

'Yes.'

'Well, I ...' She wiped a porridgy hand on the back of her jeans, adding another streak to the existing collage. 'All right.'

A half of lager for Pam and, since he was now thirsty, a pint of 'heavy' for Charles. 'How are the props? Coming together?'

'I think so. I'm spending over my budget on them.'

'D.U.D.S. will find the money.'

'I hope so.' She spoke with great care, as if the accumulated tension inside her might break out at the slightest provocation.

Charles knew that discussion of Willy's death might be exactly that sort of provocation. But it was what he had to investigate. He approached obliquely. 'Everyone settling down a bit now.'

'Yes, I suppose so. All too busy to think about it.'

'That's a blessing.'

'Yes.' Silence. Charles tried to think how he could get her back on to the subject without causing too much pain. But fortunately he did not have to. She seemed anxious to talk it out of her system without prompting. 'I don't think I'll ever get over it. It's the first time I've ever seen someone dead.'

'It is nasty. But you do forget.'

'I mean, you see it on films, and on the box and it all ... well, it doesn't seem important. But when you actually see ...' Her lower lip started to quiver.

'Don't talk about it.'

As Charles hoped, she ignored his advice. 'And the trouble is ... apart from just the shock and things, I feel responsible. I mean, I was in charge of the props, so I must have got the knives mixed up.'

'Do you really think you did?'

'Oh Lord, I just don't know now. I would have said definitely not. I remember counting them before I put them in my carrier bag. The police asked me all this and, you know, at the end I couldn't remember what I'd done. You think so much about something, after a time you just don't know what's true any more ...'

'I know what you mean.

'And it's so stupid, because I shouldn't have done the knives like that anyway. Michael Vanderzee told me what he wanted, and I thought the best thing would be to get real knives with hollow handles and unscrew them and take the blades out. And Michael said that was daft and expensive and I should have improvised and ...' Her voice wavered with the remembered rebuke. 'It's the first time I've done props. And I got it all wrong. If I hadn't done the knives that way, Willy would still be alive.'

Charles did not feel so certain of that. He felt sure that if the knives had not been to hand, the murderer would have found some other method. But it was not the moment to voice such suspicions. 'Pam, you really mustn't blame yourself. Even if you did mix the knives up. And it's quite possible that you didn't. Somebody else may have been playing about with them and made the mistake. I mean, presumably they were just lying round the house, so anyone could get at them?' He left the question hanging disingenuously in the air.

'Yes. I suppose so.'

'Toy knives have a fascination for people. Anyone might have started fooling around with them. How long were they there?'

'I was up late finishing them on Monday night. And I left them out on the table till the next morning.'

'Why? So that the paint could dry?'

'Yes, but it didn't actually. I got some awful oily lacquer that stayed sticky for ages.'

'Was the real knife with the others?'

'Yes, it was. You see, it was daft, but I was sort of rather proud of the ones I'd made because they did look so realistic. So I left them all out on the table.'

'So that people would see them when they came down to breakfast?'

'Yes.' She looked sheepish. 'I haven't made lots of things and I thought they looked good.'

'They did. Look very good.' He almost added 'Unfortunately', but realised that might be tactless. 'So then they were put away while people had breakfast?'

'Yes, I put them in a carrier bag, and I thought I left the real one in a box with my scissors and sellotape and glue and all that rubbish.'

'And they stayed in your carrier bag in the sitting-room till you brought them down to the hail at about three o'clock?'

'Yes.'

'So there was lots of time for anyone in the house to play around with them during the day and mix them up?'

'I suppose so.'

'You weren't there during the morning?'

'No, I had to go out to buy some cardboard and stuff.'

'Well, I should think that's what happened. Someone was fooling about with them on the Tuesday morning and mixed them up.' It was not what he really meant, but Pam looked reassured. What he did mean was that the knives had been on show for every member of the company, that the murderer had realised their potential and arranged the switch when the sitting-room was empty at some point during the Tuesday morning. Then he had had to wait and see what happened. Which might well have been nothing. The chances were that someone would notice the real knife before the stabbing could take place, and the murderer would have to find another method. But the impatience of the photographer at the photo-call had given no one time to inspect their weapons closely.

Though the murder method was now clear, the identity of its deviser remained obscure. From Pam's account, virtually anyone who was in the house on the Tuesday morning could have switched the knives. And that meant virtually every member of the D.U.D.S. company. Which in turn meant checking everyone's movements. Which sounded a long, boring process.

'Did you know Willy Mariello well?' Charles tried another tack.

Pam blushed. 'No, hardly at all.'

'But you must have seen him round the University.'

'What do you mean?'

'During term-time. If he was involved in the Dramatic Society.'

'Oh, but he wasn't. He was nothing to do with the University.'

'Then where did he come from?'

'He used to play with Puce.'

'What?'

'The rock band. He was lead guitar. Until they broke up earlier this year.

Oh, come on, you've heard of Puce.'

Charles had to confess he hadn't.

They walked back to Coates Gardens together. Pam seemed calmer; she had almost recaptured her customary bounce. A nice girl. No beauty, but good-natured. Needed a man who appreciated her.

She was telling him about her parents' home in Somerset as they entered the hall. At that moment Anna Duncan came out of the Office. 'Hello,' said Charles. She grinned.

Pam paused in mid-sentence: He realised his rudeness. 'I'm so sorry. I ... what were you saying?'

'Oh, it wasn't important. I'd better get on with my wall.' And she disappeared gracelessly downstairs.

'Taking other women out when you've already stood me up,' said Anna with mock reproach.

'I hardly think we'd have had a very relaxed dinner with policemen taking statements between courses.'

'No, I didn't mean it.'

'Rehearsing tonight?'

'Finishing at half past eight.'

'Shall we pretend the last two days haven't happened, and pick up where we left off?'

'That sounds a nice idea.'

'Shall I see you here?'

'No. If Mike gives us another of his rolling about on the floor workshops, I'll need to go back to the flat and have a quick bath.'

'Well, let's meet at the restaurant. Do you know L'Etoile?'

'In Grindlay Street?'

'That's the one. I'll book a table for half past nine. O.K.?'

'Fine. I must get back upstairs and pretend to be a banana.'

'Another of Michael Vanderzee's wonderful ideas?'

'Yes. The perception through inanimate transference of pure emotion.'

'Wow.'

Anna grinned again and left. Charles knocked on the office door. If Brian was back, perhaps it would be possible to arrange some rehearsal time at the Masonic Hall.

The Company Manager was wearing another executive suit, this time a beige three-piece. Charles explained his requirements and was not wholly reassured by Brian's assurance that he'd sort it out and the movement of some coloured strips on the wall-chart. There are certain sorts of efficiency which do not inspire confidence.

The efficiency had obviously been at work on the 'What the Press says about D.U.D.S.' board. It was smothered with cuttings about the death of

Willy Mariello. The one person to have made a definite profit from the killing was the disgruntled Glaswegian photographer. He seemed to have sold the pictures to every newspaper in the country. Charles felt a frisson of shock at seeing the scene again. 'You're not actually going to use those as publicity?'

'No,' said Brian regretfully, 'wouldn't be quite the thing. Not to display them. Mind you, it is an amazing spread. It's really fixed the name of D.U.D.S. in people's minds. Better than any publicity stunt you could devise. I remember last year Cambridge staged something about pretending Elizabeth Taylor was in Edinburgh. They got a girl to dress up as her and so on. Quite a lot of coverage. But nothing like this.'

The note of unashamed satisfaction in Brian's voice made Charles look at him curiously. Insensitivity of that order would be wasted in the Civil Service; he should try for advertising or television. 'I'm sure Willy would be glad to think that his life was lost in the cause of full houses for the D.U.D.S.'

'Yes, it's an ill wind.' Brian was impervious to irony.

'One thing ... I was interested to hear that Willy Mariello wasn't a member of the University.'

'No.'

'How did he come to be involved in this then?'

'I don't know. I suppose he was a friend of someone.'

'Who? Do you know?'

'No. I don't know any of them very well. I wasn't in D.U.D.S. I was Chairman of Ducker.'

'Ducker?'

'D.U.C.A. Derby University Conservative Association.'

'Oh.'

'They only brought me into this because of my administrative ability.'

The men's dormitory was mercifully empty and Charles managed an undisturbed run of *So Much Comic, So Much Blood*. He was encouraged to find how much he remembered. The intonation of the poems came back naturally and he began to feel the rhythm of the whole show. A bit more work and it could be quite good.

So he felt confident as he sat opposite Anna in the French restaurant in Grindlay Street. Her appearance contributed to his mood. The 'quick bath' back at her flat had included a flattering amount of preparation. Just-pressed pale yellow shirt with a silly design of foxtrotting dancers on it, beautifully cut black velvet trousers. Eyelashes touched with mascara, lip-coloured lipstick, cropped hair flopping with controlled abandon. All very casual, but carefully done.

'I'm looking forward to seeing the show. I'm sorry, as I said, I don't know anything about Hood.'

'Not many people do.'

'Was he Scottish?'

'No. His father came from Dundee, but Thomas himself only went there a couple of times. Wasn't very struck with it either. Particularly the cooking. "I sicken with disgust at sight of a singed sheep's head. I cannot bring myself to endure oatmeal, which I think harsh, dry and insipid. The only time I ever took it with any kind of relish was one day on a trouting party, when I was hungry enough to eat anything." Sorry, I've just been working on it, hence the long trailer.'

'What do you do in the show—dress up as Hood?'

'No, it wouldn't work. I don't like all that emotive bit—this is what the bloke was *really like*. It seems to remove the subject from reality rather than making him more real. Like historical novels about Famous People. I'm just an interpreter of Hood's work; I don't pretend to be him. Let the poems and lyrics speak for themselves. Certainly in the case of the poems, it would falsify them to read them in character. They were written as public entertainments to be recited and that's how I treat them.'

'So it's more a sort of recital than an acting thing?'

'I suppose so. It's mid-way between. And it has the great advantage that I don't have to learn it all and can actually refer to the book when I want to.'

'Handy. So you just wear ordinary clothes for it?'

'A suit, maybe. I'd look daft dressed as Thomas Hood anyway. I haven't the figure of a stunted Victorian consumptive.'

'He was another one, was he?'

'Yes. Hence the *So Much Blood* of the title. Actually there is some question as to whether it was consumption—T.B. or not T.B. It may have been rheumatic heart disease. But he spat blood, that's the main thing. It was very difficult to be a literary figure in Victorian times without spitting blood. Healthy writers started at an enormous disadvantage.'

Anna laughed. 'If he was ill, I think you're showing great restraint in not acting it out. Most actors leap at the chance of doing hacking coughs and their dramatic dying bit.'

'So do I. But unfortunately it wouldn't be right for this show. Oh, I've died with the best of them. You should have heard my death rattle as Richard II after Sir Pierce of Exton stabbed me.'

There was a moment's pause. They were both thinking the same, both seeing Willy Mariello lying on the stage at the Masonic Hall. Anna went pale.

'Sorry. Shouldn't have said that. I wasn't thinking.'

'It's all right. It's just ... so recent.'

'Yes.' Charles hesitated. He had decided to investigate Willy's death, but dinner with Anna was not intended to be part of that investigation; her attraction for him was not primarily as a source of information. On the other hand, here was someone who knew all the people involved, and the conversation had come round to the subject. The detective instinct overcame his baser ones. 'Did you know Willy well?'

'No, I wouldn't say well. I knew him.'

'I was amazed to discover that he wasn't at the University. How on earth did he get involved with your lot?'

'Oh, he ... You know he used to play with a band?'

'Yes. Puce.'

'That's right. They came and did a gig at our Student's Union. I think Willy stayed around a bit. It was just round the period the band broke up. He must have met the drama lot then.'

'And somebody asked him to do this show?'

'I suppose so, yes. Because he lived in Edinburgh and was kind of at a loose end. He wrote all the music, you see. I think he wanted to do something different, after the band.'

'*Mary, Queen of Sots* sounds pretty different. You don't know if he made any particular friends at Derby?'

'No.' She seemed to remember something. 'Oh, yes. Sam. Sam Wasserman. He's the guy who wrote *Mary*. I think Willy was friendly with him. Probably it was Sam who asked him to do the music.'

'I don't think I've met Sam.'

'No. He's not up here. On holiday in Europe somewhere. He's American so it has to be Europe rather than any specific country. They seem to think Europe is just one country.'

'So Sam's not likely to be up here at all?'

'I think he's coming up for the opening of *Mary*.'

'When's that?'

'Third week. Opens on the 2nd September.'

'Ah.' A week after Charles' engagement finished. No chance of picking Sam Wasserman's brains. The investigation did not seem to be proceeding very fast. He decided that he would forget it for the rest of the evening. 'How's your show going?'

'*Mary*'s still all over the place. We spend so much time improvising and so on, we hardly ever get near the actual script.'

'And the revue?'

'Still bits. Bits are O.K. One or two of the songs are quite exciting, but ... I don't know. See what the audience thinks on the first night.'

'Monday. I'll be there. Hmm. I wonder what I should call my opening. A first lunch?'

'Why not? I'll come and see it, rehearsals permitting.'

'Good.' Charles refilled her glass from the cold bottle of Vouvray. 'Do you want to make the theatre your career?'

'Yes.' No hesitation. 'Always have. Totally stage-struck.'

'Hmm.'

'There was a world of cynicism in that grunt. You, I take it, are not stage-struck?'

'More stage-battered at my age.'

'Don't you still find it exciting?'

'Not very often, no. I can't really imagine doing anything else, but as a profession it leaves a lot to be desired. Like money, security ...'

'I know.'

'There's a lot more to it than talent. You need lots of help. You have to be tough and calculating.'

'I know.'

'I'm sorry. I sound awfully middle-aged. I think the prime reason for that is that I am awfully middle-aged. No, it's just that I'd hate to think of anyone going into the business who didn't know what it was about.'

'I do know.'

'Yes. So you're prepared for all that unemployment they talk about, sitting by the telephone, sleeping with fat old directors.'

'I only sleep with who I want to sleep with.' She gave him the benefit of a stare from the navy blue eyes. It was difficult to interpret whether it was a come-on or a rebuff.

He laughed the conversation on to another tack and they cheerfully talked their way through coq au vin, lemon sorbet, a second bottle of Vouvray, coffee and brandy.

The Castle loomed darkly to their left as they climbed up Johnstone Terrace, but it seemed benign rather than menacing. Charles' arm fitted naturally round the curve of Anna's waist and he could feel the sheen of her skin through the cotton shirt. Edinburgh had regained its magic.

She stopped by a door at the side of a souvenir shop on the Lawnmarket. The city was empty, primly correct, braced for the late-night crowds that the Festival was soon to bring.

'Good Lord, do you live here? A flat full of kilts and whisky shortbread and bagpipe salt-cellars?'

'On the top floor.'

'That's a long way up.'

'A friend's flat. Student at the University here. Away for the summer.'

'Ah. All yours.'

'Yes. Do you want to come in?'

'What for?' Charles asked fatuously.

She was not at all disconcerted and turned the amused navy blue stare on him. 'Coffee?'

'Had coffee.'

'Drink?'

'Had brandy.'

'Well, we'll have to think of something else.'

They did.

CHAPTER FOUR

And the faulty scent is picked out by the hound;
And the fact turns up like a worm from the ground;
And the matter gets wind to waft it about;
And a hint goes abroad and the murder is out.
A TALE OF A TRUMPET

HE WAS ALONE in the bed when he awoke. There was a note on the pillow. GONE TO REHEARSAL. IF I DON'T SEE YOU DURING THE DAY, SEE YOU TONIGHT? He smiled and rolled out of bed to make some leisurely coffee.

He drank it at the window, looking down on shoppers and tourists, foreshortened by the distance, scurrying like crabs across the dark cobbles of the Lawnmarket. He thought of Anna's brown body with its bikini streaks of white, and felt good. The cynicism which normally attended his sex life was not there. An exceptional girl. Willy Mariello's death became less important.

Rehearsal for an opening in four days' time, on the other hand, was important. He finished the coffee and set out for Coates Gardens.

Martin Warburton was sprawled over a camp-bed in the men's dormitory, reading. Reading *So Much Comic* ..., Charles noticed with annoyance. The boy looked up as he entered. His expression was calmer than usual and he was even polite. 'Sorry. I shouldn't be reading this. But it was on your bed. I started it and got interested.'

Given such a compliment, however unintentional, Charles could not really complain. 'There's more to Hood than many people think.'

'I don't know. Is there? I mean he's clever, there's a lot of apparent feeling, but when you get down to it, there's not much there. No certainty. All those puns. It's because he doesn't want to define things exactly. Doesn't want anything to define him. There's nothing you can identify with.'

It was a surprisingly perceptive judgement. 'You think that's important, identifying?'

'It must be. You can only respond to art if you identify with the artist. That's how I worked. I'd read into everything someone had written, until I felt the person there at the centre. And then I'd identify. I'd become that person and know how to react to their work.'

'You're reading English, I assume.'

'No, History.'

'Ah.'

'Just taken my degree.'

'O.K.?'

'Yes, got a First.'

'Congratulations.'

'Not that it means anything.' Martin's mood suddenly gave way to gloom. 'Nothing much does mean anything. I criticise Hood for not believing in things and there's me ...' He looked up sharply. 'Have you read my play?'

'No, I'm sorry. I will get round to it, but—'

'Wouldn't bother. It's rubbish. Nothing in the middle.'

'I'm sure it's going to be very interesting.' Charles tried not to sound patronising, but was still greeted by a despairing snort. Martin rose suddenly. 'I must go. I'm late. Got to rehearse *Mary*. The composer's body not yet decomposed and we rehearse.'

'You're punning yourself, like Hood,' said Charles, trying to lighten the conversation.

'Oh yes. I'm a punster. A jolly funny punster.' Martin let out one of his abrupt laughs. 'A jolly punster and a murderer. I killed him, you know.'

'No. You were the instrument that killed him.'

This struck Martin as uproariously funny. 'An instrument. Do you want to get into a great discussion about Free Will? Am I guilty? Or is the knife guilty perhaps? Where did the will come from? The knife has no will. I have no will.'

'Martin, calm down. You mustn't think you killed him.'

'Why not? The police think I did.'

'They don't.'

'They asked so many questions.'

'It's the police's job to ask questions.'

'Oh yes, I know.'

'Why? Have you been in trouble with them before?'

'Only a motoring offence, sah!' Martin dropped suddenly into an Irish accent.

'What was it?'

'Planting a car bomb, sah!' He burst into laughter. Charles, feeling foolish for setting up the feed-line so perfectly, joined him. Martin's laughter went on too long.

But Charles took advantage of the slight relaxation of tension. 'Listen, the police can't think you did it. No one in their right mind would commit murder in front of a large audience.'

'No,' said Martin slyly, 'no one in their right mind would.' This again sent him into a paroxysm of laughter. Which stopped as suddenly as it had begun. He looked at Charles in a puzzled way, as if he did not recognise him. Then, in a gentle voice, 'What's the time?'

'Twenty-five to eleven.'

'I should be at rehearsal.' He rose calmly. 'Do try to read my play if you can.'

'I will.'

'See you.' He slouched out of the room.

Charles lay for a moment thinking. Martin seemed to be on the edge of a nervous breakdown. The end of finals is a stressful time for most students. Charles suddenly recalled the state he had been in after Schools in 1949. Three years gone and then the apocalyptic strain of assessment. How good am I? What will I do in the real world? Or, most simply, who am I?

He tried to imagine the effect of a shock like Willy's death on someone in that state. A harsh cruel fact smashing into a mind that could hardly distinguish reality from fantasy. Inside his sick brain Martin might think he was a murderer, but Charles felt sure he was not. Martin Warburton needed help. Medical help possibly, but certainly he needed the help of knowing that he was only an unwitting agent for the person who planned the murder of Willy Mariello. The facts had to come out.

And the show had to go on. He turned to the script. On sober reflection, though the day before's run-through had been promising, there was a lot that needed improvement. Particularly the Pathetic Ballads. They should have been the easiest part of the programme with their well-spaced jokes and obvious humour. But it was hard to find the balance between poetry and facetiousness. He concentrated and began to recite *Tim Turpin*.

Tim Turpin he was gravel blind,
    And ne'er had seen the skies:
For Nature, when his head was made,
    Forgot to dot his eyes.
So like a Christmas pedagogue—

'Um. I'm so sorry.' Brian Cassells was peering apologetically round the door.

'Yes?'

'Look, I'm sorry to break into your rehearsal, but I wonder if you could give me a hand to carry something.' And *So Much Comic* ... was shelved again.

Outside the Office stood Willy Mariello's forlorn guitar in its black case, leaning against a large amplifier. It had been brought up from the Masonic Hall after Tuesday's drama. By the door was a thin girl with long brown hair and those peculiarly Scottish cheeks that really do look like apples. Tension showed in the tightness of her mouth and the hollows under her eyes. 'Charles, this is Jean Mariello. Mrs Mariello, Charles Paris.'

She nodded functionally. 'I've come to collect Willy's things.'

'Yes. Charles, I wonder if you could give me a hand with this amplifier. If we just get it out on to the street, I've phoned for a taxi.'

'O.K.' Brian was patently embarrassed and wanted to get rid of Jean Mariello. His administrative ability did not run to dealing with recent widows.

They placed the heavy amplifier on the pavement. Willy's wife followed with the guitar. Brian straightened up. 'I'd better go. I've got some Letrasetting to get on with.'

'What am I going to do the other end?'

Brian paused, disconcerted by her question. Charles stepped in. 'It's all right. I'll go with you. I wanted to go over that way. Off Lauriston Place, isn't it?'

'Yes.'

'Oh ... Oh well, that's fine. I'll go and get on with the ... er ... Letrasetting.' Brian scuttled indoors.

Charles felt he should say something fitting. 'I'm sorry.'

Jean Mariello shrugged. 'Thank you.'

The taxi arrived and they travelled for a while in silence. Charles felt the need for some other inadequate condolence. 'It must be terrible for you. We were all very shaken.'

'Yes, it's been a shock. But please don't feel you have to say anything. Willy and I weren't love's young dream, you know.' The accent was Scots and she spoke quietly, but there was a hard note in her voice.

'Did you live together?'

'Up to a point. Though one or other of us always seemed to be touring or something.'

'You're a musician too?'

'Yes. I sing in folk clubs. Not Willy's sort of music. We grew apart musically as well as everything else.' She leant forward and tapped the glass partition. 'If you drop us just here ...'

Meadow Lane was lined with grey houses, considerably smaller than those of Coates Gardens. They had the dusty shabbiness of the Old Town. Most of the windows were shrouded with grey net. But on the house they stopped by the windows were clean and unveiled.

Charles let Jean pay the driver. She turned to him. 'Can you manage that on your own? It's heavy.'

It certainly was. Also an awkward size. His hands could not quite clasp round it. But he was determined to manage.

As she opened the front door, he noticed a worn stone slab over it which dated the house: 1797. Inside, however, the place had been extensively modernised. There was no sign of a fireplace in the front room, but there were new-looking central heating radiators. Everything gleamed with fresh white paint. There was even a smell of it. The room was empty of furniture, but a ladder and a pile of rubble in the corner indicated decorating in progress.

He lowered the amplifier gratefully on to the uncarpeted floor. 'Would you mind putting it against the wall there where people can't see it? The catch has gone on the window and I don't want to encourage burglars.'

Another effort moved the amplifier to the required position. He stood up. Jean Mariello had left the front door open and stood with her arms folded. He was expected to go.

And he was never likely to get such a good opportunity for finding out more about Willy. No point in beating about the bush. 'Mrs Mariello, do you think your husband was murdered?'

She was not shocked or angry, she seemed to expect the question. 'No, I don't.'

'Why not?'

'No one wanted to kill him. Listen, Willy wasn't a particularly nice person. He was mean and lazy. But those aren't reasons for anyone to murder someone.'

'No. But you can't think of anything he might have done to antagonise anyone in that Derby lot?'

'I've hardly met any of that Derby lot, so I wouldn't know. Listen, Mr

Paris, I can understand your curiosity, but the police have asked me all these questions and so has everyone I've met for the past two days. I'm getting rather bored with it, and I'd be grateful if you would stop.'

'I'm sorry, Mrs Mariello, but I do have a reason for asking.' And he told her of his encounter with Willy in the Truth Game. At the end he paused dramatically.

She did not seem over-impressed. 'You say he seemed troubled?'

'Yes.'

'Probably some horse he'd backed had been beaten.'

'No, it was more than that. I'm sure it was. Something that really went deep.'

'Nothing went very deep with Willy. That Truth Game could have meant anything. What makes you so sure it was something serious?'

He could only supply a lame 'Instinct'.

To give her her due, Jean Mariello did not actually laugh out loud. 'Well, instinct tells me, from knowing him pretty well, that the only thing that upset Willy was not getting his own way. He was spoilt. He'd had a lot of success and it went to his head. Used to be just a builder's labourer, playing guitar in his spare time. Then the group took off and suddenly he was famous. Everyone gave him everything he wanted and he started getting bad-tempered if anything didn't fail into his lap. If he was upset, it must have been that some girl had slapped his face.'

'There were a lot of girls?'

'Yes.'

'Do you know if he'd been particularly involved with anyone recently?'

'We didn't discuss it. We went our own ways. Listen, Willy was a slob. All right, I'm sorry he died, but he was no great loss.'

Charles was shocked by her honesty and his face must have betrayed it. Jean laughed. 'Yes, you're wondering why I married him. Well, I was only seventeen, I wanted to be a musician and I wanted to get away from my parents. And Willy was different then—it was before he became successful. He was less sure of himself and, as a result, less selfish. We both changed. He became a bastard and I got a lot tougher. In self-defence.'

There was a slight tremor on the last words, the first sign of human feeling that she had shown. The callous attitude to her husband's death was a protective shell, distancing her from reality. It was true that she had not loved him, but the killing had affected her. Charles changed his approach slightly. 'When did you last see him?'

'Last Friday. I went down to Carlisle to start a tour of folk clubs. Then this happened. I'll be joining the tour again as soon as I've got things sorted out.'

'And Willy didn't seem upset when you left?'

'He was exactly as usual.'

'And you've no idea what he was doing over the weekend?'

'Screwing some bird probably. Decorating here maybe. Rehearsing his bloody show. I don't know.'

The edge was creeping back into her voice. She wanted Charles to leave. She wanted to be on her own. Maybe so that she could break down and cry her heart out. There was not time for many more questions. 'Why did he get involved in the show in the first place?'

'Puce split up. Willy had delusions of grandeur—wanted to get it together as an all-round entertainer. Another Tommy Steele. No big impresario offered him a contract, but Derby University offered him a part in their tatty show. I suppose he saw it as a rung on the ladder to *stardom*.' She put an infinity of scorn into that word.

'Sounds unlikely.'

'Maybe there was some other reason. Look, Mr Paris—'

'I'm sorry. I'll go. Can I just ask you again—was there anyone you can think of, however unlikely, who might have profited by your husband's death?'

'First let me ask you—why are you so interested in all this? It's nothing to do with you.'

'No, you're right, it's just ... I was there ... I saw it ...' He petered out. Tried again. 'There are people who will feel happier when the facts are known. I mean, there's so much gossip and speculation and accusation down at Coates Gardens ...' As he spoke, he knew it was not true. In fact there had been surprisingly little discussion among the students. Once they had exhausted the inherent drama of the situation, they all seemed quite happy to accept that it was an accident and get back to the more important drama of the shows they were putting on. 'No, I'm sorry, I can't really answer your question.'

'Hmm. I'll answer yours. The only person who stood to benefit from Willy's death was his widow, who would thus get out of an unsatisfactory marriage without the fuss of divorce. In other words, the only person with a motive was me.' She laughed sharply. 'Goodbye, Mr Paris.'

He wandered disconsolately along Meadow Lane and looked back at the house. It was in a better state of repair than the others, walls and chimney repointed, missing slates replaced. And inside, was Jean Mariello as tidy and controlled? Or was she crying? He'd never know. All he did know was that she did not kill her husband. Her talk of motives had just been a contemptuous challenge to him. She had not been in Edinburgh at the time of the murder, and in the Truth Game Willy had specified that the person whose secret he had discovered was connected with the Derby group. No progress.

He felt in need of company. As a long shot, he tried the bell of Anna's flat as he passed. Just after twelve, no reason why she should be there.

She wasn't. He went into the Highland chic of the Ensign Ewart pub opposite and started drinking whisky. As he drank, the whole business of playing at detectives seemed increasingly pointless. If only there were someone around he could discuss the case with. Maybe some great detectives manage on their own, he thought as he downed the second large Bell's, but right now I'd give anything for Dr Watson to walk through that door.

But the Doctor did not come and Charles drank too much on his own. The whisky did not make him think any more clearly. He looked round the pub. The office workers of Edinburgh were in huddles with their backs to him. A loud group of American tourists was being ignored at one table. The Festival influx was not welcomed by the residents. Charles tried to get another drink, but could not attract anyone's attention. Being invisible at a bar is one of the loneliest experiences in life and he felt depressed for the first time since his arrival.

It was the interview with Jean Mariello that had done it. Up until then he had been cheerful, even buoyant after the night with Anna. But Anna was not there and it did not take long for her image to get distorted. He needed her presence to restore reality. But she was as elusive as Dr Watson.

His eyes gave up trying to catch the barman's attention and wandered over to a notice board on which the grudging management had stuck a few of the dozens of handbills which earnest theatrical groups had thrust on them. They were on a metal clip. Oxford Theatre Group on top. That was inevitable. Their headquarters was opposite the pub and so they had a head-start on that pitch in the popular Fringe game of sticking your poster over everyone else's.

Beside the Oxford bill was another that looked familiar. Good God, it was one of the greatest DUDS on the Fringe, Charles Paris' *So Much Comic, So Much Blood*, opening Monday 19th August at one fifteen p.m. He felt a sense of urgency that amounted almost to panic.

'Yes, sir, what can I get you?'

'Nothing. I've got to rehearse.' The barman's bewildered stare followed him out of the pub.

Outside in the street he realised that he had had an excessive lunch for a working actor and trod with care down the steep steps of Lady Stair's Close to the Mound. The light seemed very bright. He thought he saw the familiar figure of Martin Warburton ahead. He hurried to catch up. 'Martin!'

But the figure did not stop. It turned right at the bottom of the steps and Charles saw the beard and glasses. It was not Martin.

He awoke on his camp-bed at about five with the worst sort of afternoon hangover. The urgent rehearsal schedule he had promised himself had petered out rather quickly. He hoped that he had not been seen lying there by too many of the group. A middle-aged man asleep in the afternoon. No doubt snoring. The monotone of the piano upstairs indicated a revue rehearsal. He hoped Anna had not seen him.

A cup of coffee might help. He eased himself downstairs to the kitchen. The day's cook, a large girl with corkscrew curls, was chopping up more of the inevitable cabbage.

'Where's the coffee?'

'Over there, behind the cornflakes.'

'Oh yes.'

'I'll make you some ...'

'Thanks.' He made to sit on a chair by the table.

'... if you don't mind doing something for me.'

'What?'

'Just empty that, would you?'

'That' was a large cardboard box full of rubbish—papers, sweepings, cigarette ends, kitchen refuse. The bottom felt unwholesomely soggy on his hands. Charles Paris, haulage contractors. Amplifiers, refuse—distance no object. He negotiated the load through the kitchen door and made his way to the dustbins.

There was a little room at the top of one of them. He balanced the box on the edge and tried to let the contents slip gently in.

They all came with a rush, covering his hands with tea leaves and a yellow slime that had been food. Little scraps of paper scattered all around the bin.

He pushed down the smelly pile and bent to pick up some of the litter. A lot of the paper appeared to have been torn from a big poster photograph. He picked up a piece which had printing on it.

WI
PU

He scrabbled among the other bits until he found the adjacent one which spelled out the title.

WILLY MARIELLO
PUCE

It was a publicity poster of Willy that someone had shredded into a thousand pieces.

CHAPTER FIVE

How bless'd the heart that has a friend
A sympathising ear to lend
To troubles too great to smother!
For as ale and porter, when flat, are restored
Till a sparkling bubbling head they afford,
So sorrow is cheer'd by being poured
From one vessel to another.
MISS KILMANSEGG AND HER PRECIOUS LEG

FROM BIBLICAL TIMES the restorative properties of a young woman's body have been acknowledged, and Charles felt better after another night with Anna. He was amazed how much she affected him. She was beautiful, and she was knowledgeable in bed, but it was not just that. There was something about the honesty of her responses. No extravagant protestations of love, no questions about the future, just an acceptance that what was happening was good. Most people reveal their weaknesses in a close relationship and endear themselves by failure. But the nearer Charles got to Anna the more complete and integrated she seemed. And she made him feel complete too. Not two lost souls leaning against each other for support, but two independent people who complemented each other.

The alarm woke them at nine. Charles reached his hand round to the small of her back and kissed the elastic skin of her breasts. Anna smiled. 'Got to get up.'

'Saturday.'

'No weekend for us. The revue opens on Monday. We've got a tech. run at ten.'

'Yes, the show must go on.' She got up. Charles squatted ruefully on the bed with his elbows on his knees. Anna paused in the bathroom doorway and grinned. 'You look like a dog that's had its bone taken away.'

'Yes, I fancied a nice bit of marrow-bone jelly. Isn't that what Prolongs Active Life?'

'You needn't worry.' She closed the bathroom door. Charles smiled, gratified. He spoke up over the sound of running water. 'Hey, look, I've got a lot of rehearsal to do, too. Can I use the flat? It's so difficult to find anywhere quiet at Coates Gardens.'

A gurgle from the bathroom gave him permission. 'What are the technical lot like, Anna? All the sound and lighting people?' Another gurgle said they were fine, there was a good course in the Department of Drama. 'I hope so. I'm only getting a few hours' rehearsal in the hall—Sunday and Monday morning is all I'm allowed.'

The bathroom door slid open and Anna appeared, naked, her hair spiked with damp. 'Not fair, is it, you poor old thing?' she said as she crossed to her clothes on the chair.

He grabbed at her ankle as she passed and she flopped on to the bed. 'Got to go and rehearse, Charles.'

'Rehearse and become a big star.'

'Yes.'

'Even stars have five minutes.'

The rehearsal went well too. Given somewhere to work on his own, Charles concentrated and put more subtlety into his readings. He was very organised. Once straight through, then a laborious line-by-line analysis of what had gone wrong. Another run—improvements in individual items but too uniform a pace overall. More detailed work, and finally a run that he would not have been ashamed to show to an audience. 'There are many pleasures to be had at the Edinburgh Festival, and the greatest of these is Charles Paris' *So Much Comic, So Much Blood*.' Silly, however old and cynical he got, there were times when his mind raced and fantasies of success made him deliciously nervy and excited.

After rehearsal he found the pubs were shut and that made him feel virtuous. A brisk walk was called for. He popped into a little café aptly called the Poppin and bought a couple of floury ham rolls. Then started a leisurely stroll up to the Castle.

The Esplanade was flanked with tiers of seats ready for the Military Tattoo. The head of a statue and the point of an obelisk came up through the disciplined rows to be capped incongruously by green tarpaulin covers. But the Castle itself still looked impressive as Charles mounted the gentle incline to its heraldic gateway. 'Nemo me impune lacessit.' The motto's translation came to his mind in the accent of a Glasgow thug—'No one provokes me and gets away with it.'

It was like a pilgrimage. Every time he came up to Edinburgh, he had to look round the Castle. Climb up to Mons Meg, maybe look inside St Margaret's Chapel. Then on the level below he would lean against the ramparts and gaze down over the city, whose greys merged to distant greens. which were lost in the gleam of the Firth of Forth.

It was a clear, sparkling day. He had a beautiful girl and he felt confident about his show. And yet ...

And yet there was a nagging unease in his mind. Willy Mariello's murder. Each time he tried to dismiss it, he saw the fear in those brown eyes. And he knew that the pleasures of Edinburgh could only allay his unrest temporarily. Peace would not come until he knew the full facts.

The facts he had found out did not take him far. There were still some forty suspects who had had equal opportunity to switch the knives. Of those two had had greater opportunities than the others to stage-manage the murder—Martin Warburton and Pam Northcliffe. Martin had struck the fatal blow and he was an unstable character with strange obsessions about violence. But it seemed too obvious, and Charles felt an understanding, even an affinity with the boy's tormented mind. He could not think of him as a murderer.

The same applied to Pam. However, it was she who had actually issued the murder weapon and there were other strange features of her behaviour. He had a strong suspicion that she was responsible for the torn poster. The pieces that he had found had burst out of a paper bag full of crepe paper scraps which Pam had been using to make props. He had not challenged her with it, but he was fairly certain. So she had something to hide.

But not murder. Why not? Because I, Charles Paris, like the girl. The same goes for Martin. It is a hopelessly subjective, emotional judgement. I have an old-fashioned, middle-class view that murderers are, by definition, nasty people. Whereas, in fact, they are just nice, ordinary people who get into situations they can't cope with and take what seems to them the only way out.

Again he desperately wanted someone to talk to about his suspicions. Someone detached and objective. Not Anna. She was involved with the other students and he did not want the murder to intrude on their growing relationship. But there was always Gerald.

Gerald Venables was a show business solicitor with a childlike relish for the cloak and dagger aspect of detection. Charles had enlisted his help earlier in the year to sort out the Marius Steen affair and, when that mystery was solved, Gerald had insisted that he should be included in any future venture of criminal investigation. This looked like his opportunity.

'Hello, Gerald.'

'Who's that? Charles?'

'Yes. I think I may be on to another case.'

'Really.' Excitement sprang into Gerald's voice. 'Where?'

'Edinburgh, I'm afraid. It'd cost you a lot in fares.'

'Don't worry. I've got lots of Scottish clients. I can put it on one of their bills. What's the crime?'

'Murder.'

'Fantastic. Will it keep?'

'What do you mean?'

'Keep for a few days. I'm going to Cannes for a long weekend to stay with a client.'

'Work?'

'Well, it'll be on his bill, but I don't intend to do anything.'

'When are you back?'

'Probably Wednesday.'

'Some weekend.'

'Pity to rush it.'

'Hmm.' Wednesday seemed a long way off. Charles wanted someone there to talk to at that moment.

Gerald continued. 'And then at the end of next week—Saturday—I'm taking the family out to our villa in Corsica for a month.'

'Just the month?'

'Yes. I have to get back to work then,' said Gerald piously, not catching Charles' sarcasm.

'So you might be free for a couple of days next week?'

'Might. The case won't be solved by then, will it?'

'No, I shouldn't think so.' Depression swooped and Charles feared he was speaking the truth. 'I'll give you a buzz when you get back if there's anything left to investigate. O.K. Fine. Have a good weekend.' It was not worth saying how pointless it would be for Gerald to come up for two days. Oh, well, another good idea gone west.

'Oh, it's you, Charles.' James Milne was standing at the foot of the stairs in the hail. 'I wondered who was using the phone. That one's just an extension to mine upstairs. It's meant to be disconnected soon and I'd put it in the cupboard so that it shouldn't be used.'

'I'm sorry. It was just here on the floor when I came in.'

'Don't worry. One of the Derby lot found it, no doubt. How's Thomas Hood?'

'Fine. Positively going well.'

'Good, good.' The Laird stood with one foot on the stair, posed like an old-fashioned print. His stocky figure was dressed in a biscuit-coloured tweed suit with a Norfolk jacket. 'Can I offer you a cup of tea?'

A slow grin spread over Charles' face. 'Dr Watson,' he said.

'I beg your pardon.'

Over a cup of Earl Grey tea and chocolate-covered Bath Olivers, Charles explained. He told of his suspicions about the murder and the small progress of his investigations.

James Milne looked at him in silence for a moment. 'What an amazing idea. And what do you want me to do? Crawl around the rooftops with firearms and beard villains in their dens? I don't know whether that's quite my style. I used sometimes to try to catch poachers on my mother's estate at Glenloan, but I'm not exactly a private eye.'

'Look, all I want you to do is to address your mind to the problem. I want to hear what you think. You've met most of the people involved. You know, two heads are better than one and all that. And I'm really getting nowhere on my own. My suspicions just go round and round in circles ... I want you to be a kind of sounding board for my ideas.'

'Hmm. I think a ouija board for contacting Willy Mariello might be more useful.'

'You're probably right. What do you say?'

'Well, Charles, I'm certainly prepared to help you in any way you think might be useful. But I must say right from the start that I don't share your certainty that a murder has been committed. From what I heard it sounded like a very unfortunate accident. What makes you so sure it's murder?'

Again Charles had to fall back on his feeble cry of 'Instinct'.

' "Instinct is a great matter, I was a coward on instinct." Hmm. Dear old Falstaff. Instinct. Do the police share your instinct?'

'Not so far as I know.'

'They don't think it was murder?'

'I don't think so, though that won't really be clear until they've finished their enquiries.'

'No. Hmm. Good.'

'Why good?'

'Well, when our investigations reach their dramatic denouement, we can feel confident that Inspector Flatfoot of the Yard won't pip us at the post.'

'You mean you agree?'

'Yes, I'll be your sounding board. It could be fun.'

'Good. Thank you.'

The Laird immediately regressed to his school-mastering days. 'Right. Now have you made any notes on the case?'

'No.'

'Well, I'm sure you should.' Charles watched amazed as his Dr Watson began to organise him. 'Right, paper, fountain pen, sharp HB pencil. And a column, so. Headed 'Suspects'. And another—'Reason for Suspicion'. Now who have we got?'

'We've just been through all that.'

'No harm in doing it again. There is nothing so effective for stimulating the memory and provoking thought as writing things down.'

Charles felt he was right back in the First Form. (On his present investigative form, in the corner with a big 'D' on his hat.) But he humoured his new partner and they made out their list.

It did not take long. The 'Reason for Suspicion' column looked particularly unconvincing. 'In a sense,' said Charles, 'we're starting from the wrong end. We are putting down why we suspect someone, whereas we should be thinking, from that person's point of view, why they should want to kill Willy.'

'Would that make the list any fuller?'

Charles had to admit that it would not. 'What we've got to do is to work out who was involved with Willy—emotionally, artistically, financially. So far it seems the only person from Derby he knew well is a guy called Sam Wasserman, who is currently touring Europe.'

'You say he's the only person you can connect Willy with?'

'Except for his wife. But I can't count her because she has nothing to do with the group. Unless she has an ally who's at Derby ... A lover maybe or ...' Lack of conviction in what he was saying brought him to a halt. 'Nope.'

'And she's the only person up here with whom he seems to have had dealings?'

'Yes.'

'Oh, Charles, Charles.' The Laird shook his head pityingly. 'There's someone you've overlooked.'

'Is there?'

'Yes. And you have all the information to work out who. I know you do.' He watched for reaction and then repeated slowly, 'I know you do.'

Charles suddenly realised who was meant. 'Good Lord, yes. You. The house.'

'Exactly. You see, there is a direct financial relationship between me and Willy Mariello. He bought my house. I think I should go down on our list of suspects.'

'But that's daft. If you were the murderer, you wouldn't draw my attention to your connection with the victim.'

'Ah, Charles, I may look like the innocent flower, but be the serpent under't. You mustn't rule out any possibility. There, I've put my name down. Declaration of interests, like the Liberals keep asking M.P.s to make. Now what about you?'

'Me?'

'Your declaration of interest. Had you any motive to murder Willy Mariello?'

Charles laughed. 'No.'

'Good. Now we know where we stand.' James Milne smiled. His reserve was gone and he looked set to enjoy the game of detection. 'Now, what about the other forty-odd?'

'What indeed? Presumably I must try to meet them all and find out if any of them knew Willy well. And also what he did over the weekend before he died.'

'Yes. And how long have you got to complete this major investigation?'

'My show finishes a week today.'

'Hmm. I fear we may find time defeats us.'

'Yes. I hope not.'

'So do I. But perhaps, Charles, I hope it a little less than you.

'Why?'

'Because I don't yet fully believe that we're on to a case of murder. I'll come along with you for the ride, but I'm not convinced of the existence of a destination.'

The Laird was going to dinner with friends, so Charles left him about seven. He was no nearer the solution of the murder, but at least he had an ally. And the cataloguing power of James Milne's mind could be a useful complement to his own haphazard methods.

On the first-floor landing he paused. The revue piano had given up its usual stuck-in-the-groove repetition and was playing a whole tune. A girl was singing. He could not catch the lyrics, just hear the husky purity of her voice. Anna. He felt a strong desire to go into the room on some pretext just to see her. But no. She had said it was better they should keep their relationship a secret and she was right. He did not fancy the gossip and innuendo of forty students.

No. He still had the key to the flat. He'd go back there and wait for her to return and continue his rejuvenation. Later.

On the ground floor the only sign of human occupation was the presence of old socks, creeping like firedamp from the men's dormitory. Charles was about to leave and find a pub for the evening when he heard a slight sound from the basement. He crept down the stairs towards the glow of the sitting-room.

Michael Vanderzee was slumped on the sofa with a glass in one hand and a half-full bottle of Glenmorangie malt whisky in the other. He perceived Charles' approach blearily. 'I didn't know there was anyone in the house. Thought they'd all buggered off.'

'I've just been having a drink with the Laird.'

'Oh, that old poof,' said Michael ungraciously.

Charles did not bother to challenge the gratuitous insult, though on reflection he thought it was misplaced. He had not thought before about James Milne's sexual status, but, when he did, neuter seemed the most appropriate definition.

However, Michael was not trying to drive Charles away. On the contrary, he seemed delighted to have a witness of his lonely drinking and an audience for his self-pity.

'Charles Paris, you may work in bullshit commercial theatre, but at least you are a professional.' The drink accentuated the Dutchness of his voice as he delivered this back-handed compliment. 'Surrounded by bloody amateurs in this place. It's an impossible situation for any creative work. You can't create with amateurs.'

Charles grunted sympathetically and sat astride a chair. 'Have a drink,' said Michael, feeling that perhaps he should offer his audience some reward for its attention. 'There's a cup on the table.'

The cup was chipped and handleless, but the malt tasted good. When he reckoned that Charles was sitting comfortably, Michael began. 'No, I shouldn't have taken this job. Amateurs have no concept of theatre. Look at it. This evening I should have been working, improvising, creating something, and what happens? Half my cast are rehearsing for some bloody revue, half of them are doing some dreary Shakespeare crap, half of them aren't interested ...'

'And half of them get stabbed ...'

'Yes.' He nodded vigorously. 'Though he wasn't a lot more use to me when he was alive.'

'What do you mean?'

'Never came to bloody rehearsals. Didn't participate in the concentration exercises or movement classes, any of the workshop stuff. I mean, how can you build an ensemble with people like that? He hadn't any acting talent anyway.'

'Then why did you cast him in your show?'

'I didn't cast him. Look, I'm offered this job—'

'You mean you're nothing to do with the university?'

'Good God, no.' Michael was severely affronted. 'I'm a professional director. They booked me to get some professional feel into their production.

And then like bloody amateurs they don't give me enough time to get it together properly. Everyone off for other rehearsals. Do you know how long it takes to build up an ensemble?'

'About four years?'

'Well, four weeks anyway. And four weeks' work. Not four weeks doing bourgeois revues and middle-class Shakespeare.'

'No, of course not. You were saying how Willy Mariello came to be in the show ...'

'Yes. O.K., I take the job. I go to Derby to hold auditions. And already I'm told that Willy is doing the music and, since Rizzio's a guitarist and he has a couple of songs, O.K., he's playing Rizzio too.'

'Who told you this?'

'Sam Wasserman, the guy who wrote this crappy play.'

'Is it crappy?'

'Yes, but it doesn't matter.'

'Why not?'

'My style of direction doesn't need a good play. In fact the play can get in the way. It's only a starting point from which the totality emerges—the iron filing dropped into the acid which produces the perfect crystal.' He added the last image with great satisfaction, albeit dubious chemistry. Then he looked at Charles with pitying contempt. 'I suppose you still think a play has got to have words.'

Charles smiled apologetically. There was no point in alienating such a ready source of information. 'Yes, I am a bit of an old fuddy-duddy on that score. I expect Sam Wasserman probably thinks words are quite important too.'

'Maybe.'

'He sounds an interesting bloke. I'd like to meet him.'

Michael gave a snort of laughter that could have meant anything. 'You should get a chance quite soon. He's coming up to Edinburgh.'

'For the opening in the Third Week?'

'No, before that, I hope. We've been sending telegrams all over Europe for him. He's going to come up and take over the part of Rizzio.'

'Oh really.' That was very interesting. 'He plays guitar too?'

'Yes. He was going to do the music for the show himself until Willy was brought in.'

'Ah.' That was also interesting. 'So everything's back to where it started?'

'I suppose so. More drink?'

'Thank you.' Charles held out his cup and the malt was sloshed in like school soup. Trying desperately to sound casual, he asked, 'What did you think of Willy Mariello?'

'Useless, unco-operative bastard. Ruining my production. From my point of view, his death was the best thing that could have happened.'

It was an uncompromising statement of hatred. So much so that Charles felt inclined to discount it. A murderer would be more guarded ... Unless it was an elaborate double bluff ... Oh dear. The further he got into the business of detection, the further certainty seemed to recede. Still, keep on probing. Try to find out some more hard facts. Again he imposed a relaxed tone on his voice. 'Were you rehearsing last weekend?'

'Of course. I rehearse whenever I can get my cast together. I am trying to create something, you know.'

'Of course. So Willy was rehearsing all weekend?'

'No. That's a good example of what I mean. He rehearses on Saturday with his usual bad grace. Sunday—no sign of him. Monday he is not there and I am so furious I break the rehearsal and I go up to his house to drag him back—by force if necessary.'

'Was he there?'

'Oh yes, he's there. Calmly decorating. Plaster dust everywhere, paint brushes, so on and so on.

'Did you get him to rehearsal?'

'Yes, till mid-afternoon. Then he slipped off again when we had a break.'

'Hmm. Perhaps he wanted to get back to his decorating.'

'Yes. Or to the girl.'

'Girl?'

'Yes. When I finally got him out on the Monday morning, he called out "Goodbye" to someone upstairs.'

CHAPTER SIX

In they go—in jackets, and cloaks,
Plumes, and bonnets, turbans and toques,
As if to a Congress of Nations:
Greeks and Malays, with daggers and dirks,
Spaniards, Jews, Chinese, and Turks—
Some like original foreign works,
But mostly like bad translations.
MISS KILMANSEGG AND HER PRECIOUS LEG

BY SUNDAY 18TH AUGUST Edinburgh was beginning to feel the Festival. Over-night the city was full of tourists— tweedy music-lovers on leisurely promenades, earnest Americans decked with rucksacks and guide-books, French and Japanese drawn by the twin attractions of culture and Marks and Spencer pullovers. The residents who had not escaped on holiday wore expressions of resignation, hardened to the idea of their streets clogged with ambling foreigners, their early nights troubled by returning revue audiences and the distant massed pipes and drums of the Military Tattoo.

Because that Sunday was the day when it all started officially. In the words of the Festival brochure, 'The twenty-eighth Edinburgh Festival will be opened with a Service of Praise and Thanksgiving in St Giles' Cathedral on Sunday 18th August at 3 p.m. Later, starting from the Castle Esplanade at 9.45 p.m., relays of torch-bearing runners will light a bonfire on Arthur's Seat.'

And in the little halls of Edinburgh on that Sunday morning would-be cultural torch-bearers blew earnestly at the smoulderings of what was in many cases incombustible material. Experimental and university groups realised that their rehearsal time was running out and put on a spurt to justify the extravagant claims of their publicity. There were dress rehearsals for at least a dozen 'funniest revues on the Fringe', some twenty 'revolutionary new plays', and three or four 'new artistic concepts which would flatten the accepted barriers of culture'. If all these ambitions were realised, British theatre would never be the same again.

In the Masonic Hall in Lauriston Street Charles Paris was trying to realise more humble ambitions and finding it hard work. The lighting technician he had been allocated was a fat and contemptuous youth, whose blue denim had faded and dirtied to the colour of sludge. He was known as Plug, and Charles found it difficult to call anyone 'Plug'.

It had been made clear that, considering the exacting demands of creative amateur theatre, there was not going to be much time or effort left for him, a mere professional. 'Um ... Plug?' he said exploratively, 'I wonder about the chances of moving the back-projector round. If it stays there, I'm going to be masking the slides.'

'That'd mean moving the screen too,' Plug grunted accusingly.

'Yes, it will.'

'Can't be done. Haven't got the extension leads.'

'Can't you get them?'

'Shouldn't think so.'

Charles bit back his anger. It was difficult dealing with amateurs. In a professional context, no problem; he could have bawled the guy out, justified because a service that was being paid for was not being provided. But the amateur relies on goodwill and there did not seem to be much of it in evidence.

So he gritted his teeth and played stupid, apparently bowing to Plug's technical expertise and working the youth round till he did what was required as a demonstration of his abilities. It was important, Charles had gone to considerable trouble to have slides made of Hood's woodcuts. They had originally been printed with the poems and the crude humour of the pictures extended the range of the verse. In a one-man show it is important to give the audience as much varied stimulus as possible.

By application of simple child psychology he got the back-projector and screen moved and started a run. It was not easy. With only two stage areas in use, the lighting plot was simple. But Plug refused to rehearse the cues on their own, saying that he would pick them up on a full run. Then, in spite of the carefully marked-up script that Charles had given him, he proceeded to get every single effect wrong.

The one benefit of the run was that it tested Charles' knowledge of his words, because whether he moved to the table or the lectern, there was a guarantee of total darkness on that area. And whenever he turned to the back-projection screen, he was confronted either by a blank or the wrong slide.

It was also a useful concentration exercise. In the darkness beyond the stage people kept wandering in and out. Plug greeted them all loudly and conducted irrelevant conversations at the top of his voice. Charles was ignored like a television in the corner of the room.

The show limped to its close. As he stood at the lectern to read the final *Stanzas*, 'Farewell, Life! My senses swim ...', he was amazed to find the light was actually where it should be. It had taken the whole show to get one cue right, but at least it offered hope. Encouraged, he put more emotion into the poem. It approached its end with the dying fall he had intended.

> 'O'er the earth there comes a bloom—
> Sunny light for sullen gloom,
> Warm perfume for vapour cold—'

then, before 'I smell the Rose above the Mould', the pause held long & dramatic.

Too long. Too dramatic. Plug snapped the lights out before the line was delivered.

Charles' reserves cracked. 'Oh, for Christ's sake!'

'What's up?' Plug grunted from the darkness.

'That's not the cue. There's another line.'

Plug did not seem unduly concerned. He brought up the house lights. 'Never mind.'

'And then, after the last line, there's supposed to be a three-second pause and a five-second fade down to black.'

'Oh.'

'It's clearly marked in the script.'

'Yes.'

Charles decided there was little point in concealing his feelings. 'That was pretty abysmal.'

Plug nodded sympathetically, unaware that the comment referred to him. 'Hmm. Perhaps you need more rehearsal.'

'I think it's you who needs more rehearsal. None of the cues were right.'

Plug's silence indicated that this was an unworthy attack on his life work. Charles continued, 'So let's have one run-through of just the cues and then do the whole show again.'

'There's not much point.'

'Why not? The show opens tomorrow.'

'Yes, but I won't be doing the lights then. I'm only here for the rehearsal.'

Charles tried to find out what would be happening about his lights in the actual show from the Company Manager, and Brian Cassells was confident that everything would be all right. Charles, who found Brian's confidence increasingly unnerving, was not convinced.

'Oh, incidentally, Charles, will you be going down to the Fringe reception?'

'What's that?'

'At five o'clock. Royal Mile Centre. It's sort of to launch everything. You know, Press'll be there and all that.'

'Then I'll certainly come.' Any chance of publicity must be taken. He was not too optimistic of the 'DUDS of the Fringe' poster bringing audiences flocking to see him.

Since the pubs were not open on Sunday, he had cabbage lunch with the rest of the group. The conversation was all of the coming shows. Willy Mariello's death had been almost forgotten. Charles looked round the table. Anna was not there. He suddenly wished she was, or wished that he was with her somewhere keeping the blues at bay.

The loud T-shirted crowd joked and attitudinised. He felt old and envious. Their values were so simple. What they were doing on the Fringe was the most important thing that had ever happened; that was all there was to it. Their shows consumed all their thoughts and energies.

Except for the thoughts of one person—the murderer. He or she must be feeling regret or anxiety or something. But the lunch time crowd showed no signs of guilty conscience. They all seemed interchangeably brash and cheerful. Pam Northcliffe was up the far end of the table as nervously bright and giggly as the rest. Communal excitement had replaced the short tempers of earlier in the week.

Martin Warburton was not there. Charles wondered if he would be sharing in the group gaiety if he were. There was still a lot to be found out about Martin Warburton. That afternoon might be a good opportunity to read *Who Now?*—a Disturbing New Play.

It was disturbing. The language was good, there was some sense of structure, but the content was frightening. As the title implied, questions of identity figured large. None of the characters seemed to have a fixed personality; they were chameleons who took on the colour of different forms of violence. There was a woolly Leftish political message coming through the monologues that made up the play. Its main tenet seemed to be that, come the Revolution, the bourgeois would be destroyed. But it was the way in which they were going to be destroyed that was disturbing. Images of bombings, secret beatings and firing squads abounded. Continually blood welled, bones cracked, corpses twitched and entrails spilled. So much blood.

Under normal circumstances, Charles would have put it down to over-writing. Some of the extended metaphors even reminded him of his own adolescent literary excesses. But even so, and even given a young person's insensitive ignorance of the real facts of death, there was something obsessive about the play. A morbid preoccupation with violence unbalanced the writer's considerable natural talent.

And became uncomfortably relevant in the light of Willy Mariello's death.

About half past four Martin Warburton suddenly appeared in the men's dormitory. He seemed in a hurry and had dropped in to collect something from his suitcase. Charles was lying on his camp-bed checking through *So Much Comic ...*

'Oh, Martin, I've read your play.'

'Ah.' He seemed embarrassed.

'I'd like to talk about it.'

'Ah.'

'Now? If you're walking down to this reception, we could chat on the way.'

'I'm not going to the reception.' Martin hesitated. He was improvising. 'I'm going to meet someone down at ... er ... Dean Village.'

'Oh. O.K. Well, some other time.'

'Yes.'

Charles started off with some of the *Mary* cast to walk to the Royal Mile Centre. Just as they were about to cross Princes Street to go up the Mound, he realised that he had not brought any of his hand-outs. Even a playbill offering one of the DUDS of the Fringe was better than no publicity. Brian Cassells would not have thought to take any. With some annoyance, because it was a warm afternoon, he started back along Princes Street.

He was waiting for the lights to cross Charlotte Street when he saw Martin over the other side striding purposefully along Lothian Road. In the opposite direction from Dean Village.

Charles was not aware of making the decision, but it seemed natural to cross over Princes Street and follow. He was some fifty yards behind his quarry and there were enough meandering tourists about to make the pursuit look casual. He kept his eyes fixed on the blue denim back ahead.

Martin turned left along Castle Terrace which skirts the great Castle rock, then crossed over Spittal Street and climbed up towards Lauriston Place. Maybe going to the Masonic Hall. The scene of the crime. There were no rehearsals that afternoon. Everyone was going down to the reception. Or perhaps Martin was aiming for the Mariello's house in Meadow Lane. Charles felt a spurt of excitement.

There were less people about in this part of the old town, so he dawdled. He did not want to be noticed if Martin stopped suddenly.

But the boy did not stop. The blue denim back continued its progress. Past the Masonic Hall, no hesitation. Past the Meadow Lane turning. On past the Infirmary, looking neither left nor right. Charles began to feel it was a long walk.

And it continued. On past the University Union with its cloth banner advertising Russell Hunter in *Knox*. On to Nicholson Square and then suddenly right, along the broad pavement of Nicholson Street. Martin still kept up his even, preoccupied pace, with Charles alternately lingering and hurrying along behind.

The whole thing seemed pointless. Charles could not really think what he was doing, playing this elaborate game of cops and robbers when he should be snatching much-needed publicity at the reception. Perhaps Martin was just going out for a walk. Something innocuous. Something—

Martin had disappeared. The fact jerked Charles out of his reverie. One moment the denim back had been moving smoothly along, the next it was gone. In the middle of a parade of shops. No chance of having turned up a side street.

Cautiously Charles moved forward to where he had last seen Martin. All the shops were Sunday shut. Their fronts were separated by doors which served the flats above. Gently Charles pushed the one nearest to where he had last seen Martin.

It was a heavy door, but it gave. The stone hall was dark and suddenly cool. A pram. A bicycle. Stone stairs, a metal rail. And attached to the top of the door a heavy chain that was part of some antiquated system to open it from the flats above.

Just an ordinary hall of an ordinary tenement block. Silence. He could not start barging into private flats at high tea time on an Edinburgh Sunday afternoon. Anyway, what was he looking for? He went out into the street again.

The names on the old-fashioned bell-pushes told him nothing. McHarg,

Stewart, Grant, Wilson. He waited for about five minutes, apparently intrigued by a display of dusty Pyrex in an adjacent shop. Martin did not re-emerge. It was after half past five. Charles set off for the Royal Mile Centre.

At the entrance he was asked to identify himself.

'Charles Paris.'

'Not your name. Who are you with?'

'Oh, Derby University Dramatic Society.'

The result was that he entered the upstairs assembly room with a red card badge bearing the legend 'D.U.D.S.'. It did not seem very positive advertising.

Entering the room was difficult; it was so full that he had to ease one shoulder in as a wedge and wriggle the rest of his body in after it. Some people had glasses of drink. Infallible instinct tracked its source and he slid and sidled over to a long table.

The drink was a pink wine-cup of minimal alcoholic content. Charles looked out across the throng. A swarm of cultural locusts was buzzing loudly and milling round the red badges which bore the names of newspapers, radio or television companies.

Everyone had a badge. *Radio Clyde* bounced on the forceful breasts of a young reporter. *Bradford* clung to chain mail worn to publicise their play *The Quest*. *B.B.C.* flopped on well-cut mohair. *Nottingham* sagged on a dirty T-shirt.

And everyone forced literature on everyone else. Charles had only to stand there to become a litter-bin for hand-outs and programmes. He kicked himself for wasting time following Martin and not getting his own publicity.

A glance at the cultural treats the literature offered revealed that there was not much he would want to see, but it was at least varied. There was *Problem 32* by Framework Theatre—'ten young designers creating an hour's theatre in their own terms'. The World Premiere of *ScotsWha Hae*, a new Scots comedy from the group that brought you *The De'il's Awa'* and *Cambusdonald Royal*. Paris Pandemonium Projects offered *Chaos, Un Collage de Comédie*. Under the intriguing title *Charlotte Brontë and her Scotsmen*, Accolade were presenting 'psychological deduction of her relations with men in her last years (reduced prices for students and Old Age Pensioners)'. Or there was Birkenhead Dada with *We Call for the Decease of Salvador Dali*—'Shocks, poems and perversions; indefensible personal attacks; new levels of tastelessness.'

In other words the Fringe was much as usual. But with decreasing conviction. Charles remembered the heady days of the late fifties and early sixties when Edinburgh was the only outlet for experimental drama in Britain. The recent spread of little theatres in London and other major cities had eroded that unique position. And the Edinburgh Fringe seemed less important. Less truly experimental. Too many of the university groups were doing end-of-term productions of classics rather than looking for new ideas.

'Not a lot, is there, Charles?'

marvellous and bought posters and ...' She looked up defiantly. 'It's terrible emotional immaturity, I know. But I am emotionally immature. Thanks to a middle-class upbringing. It was just a schoolgirl crush.'

'Did you know him well?'

'No, that's what makes it so pathetic. I mean, I knew him to say hello to, but nothing more. He didn't notice me.'

'You never slept with him?'

Her eyes opened wide. 'Oh Lord, no.'

'So why the rush to get rid of the poster?'

'I don't know. That was daft. I was just so confused— what with the death, and the police asking all those questions ..., and then you asking questions ... I don't know. I got paranoid. I thought somehow if my things were searched and they found the poster that I'd be incriminated or ... I don't know. I wasn't thinking straight.'

It rang true. The brief mystery of the poster was explained. But there must be more to be found out from Pam. 'What did you feel about Willy when he was dead?'

'Shock. I mean, I hadn't seen a dead body before.'

'Nothing else?'

'No, I don't think so.'

'No sense of loss?'

'Not really. I mean, it wasn't real love, just something I'd built up in my mind. In a way his death got it out of my system, made me realise that I didn't really feel a thing for him. Anyway, it had been fading ever since we came up here.'

'As you saw more of him?'

'Yes.' She grinned ruefully. 'He became more real. Just an ordinary man. And perhaps not a very nice one. Anyway, I didn't really feel the same about him after that business with Lesley ...' Charles picked up the last few words as if they were the ash of a vital document in a murderer's fireplace. 'Business with Lesley?'

'Yes, I ...' well, I haven't mentioned it to anyone, but ... it may be nothing, just the way it seemed ...'

'What?'

'It was after we'd been up here about a week. Willy suddenly started to take an interest in Lesley—that's Lesley Petter who—'

'I know about her. Go on.'

'I think he was probably after her, fancied her, I don't know. Anyway, one evening, after we'd been rehearsing, we were all having coffee back at Coates Gardens and Willy said he was going for a walk up to the Castle and did anyone want to come with him. Well, I said yes sort of straight off, because, you know, I thought he was marvellous and ... But then I realised that he'd only said that as a sort of prearranged signal to Lesley. It was meant to be just the two of them.

'I was awfully embarrassed, but I couldn't say I wouldn't go when I realised. So the three of us set off and I dawdled or went ahead or ... wishing like anything I wasn't there.

'We went up to the Castle Esplanade and wandered around, and I, feeling more and more of a gooseberry, went on ahead on the way back. I started off down the steps that go down to Johnstone Terrace.'

'Castle Wynd South.'

'Is that what it's called, yes. Anyway, I was nearly at the bottom, and suddenly I heard this scream. I turned round and saw Lesley, with her arms and legs flailing, falling down the steps.'

'And that was how she broke her leg?'

'Yes. I rushed up to where she'd managed to stop herself, and Willy rushed down. She was in terrible pain and I shot off to phone for an ambulance. But just before I went, I heard her say something to Willy, or at least I think I did.'

Charles felt the excitement prickling over his shoulders and neck. 'What did she say?'

'She said, "Willy, you pushed me."'

CHAPTER SEVEN

"Be thou my park, and I will be thy dear,"
(So he began at least to speak or quote;)
"Be thou my bark, and I thy gondolier,"
(For passion takes this figurative note;)
"Be thou my light, and I thy chandelier;
Be thou my dove, and I will be thy cote;
My lily be, and I will be thy river;
Be thou my life—and I will be thy liver."
BIANCA' S DREAM

THE SHOW BIZ RAZZMATAZZ of first nights was invented before the development of lunch time theatre. There is something incongruous about flowers and telegrams for a first lunch. Charles did not get any, anyway. There was no one to send them. Maurice Skellem was the only person outside Edinburgh who knew the show was happening and he was not the sort to spend his client's money on fulsome gestures. Charles deliberately had not told his ex-wife Frances that he was going up to the Festival as another hack at the fraying but resilient umbilical cord that joined him to her.

But the first night excitement was there. He walked from Coates Gardens to the Masonic Hall with a jumpy step, a little gurgling void of anticipation in his stomach. To his relief, the odious Plug had been replaced by an amiable young man called Vernon, who was not only efficient in the rehearsal but was also staying for the show. It made Charles feel more confident. And more scared. With the technical side under control, no excuses were possible; it was his responsibility entirely.

He calmed himself by hard work. One run of the show for Vernon's benefit, to get the cues right; then a quick double-check through all the slides; finally an as-per performance run which was depressingly pedestrian. As it should be. Charles believed in the old theatrical adage about bad dress rehearsals leading to good first nights.

A few more details checked, then down to the pub about twelve-thirty for a quick one. Just one; mustn't risk slurring. Vernon was quiet and reassuring, a good companion for last-minute anxieties. Yes, he would hold the last fade. Yes, he would anticipate the slide of *The Last Man* sitting on the gallows. No, he didn't think there was too much serious stuff in the programme. No, he didn't think the dark suit was too anonymous.

Back at the hall Brian Cassells was in charge as Front of House Manager. Apparently he felt that evening dress was obligatory for this róle, though he looked a little out of place penguined up at lunch time. He admitted to Charles that advance sales were not that good (three seats), but he had great hopes for casual trade during the next twenty minutes.

Sharp on one fifteen the show started. Charles had felt on the edge of nausea as he waited to enter in the blackout, but as usual actually being onstage gave him a sense of calm and control.

The imperfect masking of the hall's windows meant that the audience was visible, but he did not dare to look until he had received some reaction. The watershed was *Faithless Nellie Gray*; nothing expected on *I Remember, I Remember* and the rest of the preamble. But the first Pathetic Ballad should get something.

Ben Battle was a soldier bold,
And used to war's alarms;
But a cannon-ball took off his legs,
So he laid down his arms.

Yes, a distinct laugh. And the laughs built through the ensuing stanzas. Not a big sound, but warming.

Emboldened, he inspected the audience as he recited. About twenty, which, on the first day of the Festival, with negative publicity, was not bad. On a second glance he realised that a lot of it was paper, members of D.U.D.S. who had been allowed in free. There was a little knot of revue cast, dark figures grouped around Anna's shining head. James Milne leant forward in his seat with intense concentration. There were only about eight faces Charles did not recognise. And some of those might be complimentaries for the critics. Maurice Skellern was not going to be over-impressed by ten per cent of fifty per cent of that lot.

But it was an audience. And they were responding. Charles enjoyed himself.

The Laird insisted on taking him out to lunch. They went to an Indian restaurant on Forrest Place and managed to persuade the waiter it was still early enough for them to have a bottle of wine. After a couple of glasses Charles felt better. The immediate reaction after a show was always emptiness, even depression, and the ability to remember only the things that went wrong. Gradually it passed; alcohol always speeded the process.

So did enthusiastic response to the show. And James Milne was very enthusiastic. He had only known the familiar poems of Hood, the ones which have become cliches by repetition, *November*, *A Retrospective Review*, *The Song of the Shirt* and the inevitable *I Remember, I Remember*. The broadening of the picture which Charles' show had given obviously excited him. The punning and other verbal tricks appealed to his crossword mind. 'I had no idea there was so much variety, Charles. I really must get hold of a *Complete Works*. Is there a good edition?'

'There's an Oxford one, but I don't know if it's in print.' You might be able to pick up a second-hand one somewhere. Or there are some fairly good selections. But look, if you want to borrow mine, do. I should know my words by now.' He held the copy across the table.

The Laird was touched. By his values, lending a book was the highest form of friendship. 'That's very kind. I'll look after it.'

'I know you will.'

'And I'll make it a priority to find one for myself. Oh, you know I envy that kind of facility with words. Not just the facility—we all happen on puns occasionally—but the ability to create something out of it. It must be wonderful to be a writer.'

'I don't know. It was hard graft for Hood. If he hadn't had to work so hard, he might have lived longer.'

'Yes, but at least it's congenial graft. I mean, writing, you're on your own, you get on with it, you don't have to keep getting involved with other people. You just write and send your stuff off and that's it. A sort of remote control way of making a living.'

Charles laughed out loud. 'James, you've got it all wrong. Hood would disagree with you totally. He didn't just sit at a desk toying with his muse and packing the products off in envelopes to editors. All his life was spent scurrying round, selling his own work, sub-editing other people's, setting up magazines. No question of remote control, his Liveli-Hood, as he kept calling it, was very much involved with other people.'

'But some writers don't have to do all that, Charles.'

'Very few. In my own experience of writing plays, about ten per cent of the time is spent actually writing; ninety per cent is traipsing round like a peddler, hawking the results to managements or television companies.'

'Oh dear. So what you are saying is that a writer's life is just as sordid and ordinary as everyone else's?'

'If not more so. Hood himself, in his *Copyright and Copywrong*, said of writers, "We are on a par with quack doctors, street preachers, strollers, ballad-singers, hawkers of last dying speeches, Punch and Judies, conjurers, tumblers and other diverting vagabonds."'

'How very disappointing. I think I'd rather forget you told me that and keep my illusions of ivory towers and groves of Academe.'

They talked further about writing. James Milne admitted that he would have liked to produce something himself, but never got around to it. 'Which means perhaps that I haven't really got anything to say.'

'Maybe. Though writing doesn't have to say anything. It can just be there to entertain,' said Charles, reflecting on his own few plays.

'Hmm. Perhaps, but even then the writer must get a bit involved. Begin to identify with his characters.'

'Oh, inevitably that happens.'

The Laird paused for a moment, piecing his thoughts together. 'I was wondering if there could be anything of that behind this murder.'

'What do you mean? Anything of what?'

'Identification. I mean, if there's anything in the actual situation of the killing, the way it happened.'

'I'm still not with you.'

'Willy Mariello was playing David Rizzio in a play based on the life of Mary, Queen of Scots. Now there are certain obvious parallels between Willy and Rizzio. There's the Italian name, for a start. I know there are lots of Scots with Italian names, but it's a coincidence. Then they both played the guitar.'

'So what you're suggesting,' Charles said slowly, 'is that someone got obsessed with the whole Mary, Queen of Scots story and identified with Rizzio s murder and ... Incidentally, who did kill Rizzio?'

'A lot of people, I seem to recall. I think Darnley was the prime mover. Who's playing Darnley in the show?'

'I don't know. I could check. And you think when we've got that name we've got our murderer?' He could not keep a note of scepticism out of his voice.

'It's just another possible line of enquiry. Something that struck me.'

'Hmm.'

'Well, we're not getting far on any other tack, are we?'

Charles hesitated. 'No.'

'You haven't found out anything else, have you?'

'No,' he lied. For some reason he did not want to tell anyone about Pam Northcliffe's story of Willy and Lesley. Not yet.

The Laird was going to browse round some book shops, but Charles did not feel like it. He was still wound up after the performance, and, since licensing hours did not permit his usual method of unwinding, he decided an aimless stroll round Edinburgh might do the trick.

The stroll soon ceased to be aimless. He had only gone a few hundred yards and was turning off George IV bridge into Chambers Street when he saw Martin Warburton. Striding along on the opposite side of the road with the same expression of blinkered concentration that he had had the day before. And again heading for Nicholson Street.

It is a lot easier following someone when you know where he is going and Charles felt confident of Martin's destination. He was right. The boy again disappeared behind the blue door.

The excitement of seeing the same thing happen two days running quickly gave way to confusion as to what should be done about it. Charles still did not know which flat Martin had gone into and did not feel in the mood for an elaborate masquerade as a reader of gas-meters to gain access. Apart from the risk of illegal impersonation, what would he say if he did find Martin? There was probably some simple explanation for the boy's actions. He had friends living in the flats. Maybe even a girl-friend. Something quite straightforward. Charles was just letting his imagination run riot and suspicion was clouding his judgement.

But he did not want to go. He might be on the verge of some discovery.

Better join the bus queue opposite while he worked out a plan of campaign.

As he stood with the laden housewives and noisy schoolchildren he knew it was not really getting him anywhere. No plan of campaign emerged. If he really wanted to find out what Martin was doing, then the only course was to enter the flats. Otherwise he might just as well give up the whole business, leave Willy Mariello to the police and forget any detective fantasies he might be nurturing.

A bus arrived and the queue surged forward, canny housewives wedging themselves into good seats and practised schoolchildren scampering upstairs to good fooling-about positions. One or two of them gave curious looks to the man at the stop who still queued altruistically without taking his due prize of a seat. The maroon and white bus passed on.

Charles felt exposed and ridiculous on his own at the bus stop. He turned to go, determined to chuck the whole business and resign himself to just being an actor, when he heard the bang of a door on the other side of the road.

It was the blue one, and a thin figure was walking away from it towards the centre of the city. Walking with a determined gait, but not walking like Martin Warburton. It was a slightly unnatural heavier step.

And not looking like Martin Warburton either. A woollen hat gave the impression of short hair. A beard and moustache. Glasses. Dressed in an old donkey jacket and shapeless twill trousers. A khaki knapsack slung across one shoulder. And this strange ponderous walk.

It was the figure whom Charles had seen the previous week on the steps down to the Mound. And it was Martin Warburton in disguise.

By eleven o'clock that evening Martin's identity games did not seem very important. One reason was that the afternoon's adventures had not led to anything. Charles had continued tailing his disguised quarry half-way across Edinburgh until Martin had disappeared inside the Scottish National Portrait Gallery in Queen Street. Rather than risk raising suspicions by a confrontation inside the building, the self-questioning sleuth had waited twenty minutes some way down the road. Then he had followed the donkey jacket back to Nicholson Street, missed a few more buses while the young man was reconverted into Martin Warburton and trailed behind that familiar figure back to Coates Gardens. All of which left Charles with sore feet and the feeling that if Martin wanted to do his Edinburgh sightseeing in disguise, that was his own affair. And that Charles Paris needed a drink.

Which accounted for the other reason why Martin's behaviour seemed unimportant. Charles was satisfyingly pissed.

After solitary refuelling at the pub, he had found Anna with the rest of the revue team at Coates Gardens. He had taken her out for a meal, to celebrate the opening of his show and keep her mind off the opening of hers. They went to the Casa Española in Rose Street and, since Anna was in a high state of nerves, he had to eat most of a large paella and drink all of the wine. A fate which he embraced with fortitude and which contributed to his present well-being.

It had also been encouraging to see Anna nervous. She was as jumpy as a kitten and it was the first time he had seen her lose her cool at all. Which made her seem more human. And even nicer.

Charles thought of her warmly as he sat in the Masonic Hail and fingered her key in his pocket. He had the drunkard's feeling of sexual omnicompetence and longed to be with her in the bed over the Lawnmarket. It would not be long. After the revue. He would go discreetly back to the flat and then, after the company giggles and congratulations, she would join him.

The lights dimmed. Not bad; the house was two-thirds full. He sat back in the right mood to enjoy *Brown Derby*—'Simply the Funniest Late-Night Revue on the Fringe.'

If it was, it did not say a lot for the others. Brown Derby was a hotch-potch of styles. Decrepit jokes that should have been allowed quiet deaths were resuscitated and paraded as new. Dull irrelevant puns were presented as wit. The ill-digested influence of television comedy made for uncomfortable production. Though there were flashes of humour, the show was heavy going, and never heavier than in its topical material. The comments on the British political scene showed neither insight nor understanding and the piece on the American presidency was frankly embarrassing. Ten days after President Nixon's resignation was not the time for a naive and tasteless parody of Adolf Hitler in his bunker (including some pretty tired jokes about golf).

And it was not a case of a brilliant new team struggling valiantly against unworthy material. The cast was not good. If acting at its most basic is making oneself heard and not bumping into the furniture, they failed as actors on two counts. They were rarely audible and kept tripping over chairs (especially during the extended blackouts between sketches, with the result that the lights usually came up on some puzzled youth lying full length on the upturned furniture). They had almost no talent.

Except for Anna. She was extraordinarily good and, given the lack of competition, dominated the show completely. Singing, dancing, flashing through a variety of accents and costumes, she was the only person onstage with any concept of pace or comedy. The direness of the material she had to perform only highlighted her skill.

Charles was amazed. Anna was a beautiful girl, but onstage she was animated by an extra charge that intensified her beauty. A real stage presence. He could feel the men in the audience responding to her. When she came on for her last number *A Bunny Girl's Lament* (a reasonable idea, marred by flabby lyrics), dressed in full Playboy Club kit, showing her long brown legs, the audience broke into spontaneous applause. It was not just that she looked sexy; she managed to incorporate an archness which distanced her from her material and was also extremely funny. Anna Duncan was that rare creature, a woman who can be funny onstage without sacrificing either her dignity or her sex appeal.

It was late when she tapped on the door of the Lawnmarket flat. The first night junketings must have gone on a bit. Perhaps the Brown Derby cast had been drowning their sorrows. Or perhaps they were celebrating, thinking that the enthusiastic final applause for Anna was meant for all of them.

She looked him straight in the eye. 'Well, what's your cool professional assessment?'

'Can you take it?'

'Yes.'

'Well, I'm afraid I thought the show was terrible. The only constructive suggestions that I can make are that your writers should go and sell vacuum cleaners, your male cast should join the Army and your director should become a monk.'

'Hmm.' The navy blue eyes kept their level gaze fixed on him. She knew there was more to come.

So he let it come. 'I would also like to say that you are one of the most talented young actresses I have ever seen.

She smiled and allowed herself a slight relaxation of relief. 'Charles, I asked for your cool professional assessment.'

'That was my cool professional assessment.'

'Hmm. Sounds biased.' But she was obviously delighted.

'Biased nothing! I may also happen to think you are the best screw in the world, but I do genuinely believe that you are exceptionally talented as an actress. Now come and make love.'

She grinned suddenly. 'You talked me into it.'

It was even better. They were completely together. He rolled apart from her and cradled the strong slender body in his arms. Her breasts were slack against his ribs, her breath soft on his shoulder. He recited gently into her hair.

' "O, happy times! O happy rhymes!
For ever ye're gone by!
Few now—if any—are the lays
Can make me smile or sigh." But you're one of them. You can make me smile and sigh.'

'I don't think Thomas Hood meant "lay" that way,' she murmured lazily.

'No, I don't think he did.'

'Incidentally, I liked your show. I think I was too uptight over dinner to mention it.'

'Thank you. Mutual admiration society.'

'Hmm.' There was a long pause. He wondered if she had gone to sleep. But she spoke again. 'Do you really think I'm good?'

'Yes.'

'Good enough to make it in the professional theatre?'

'Yes.'

'In spite of all you said about needing to be tough and calculating, and needing lots of help?'

'I'll help you, Anna.'

Soon she was asleep. Charles lay thinking. He could help her. Get her work, maybe. Even cast her in plays he was directing. He felt useful and wanted to give to her. To give a lot. Was it so ridiculous for a man of nearly forty-eight to go round with a girl in her early twenties? His experience could help her. He felt something for Anna that he had not felt for a long, long time. Possibly even love.

CHAPTER EIGHT

O William Dear! O William Dear!
My rest eternal ceases;
Alas! my everlasting peace
Is broken into pieces.
MARY'S GHOST

TUESDAY 20TH AUGUST was an unsettling day.

It started all right. Charles felt at one with Anna and at one with the world. She left the flat at about half-past nine. (Michael Vanderzee was champing at the bit to get his workshop sessions restarted after the lay-off caused by the revue's opening.) Charles had a leisurely breakfast of floury bacon rolls at the Poppin and then, as a token gesture to detective work, he went back to the Scottish National Portrait Gallery to see if he could work out the reason for Martin's visit.

The Gallery was well laid out and should have been interesting, but he was not in the mood for inspecting the faces of people he had never heard of. The whole business of searching for clues and motives was beginning to bore him.

He was gazing at a wax model of William III when he remembered the newspapers. The day after a first night (or at least a first lunch) and he had not yet checked to see if there were any notices. The rest of the portraits could wait. He hurried out under the disapproving glare of the large nosed-faces of Scotland's heritage.

There was a big newsagents on Princes Street. Rather than behaving logically and starting with just the *Guardian,* he went mad and bought every available daily. Which meant a great deal of waste paper; *So Much Comic* ... had so far failed to capture the interest of the nationals.

He stood in the street reading and dropped the inadequate newspapers one by one into a litter-bin. Nothing in the *Guardian*; so much for his conversation at the Fringe Reception. Charles realised he was being naively optimistic to expect to be noticed on the first day of the Festival, particularly with negative advertising.

Only the *Glasgow Herald* left. He opened it without hope, and on the review page, there it was.

So Much Comic, So Much Blood, Masonic Hall, Lauriston Place. Thomas Hood is now remembered, if at all, for about three poems which recur in anthologies. It was therefore a pleasant surprise to get a broader view of the poet's work from this enchanting lunch-time show. Charles Paris has compiled a skilful programme from poems and letters, which maintains a fine balance between humour and pathos without ever slipping into sentimentality. He performs the show with the clarity and understatement which are the hallmark of real talent. Do try to catch this. It's only on for the first week of the Festival and I guarantee more laughs than in most of the late-night revues.

Charles could not control an ebullient smile. What he held in his hands was a good old-fashioned rave.

Thanks to the review and a couple of large Bell's, he arrived at the Masonic Hall at a quarter to one in high spirits and totally devoid of nerves. He felt confident as he waited in the wings for the lights to go down.

From that point on the day deteriorated. For a start, the show did not go well. A second performance is always difficult, because of the feeling of anticlimax. And the size of the audience did not augur well for the circulation figures of the *Glasgow Herald*. There were about twenty, apparently under doctor's orders that laughter was injurious to health. Puns and wisecracks vanished into the spongy void of the hall.

And, to add to that, Frances was in the audience. The woman he had married, to whom he had given the unfortunate name of Frances Paris. He recognised her as soon as the show started from her loyal, and solitary, laughter. When he stopped to consider, it was quite logical that she should be in Edinburgh. She came up most summers to give a couple of her sixth formers a quick cultural immersion. There were two girls sitting with her, one black and one white.

Charles was very fond of Frances, but he wished she was not there. Since he had walked out on her twelve years before, they had remained friendly and he had even gone back to her from time to time. She made no demands on him, but her presence, just when he was feeling secure of his relationship with Anna, was embarrassing.

He tried not to be too off-hand when she came round backstage; he had no desire to hurt her. She looked harassed and was obviously having difficulty controlling her two charges outside the school context. The white girl was dumpy and called Candy; the black girl was splendidly tangible and called Jane; both regarded Edinburgh as an opportunity to be emancipated and *meet men*.

Husband and wife exchanged Edinburgh addresses and parted amicably with vague intentions to meet up again. The encounter brought a little cloud of depression into Charles' sunny outlook.

It was not until about half past six that the cloud started to look stormy. The Mary cast had been rehearsing all afternoon, but most of them were released for the evening, because Michael Vanderzee wanted to work on the Mary/Bothwell scenes for an hour until Anna had to go to the revue. After a cabbage supper at Coates Gardens, the actor playing John Knox (nicknamed 'Opportunity Knox' by the rest of the cast) suggested a trip to the pub. Darnley, Ruthven and Cardinal Beaton thought it was a good idea. So did the new David Rizzio, Sam Wasserman. Charles decided that he too would like a drink.

In the Haymarket pub, he discovered that student unrest manifests itself in reluctance to be first to the bar, so he bought the round. Without conscious engineering, he found himself alone at a table with Sam.

The author of *Mary, Queen of Sots* was a young American with fine blond hair, a woffly ginger moustache and black-rimmed round glasses. He wore a thick check lumberjack shirt, the inevitable blue jeans and yellow-laced brown boots. He had arrived in Edinburgh that day, just in time to hear the boom of the one o'clock gun fired from the Castle and become immediately embroiled in one of Michael Vanderzee's workshops.

'That was after two solid days' travelling. I got Mike's telegram from the Poste Restante in Brindisi, and I just dropped everything and came. I mean, my God. I really care about this show ...'

As soon as Sam started speaking, Charles realised why the tête-a-tête had been so easily arranged. Sam Wasserman was a bore, one of those instantly identifiable bores who has the ability to make the most interesting anecdote tedious, who can destroy by endless detail. But as well as qualifying as one of this international type, Sam also demonstrated that refinement of the quality which is peculiar to earnest young American academics. A glaze crept over Charles' eyes as the monologue continued.

'... In fact, *Mary, Queen of Sots* derives directly from the presentation techniques I developed in a show based on the Boston Tea Party for my Master's thesis at U.S.C. ...'

'U.S.C.?' Charles queried weakly.

'University of Southern California. I did my Master's there before coming to Derby. In Drama and Creative Writing. When I say my project was based on the Boston Tea Party, I mean of course loosely based. It concentrated on the ethnico-political problems of the American Indians. Viewed of course from a Socialist standpoint. The central allegorical symbol was the fact that the Boston Tea Party was perpetrated by white men disguised as Indians. White usurping the place of red. Like corpuscles. I used the analogy of leukaemia.'

Charles concentrated and tried to nudge the conversation in the direction he wanted. 'But you come to this show in rather macabre circumstances.'

The nudge was insufficient; Sam needed actual derailment. 'The macabre is very much an integral part of my writing. And the bizarre. Another image I developed in the U.S.C. show,' he steamrollered on, 'was the unusual ability of the Navajo Indians to walk along girders at great height as if they were on the ground. It's a different spatial concept. I related that to the myopic nature of the social services ...'

'Oh.' Charles found himself nodding like a toy dog in the back of a car. He made another supreme effort to manhandle Sam off his monologue. 'What I meant was that Willy Mariello was killed with a knife and that's why you're here actually taking part in *Mary, Queen of Sots*.'

For a moment it seemed to have worked. Sam looked straight at him and was silent for a long time before his continuation showed that Charles had failed. 'Well, of course, *Mary* is an entirely different proposition, in spite of certain similarities of technique. And in fact, from an allegorical point of view, it's very apt that the show should be born in an atmosphere of violence.

'You see, the basic allegory of *Mary, Queen of Sots* is the historical parallel. The original Mary's life was stained with blood. In my version, Mary, Queen of Scots represents Scotland and the natural wealth of her oil resources.'

'Oh yes,' Charles mouthed, wilting.

'Yes,' said Sam, as if it were a surprising affirmation. 'Now Mary's two husbands, Lord Darnley and the Earl of Bothwell, I take to represent England and the good old U.S. of A., the two countries who want to control her wealth. Queen Elizabeth, who ordains her execution, is the Arab states, who hold the real power in oil politics. Neat, huh?'

Charles, suffering from mental indigestion at the thought of this laboured allegory being expounded in Creative Writing, nodded feebly. But he saw a slight chance. 'Where does David Rizzio fit into this scenario?'

'David Rizzio represents the ecological lobby who might argue against the exploitation of oil resources in favour of a more medieval economic structure. For that reason, he gets killed off pretty early.' Sam chuckled at his own intellectual audacity.

It might be a tiny lever to shift the conversation and Charles seized it. 'But not killed off as early as Willy Mariello was.'

'No.'

Before Sam had time to relate the death to one of his allegories, Charles pressed on. 'You must have been pretty cut up to hear about Willy.'

'Shocked certainly. I mean one is always shocked to hear of a young person's death; it's a kind of suspension of continuity. And obviously there was a dramatic element in this particular event.'

'But you must have felt this more. To lose a friend ...'

'I didn't know Mariello that well.'

'I thought it was through you that Willy came to be in this show in the first place.'

'That's true, but only indirectly. I suppose the suggestion that he should do the music came from me—I put it up to the D.U.D.S. committee—but that was on the recommendation of someone else.'

'Who?'

'A girl involved in the society suggested it. I thought it was a good idea, because, you know, he was a professional musician and into rock music and I, well, I've got a kind of basic musical knowledge, but really my talent lies with *words*. And certainly the settings Mariello did for my lyrics were infinitely superior to anything I could have done. He changed the odd word here and there and I had to pull him up on that, but basically it was great. Besides, I believe very strongly in people working together under a kind of creative umbrella unit.'

'Why do you think the girl recommended Willy to you?' Charles asked slowly.

'Well, like I say, he was very good. And he'd been hanging round the Derby campus for a bit and apparently, after the group he was with split up, he wanted to try something different ...'

'And?'

'Well, I kind of got the impression that there might be a kind of thing going on between him and this girl. They both played it pretty close to the chest, but I sort of got this feeling that they wouldn't mind being involved in something together.'

'Oh,' said Charles, and then asked the question he had been putting off. 'Who was this girl?'

'A girl called Anna Duncan. She's now playing Mary in my show. I don't know if you know her.'

'Oh yes,' said Charles, 'I know her.'

That evening he met James Milne back at Coates Gardens and found the Laird eager for another Dr Watson session. Charles had suddenly become unwilling to pursue the business of detection, but he could not avoid a cosy chat over malt whisky.

Sherlock Holmes was always way ahead of Dr Watson in his deductions, but he rarely actually withheld information from his sidekick. Charles Paris did. There were things he wanted to be sure of, half-formed ideas that could not be shared until they had hardened into facts.

They talked mostly about Martin Warburton. Charles told of his long tracking expeditions and the discovery of Martin's second identity.

'But surely that makes him our number one suspect?'

'I suppose so.' Charles hoped he sounded convinced.

'It's fairly bizarre behaviour.'

'Yes, I agree. Certainly Martin is in a very strange mental state. He's all mixed up and he has some violent fantasies. I think he's probably suffering from overwork—you know, just taken finals—but that doesn't make him a murderer. His disguise may be for criminal purposes, or it may just be that he needs to escape into another identity.'

'Hmm. That sounds like psychological claptrap to me.'

'You don't subscribe to a psychological approach to crime?'

'I dare say it's very useful in certain cases, but I think it's often used to fog perfectly straightforward issues. Every action has some sort of motive, and I'm sure that Martin Warburton has a real motive for dressing up as someone else.'

'And you don't regard an inadequacy in his personality as a real motive?'

'I regard it as a formula of words. A motive is theft or blackmail, that sort of thing. Revenge even.'

'But Martin might take on another identity because there's something in his own that he can't come to terms with.'

'I don't really know what you're talking about.'

It was so easy for the Laird, insulated from life in his library, just as he had been insulated with his mother at Glenloan House and insulated in the staffroom at Kilbruce School. Because he had never encountered any unpleasant realities, he assumed they did not exist. Or if they did, they were simple things that could be cut up like sheets of paper, not made of material that frayed and tore and could never be properly divided.

'But, James, come off it. When we last spoke you were talking of an obsessional killer, someone for whom the Mary, Queen of Scots story had a macabre significance.'

'I didn't quite say that.'

'You were moving in that direction. And an obsessional killer hasn't got one of your nice neatly defined motives like theft or blackmail or revenge.

'Yes, he has. The very obsession is the motive. It's not a sane motive, but it's real to the murderer.'

'Therefore you've got to understand the psychology of the murderer.' Charles felt that it was a mild triumph.

'Yes, but the process is simple. Assume an inverted logic, and the motivation makes sense. You don't have to delve into inadequacies of personality and compensation and all that humbug.'

'I don't think we're going to agree on this point.' Charles was beginning to lose the little interest he had in their discussion. His mind was elsewhere, and not enjoying the trip. But he felt he should simulate some concern. 'So if Martin, say, is an obsessional killer, what do you reckon is the motive for his walking round the city of Edinburgh in disguise?'

'It must be something to do with the planning of his next crime.'

'I see.' Charles tried not to sound contemptuous. 'So what do you think we should do about it?'

'I think we should keep a close eye on him.'

'Yes, fine. I must go.' He rose with almost rude abruptness. 'I've got to ... um ... go.' He could not think of a polite excuse. He could not think of anything except the ordeal ahead of him. The ordeal of seeing Anna.

When it came, it was not really an ordeal. She arrived, flushed and excited after the revue. There had been a B.B.C. producer in the audience who (according to Brian Cassells, who had buttonholed the poor man departing and forced an opinion out of him) had liked Anna's performance. She was very giggly and charming as she described Brian's earnest relaying of the news and imagined his clumsy handling of the encounter. Charles warmed to her in spite of himself.

But he felt detached because of the tiny infection of suspicion inside him. He kept wanting to ask her about Willy, to know if they had had an affair and, by doing so, cauterise the wound before it spread to dangerous proportions.

But he could not do it. Not when she was so lovely. It would spoil everything.

They drank some port that Anna had bought and giggled into bed. And they made love. As good as ever, tender, synchronised, good. Except that Charles felt he was watching the two of them like a picture on the wall. Immediately after, they switched off the light and Anna, who was exhausted by *Mary* rehearsals and the revue, slipped easily into sleep.

Charles did not. He felt better for having seen her; his imagination could not run riot while she was actually there. But the doubt remained. He wanted to excise it, cut it out of his mind. The only way to do that was to ask her point-blank. But he knew he couldn't. Not to her face. He contemplated ringing her up, even ringing her up in a different identity, pretending to be a policeman or ... No, that was stupid.

He reasoned with himself. All right, so say she had been having an affair with Willy Mariello. So what? Charles had no particular claim on her and, anyway, he never worried about a woman's previous lovers; they didn't concern him. Jealousy over something that was over was pointless. And a lover couldn't be more over than Willy.

That was the worrying bit. Not that Anna had slept with the Scottish lout, but that he had been murdered. Again Charles reasoned with himself and calmed himself with thoughts that there might be no connection between the two facts. Indeed, they weren't both definitive facts yet. And they could be investigated.

Yes, a bit of investigation would put his mind at rest. He plumped up his pillow and turned over. Anna's breathing had a soporific rhythm. But he did not sleep.

CHAPTER NINE

There's some have specs to help their sight
Of objects dim and small
But Tim had *specks* within his eyes,
And could not see at all.
TIM TURPIN

THE FIRST PART of the investigation to set his mind at rest was another call on Jean Mariello.

She opened the door and leaned against it uninvitingly. 'What do you want? There's nothing more I can tell you.'

'Please, just a couple of questions. I think I'm on to something.'

'Big deal. Listen, Mr Paris. I'm very busy packing. The only thing that interests me about Willy is how soon I can forget he ever existed. And I don't want to play cops and robbers.'

'Please give me five minutes.'

'Oh ...' She hovered between shutting him out and letting him in. Then she drew back. 'Five minutes.' She looked at her watch.

Charles entered the hall and moved into the front room. Jean Mariello gained some of the satisfaction she would have got from slamming the door in his face by slamming it behind him. 'Right. Ask.'

Charles looked round. There were suitcases and cardboard boxes brimful of belongings. In the corner household rubbish and decorating rubble was swept into a neat pile. 'You're going?'

'Yes, the house is on the market. I'll never come back here.'

'You're leaving Edinburgh?'

'Yes. I'm moving in with a man in the folk group. In Newcastle.'

'Won't you miss it?'

'Edinburgh, yes. This house I hope I never see again.'

'It's a nice enough house.'

'Look, I never lived here. Willy only bought the place a few months ago. I've been on tour. The only times I ever saw it, it was covered with paint brushes or plaster dust or other evidence of Willy's latest ideas of home decor. He had the knack of converting every place we lived in into a pigsty. He'd suddenly get sick of his surroundings and want to change it all—smother everything with paint, take down a door ... and never finish the job. We got turned out of one flat after he decided to take down the partition between the bedroom and sitting-room. Living with Willy was not an experience that gave one a feeling of home. I feel nothing for this place.'

'Oh well, it's in reasonable condition. You should get a good price for it.'

She snorted contemptuously. 'The building society should get a good price for it.'

'Ah. Still, Willy ...'

She shook her head. 'Willy had no money. He spent everything he made with Puce, not that there was much left after all the agents and managers had taken their bites. There may be a few royalties to come, but they'll go on the bank loan he got for the deposit on this place and the arrears on the mortgage.'

'Arrears?'

'Yes. Willy got the mortgage on the basis of his earnings last year and the assumption that that level of income would continue. Then the band split up and he had virtually nothing. I don't think one single repayment has been made to the building society. Mind you,' she added bitterly, 'I only discover this when he's dead and I have to go through his mail.'

'So you're not exactly a rich widow?'

He got a scornful 'Huh' for that. 'Mr Paris, I can't believe that you came here to talk homes and gardens and mortgages. And if you didn't, your five minutes and my patience are running low.'

'I'm sorry. But just before I ask what I really came for, tell me why Willy bought this house.'

'It fitted the image of what he wanted to be. Saw himself as the great landowner, in his ancestral home in front of his blazing fire. The man of property, Willy, like all social upstarts, couldn't wait to be rich enough to be Conservative. The Socialist pose, the sub-hippy world of rock music—that meant nothing to him really. It was only a stage he had to go through. He wanted to be stinking rich with servants to do everything for him. Trouble was, he was a bloody awful business man and couldn't keep any money for more than five minutes.'

There was a pause. Jean Mariello looked at her watch and Charles realised he could not beat about the bush any longer. 'I really wanted to ask you about Willy's sex life.'

'Oh. Well, of recent years I'm not really an expert on that.'

'No.1 wanted to know about another woman.'

'I didn't take a great deal of interest in his other women either.'

Charles ignored the rebuffs and ploughed on. 'When he was in Derby—you know, he stayed after the band had played there—do you know if he had a girl then?'

'I assume so. I can't think he stayed for the scenery.'

'He never mentioned a girl?'

'No. We didn't discuss our private lives.' She glanced at her watch.

'Do you know if he had a girl around recently? You know, in the week before he died?'

She laughed incredulously. 'I wasn't here much of the time. You know that. What do you want me to do—say if I found stains on the sheets or hairs on the pillow?'

'Yes, if necessary.

That took her aback. She paused and then said in a softer voice. 'All right then, I would say, from the evidence of dirty laundry, that Willy did commit yet another desecration of our marriage bed between the Friday when I left and the Tuesday when he was killed.'

'Yes?'

She spoke slowly, as if unwillingly dredging her memory. 'Oh yes, he'd had someone. Hairs on the pillow, all the old familiar signs.'

'What colour hairs?' asked Charles breathlessly.

'Blonde.' She looked at her watch. 'Five minutes. Goodbye, Mr Paris. We won't meet again.'

The audience for *So Much Comic, So Much Blood* was larger and they saw a competent performance by Charles Paris. There were some laughs, although the show had no more animation than a slot-machine. As Charles' voice wove its way through Hood's tortuous puns, his mind was elsewhere.

After the show, he gathered his possessions together for a quick exit. There was something important that had to be done before three o'clock.

The women's wards in the Royal Infirmary off Lauriston Place are much the same as in other hospitals. The one Charles entered had the usual mixture of patients. An old lady stared ahead with liquid blue eyes, her long white hair radiating over the pillows. A plump bed-ridden blonde chattered to a morose husband. A homely housewife's face still registered surprise at being hospitalised and half-listened to the sympathy of a lady in a hat. Screens hid one bed and prompted unhealthy thoughts. A thin, thin woman with shiny skin lay as still as her pillow. And, in the corner bed, was a young girl with her plastered left leg raised on a pulley.

Visiting ended in ten minutes; no time to waste. 'Hello. Are you Lesley Petter?'

The girl looked up and acknowledged that she was. Brown hair, shrewd brown eyes, well-proportioned but unremarkable features. Hers was the sort of face that needed emotion to animate it; in repose it was ordinary.

Charles' approach had brought some light into her eyes. Anything was more interesting than the pile of magazines, thrillers and ragged-edged French novels.

'I'm Charles Paris.'

'Oh. You've taken over my lunch time show.'

'Yes. It's an ill wind.'

She laughed wryly. 'How's it going?'

'O.K.'

'It's about Thomas Hood, isn't it?'

'Yes.' He did not want to elaborate, though the girl's intelligent eyes indicated sensible opinions on the subject. 'I'm really here for a purpose.'

'Of course.' She was disappointed, but philosophical. 'Though I can't think what purpose of yours could involve me.'

'No. Maybe it doesn't involve you.' He tried to think of a way to phrase his questions. 'I ... there's ... I don't know, your group ... D.U.D.S., there's something strange going on there.'

'It must seem strange to an outsider coming in.'

'No, I expect that, as a middle-aged man with a bunch of whizz-kids. I mean strange in ... well, there's Willy Mariello's death.'

A shutter of caution flicked across her eyes. 'Yes. That was terrible.'

'And, of course, your accident.'

'Yes.' She seemed anxious to move the dialogue into a more flippant direction. 'Somebody must have whistled in the dressing-room or quoted Macbeth or had real flowers onstage or broken another of the show business taboos.'

Charles laughed. He was also relieved at the postponement of his questions. 'You know it all. Do you want to go into the theatre?'

'Yes, I did. But ... I don't know how good I am as an actress. Oh, I'd done bits all right, but the thing I'm really good at is dancing: She looked down the bed at the grotesque suspended limb.

'It'll heal all right.'

She patently did not believe his diagnosis, though she said 'Oh yes' as if there were no question.

Charles retreated to safer ground. 'Anyway, I'm sure you must be a good actress. I mean, you were playing Mary and doing the revue and ...'

'I got the parts, yes. I don't know how I'd have done them, whether I'd have got good press or ...'

'Well ...' He could not think of anything suitable. 'Anna got a very good notice for the revue.' It was just a statement, without malice or jealousy.

'Yes, I gather she did.' Charles instinctively and defensively made it sound as if he hardly knew who was being referred to.

'And I think she'll be better than I would have been in *Mary*.'

'Who knows.' He found himself blushing. 'As I said, it's an ill wind.'

'Yes.'

There was a slight pause. A bell sounded, muffled, from an adjacent ward and he blurted out his question. 'Lesley, did Willy Mariello push you down those steps?'

She looked at him in amazement and opened her mouth to reply. But she swallowed the instinctive answer and said in a controlled voice, 'No. No. Why should he?'

It was too controlled. Charles was not convinced. 'Are you sure he didn't? I heard a rumour to the contrary.'

'People shouldn't spread rumours,' she said sharply. There was confusion in her face. 'Listen, Willy's dead. My leg's broken, there's nothing can be done about that. Does it matter?'

'Yes, it does.'

'Well, I don't know. To be quite honest I don't.' She was floundering, an essentially nice girl unable to come to terms with something unpalatable. 'I was confused when it happened and I suppose I turned on the nearest person.

I ... I don't know. I mean, would Willy do something like that? What had he possibly got to gain from doing it?'

Charles restricted himself to answering the first question. 'Willy was capable of that sort of thing; he was a lout.'

She looked shocked at this speaking ill of the dead. A bell was rung loudly in the corridor outside the ward. There was a rustle of parcels and final messages from the other visitors. Lesley looked at Charles pleadingly. 'If he did it, I'm sure it was only high spirits, or horseplay or ...'

'You mean he did do it?'

'I don't know. I ...'

'Did he push you?'

'Yes, he did.'

Charles left her with assurances that he would try to visit again. And he meant to. Poor kid, stuck in hospital in a strange city where all her friends were too busy to remember her.

The brown eyes were troubled when he left. And it was not just loneliness. She had managed to convince herself since the accident that it really had been a mistake, an unfortunate overflow of youthful exuberance. Now she had been forced to destroy that illusion and her kind nature was finding it difficult to believe that anyone could be so evil.

Charles had no difficulty in believing it. To him the human capacity for evil suddenly seemed infinite.

CHAPTER TEN

Thus Pleasure oft eludes our grasp
Just when we think to grip her;
And hunting after Happiness,
We only hunt a slipper.
THE EPPING HUNT

TWO THINGS WERE clear. One, a confrontation with Anna was now unavoidable. And two, he could not face that confrontation himself. He still treasured a hope that everything would be all right, that there was an innocent explanation for the disturbing chain of events that his logic was joining up. And, if his suspicions proved unfounded, he did not want to let them blight his budding relationship with the girl. There was too much at risk. She was the first woman to touch his emotions for years.

He considered the possibilities of disguise, but rejected them. As an actor, he was capable of convincing physical transformations, and he had used disguise before to gain information. But then he had not been trying to hide his identity from people he knew; here he would be trying to fool a girl he had been sleeping with. No disguise would work at close quarters under those circumstances. Even the varied wardrobe of Edinburgh's many old clothes shops and the wizardry of film make-up with foam rubber padding, latex masks and coloured contact lenses would not stand close scrutiny.

He regretted that he could not use the excitement of dressing up to take his mind off the depressing tracks it was moving along. And, like most actors, he found it easier to perform difficult tasks in character than as himself. He visualised appearing to Anna in a total disguise, confirming her innocence by a few well-placed questions, then unmasking and making a joke of it.

But it was just a fantasy. He was being influenced by Martin Warburton and the strong attraction of channelling unpleasant parts of himself into another identity. The fact remained that dressing up would not work.

He contemplated interrogation by telephone. A disembodied voice could be convincingly disguised. But that introduced the problem of an identity. Who would Anna be likely to give information to in a telephone conversation? There were only two answers—someone she knew or a policeman. The first was out and Charles did not feel inclined to risk the second. On a previous occasion he had had it pointed out to him that impersonation of a policeman is a serious offence. And if Anna did have something criminal to hide, the last person she would tell about it was an investigating officer of the law. What was needed was an interrogator who had some other justifiable reason for meeting her and who could introduce relevant questions into the conversation with some pretence at casual enquiry.

Which meant an accomplice. It was Wednesday. Gerald Venables should be back from his weekend in Cannes. Charles rang his Grosvenor Street office from a call-box in the Royal Mile.

Gerald was back. 'How's the sleuth-work going, Charles?'

'I don't know really. I might be on to something.'

'Anything I can do?' There was immediate excitement in the voice. Gerald, who spent his entire life dealing with the peccadilloes of contract-breaking in his show-business legal firm, was fascinated by what he called 'real' crime. He had a Boy's Own Paper enthusiasm for anything shady. 'Wills to check out, blood samples to analyse, stool pigeons to third degree, hit-men to rub out? You name it, I'll do my best.'

Charles wished he could share this detective fiction relish for the case; it all seemed depressingly real to him. 'There is something you can do for me. I'm afraid it involves coming up to Edinburgh.'

'That's all right. One of my clients is in the Actors' Company *Tartuffe*. There's a film contract on the way for him. I could arrange to have to come up and discuss it.'

'Is it urgent?'

'No. But he's not to know that.'

'You mean he's going to be footing your bill?' Charles had to remonstrate on behalf of a fellow actor.

'Don't worry. You should see the money they're paying him for the movie. And he can set me against tax. Really I'm doing him a service.'

'Hmm.' There was never any point in arguing with Gerald on money, it was a subject he had made his own. 'Look, how soon do you think you can get up?'

'If Polly can fix me a flight, I'll be up this evening.' It was typical of Gerald that he would not insult his client's money by contemplating rail travel.

But it was good from Charles' point of view. 'Good. If you can make it, there's a revue I'd like you to see at eleven o'clock. Oh, and could you bring one of your little cassette recorders?'

'Conversation you want to tape?'

'That's it.'

'Secretly?'

'Exactly. Do you think you'll be able to make it tonight?'

'Do my best. Can I ring you back?'

'No, I'm in a call-box.'

'Ring me again in an hour and I'll tell you what gives.'

Charles had decided that he could not face another night with Anna until his suspicions had been exorcised. Then, he kept telling himself, then we can bounce back together again and it'll be even better. Maybe he'd stay in Edinburgh longer than his week. Maybe even away from Edinburgh they could ...

But not till this was sorted out.

He left the call-box and went down Cockburn Street to the Accommodation Bureau. He picked up his bag from Coates Gardens and by five o'clock was installed with Mrs Butt in the Aberdour Guest House in Dublin Street, booked for two nights.

He rang Gerald's office from Mrs Butt's pay-phone. Polly's efficiency had worked wonders and her boss was already in a taxi on the way to Heathrow. He would reach the Princes Street terminal in a coach from Edinburgh (Turnhouse) Airport at about ten.

The next move involved seeing Anna. After a couple of bracing whiskies in a Rose Street pub, he went back to Coates Gardens, where, as he anticipated, another cabbage dinner was drawing to its blancmangy end. He signalled to Anna, who left the table discreetly and met him in the empty hall.

The lie slipped out easily. 'Look, I'm sorry. Can't come tonight. An old friend called Alastair Newton came to see the show at lunch time. He's invited me to dinner at his place. It's some way outside Edinburgh, so he suggested I stay the night there and he'll give me a lift in in the morning. It's a bugger, but I can't really get out of it.'

Anna looked disappointed, which did not make the deception any easier. Then she grinned. 'I could do with some sleep, anyway.'

He grinned too. She was beautiful and the navy blue eyes looked so open and honest, he wished the script of the last few days could be rewritten and all the promptings of suspicion cut out. He felt confident that it would be all right. Probably they would even be able to laugh about it afterwards.

'But tomorrow...' he hazarded, 'be O.K. if I come round after the revue as per usual?'

'As per usual. Of course.' There was a lot of warmth in her voice. But she was still discreet and did not want them to be seen together. 'Better get back.'

As she turned to go, he took her hand and leant forward to kiss her. Their lips came together.

A creak on the stairs from the basement made Charles recoil guiltily. Anna as usual kept her cool and glanced towards the person who was staring at them. She looked back at Charles. 'See you then, then.' With unruffled poise she went back to the dining-room. Martin Warburton stood aside to let her pass, looked at Charles, gave one of his abrupt laughs and hurried out of the front door, slamming it behind him.

It didn't matter. Anna was the one who wanted to keep the affair quiet, and somebody was bound to twig sooner or later.

Charles remembered that he had left his toothbrush in the first-floor bathroom. On the landing he met James Milne hurrying angrily downstairs. 'Oh hello, Charles. I've spoken to them before about slamming that door. Not only is it bad for the actual door, it also disturbs the neighbours and I get complaints. Did you see who it was?'

'It was Martin Warburton.'

'Ah.' The Laird's tone changed from angry to confidential. 'Actually I wanted to talk to you about Martin Warburton. Come upstairs and have a drink.'

'Have to be quick. I've got to go out to dinner.' It was important to maintain the lie.

'Won't take long.'

More malt in the leather-bound library. The Laird stood by his marble mantlepiece to give drama to his pronouncement. 'Further to our discussion about Martin's disguise, I followed him this morning.'

'From here?'

'Yes, all the way to Nicholson Street as you described. I waited and he came out with the beard and what have you, and then I followed him again. Guess where he went this time?'

'Not a clue.' Charles found it difficult to get excited about Martin's bizarre doings. He had decided that they were irrelevant to the investigation.

'The Palace of Holyroodhouse,' said James Milne dramatically. 'Now why should he go to the National Portrait Gallery and Holyrood in disguise?'

'I don't know. Maybe he's embarrassed about being a tourist.'

This flippant answer was not well received by the Laird who thought that Martin was definitely the murderer. Charles wished he could share that simple faith; it would be a relief from the forbidding tangle of thoughts that filled his head. But he did not feel inclined to tell his confidant what he knew. It would be better to play along with this Martin theory.

James Milne elaborated. 'I think there's some strange tie-up in his mind. It's all connected with the Mary, Queen of Scots story, I'm sure. Rizzio was only the first of a sequence of murders of people close to that particular lady.'

'I'm a bit hazy about the details of her life. I just remember that she was very tall and when they executed her they lifted the head up and her wig came off.'

'What unusual details you pick on, Charles. I'm sure one of your psychologists would have something to say about the selective processes of your mind. But let me tell you, there's quite a lot more significant stuff in the unfortunate queen's story. I know it fairly well—as a schoolboy I spent one long wet holiday at Glenloan reading everything available on the subject. As you probably know, Mary was the daughter of James V of Scotland and Mary of Guise—'

Charles was in no mood for a schoolmaster's lecture. Worry made him less tolerant than usual. 'James, I'm sorry. I do have to go.

'Well, let me lend you a book on the subject. I won't give you one of my heavy schoolboy tomes. But there's Antonia Fraser's biography. Popular, but none the worse for that.' His mental catalogue took him straight to the right volume on the shelf.

Charles was eager to leave now. He reached out for the book with muttered thanks, but James Milne kept hold of it and said with a twinkle, 'If I might quote from the Great Unknown, Sir Walter Scott, "Please return this book; I find that though many of my friends are poor arithmeticians, they are nearly all good bookkeepers." Not a bad joke, considering the source.'

Charles smiled politely and managed to leave. He was in no mood for swapping literary references. He found a pub in Dundas Street where he was unlikely to meet any of the D.U.D.S. and whiled away the time till Gerald's arrival with the co-operation of Bell's Whisky, Ltd.

The solicitor arrived at the terminal immaculate in a Prince of Wales check three-piece suit. He carried an overnight bag that looked like a giant pigskin wallet and obviously contained the neatly pressed shirt and pyjamas of a travel advertisement. 'Hello, buddy. Wise me up on the gen.'

Charles cringed at the number of thrillers Gerald must have read, and suggested that they talk in a pub.

'Why not in the hotel bar? Then I can check in and dump the bag.'

'Which hotel?'

'The North British.' It had to be. Typical of Gerald. Polly had managed to fix it, and somehow the client would manage to pay for it.

Posh hotels were not Charles' usual style, but whisky's whisky anywhere. They sat in a dark corner and Gerald leant towards him conspiratorially. 'O.K. Spill the beans,' he whispered unsuitably.

'Listen, is your firm engaged in any big film productions at the moment?'

'We always are. Setting up a colossal Hudson movie out in Spain. Starts filming in September if we get the contracts sorted out.'

'Have you got a stake in it?'

'The firm has.' The answer was discreet. Gerald never admitted his dabbling in film production, though it was common knowledge that he doubled his already considerable income by judicious investment.

'So it wouldn't be too difficult for you to pose as a film producer?'

'It would hardly be a pose,' he replied smugly, and then realised that this was tantamount to an admission of financial interest in films. 'That is, I'm sure I could manage.'

'Right. What I want you to do is to go to a revue called *Brown Derby* at the Masonic Hall in Lauriston Place. It starts at eleven. Now there's a girl in that show called Anna Duncan. She's a good actress, but even if you don't think so, I want you to go round after the performance, introduce yourself as a film producer, say you'd like to talk to her about various ideas and would it be possible to meet for lunch tomorrow.' His treachery tasted foul on his tongue, but it was necessary. He had to know.

Gerald's eyes were sparkling with excitement. 'And tomorrow?'

'You take her out for lunch. I'll fill you in on what to ask her.'

'O.K. And that's the conversation you want recorded?'

Charles nodded. 'If it can be done.'

'No sweat.' The colloquialism again seemed to run counter to the Prince of Wales check. 'Do you think I should use a pseudonym?'

'Don't see why you shouldn't use your own name. If you don't mind.'

'No, of course not.' He was a little crestfallen at losing this dramatic element, but brightened again immediately. 'Is this girl Anna Duncan your Number One Suspect?'

Charles could not bring himself to answer that question, even in his own mind. 'I wouldn't say that. Just need some information from her, that's all. But it's difficult for me to get it myself.'

'Aren't you going to give me all the details of the case so far?'

'Tomorrow. There's no time now. You've got to get to the revue.'

They made a rendezvous for the next morning and Charles went back to the Aberdour Guest House. A half-bottle of Bell's did not go far enough and he spent a long miserable night with patches of sleep.

Daylight did not speed time up much, and Gerald's arrival at Dublin Street at half-past ten added another delay to the programme. Anna had a tight rehearsal schedule for Mary and would not have much of a break for lunch. The assignation had therefore become a dinner date, which extended the agony of waiting by eight hours. Apart from that, all had gone well the previous evening.

Charles then gave Gerald an edited version of the events surrounding Willy Mariello's death and indicated the information he required, with some hints as to what he considered the most effective way of doing it. He hoped that he was judging Anna's character right, and that she would respond in the way he anticipated. But all the time he felt increasingly despicable for the elaborate deception.

At one fifteen he did a performance of *So Much Comic, So Much Blood* without thinking about it. The audience had swelled to nearly eighty and seemed appreciative, but he hardly noticed. He even had a discussion with some dreary Welsh academic about whether Hood's work contained High Moral Seriousness, but only the reflexes of his mind were working. The rest of it was churning with guilt and anxiety.

In the afternoon he tried to pull himself together and entertain thoughts of the other possibilities of the case. What he should really do was to retrace Martin Warburton's visit to Holyrood and see if it prompted any ideas. But even as he thought of it, he knew he could not be bothered. All his thoughts centred on Anna.

As he meandered through the city, he met Frances sitting on a bench in Princes Street Gardens. She had managed to lose Candy and Jane on a sightseeing coach tour of Edinburgh, and was appreciating the break. Charles knew she could tell he was upset, but he refused to unburden himself to her. He knew she would be understanding and reassuring. That was her most infuriating quality, the way she understood him. It was an option he did not want to take. Guilt about Frances joined the mess of unpalatable thoughts in his head.

He hardly listened to what she said. Most of it was about Candy and Jane, the shows they had seen, how exhausting she was finding it, how she'd need a proper holiday after this, how she even thought of staying up in Scotland for a few days to recuperate after the girls had gone. Charles sat, half-hearing and restless. Suddenly he created an appointment and rose. They made vague plans to meet for dinner in the next couple of days when he was clearer about his movements, and he slouched off, not daring to look back at the pain in her eyes.

It was still a long time till the pubs. He approached a cinema, but when he got there changed his mind and continued his aimless perambulation.

At last five o'clock arrived. The whisky did not work. It was as if he had a heavy cold and was numb to its powers. Half past seven came and he thought painfully of Gerald and Anna meeting in the Cosmo Ristorante in North Castle Street. He felt powerless, as if he was watching an accident from too far away to prevent it.

It was nearly ten o'clock when Mrs Butt grudgingly admitted Gerald Venables to the Aberdour Guest House. He was flushed with excitement or wine and carrying a briefcase which contained his cassette recorder. 'Got a specially long tape. I don't know what the quality will be like. I could only put the case on the table and hope for the best.'

Charles was not in the mood for talking. 'Let's hear it.'

Gerald produced the recorder with all the pride of a schoolboy showing his Cycling Proficiency Certificate. He switched the machine on and wound the tape back. Then, as it started, he fiddled with the dials to get the optimum sound.

The quality was not bad. Gerald's own voice was distant because the microphone had been pointing away from him, but he filled in where his original questions were inaudible. There was a lot of interference from dishes being delivered and cutlery clattering, but most of Anna's answers were perfectly clear. Charles got a strange frisson from hearing her voice. It was not attraction exactly, and it was not guilt, but a mixture of emotions he had never encountered before.

The tape started with an amusing dialogue between Gerald and the waiter, who felt certain that Signor would prefer to put his case on the floor. This was followed by the detailed business of ordering. Gerald did not stint himself, and, encouraged by example, nor did Anna. The client in the Actors' Company was certainly going to pay for advice on his film contract.

After these preliminaries, Gerald started explaining why he was in Edinburgh. As a film producer, he was setting up a new movie, meeting some of the other backers, enjoying the Festival ... and possibly even doing a bit of casting.

Anna's reaction to this was non-committal and Charles began to feel redoubled guilt. If she were innocent what he and Gerald were doing was unforgivable. No aspiring actress should have her hopes manipulated in such a way.

Gerald's distant voice then started to outline the plot of the film he was setting up, according to their plan. He dropped a few suitably substantial names and spoke airily of the locations in Spain and Finland. In fact, it was not all untrue; it was based closely on the film that he really was setting up. The only bit that was complete fabrication was that one part remained uncast.

The part of a young girl, whose lover (a considerable film star was playing the part), a terrible lout, treats her cruelly and is stabbed to death halfway through the film. 'Of course,' purred the distant voice, 'that's going to be really difficult, that's the bit that'll call for real acting. The girl's got to express this complex emotion when he's killed. She knows he's a slob, but ... tricky. I think they should go for Diana Rigg or someone of that stature, but the director's got this crazy idea about finding an unknown. He must've read too many film magazines.'

The first course was delivered. Gerald expertly checked the wine and the sound of Niagara Falls showed that Anna's glass had been adjacent to the microphone. Nothing much happened for a while except for eating and pleasantries. The waiting was purgatory for Charles. Then Gerald's voice resumed its tactics. 'I'm sorry. All this talk of people being stabbed. I read in the papers about that terrible accident in your group. I shouldn't talk about it.'

'It's all right.' Anna's voice came through, very clear and controlled. But was the control genuine, or was there just a fraction too much, a hint of acting?

Gerald continued apologising. 'No, I'm sorry. Shouldn't have mentioned it. It's just that that kind of thing's such a shock. You must have all felt that. But think how much more terrible it must be if the person who dies is a lover or someone close. It doesn't bear thinking of.'

'No. It's terrible.' Charles tried to prise apart the layers of intonation to understand what she meant. Was she rising to the bait? He was torn between the desire to vindicate her and the intellectual satisfaction of having his psychological approach proved right.

Gerald's voice went on, more subdued than ever. 'That's the trouble. Every tragedy leaves someone behind. I suppose this ... Mariello, was that his name? ... I suppose he had a girl somewhere ... oh, it's ghastly ...'

'Yes, he had a girl ...' There was no question about the way she said the line. She played it subtly, wasting none of her talent for drama. But its meaning was undeniably clear. Charles Paris understood that meaning and understanding hurt like physical pain.

Gerald's recorded reactions were unnecessary, but the tape ploughed relentlessly on. 'You mean ... you?'

'Yes. Willy and I were lovers.' The voice was very soft, genuinely moving. There was a long intake of breath and a sob. 'Were ... lovers.'

'I'm so sorry. I had no idea. I wouldn't have raised the matter if I'd had an inkling ...' Gerald's lying protestations continued and Anna's tearful assurances that she had got over it mingled with them. She was playing the scene for all it was worth.

Her unfinished antipasta was taken away and she calmed down sufficiently for the gentle questioning to begin again. 'That must have been absolutely terrible for you. To be there and.., oh, I'm sorry. And it wasn't that you had been lovers? I mean, you still were right at the end?'

There was a long pause which Charles interpreted as Anna being thrown by the question and not knowing which way to jump. Eventually, the voice came back, quiet, but well projected. 'Yes, right at the end.'

'Good God.' The shock sounded genuine. Gerald had played his part well too. 'You've been thrown into almost exactly the same situation as the girl in this film. It's amazing.' Charles no longer felt guilty about the deceit. Guilt was being forced out of his mind by swelling anger as he listened to Gerald laying the next snare. 'Bereavement is an awful thing. It's so difficult to explain to anyone what you really feel, the true nature of your emotions.

'And of course it's even more complex for the girl in this film. Her lover is, as I said, not very loving. A real bastard, in fact, keeps doing crazy things, cruel things, criminal things. I think the character's overdrawn. No woman would stay with a man like that.'

'I don't know ...' Again just a simple remark infused with all the art her considerable talent could muster.

'But surely ...'

'What, all that not speaking ill of the dead business? Why should I worry? He's dead, and when he was alive, it was not his goodness I loved him for. I knew his faults. He could be cruel, oh yes, and evil.' She was warming to her performance. 'He'd do crazy things. Wicked things, and he'd say he'd done them for me.'

Gerald had only to grunt interest; she needed no prompting. 'I mean, take an example. Recently, he nearly killed someone for me. Yes.' She let the drama of it sink in. 'There was a girl in our group who would have been in the revue. She had the part I'm playing. And one day I must have said to Willy that I envied her. I don't mean I was jealous; she was a sweet girl, I liked her—but I must have said what a super part she had or something. And do you know what Willy did?'

'No,' said Gerald, on cue.

'He pushed her down some stone steps.'

'Good God.'

'Yes. It was so cruel. No, I'm sorry, you were wrong when you said I didn't know what it was like to love a bastard. I do, to my cost.'

Charles rose suddenly and switched off the machine.

'She really was very moving,' said Gerald. 'Very. And you reckon this is all significant information? *Cherchez la femme*, that's what they always say in detective stories. Frailty, thy name is woman. Is it Raymond Chandler who calls them frails?'

'Is there much more?' Charles snapped.

'A couple of courses. She did perk up a bit after that.'

'After she'd finished her audition.'

'Yes, I suppose you could say that.'

'I'll spool through and see if there's anything relevant.'

'No, I'll do it, Charles,' said Gerald hastily. 'Incredibly pretty girl, I must say. Sort of navy blue eyes. Do you know her well?'

'I thought I did.'

'Oh.' Understanding dawned. 'Oh.' Gerald busied himself spooling on and playing snatches of the tape. It was mostly general talk about films and the theatre. At one point Charles' ears pricked up.

'... had a lot of experience acting?' asked Gerald's voice.

'Yes. Only at university level, of course.'

'But you want to go into the professional theatre?'

'Oh yes. I've had one or two offers.'

'What sort of thing?'

'Well, I've been asked to play Hedda Gabler at the Haymarket, Leicester ...'

'The cow!' Charles shouted inadequately. With the unquestionable logic of the last piece of a jigsaw puzzle, his own role in the proceedings dropped into place. He was just a prop in the oldest theatrical scene of all—the casting couch.

Gerald spooled on and started playing another extract. 'Well, as you know, from last night,' said Anna's voice, 'the show comes down about twelve fifteen and— ' He stopped the tape abruptly.

'What was that?' asked Charles.

'Nothing.'

'Switch the damned thing on!' Gerald was powerless against this outburst of fury and sheepishly pressed the button. Anna's voice continued, 'We could meet after that if you like.'

'I'm at the North British down on Princes Street. If you meet me in the foyer, say twelve thirty ...' Gerald grinned weakly at the sound of his own voice.

'O.K. See you then.' Anna's tone was poisonously familiar.

Charles switched off the recorder and turned to his friend. 'Ah,' said Gerald, 'now don't get the wrong impression. What I thought was, if you were planning a confrontation with her, you d want to know where she was, and I thought that'd be handy. I mean, for heaven's sake, you didn't think that I'd ...? I mean, I'm a married man. Kate and I have a perfect relationship and ...'

He was still mumbling apologetically as Charles stormed out of the room.

At first he just walked furiously without noticing where he was going, but eventually calmed down enough to think of what his next step should be. It was midnight and now a confrontation with Anna was unavoidable. All the delicate feelings which had held him back before had been driven out by anger.

He knew her movements well by now. At twelve fifteen the show came down; he could meet her then at the Masonic Hall. Or he could go back to her flat to wait. But a perverse masochism made him reject both possibilities. At twenty past twelve he took up his position outside the North British Hotel. He leant against the corner of the building, at the top of the steps down to Waverley Station, and prayed she would not come. That at least would spare him the final twist of the knife in his wound. The idea of her deceiving him with Gerald was the most intolerable of all the foul thoughts he was suffering. He would wait till a quarter to one and then go up to the flat.

At twelve thirty she came. He heard the clack of heels and saw the familiar figure walking purposefully along Princes Street towards him. She was wearing the pale yellow shirt with fox-trotting dancers on it and the velvet trousers she had worn when he first took her out to dinner. That made it worse.

As she came close, he shrugged his back off the wall and stepped forward to face her. The pain was too intense for him to find words. He just stood there, rocking on his heels.

Anna did a slight take on seeing him, but when she spoke, her voice was even. 'Charles. Hello. I thought we'd arranged to meet up at the flat.'

He managed to grunt out, 'Yes'.

'It's just as well I've seen you actually, because I won't be there till later. I've got to meet someone in the North British.'

He almost felt respect for the directness of her explanation until the lie followed. 'It's an aunt of mine who's up in Edinburgh very briefly.'

'You're visiting your aunt at twelve thirty a.m.?'

'Yes. I've been rehearsing all day, so there hasn't been another opportunity. I'll get back to the flat as soon as I can.' She smiled. It was the same smile, the one he had warmed to all week. He realised suddenly that Anna was a perfectly tuned machine. She had all the charm and skills of a human being and knew how to use them like a human being, but inside, controlling everything, was the cold computer of selfishness. Sex, emotions, other people were nothing but programmes to be fed in to produce correct results quickly. Charles knew that he could never again believe anything she said. She was not governed by ordinary principles of truth, but by the morality of advantage.

'You're lying,' he said sharply. 'You're going to the North British to see Gerald Venables. You're going to see him because you think he's a big film producer and can help your career. In the same way that you slept with me because I direct plays, and with Willy Mariello because he was a pop star and might have useful contacts.' He wished the accusations carried some dignity rather than sounding clumsy.

A spark of anger came into the navy blue eyes when she started to speak, but it was quickly smothered. Her voice kept its level tone. 'I see. You set Gerald Venables up?'

'Yes.'

'And he isn't really a film producer? The part he was talking about doesn't exist?'

'He is a sort of occasional film producer. But no, the part doesn't exist.'

She flared. He had hit her where it hurt most, in the career. 'That was a dirty trick.'

For a moment he almost felt a twinge of guilt until he reminded himself of the situation. Anna carried such conviction in her acting. She went on. 'I suppose I should have realised that it was unwise to mix with old men. They only get clinging and jealous.'

That stung him. 'Good God! Do you think I set all this up as some elaborate charade to test your affection for me?' He almost shouted the words. A tweedy middle-aged couple who were passing turned curiously.

'I can't think of any other reason why you should do it.'

That sounded genuine, but then everything she said sounded genuine. Charles was not going to be stopped now. It was a time for truths. And accusations.

'I set Gerald up to get certain information from you.'

'Like what?'

'Like the fact that you and Willy Mariello were lovers.'

'So what? At least he was my age. You see, you are jealous. Jealous of someone who's dead. Anyway, Willy and I were finished. It happened while we were in Derby. We thought it would continue while we were up here, but it didn't.'

'You told Gerald it did, right up to Willy's death.'

'Oh, you've been spying carefully. That wasn't true. I just said that to sound more like the girl in the film.'

That again sounded plausible. The set-up may have been too heavy, and Anna may just have given any information that seemed likely to help her to the part. But Charles was not checked. 'Did Willy want the affair to end?'

'No. He got clinging too. Kept trying to win back my affections. But I'd outgrown him.'

'How did he try to win back your affections?'

'Silly things.'

'Like pushing Lesley Petter down the steps by the Castle?' That did shake her. There was a long pause before she replied. 'Yes. I suppose that was an attempt to get me back.'

'Did you suggest it?'

'No, I did not!' she snapped. 'I may have mentioned that I was understudying her, that the parts she was playing were good ones, but no ...'

Charles could imagine her 'mentioning' with all the innocence of Lady Macbeth. 'Listen, Anna, you're in serious trouble.'

'What on earth do you mean?'

'Murder is a serious business.'

'What? Are you accusing me of murder?'

'Yes.'

'You're off your head. Whom am I supposed to have murdered?'

'Willy.'

'Good God.' Now she really did look lost, stunned by the accusation. 'It never occurred to me that he was murdered. And how in heaven's name am I supposed to have done it? And why, for God's sake?'

'Why first. You incited Willy to nobble Lesley.'

'That's not true. It was his idea.'

'Quite! He did it, thinking that you'd be grateful and bounce back into his arms. It gave him a hold over you and you were forced to go back to him.'

'I didn't.'

'But then he became, as you say, clinging. He was a nuisance, he proved to be without influence in show business circles, but he was not easy to shake off because of your shared guilt over Lesley. So you killed him.'

She was staring at him now in frank amazement. 'And how am I supposed to have done the murder?'

He recapitulated all the business of the knives lying unattended at Coates Gardens before the killing. 'It was a long chance. The switch was likely to be discovered before the photo-call. But it might work. And it did.'

Anna gave a slight smile. 'But surely, if, as you say, Willy and I were back together, I would have been sleeping at his place and gone straight to the Hall for rehearsal. I wouldn't have gone to Coates Gardens at all during the relevant period.'

That was a blow to Charles' logic. But she had lied so much that she might be lying over that as well. 'You could have crept out in the night.'

'Oh yes, informed by some psychic source that the knives were lying there?'

'Yes,' he asserted, conviction wavering.

'Well, you're wrong. I wasn't sleeping with Willy. But I do have an alibi for the period. I spent that night in the Lawnmarket flat with someone else.'

'Who?'

'Its owner. A bloke called Lestor Wanewright. He was the reason I broke off with Willy. I met him out in Nice while I was on holiday. He has a villa there. We came back here together and he stayed until he had to return to London on business. That was on the morning of Willy's death. Lestor went straight to Waverley Station and I went straight to the Masonic Hall for rehearsal.'

'Why should I believe that?'

'You can check it. Lestor works for his father in London. Wanewright's, the merchant bank.'

'But you took up with me only two days later.'

She shrugged. 'Aren't you flattered?'

'No. You only wanted me for what I could do for you.'

'Yes. I quite liked you too.'

'Oh yes.' There was no danger of his believing anything she said now. Except about Lestor Wanewright. That rang true. If she just wanted an alibi, she had got it with Charles' own assumption that she had been with Willy (a flaw he had overlooked in his argument). The fact that she gave a checkable alibi with Lestor Wanewright meant it was true.

'Goodbye. Charles. I don't think we'll see a lot of each other now.

'No.'

She walked off, still brisk and purposeful. Lovely, but not human. Charles leant back against the North British Hotel wall and let the warring emotions inside him fight it out for themselves.

One thing he was sure of. Anna Duncan was a dishonest bitch and a whore. But she was not a murderer.

CHAPTER ELEVEN

Even the bright extremes of joy
Bring on conclusions of disgust,
Like the sweet blossoms of the May,
Whose fragrance ends in must.
ODE TO MELANCHOLY

WHEN THE LONG night ended and light returned, Edinburgh had lost its charm. The bubbling spirits with which Charles had arrived had been ebbing for days and the previous evening's events had finally flushed them away. Unsustained by hope and excitement, he felt tired and miserable. And above all, he felt stupid. He saw himself from the outside—a middle-aged man infatuated with a young girl, thinking she could halt the processes of time. He was a figure of fun from a Restoration comedy, the elderly dupe, no doubt dubbed with some unsubtle name like Sir Paltry Effort. The more he thought about the fantasies he'd had of himself and Anna, the way his mind had raced on, the more depressed he felt. Overnight his new lease of life had been replaced by an eviction order.

At about nine he rang Frances. He convinced himself he rang so early to catch her before she went out to the eleven o'clock concert of Mahler songs at Leith Town Hall; not because in his abject state he needed her understanding.

They fixed to meet for dinner, as if it were a casual arrangement. But she knew something had happened and he rang off curtly to stem the flow of sympathy down the phone. He was not ready for that yet.

Then there was Gerald to sort out. Charles did not want to lose a friend over some bloody woman at his age. He went to the North British and summoned the solicitor from a late breakfast.

Gerald came into the hotel foyer wiping his mouth and blushing vigorously. 'Charles, hello,' he said with manufactured bonhomie.

'Hello. I came to thank you for last night.'

'Oh ... um. It was ... er ... nothing. I hope I got you the information you wanted.'

'Yes. It proved I was on the wrong track.'

'Oh, I'm sorry.'

'Mind you, that was a relief in a way.'

'Ah.' Gerald looked at him in silence, uncertainly, as if he half-expected to be punched on the nose. 'Look, old man, about the ... er ... other business ...'

'Forgotten it already.'

'Oh good. But, you know, it's the sort of thing that ... er ... well, it was just a joke, but it's the sort of thing ... I mean, the girl did seem to be virtually offering herself ...'

'I know.'

'Yes. But it's sort of ... not the sort of thing to make jokes about. I mean, say you were at home ... with us. Kate's got a ... you know ... a rather limited sense of humour in some ways.

'It'll never be mentioned.'

'Oh good.' Relief flooded into Gerald and he seemed to swell to fill his expensive suit. 'Care for a cup of coffee?'

When they were seated with their cups, the solicitor started asking about the case.

'I don't know,' Charles replied despondently. 'I was working on the theory that Anna had done it.'

'Good God. I thought you just wanted information out of her.'

'Otherwise you wouldn't have been so anxious to lure her back to your bed?'

'Charles! You said you wouldn't mention it.'

'I'm sorry.'

'So who's the next suspect? Who are you going to turn the heat on now?'

'God knows. I can't think beyond Anna. All my other lines of enquiry are confused. Anyway, my last performance is tomorrow. Now all I want to do is get the hell out of Edinburgh.'

'But what about the case?'

'I don't even know if there is a case. Suppose Willy Mariello died by an accident? That's what everyone else thinks. Why shouldn't they be right?'

'But Charles, your instinct—'

'Bugger my instinct. Look, even if it wasn't an accident, who cares? No one's mourned Willy much. One slob less, what does it matter if he was murdered? It's certainly not my business.'

'You mustn't take that attitude.'

'Why not?' he snapped. 'I'm an actor, not a detective. If I were a detective, I'd have been sacked years ago for incompetence. There are some things one can do and some one can't. It's just a question of recognising that fact before you make a fool of yourself. And I now know that I have as much aptitude for detective work as a eunuch has for rape.'

'So you don't think you'll pursue the case?'

'No.'

'Hmm. I'm getting a plane back shortly.'

'Yes. Well, thanks for your help.'

'It was nothing.'

'See you in London, Gerald.'

'And if you change your mind, and do go on investigating, let me know how you get on.

'Sure. Cheerio.' Charles slouched out of the hotel.

Apparently he did a reasonable performance of *So Much Comic, So Much Blood* to an audience of one hundred and twenty at lunch time. He did not really notice it. All he was thinking was how soon he could get out of Edinburgh.

That involved tying up professional loose ends. Which meant a call on Brian Cassells at Coates Gardens. Charles hoped that the *Mary* cast were rehearsing at the Masonic Hall; he did not want to meet Anna Duncan. Ever again.

His hope proved justified. The house was unusually quiet. The Company Manager was in his office, as usual pressing Letraset on to sheets of paper. 'Thought we might need a bit of puff for *Who Now?* Opens on Monday in your lunch time slot. Got to keep ahead in the publicity game or no one knows a show's on.'

'No, they don't,' said Charles pointedly, thinking of the publicity his show had got.

But irony was wasted on Brian. 'I've changed "A Disturbing New Play" to "A Macabre and Bloody Exposition of Violence by Martin Warburton". Pity I have to hint; I'd like to add "...who stabbed Willy Mariello". That'd really bring the audience in. Still, the police are probably still investigating, so we may get some more publicity.'

Charles searched the Company Manager's face for a trace of humour after this pronouncement, but it was not there. ' "Stabbed to death" rather implies a positive act, like murder, Brian. Doesn't fit in with an accident.'

It was a half-hearted attempt to see if the average member of D.U.D.S. harboured any suspicions about Willy's death. Brian obviously did not. 'Oh, that's just semantics. You mustn't get too hung up on meaning, you've got to think of the impact of words.'

'Hmm. Are you going into advertising?'

'I might think of it if I don't get this Civil Service job I'm up for.'

'You'd be very good at it.'

'Thank you.' Again totally unaware that a remark could be taken two ways.

'Actually I wanted to talk about money.' They arranged that Brian would send a cheque to London when the miserable fifty per cent of the miserable box office was worked out. Charles was not expecting much; in fact he could work out exactly how much by simple arithmetic; but he preferred not to. That always left the possibility of a pleasant surprise.

But he knew the payment would not begin to cover his expenses. It hurt to think how much lavish meals for Anna figured on those expenses. The classic fall-guy, the duped sugar-daddy—he felt a wave of self-distaste.

Have to make some more money somehow. Maybe the B.B.C. P.A.s' strike would soon be over and the telly series would happen. It was the first time he had thought outside Edinburgh since he arrived. A line echoed in his mind. 'There is a world elsewhere.' Was it Shakespeare? He could not recall. But it was melancholy and calming.

He hoped to leave Coates Gardens without meeting James Milne, but failed. So he was left with the unattractive prospect of Sherlock Holmes telling Dr Watson that he had given up investigation.

'Anything new?' the Laird hissed eagerly as they met in the hall. He swivelled his white head left and right in an elaborate precaution against eavesdroppers. Charles was getting sick of enthusiastic amateur sleuths—Gerald with his inept slang, James Milne with his melodramatic whispering.

'No, not a lot.' He tried unsuccessfully to make it sound as if that exhausted the subject.

'You haven't been following Martin again?'

'No, I've ... er ... no.' He had not mentioned any suspicions of Anna to his confidant and it seemed pointless to start just as the Dr Watson role was becoming redundant.

'But you must have been following some line of investigation the last couple of days.'

'Yes, I have, but I ... don't really want to talk about it.'

'Something personal?'

'Yes, I found it involved someone I knew well and ...' He hoped that might edge the conversation in another direction. The Laird's old-fashioned values would surely respect a chap's discretion about his private affairs. I mean, dash it all, when there's a lady in the case ...

But James Milne's curiosity was stronger than his gentlemanly outlook. 'And where are those suspicions leading you?' he asked with some excitement.

'Nowhere. Well, I mean they've led anywhere they're going to lead. And produced nothing. I just want to forget about the case now.'

The Laird looked at him quizzically. 'But you were so keen on it before. I mean, it was your idea that there was anything to investigate. And now you've managed to persuade me there's something in it. You can't just drop it.'

'I can. I have.'

'But don't you think we ought to do some more investigation of Martin's movements and behaviour?'

'Sorry. I've lost interest.'

'Oh. And you're leaving tomorrow?'

'Yes.'

'Ah. Well, I'd better return your Hood.' James Milne ignored Charles' remonstrance that it didn't matter, found the volume immediately and handed it over.

'Enjoy it?' Charles saw a way out of the awkwardness into the impersonal area of literary criticism.

'Yes,' came the morose reply.

'Amazing feeling for words.'

'Yes.'

'There's a lot of discussion as to whether it's a purely comic gift. I mean, in some cases a pun does reinforce a serious statement. You know, like that line from *A Friendly Address to Mrs Fry*. "But I don't like your *Newgatory* teaching." '

'Yes.' The Laird responded in a predictably brighter tone.

Charles pressed home his advantage. 'And some of the wholly serious poems aren't bad. Did you try *The Plea of the Midsummer Fairies*?'

'Yes. Sub-Keats, I thought.'

'Right. But *The Song of the Shirt's* O.K. if hackneyed, and *The Bridge of Sighs* is quite moving. And did you read *The Dream of Eugene Aram*?'

'No,' said the Laird, 'I've never heard of it,' and relapsed into gloom. Charles felt churlish for his proposed defection. He needed to soften the blow of his departure. 'Look, let's meet for a farewell drink in the morning. At the pub by the Masonic Hall. See you there about eleven. Before my last lunch time. O.K.?'

The Laird nodded, but he looked downcast and Charles felt that he had let the man down.

Dinner with Frances was refreshing in that, unlike Gerald Venables and James Milne, she did not encourage him to continue with his detective work. In fact, when he gave her a selective résumé of his investigations, she positively discouraged him. Murder, in her view, was an extremely unpleasant business, and when inadvertently it did occur, it belonged by right to the police and not to untrained amateurs. It could be very dangerous. Although they were separated, Frances retained a maternal protective instinct for her husband. This regularly manifested itself in warm socks and sensible Marks and Spencer shirts for birthdays and Christmas.

They ate in Henderson's Salad Bar, a bit of a comedown from the places where he had squired Anna, but excellent food and better value. Charles began to relax. As he did, the exhaustion that had been stalking him all day caught up. He nearly nodded asleep into his lentil stew. Frances reached out and held his hand. 'You're dead.'

'Mmm.'

'Been overdoing it.'

'I suppose so.

'Early night.'

'Good idea.'

'I'm pretty exhausted too. Those two girls have been leading me such a dance. Still, thank God they get a train back tomorrow. It can't come soon enough. I think I might stay in Scotland for a bit.'

'Don't you have to chaperone them home?'

'No. Put the two little horrors on the London train and from that moment they're on their own.'

Charles smiled weakly at the incipient relief in her voice. 'And then you'll have a few days' holiday?'

'Yes. Bliss. Before term starts.' She hesitated. 'I don't suppose ...'

'What?'

'I don't suppose you'd fancy a few days' holiday. If we could book up somewhere ...'

It was strange to see her blushing. Blushing for propositioning her own husband. He felt the familiar ridge of the kitchen-knife scar across her thumb. His eyelids were heavy with sleep as he replied. 'I've heard worse ideas.'

There was quite a party at the pub before Charles' performance on the Saturday. A lot of the D.U.D.S. who had never said hello to him decided they had an obligation to say goodbye, and any money that the show might have made was anticipated in large rounds of drinks for people he did not know.

But Charles didn't mind. A night's sleep had done wonders. Alcohol and company meant that he only felt the occasional twinge from thoughts of Anna or Willy's death. Recovery from both obsessions would take time, but it was possible.

Frances was there, celebrating the departure of a King's Cross train from Waverley Station. And, by a stroke of incredible luck, they had arranged a holiday. Stella Galpin-Lord, who was in the party, justified the expense of the vodka and Campari she ordered by fixing them up in a hotel at Clachenmore on Loch Fyne. In fact she had been booked in for a week herself, but had just heard that the acting friend who was meant to join her had got a part in a film and had to cancel. The need for a consoling drink after this disappointment explained her presence in the pub. But her loss was Charles' and Frances' gain. A phone call clinched the change of booking. Charles was so excited about the speed with which it happened that he did not have time to question the wisdom of going on holiday with his ex-wife.

He felt affectionate towards all of the Derby crowd and, now that his departure was imminent, even indulged himself in a slight regret that it was over. Sam Wasserman was talking earnestly (and no doubt allegorically) to Pam Northcliffe. She had her back to Charles, but he could imagine the glaze of boredom slowly covering her eyes. Frances was gamely trying to conduct a conversation with the lighting man Plug (who'd got to do the sodding cue sheets for *Who Now?*, but who'd heard there was a free drink going). Martin Warburton was gesticulating wildly as he expounded one of his theories to Stella Galpin-Lord. They all seemed animated and cheerful except for James Milne who sat slightly apart with a half of 'heavy'.

Since the Laird was the first person he'd invited to the get-together, Charles felt he should not neglect him and sat down at the same table with his pint.

'Are you really giving the investigation up, Charles?'

He found it difficult to meet the older man's eyes. 'Yes.'

'I'm sure we ought not to. I mean, if something else happens, we'll feel terrible.'

'What else can happen?'

'Another crime.'

'Why?'

'I don't know. It's just ...' The Laird leant closer and whispered. 'I am convinced there's something odd about Martin's behaviour. We ought to find out more. We can't just leave it.'

This was unsettling. Deep down Charles agreed. But he had managed to push that agreement so far down that it hardly troubled him. He would have to make some concession to his conscience. 'What, you mean investigate the flat in Nicholson Street?'

'Something like that, Charles.'

'How about Holyrood?' With sudden inspiration. 'We'll go this afternoon.' The Laird looked relieved that something was being done and Charles felt it was a satisfactory solution. It gave the illusion of interest on his part and was a pleasant way of spending an afternoon. A visit to Edinburgh's famous palace would be a fitting farewell to the city.

'Drink?' The word was spoken sharply close behind Charles. He turned to see Martin Warburton holding a couple of empty glasses. 'I'm getting a round.'

Charles looked at his watch. 'Better not have any more. I'll want a pee in the middle of the show.'

James Milne also refused politely, but Martin did not turn away immediately. He stood still for a moment and said, almost to himself, 'Holyrood.'

'Yes,' said Charles. 'We're going down there this afternoon.' And then, as an explanatory probe, 'Have you ever been there?'

'Oh no,' Martin replied slowly. 'No, I haven't.'

The last performance of *So Much Comic, So Much Blood* went very well; it justified the *Glasgow Herald*'s enthusiasm. It was possibly helped by the alcoholic relaxation of its presenter, and certainly by the vigorous reactions of an alcoholic contingent in the audience. Charles was left with the melancholy emptiness that follows a good show, and an urgent awareness that the pubs closed at two thirty.

A few more drinks and he parted with the D.U.D.S. in a haze of goodwill. Frances went off to scour Edinburgh for gumboots which she assured Charles would be essential for the West Coast of Scotland. James Milne waited for him outside the Masonic Hall while he slipped in to have another pee and pick up his belongings.

The stage crew were already in, setting up the scenery for a lighting rehearsal of *Who Now?* Martin Warburton, as writer, was deep in conference with Plug, the electrician. Charles picked up the holdall that he had left onstage. 'Did all the slides go in, Plug?'

'Sure.'

'Cheerio then.'

'Bye.' Charles swung the holdall cheerfully on to his shoulder.

'Goodbye, Charles Paris,' said Martin Warburton.

The guide at the Palace of Holyroodhouse was a jovial gentleman with a green cap, green jacket and tartan trews. The effort of showing a mixed bag of international tourists round the old building ten times a day (or even more during the Festival) had not blunted his good humour, though it did give a staged quality to some of his jokes.

Charles let it all wash pleasantly over him. He even felt confident that the alcohol would not wear off until the pubs opened again at five. After the stresses of recent days he owed himself a real Saturday night blinder.

Meanwhile information about Scotland's history and art poured out from the guide. Charles II rebuilt the palace ... George IV wanted to be painted wearing a kilt ... you can tell the carving's by Grinling Gibbons because of his signature of five peas in a pod ... the present Queen holds garden parties in the gardens here ... the harpsichord by Johann Rucker of Antwerp is still in working order ... the portraits of fictitious kings of Scotland are by Jacob de Wet ... and so on and so on.

Occasionally Charles would be shaken from his reverie by a hiss from the Laird. 'Do you think that might be significant?'

'What?'

'Sixteenth-century tapestry of the Battle of the Centaurs.'

'Why?'

'Well, it's violent, isn't it? And Martin's very obsessed with violence.'

Charles would feign interest for a moment and then mentally doze off again. With the confidence of alcohol, he knew that so far as he was concerned the Mariello case was over. The relief of that decision gave him the freedom to look at the case objectively. He saw the long trail of his mistaken suspicions dragging on like a Whitehall farce, with him as the overacting protagonist, always opening the wrong door after the crooks had fled, after the pretty girl had put her clothes back on again, or after the vicar's trousers had been irrevocably lost.

And, without the pressure of having to think about it, a new logic crept into the case. First, the greatest likelihood was that Willy Mariello had died accidentally. And if he had not, then the only person with whom he was directly connected was James Milne, through the house sale. Perhaps there had been some motive there; perhaps even (taking a cue from Michael Vanderzee's insinuation) there had been a homosexual liaison between Willy and the Laird. Perhaps, perhaps. Motivations and suspicions took on the expendable and detached fascination of a crossword. Perhaps one day someone would make the effort to find out the facts. Preferably a policeman. Certainly it would not be Charles Paris. Detective work, he reflected, was a slow and unrewarding business, like reading Dickens for the dirty bits. Not for him. He followed the guide through a film of alcohol.

The oldest parts of Holyroodhouse, in the James IV Tower, are kept till last in the guided tour. These are the apartments of Mary, Queen of Scots and her second husband, Lord Darnley, and it is impossible to enter them without a sense of excitement.

Darnley's bedroom is downstairs and there is a little staircase that leads up to the Queen's room. Next door is the supper room where David Rizzio, her Italian secretary, musician and companion, was murdered by Darnley, Patrick Lord Ruthven and other disaffected noblemen. On his body there were found between fifty and sixty dagger-wounds.

'And there,' said the guide dramatically, 'is the very spot where it happened.' Then, with a quick switch into the practised joke, 'There's no use looking for bloodstains. There's only a brass plaque there and it's a different floor. But everything else is just as it was.'

'Everything?' Charles queried facetiously. 'Is it the same clock?'

'What clock?' asked the guide, confused for the first time on the tour.

'Well, the clock ...' Charles turned slowly round the room. There was no clock. 'Then what's the ticking?'

He looked slowly down at his holdall, lowered it to the floor and, with great care, unzipped it. The other tourists watched with frozen fascination.

There was no question. He had seen enough newspaper pictures from Northern Ireland to recognise the untidy arrangement of a clock face and wires.

So had the rest of the party. In the panic and screams that followed as they all rushed for the narrow spiral staircase, he could hear the Laird's voice, high with fear. 'A bomb! He could have killed us all! A bomb!'

CHAPTER TWELVE

The dog leapt up, but gave no yell,
The wire was pulled, but woke no bell,
The ghastly knocker rose and fell,
    But caused no riot;
The ways of death, we all know well,
    Are very quiet.

JACK HALL

BOMBS IN PUBLIC places are police matters, and cannot be well investigated by half-hearted amateurs. Charles found it a great relief when the blue uniforms moved in. He felt he could have gone on snooping in the dark for ever; the police had the advantage that investigation was their business. And they got on with it very efficiently.

An Army bomb disposal expert saved Queen Mary's historic apartments from destruction. As Charles sat waiting to be interviewed at the Edinburgh City Police Headquarters in Fettes Avenue, he wondered what would have happened if the device had gone off. The wholesale destruction of twenty-odd tourists and a guide might have put Rizzio's murder in the shade. And it would have needed a hell of a big brass plaque.

He had assumed that the bomb had not reached its detonation time when it was discovered and received an ugly shock when the findings of the bomb disposal expert were communicated to him. It had been set for twenty minutes earlier. The minute hand on the clock had reached its brass contact screw fixed in the clock face; it was only luck that had prevented it going off. The device's construction was amateur and the motion of Charles' holdall appeared to have broken one of the inadequately soldered joints in the wiring. But for the cavalier, drunken way he had manhandled the bag, the bomb would have worked.

He found its failure small comfort. The intention was no less destructive. The bomb was an unsophisticated weed-killer and acid device, which might not have been too devastating in the open, but in an enclosed space like the supper room ... He didn't like to think about it. Particularly as he had been carrying the thing. Even in the unlikely event of his surviving the blast, he would have been typecast for the rest of his life as Long John Silver or Toulouse Lautrec.

When he talked to the police, he was amazed at how much they knew. The assumption that they had written off Willy Mariello's death as an accident and were just waiting for this to be officially confirmed in the Procurator-Fiscal's report proved to be naive. Ever since the stabbing they had been investigating and keeping an eye on the D.U.D.S. They knew about Martin's dual identity and had been following his movements with particular interest.

It all made Charles feel crassly amateur. Not only because his own stumbling investigations seemed so pathetic, but also because it showed he had an outdated image of the police as thick village constables whose only function was to have rings run round them by the brilliant amateur sleuth. That was the way it was in most of the plays he had ever been in, and plays were about his closest contact with the police. What he had taken in this case to be their lethargic inactivity had been discreet investigation, gathering together sufficient evidence for an arrest.

And they reckoned the bomb was probably enough evidence. Certainly enough to justify a search of the flat in Nicholson Road.

There was no question in the police's mind of investigating anyone but Martin. Like the Laird, they reckoned that his behaviour was suspicious and, unlike Charles, they were not held up by vague woolly liberal notions that the boy was misunderstood and must have other explanations for his actions. Charles felt as he had in Oxford when, after an elaborate midnight climb back into college over walls, across roofs, down drainpipes and through dons' bedrooms, he had discovered that the main gate was open.

He also felt rather out of it, though at the centre of operations. At least on his own abortive investigations he could maintain the illusion of doing something important in his own right. Here at the police headquarters he was just a source of information, politely asked to wait, filed for reference when necessary. They were interested in what he knew, not what he thought.

So rather than stage-managing dramatic denouements himself, he found out at second hand what had happened. The search at Nicholson Street had provided plenty of evidence to convict Martin. It was a positive bomb factory, chemicals and components scattered around on tables without any attempt at concealment. There was also an unpleasant collection of knives and other weapons, including a meat cleaver. The boy's fantasies of violence took a disturbingly tangible form.

What the police did not find at the flat was Martin Warburton himself. And, though they found a bottle of spirit gum substitute and a brush, there was no sign of his false beard or glasses. So it was possible that he was somewhere in Edinburgh in his disguise.

They tried the obvious places, which were Coates Gardens and the Masonic Hall, but he was not at either. Apparently he had left the theatre after a disagreement with Plug over some lighting effect. That was shortly before three, and nobody had seen him since.

The case had changed from a whodunnit to a manhunt.

Charles was thanked courteously for his co-operation by the police and asked to keep them informed of where he would be contactable if he left Edinburgh.

It was then about seven o'clock. Frances, he knew, had got a ticket for the Scottish Opera's *Alceste* at the King's Theatre. Denied her calming therapy for his shattered nerves, he saw no reason to change his plans of earlier in the day, and got drunk.

*

At the Police Headquarters James Milne and Charles had arranged to meet for coffee in the flat the next morning to talk through what had happened. Charles had found the truth of Dr Johnson's dictum about the proximity of death concentrating a man's mind wonderfully, and regained his flagging interest in the case.

About eleven on the Sunday he arrived at Coates Gardens. 'Do you mind if I have something a bit stronger than coffee?'

'Still in a state of shock? So am I.'

'Well, mine's only an indirect state of shock, James. I was so shocked yesterday that I had to have a great deal to drink for medical reasons. That's why I need something stronger now. Hair of the dog.'

The Laird chuckled and reached for the malt whisky bottle. 'Well,' he said when they were sitting and the first gulp was irrigating Charles' dehydrated head, 'it seems that I was on the right track.'

'About Martin?'

'Yes.'

'Hmm. Of course, I knew there was something wrong with him right from the start. Now I come to think of it, the first night I was here, I heard someone crying in the bathroom—I'm sure it was him. Obviously in the throes of a nervous breakdown. A schizoid condition, aggravated by overwork for his finals.'

'All work and no play ...'

'Makes Jack a nutter, yes.'

' "Much study had made him very lean..." '

' "And pale and leaden-eyed." ' Charles completed the quotation automatically without thinking. Martin's case seemed more relevant than literary games. 'What surprised me was that all his fantasies manifested themselves in a real way. Usually with that type all the action's in their minds.'

'Not, it seems, in this case, Charles.'

'No.' He paused for a moment, ruefully. 'Poor kid. He was so mixed up. He seemed so much the obvious suspect that I never really considered him.' He laughed. 'I must get a less subjective view of criminals.'

'What do you mean?'

'Look at me—on this case I miss out the obvious solution just because Martin's someone I like and feel sympathy for. Instead I go off into wild suspicions of more or less everyone else I meet.' The atmosphere between them was friendly enough for a confession. 'Do you know, I even suspected you at one point.'

'Really? Why?'

'God knows. My mind wasn't working very well. I suspected everybody. Still, even if we didn't know about Martin's bomb factory, I think I'd have to cross you off my list now. The average murderer doesn't deliberately try to get himself blown up.'

'No.' They laughed.

Then Charles sighed. 'I wish I'd got it all a bit more sorted out in my mind. I mean, it's now clear that Martin planted the bomb, and presumably planned Willy's death as well, but I still don't see exactly why.'

'He was unbalanced.'

'Yes, but ... I don't know. I suppose I've got a tidy mind, but I'd like to find some sort of method in his madness, some logical sequence.

'What about the Mary, Queen of Scots thing I suggested a few days ago?'

'That would explain the Mariello stabbing, I suppose. Willy was playing Rizzio, so there might be some identification there, but what about the bomb?'

'Darnley was blown up with gunpowder, Charles.'

'Was he? Good God.'

'Yes, I'm sure he was. At the instigation of Bothwell, as I recall.'

'Bothwell? But that's who Martin's playing in *Mary, Queen of Sots*. And ... yes ... he talked to me once about how easy it was to identify with people from history.'

'There you are then.'

'Let's work it out. He's in this show about Mary, Queen of Scots and gets obsessively involved with her life ...'

'A life surrounded by intrigue and murder.'

'Exactly. He identifies with Bothwell and—I say, it's just struck me. I bet there's a portrait of Bothwell in the Scottish National Portrait Gallery.'

The Laird nodded excitedly. 'There is. It's a miniature. And it's the only extant picture of him.'

'Yes.' Charles pieced it together slowly. 'Right. Martin identifies so completely that, in his confused mind, he becomes Bothwell and Sam Wasserman's awful play becomes reality. And that reality suits his existing obsessions about violence.'

'So Rizzio has to be stabbed. Willy Mariello doesn't exist for Martin; he actually is David Rizzio. And Martin must have said something that made Willy afraid of him, which explains what Willy told me in the Truth Game. By a stroke of luck, the stabbing looks like an accident, and so Martin is free to plan his next murder, that of Darnley ...' His racing thoughts were suddenly brought up short. 'But that's strange. If he was living the reality of the play, why did he identify me with Darnley and not the bloke who's actually playing the part?'

'Perhaps he was just getting a bit confused,' the Laird offered.

'That's a bit lame. I'm sure if the obsession's as complicated as it seems to be, there must be some logic behind it, some sort of crazy justification for his action.'

'You don't think there's anything missing in the historical Mary story?'

'I don't know. What happened to Bothwell in the end?'

'I think he died in prison. Insane.'

Charles smiled grimly. 'I'm afraid that part of the identification could be horribly apt too. No, there's something we're missing. Why does he turn on me as Darnley?'

'Because he thinks you're on his trail?'

'Doesn't really fit the historical obsession bit. Unless ...' The solution flashed into his mind. 'Good God! Anna!'

'What?'

'Anna Duncan. She's playing Mary. And Willy Mariello had an affair with her. Martin must have seen them together and killed him out of jealousy. And then me. He saw us together downstairs a couple of days ago.'

'You and Anna?'

Charles felt himself blushing, but the picture was developing too quickly for him to be discreet. 'Yes, we were having an affair, and after he saw us together, he started to identify me with Darnley. So I had to be blown up.'

'Leaving Anna to him?'

'I suppose so. But don't you see, James, this may give us a lead on what he's likely to do next.'

'Why?'

'Who's the next person to be murdered in the Mary, Queen of Scots saga?'

The Laird pondered with infuriating slowness. 'Well, I think actual murders are a bit thin on the ground after Darnley. There are plots and battles, but I don't think any more major figures were actually murdered.'

'None at all?'

'No. Well, not until Mary herself had her head cut off. There are a lot of Scots who still regard that as a murder.'

Charles sprang to his feet with a feeling of nausea in his throat. 'No! I must get to the Lawnmarket.' All he could think of was the fact that among other weapons in the Nicholson Street flat the police had found a meat cleaver.

He was so relieved to see Anna open the door of the flat that it took a moment before he realised the situation's inherent awkwardness. She looked at him and the Laird without emotion. 'Good morning.'

Urgency overcame Charles' embarrassment. 'Have you seen Martin?'

'Yes.'

'What, here?'

'Yes, he was here.'

'When?'

'He left about half an hour ago.'

'And how long had he been here?'

A hard look came into the navy blue eyes. 'Listen, if you're playing another of your elaborate games—'

'I'm not. This is serious. We've got to find Martin. He's in a dangerous state.'

'Certainly in a strange state. He was babbling on about the police being after him or something.'

'That's true.'

'Why?'

'They want him for the murder of Willy Mariello and the attempted murder of Charles Paris.'

Her mouth fell open and an expression of frozen horror came over her face. Charles realised it was the first spontaneous reaction he had ever seen from her.

'Where is he now?'

'I don't know, Charles. He came here last night in an awful state and begged to stay. I thought he was mad, so I didn't argue.'

'Just as well. I think you were next on his list.'

'What?' She started to cry with shock, and looked human and ugly. But Charles did not have time to notice. 'Have you any idea where he was going?'

'No, but he was dressed up.'

'Disguised?'

'Yes. I thought he was joking when he suggested it, but he was so fierce and insistent that I let him have the stuff.'

'What stuff?'

'A smock and a handbag of mine. And a curly dark wig I've got. And my sunglasses.'

'He was wearing all that when he left?'

'Yes.'

'Thank you.' He turned to rush away.

'Charles?' she whispered.

'Yes.'

'Do you think he really might have murdered me?'

'Yes, Anna. I do.'

As he ran down the steps from Lady Stair's Close towards Waverley Station, he knew it was a long chance, but he could not think of anywhere else to go. If Martin wanted to get out of Edinburgh, that was the quickest way. Charles had a feeling that there was a London train at two o'clock. In twenty minutes.

The cold sweaty feeling of his hangover mixed with the hot sweaty feeling of running. Ambling tourists turned bewildered faces towards the middle-aged man pelting down the road in the calm of a Sunday afternoon. James Milne was a long way behind him, doing the ungainly penguin run of a man with things in his pockets.

Charles sped down the taxi-ramp into Waverley Station and halted in the sudden cool shade, gasping to get his breath. Then he moved slowly towards Platform 1/19 where the London train would leave. It had not yet arrived.

He stalked along the railings that ran the length of the platform and peered through at the passengers, who stood waiting with their luggage. They all looked extremely ordinary. He walked on. The women were very womanly.

He stopped and looked at one back view again. The clothes were right. Red smock, blue jeans, curly hair, handbag dangling casually from one hand. It must be.

But he hesitated. There was something so feminine about the stance. And no trace of anxiety.

But it must be. Martin's chameleon-like ability to take on another personality would enable him to stand differently, to think himself so much into the part that he was a woman. Any actor could do it to a degree and a psychopath could do it completely.

Charles moved with organised stealth. He bought a platform ticket and walked through the barrier. Then he advanced slowly towards the 'woman'. People peered along the line and started to gather up their luggage. The train was coming. He quickened his pace.

He was standing just behind his quarry when the train slid protesting into the station. Even close to, the figure looked womanly. Charles waited a moment; he did not want to risk a suicide under the oncoming wheels. But as the passing windows slowed to a halt, he stepped forward. The curly head was close to his face. 'Martin,' he said firmly.

The violence of the blow on his chest took him by surprise. He had time to register the skill of the boy's make-up as he fell over backwards.

The shove winded him and it was a moment before he could pick himself up again. By that time Martin had charged the barrier and was rushing through the dazed crowd in the main station. Charles set off in gasping pursuit.

The boy was at least two hundred yards ahead when Charles emerged into the sunlight, and running up the hill which the older man had just descended. Martin was young and fit and moving with the pace of desperation. Charles was hopelessly out of condition on the steep gradient and could feel the gap between them widening.

Then he had what seemed like a stroke of luck. Martin was keeping to the right of the road as if he intended to veer off down the Mound into Princes Street where he would soon be lost in the tourist crowds. But suddenly he stopped. Charles could see the reason. James Milne was standing in his path. Martin seemed frozen for a moment, then sprang sideways, crossed the road and ran on up the steps to the Lawnmarket, retracing Charles' footsteps.

In fact, going straight back to Anna's flat.

Realisation of the girl's danger gave Charles a burst of adrenalin, and he surged forward. As he passed the Laird on the steps he heard the older man gasp something about getting the police.

Martin was spread-eagled against the door in Lawnmarket when Charles emerged from Lady Stair's Close. The boy was hammering with his fists, but Anna had not opened the door yet. No doubt she was on her way down the five flights of steps. Charles screamed out Martin's name, turning the heads of a party of Japanese in tam o'shanters.

The youth turned round as if he had been shot and froze again like a rabbit in a car's headlights, unable to make up his mind. Charles moved purposefully forward. It had to be now; he had no energy left for a further chase.

He was almost close enough to touch Martin, he could see the confusion in the young eyes, when suddenly the youth did another side-step and started running again. Charles lumbered off in pursuit, cursing. If Martin made it down to the Grassmarket, he could easily lose his exhausted hunter in the network of little streets of the Old Town.

But Martin did not do that. He did something much more worrying.

Instead of breaking for the freedom of the Grassmarket, he ran back across the road and up towards the Castle. In other words, he ran straight into a dead end. With a new cold feeling of fear, Charles hurried after him, up between the Tattoo stands on the Esplanade and into the Castle.

The fear proved justified. He found Martin standing on the ramparts at the first level, where great black guns point out over the New Town to the silver flash of the Firth of Forth. A gaping crowd of tourists watched the boy in silence as he pulled off the wig and smock and dropped them into the void.

Charles eased himself up on to the rampart and edged along it, trying not to see the tiny trees and beetle people in Princes Street Gardens below. 'Martin.'

The look that was turned on him was strangely serene. So was the voice that echoed him. 'Martin. Yes, Martin. Martin Warburton. That's who I am.' The youth wiped the lipstick from his mouth roughly with the back of his hand. 'Martin Warburton I began and Martin Warburton I will end.'

'Yes, but not yet. You've got a long time yet. A lot to enjoy. You need help, and there are people who will give you help.'

Martin's eyes narrowed. 'The police are after me.'

'I know, but they only want to help you too.' This was greeted by a snort of laughter. 'They do. Really. We all want to help. Just talk. You can talk to me.'

Martin looked at him suspiciously. Charles felt conscious of the sun, the beautiful view of Edinburgh spread out below them. A peaceful Sunday afternoon in the middle of the Festival. And a young man with thoughts of suicide. 'Don't do it, Martin. All the pressures you feel, they're not your fault. You can't help it.'

'Original Sin,' said the boy, as if it were a great joke. 'I am totally evil.'

'No.'

For a moment there was hesitation in the eyes. Charles pressed his advantage. 'Come down from there and talk. It'll all seem better if you talk about it.'

'Talk? What about the police?' Martin was wavering.

'Don't worry about the police.'

Martin took a step towards him. Their eyes were interlocked. The boy's were calm and dull; then suddenly they disengaged and looked at something over Charles' shoulder. Charles turned to see that two policemen had joined the edge of the growing crowd.

When he looked back, he saw Martin Warburton launch himself forward like a swimmer at the start of a race.

But there was no water and it was a long way down.

And Brian Cassells got another good publicity story.

CHAPTER THIRTEEN

A plague, say I, on all rods and lines, and on young
　　or old watery danglers!
And after all that you'll talk of such stuff as no harm
　　in the world about anglers!
And when all is done, all our worry and fuss, why,
　　we've never had nothing worth dishing;
So you see, Mr Walton, no good comes at last of your
　　famous book about fishing.

A RISE AT THE FATHER OF ANGLING

CHARLES WATCHED THE sun-gold surface of the burn change in seconds to dull brown and then become pockmarked with heavy drops of rain. He heard a rustle of P.V.C. behind him as Frances tried to rearrange her position at the foot of the tree to keep the maximum amount of water off her book. The rain was no less cheering than the sun.

As he knew from previous experience, if you do not like rain, there's no point in going to the West Coast of Scotland. The whole area is wet. Wet underfoot like the surface of a great sponge. Everywhere the ground is intersected with tiny streams and it is never completely silent; there is always the subtle accompaniment of running water. The wetness is not the depressing damp of soggy socks and smelly raincoats; it is stimulating like the sharp kiss of mist on the cheek. And it is very relaxing.

Charles twitched his anorak hood over his head and thought how unrelaxed he still felt. Suffering from anoraksia nervosa, his mind suggested pertly, while he tried to tell it to calm down. But it kept throwing up irrelevant puns, thoughts and ideas. He knew the symptoms. It was always like this after the run of a show. A slow process of unwinding when the brain kept working overtime and took longer than the body to relax.

The body was doing well; it appreciated the holiday. Clachenmore was a beautiful place, though it hardly seemed worth putting on the map, it was so small. Apart from a tiny cottage given the unlikely title of 'The Post Office', there was just the hotel, a solid whitewashed square with a pair of antlers over the door. Every window offered gratuitously beautiful views—up to the rich curve of the heathery hills, sideways to the woods that surrounded the burn (free fishing for residents), down over the vivid green fields to the misty gleam of Loch Fyne.

So the situation was relaxing. And being with Frances was relaxing. Arriving at a strange hotel with an ex-wife has got the naughty excitement of a dirty weekend with a non-wife, but with more security. And Frances was being very good, not talking about defining their position and not saying were they actually going to get a divorce because it wasn't easy for her being sort of half-married and half-unmarried and what chance did she have of meeting someone else well no one in particular but one did meet people, and all that. She seemed content to enjoy the current domestic idyll and not think about the future. A line from one of Hood's letters came into his mind. 'My domestic habits are very domestic indeed; like Charity I begin at home, and end there; so Faith and Hope must call upon me, if they wish to meet.'

But he did not feel relaxed. He did not mind lines of Hood flashing into his head; that was natural; it always happened after a show; but there were other thoughts that came unbidden and were less welcome. He closed his eyes and all he could see were the writhing coils of the fat grey earthworms he had dug for bait that morning. That was not good; it made him think of worms and epitaphs. What would Martin Warburton's epitaph be? He opened his eyes.

The fish seemed to have stopped biting. Earlier in the day he had a good tug on his borrowed tackle and with excitement reeled in a brown trout all of five inches long. Since his most recent experience had been of coarse fishing, he had forgotten how vigorous even tiny trout were. But since then they had stopped biting. Perhaps it was the weather. Or he was fishing in the wrong place.

Even with the rain distorting its surface, the pool where he was did not look deep enough to contain anything very large. But there were supposed to be salmon there. So said Mr Pilch from Coventry who came up to Clachenmore every summer with the family and who liked to pontificate in the lounge after dinner. 'Oh yes, you want to ask Tam the gamekeeper about that. Actually, he's not only the game-keeper, he's also the local poacher. Only been working on the estate for about five years, but he knows every pool of that burn. Good Lord, I've seen some monster salmon he's caught. They put them in the hotel deep-freeze. Mind you ...' Here he had paused to attend to his pipe, an aluminium and plastic device that looked like an important but inexplicable electronic component. He had unscrewed something and squeezed a spongeful of nicotine into the coal-bucket. 'Mind you, what you mustn't do is ask *how* Tam catches the fish. Oh no, I believe there are rules in fishing circles. But, you know, he goes through the water in these waders stalking them, and he can tell the pools they're in—don't know how he does it, mind—and he's got these snares and things, and his ripper. It's a sort of cord with a lot of treble hooks on. Well, he whips them out of the water on to the bank and then gets the Priest out— you know why it's called the Priest? It gives the fish their last rites. Vicious little device it is, short stick with a weighted end. Anyway, down this comes on the fish's head and that's another for the deep freeze. Highly illegal, but highly delicious, eh?'

However the salmon were playing hard to get. So were the trout. So, come to that, were any fresh water shrimps that might be around. Obviously the recommended bunch of worms on a large hook ledgered to the bottom was an insufficient inducement. Charles turned to Frances, and put on his schoolboy party-piece voice. 'A recitation—*The Angler's Farewell* by Thomas Hood.

"Not a trout there be in the place,
Not a Grayling or Rud worth the mention,
And although at my hook
With *attention* I look
I can ne'er see my hook with *a Tench on*!"'

Frances clapped and he bowed smugly. 'IthangyouIthangyou, and for my next trick, I was thinking of going for a walk to work off some of Mrs Parker's enormous breakfast in anticipation of her no doubt enormous lunch. Do you want to come?'

'I'm nearly at the end of this book actually and I'm quite cosy.' She looked cosy, tarpaulined in P.V.C. mac and sou'wester, crouched like a garden gnome at the foot of the tree.

'O.K. What are you reading?'

'Your *Mary, Queen of Scots*.'

'Oh Lord. That's not my book. I should have given it back. Borrowed it from someone in Edinburgh. Ha, that reminds me of Anatole France.'

'Hm?'

' "Never lend books, for no one ever returns them; the only books I have in my library are those that other people have lent me." A quote.'

'I didn't know you were given to gratuitous quotation.'

'The bloke who lent me the book would have appreciated it.'

Some Victorian spirit of Nile-source-searching prompted him to go upstream towards the spring that fed the little burn. Any hopes of finding the source before lunch were soon dashed by the stream's unwillingness to get any narrower and the steepness of the gradient down which it came. Centuries of roaring water had driven a deep cleft into the rock. Tumbled boulders enclosed dark brown pools, fed from above by broad creamy torrents or silver threads of water.

The banks were muddy and the rocks he had to climb over shone treacherously. More than once he had to reach out and grasp at tussocks of grass to stop himself from slipping.

At last he came to a part of the burn that seemed quieter than the rest. There was still the rush of water, but it was muffled by trees arching and joining overhead, which spread a green light on the scene. Here were three symmetrical round pools, neatly stepped like soup plates up a waiter's arm.

He identified the place from Mr Pilch's descriptions in the lounge after dinner. 'Some of the pools up there are incredibly deep, just worn down into the solid rock by constant water pressure. Makes you wonder whether we take sufficient notice of the potential of hydro-jet drilling, eh? Mind you, it takes a few centuries. Still, some of those pools are supposed to be twenty feet deep. Tam claims to have caught salmon up there, though I can't for the life of me imagine how they get that high. Maybe by doing those remarkable leaps you see on the tourist posters, eh?'

But Charles did not want to think about Pilch. The enclosing trees and the muffled rush of water made the place like a fairy cave. It was magical and, in a strange way, calming. Puffed by the climb, he squatted on his heels at the foot of a tree, and started to face the thoughts which regrettably showed no signs of going away.

He knew why he was restless. It was because the explanations he had formed for recent events in Edinburgh were incomplete. Now Martin Warburton was dead, that situation looked permanent. The frustration was like getting within four answers of a completed crossword and knowing from the clues that he had no hope of filling the gaps. He could put down any combination of letters that sounded reasonable, but he would not have the satisfaction of knowing he was right. And with this particular crossword, there would not be a correct solution published in the following morning's paper.

It was partly his own fault for wanting a clear-cut answer rather than the frayed ends of reality. A basic misconception, like his idea that the police were way behind on the case.

But he could not get away from the fact that the tie-up of Martin's motivations which he and the Laird had worked out was unsatisfactory. There were too many loose ends, stray facts that he had found out and still required explanations. Though the main outline was right, there were details of Martin's obsessive behaviour that were not clear.

He worked backwards. Martin's suicide demonstrated that, at least in his own mind, the boy was guilty of something. The discovery of the Nicholson Street bomb factory made it reasonable to suppose that one of the causes of his guilt was the device planted in Charles' holdall.

But what evidence was there that he was also responsible for killing Willy? Certainly in retrospect it looked likely. Martin had actually wielded the murder weapon and Rizzio was an obvious first victim in his macabre game of historical reconstruction. But if the murder was carefully planned, the actual execution was a bit random. Assuming Martin had switched the real knife for the treated one, he still had no guarantee that he would be given that one for the photo call. Willy might have been killed by another unsuspecting actor, but would that have given Martin the requisite thrill? Charles felt ignorant of how accurate a psychopath's reconstruction of events has to be for him to commit a murder; it is not a well-documented subject.

But at least he had faced the fact that he wanted to tie up the loose ends. Just for his own satisfaction. After lunch he would be organised like James Milne, sit down with a sheet of paper and make a note of all the outstanding questions of the case. Feeling happier for the decision, he set off down the hill to the hotel.

*

'Three days ago, you know, I wouldn't have believed it possible to eat one of Mrs Parker's lunches within gastronomic memory of Mrs Parker's breakfast, and certainly not with the prospect of Mrs Parker's dinner looming deliciously like an enemy missile on the horizon.'

Frances laughed as she watched him put away his plateful of cod and chips without signs of strain. 'It's the famous Scottish air. Sharpens the appetite.'

He took a long swallow from his second lunch time pint of Guinness. 'Did you finish the book?'

'Yes.'

'Good. Then you can tell me. I want some details about the Earl of Bothwell.'

'All right.' She sat expectant, her schoolmistress mind confident of its recently acquired knowledge.

'Well, we know Bothwell killed Darnley by blowing him up at Holyrood. What I want to—'

'We don't know any such thing. Holyrood's still standing. The house where Darnley was staying, the one that was blown up, was in the Kirk o'Field. And anyway, Darnley wasn't blown up; he was strangled.'

'Really.' Charles took it in slowly. 'Then what about the murder of David Rizzio? Bothwell didn't do it on his own, I know. Who was with him on the—'

'Bothwell wasn't involved in the murder of David Rizzio. Really, Charles, I thought you had a university education.'

'A long time ago. And I read English.'

'All the same. My fourth formers could do better. Rizzio was savagely murdered by Lord Darnley, Patrick Lord Ruthven (who rose from his sick bed), Andrew Ker of Fawdonside, George Douglas, um ...' Her new storehouse of information ran out.

'Really?' said Charles, even more slowly. 'Really.' Martin had read History at Derby. If he were in the grip of psychopathic identification with an historical character, surely he would at least get the facts of his obsession correct. Charles began to regret the glibness with which he had assumed that Willy's death and the bomb were automatically connected.

'Hello. Everything all right?' Mr Parker, who owned the hotel and was owned by Mrs Parker, appeared at their table with the glass of whisky that was a permanent extension of his hand.

Charles and Frances smiled. 'Yes, thank you,' he said, tapping a stomach that surely could not take many more of these enormous meals without becoming gross. 'Excellent.'

'Good, good.'

'Can I top that up for you, Mr Parker?'

'Well ... if you're having one.'

'Why not? I'll have a malt.'

'Mrs Paris?'

'No, I'll—'

'Go on.'

'All right.'

It started to rain again heavily. Long clean streaks of water dashed against the window panes. It was cosy over the whisky.

Charles proposed a toast. 'To Stella Galpin-Lord, without whom we wouldn't be here.'

'Stella Galpin-Lord,' said Mr Parker, and chuckled. 'Yes, Stella Galpin-Lord.'

'You know her well?'

'She's been here four or five times. Stella the Snatcher we nickname her.'

'Snatcher?'

'Oh, I'm sorry. Perhaps she's a friend of ...'

'No,' said Charles in a mischievous way to encourage indiscretion.

'Well, we call her the Snatcher, short for cradle-snatcher. Let's say that when she comes here it tends to be with a young man.'

'The same young man?'

'No. That's the amusing thing. Always books as Mr and Mrs Galpin-Lord, but, dear oh dear, she must think we're daft or something. I mean, I can't believe they're all called Galpin-Lord.'

'It is a fairly unusual name.

Mr Parker chuckled. 'It's not our business to pry. I mean, I don't care about people's morals and that, but I must confess Mrs Parker and I do have a bit of a giggle about the Mr and Mrs Galpin-Lords.' He realised that this sounded like a lapse of professional etiquette. 'Not of course that we make a habit of laughing at our guests.'

'No, of course not,' Charles reassured smoothly. 'But you say it's always younger men?'

'Yes, actors all of them, I think. Mutton with a taste for lamb, eh? Sorry, I shouldn't have said that.'

'Hmm. And thanks to her latest actor getting a job, here we are.'

'Yes.'

'All the more reason to toast her in gratitude. Stella Galpin-Lord.'

Mr Pilch edged over from the table where Mrs Pilch and the little Pilches were finishing their apricot crumble. 'Oh, er, Mr Paris. Tam the gamekeeper's going to take me up the burn to see if we can bag a salmon. With the right sort of fly, of course.' He winked roguishly at this. 'I wondered if you fancied coming ...?'

But Charles felt rather full of alcohol for a fishing trip. And besides, he wanted to start writing things down on bits of paper. 'No thanks. I think I'll have a rest this afternoon.'

'Perhaps there'll be another chance.' Mr Pilch edged away.

'Sure to be, Mr Paris,' whispered Mr Parker confidentially. 'I'll ask Tam to take you another day. See what you can get. Actually, when our Mrs Galpin-Lord was here last summer, she went off with Tam and they got a fifteen-pounder. Not bad.'

'And did the current Mr Galpin-Lord go with them?'

'Oh no.' Mr Parker laughed wickedly. 'I daresay he was sleeping it off. Eh?'

The rest of the afternoon seemed to lead automatically to making love, which, except for the Clachenmore Hotel's snagging brushed nylon sheets, was very nice. 'You know, murmured Frances sleepily, 'we do go very well together.'

He gave a distracted grunt of agreement.

'Do you think we could ever try again?'

Another grunt, while not completely ruling out the idea, was not quite affirmative.

'Otherwise we really ought to get divorced or something. Our position's so vague.' But she did not really sound too worried, just sleepy.

'I'll think about it,' he lied. He did not want to think about the circle of going back to Frances again and things being O.K. for a bit and then getting niggly and then him being unfaithful again and her being forgiving again and and and ... He must think about it at some stage, but right now there were more important things on his mind.

The lunch time alcohol had sharpened rather than blunted his perception and he was thinking with extraordinary clarity. The whole edifice of logic he had created had been reduced to rubble and a new structure had to be put up, using the same bricks, and some others which had previously been discarded as unsuitable.

Thinking of the two crimes as separate made a new approach possible. Blurred and apparently irrelevant facts came into sharp focus. Red herrings changed their hue and turned into lively silver fish that had to be caught.

It came back again to what Willy was doing over the few days before he died. The melodrama with Anna and subsequent events had pushed that line of enquiry out of his mind, but now it became all-important and the unexplained details that he had discovered were once more significant pieces in his jigsaw.

He slipped quietly out of the brushed nylon sheets without disturbing the sleeping Frances, then dressed and padded downstairs to the telephone in the hotel lobby.

First he got on to directory enquiries. Then he took a deep breath, picked up the phone again and dialled the operator. London could not be dialled direct, which made his forthcoming imposture more risky, but he could not think of another way. By the time he got through, the Glachenmore operator, the London operator, Wanewright the Merchant Bankers' receptionist and Lestor Wanewright's secretary had all heard the assumed Glaswegian tones of Detective-Sergeant McWhirter. If it ever came to an enquiry by the real police, there was a surfeit of witnesses to condemn Charles Paris for impersonating a police officer.

Fortunately Lestor Wanewright did not show any sign of suspicion. When the Detective-Sergeant explained that, in the aftermath of the deaths in Edinburgh, he was having to check certain people's alibis as a matter of routine, the young merchant banker readily confirmed Anna's statement. They had been sharing his flat in the Lawnmarket from Sunday 4th August when they had arrived back from Nice until Tuesday 13th August when he'd had to go back to work again. Yes, they had slept together over that period. Charles Paris felt a slight pang at the thought of Anna, but Detective-Sergeant McWhirter just thanked Mr Wanewright for his co-operation.

Charles stayed by the phone after the call, thinking. He had two independent witnesses to the fact that Willy Mariello had slept with a woman at his home during the three or four days before his death. Jean Mariello had spoken of blonde hairs on the pillow and she had no reason for making that up. And, according to Michael Vanderzee, Willy had called goodbye to someone upstairs when dragged off to rehearsal on the Monday before he died.

True, Willy's sex life was free-ranging and the woman might have been anyone. But Charles could only think of one candidate with, if not blonde, at least blonded hair, and a taste for younger men.

It was nothing definite, but he still felt guilty about Martin's death. If there was anything that invited investigation, he owed it to the boy's memory to investigate it.

With sudden clarity, Charles remembered the first time he had seen Willy Mariello, on the afternoon of his death. He saw again the tall figure striding ungraciously into the Masonic Hall. Followed a few moments later by Stella Galpin-Lord, who was sniffing. Had she been crying? The memory seemed to be dragged up from years ago, not just a fortnight. But it was very distinct. He remembered the woman's face contorted with fury in the Hate Game.

That decided him. He picked up the phone again and asked for an Edinburgh number.

At first there seemed to be a crossed line, a well-spoken middle-aged woman's voice cutting across James Milne's, but it cleared and the two men could hear each other distinctly. 'James, I've been thinking again about some aspects of the case.'

'Really. So have I.'

'It doesn't all fit, does it?'

'I think most of it does.' The Laird's voice sounded reluctant. He and Charles had worked out a solution that was intellectually satisfying and he did not want their results challenged. It was the schoolmaster in him, the academic hearing that his theory has just been superseded by a publication from another university.

'You may be right, James. But for my own peace of mind, there are one or two people I'd just like to check a few details with. So I'm coming back to Edinburgh.'

'Ah. And you're asking me to put my Dr Watson hat back on?'

'If you don't mind.'

'Delighted. You'll stay here, of course?'

'Thank you.'

'When are you arriving?'

'Don't know exactly. It'll be tomorrow some time. As you know, I'm out here at Clachenmore and getting back involves a taxi to Dunoon, ferry across the Clyde to Gourock, bus to Glasgow and God knows what else. So don't expect me till late afternoon.'

'Fine. And you'll tell me all then?'

'Exactly. Cheerio.'

Then something odd happened. Charles heard the phone put down the other end twice. There were two separate clicks.

Two separate clicks—what the hell could that mean? He was about to dismiss it as a vagary of the Scottish telephone system when a thought struck him. There were two extensions of the same telephone at Coates Gardens, one in the Laird's flat and one in the hall. Perhaps what he had taken to be a crossed line at the beginning of the call had been someone answering the downstairs telephone. And the first click was that person putting their receiver down. In other words, someone could have heard all of the conversation.

Only one woman likely to be in Coates Gardens had a middle-aged voice.

The journey to Edinburgh developed another complication when he tried to order a taxi. The only firm for miles was in Tighnabruiach and there was a funeral there the following morning which was going to appropriate every car; they could not get one to the Clachenmore Hotel until half past two in the afternoon.

There was nothing to be done about it. It just meant another morning's fishing and another of Mrs Parker's gargantuan lunches. There were worse fates.

The next morning was very, very wet. Rain fell as if God had upturned a bottomless bucket. Frances decided that she would not venture out; she curled up on the sofa in the Lounge with *Watership Down*.

'What do you think about fishing?' Charles asked, hoping Mr Parker's reply would excuse him from going out.

'Yes, not bad weather for it.'

Damn. Charles started to pull on his anorak. 'Actually,' Mr Parker continued, 'Tam was asking if I thought you'd like to go after some salmon.'

That sounded a lot more attractive than pulling worms out of damp clods in the hope of another five-inch trout. 'Really? Is he about?'

'Was earlier. There was a phone call for him. I'll see.'

Tam was found and was more than willing to conduct a guided tour of the salmon pools (no doubt in anticipation of a substantial tip). His only reservation, which Mr Parker interpreted to Charles, was that he did not approve of women being involved in fishing, and did Mrs Paris want to come? Charles set his mind at rest on that point, and then took stock of his guide.

The gamekeeper was a man of indeterminate age and impenetrable accent. His face was sucked inwards and shrivelled like perished rubber. He wore a flat cap and a once-brown overcoat with large pockets on the outside (and no doubt even larger ones on the inside).

Tam's mouth opened and uttered strange Scottish sounds which might have been asking if Charles was ready to go straight away.

'Yes,' he hazarded. 'Will I need a rod?'

Tam laughed derisively. Legal fishing methods were obviously a myth created for the tourists.

They set off, following the burn up the hill. Conversation was limited. Tam would occasionally comment on things they passed (a dead sheep, for example) and all Charles' acting skill would be required to choose the right 'Yes', 'Really?', 'Too true', 'Did they indeed?' or omnipurpose grunt. He did not have the confidence to initiate subjects himself, reacting was safer. Mr Pilch's words came back to him. 'They're a proud lot, the locals. Oh yes, you have to be careful what you say. And they have this great loyalty to their masters. In many ways, it's still an almost feudal society. Very poor though, I'm afraid. Not a lot of jobs available round here. It'll change of course when the oil comes—if it comes, which heaven forbid. You know there are plans to put up platforms just outside Loch Fyne? I hope they don't ruin the West Coast. Eh?'

None of that offered very promising conversational topics. What's it like being proud? Or living in a feudal society? Are you really very poor? What is your feeling about the proposed development of natural oil resources off the West Coast of Scotland? Somehow none of these seemed quite the right question to ask Tam, and fortunately the gamekeeper did not appear to find the silence irksome.

At last he indicated that they had reached their destination. It was the linked series of pools where Charles had been the day before. Again the trees overhead changed the note of the running stream and the heavy dripping of rain was muffled.

'Do the salmon really get up this far?'

Tam managed to communicate that they certainly did. He had got a twenty-pounder out a good half mile farther up into the hills.

'Whereabouts do they go? Do we just look for them swimming about in the pools?'

Apparently not. In these conditions they lay still just under the bank. The skill was to spot them and whip them out of the water quickly. Tam would demonstrate.

They edged slowly down the slippery rocks to the waters edge. As they drew closer, the noise of the water increased. Swollen by rain, the cataracts pounded down on the rocks below. It was easy to see how the deep cleft had been worn down into the rock over the years.

Silently and efficiently, Tam lay down on the rocks at the waterside and peered into the bubbling green depths.

'Anything?' Charles hissed and was reprimanded by a finger on Tam's lips. The gamekeeper slid crabwise along the rocks, still looking down. Then he froze for a moment and got up.

'Big one,' he whispered. Either Charles was getting used to the accent or it was clearer close to.

'Where?'

'Directly under that rock. Have a look. But be quiet and don't move suddenly.'

Charles eased himself down to a kneeling position and, with his hands gripping the slimy edge of the pool, moved his head slowly out over the water.

At that moment his left hand slipped. It saved his life. As his body lurched sideways, he saw the flash of the brass head of Tam's Priest as it came down. The blow aimed to the skull landed with agonising force on Charles' shoulder.

The shock of the attack stunned him even more than its violence. For a moment he lay there, the rocks hard under his back, his hair soaked with spray from the pounding water just below. Then he saw Tam advancing towards him with the Priest again upraised.

The gamekeeper must have thought he had knocked his victim out; he was unprepared for the kick in the stomach that Charles managed from his prone position. Tam staggered back clutching himself, reeled for a moment at the water's edge, then fell safely on to the rocks.

Charles had one aim, which was to get the hell out of the place. Winding his assailant had given him the opportunity. He scrambled manically over the slimy rocks, grabbing at tussocks and branches to heave himself up the gradient. His right arm screeched with pain like a gear lever in a broken gearbox. But he was getting away.

He turned for a moment. Tam was standing now, but Charles had the start. Then he saw something whip out and uncoil from the gamekeeper's hand. As the treble hooks bit into his leg and he felt the inexorable pull down towards the boiling cauldron below, Charles knew it was the ripper.

CHAPTER FOURTEEN

O'er all there hung a shadow and a fear;
A sense of mystery the spirit daunted,
And said, as plain as whisper in the ear,
The place is Haunted!
THE HAUNTED HOUSE

IN THE TRAIN from Glasgow to Edinburgh Charles said a little prayer of thanks, and reflected how frustrating it must be for God only to be in demand in times of danger, like a brilliant tap-dancer waiting for tap-dancing to come back into fashion. Still, God had saved his life and Charles Paris was suitably grateful.

There was no other explanation than divine intervention. The pain from his shoulder and the long furrows gouged in his left leg made the scene hard to forget. He could see the bank slipping past him as he was dragged painfully down to the water. He could feel the kick in the stomach with which Tam had immobilised him, and see the Priest again raised for a blow that was not going to miss.

And then, as Charles closed his eyes and vainly attempted to put his mental affairs in order, the threat vanished. Almost literally. The blow seemed a long time coming, so he crept one eye open. And Tam had disappeared.

The gamekeeper's foot must have slipped on the rocks and, caught off balance, he had fallen into the water. The force of the stream had swept him over the ledge of one pool and into the next, where he floated round like a giant face-cloth with a bubble of air caught in it.

Charles had tried to disengage the ripper from his leg, but the pain was too great, so he used a long stick to guide the body to the water's edge. Then, using both arms (though the right one felt as if it was being severed from his torso with a blow lamp), he had heaved the sodden mass on to the bank.

To his amazement, he found that Tam was still alive, unconscious, but with a strong heartbeat and pulse. Rediscovering a scrap of knowledge that had lain dormant since some aunt had given him a Boy Scout diary in his teens, Charles turned the body over and, after working the shoulders for a few minutes, was rewarded by a flow of water from the injured man's mouth. He then reckoned it was safe to leave Tam there; there was no danger of either death or escape. The body was propped up against a mossy bank and Charles started his painful course back to the hotel.

Mr Parker took control with instant efficiency. Suddenly Clachenmore did not seem so isolated. A doctor was summoned and a party of local forestry workers who were in the bar went off to fetch Tam.

The doctor did not comment on the story of two men slipping on the bank, Tam falling into the water and Charles getting tangled in the hooks and banging his shoulder on a rock; he just got on with the job. Removing the barbs of the hooks was the worst bit, but he was used to it. He explained that a pair of pliers was an essential part of a doctor's equipment in that area, though most of the hooks he came across tended to be lodged in the cheeks of people walking behind over-enthusiastic fly-fishermen. Treble hooks, he admitted, were trickier, but the principle was the same—push the hook through until its barb stood clear of the flesh, snip it off with the pliers, and then work the remains of the hook out. While this excruciating operation was conducted, Charles made a rash vow that he would give up fishing; he had never thought what it felt like for the fish before.

In spite of the pain they caused, the scrapes on his leg were not deep. The highest one needed a couple of stitches, but the others were just cleaned and dressed. The shoulder presented even less problem. There was nothing broken, just severe bruising. The doctor strapped it into a sort of sling and went to tend the still-unconscious Tam, who had just been brought back.

Charles was patched up in time for lunch. Frances sat opposite him, looking anxious, but respecting his promise to explain everything in detail when it was over. There was an atmosphere of shock in the dining-room. Even Mr Pilch was subdued and did not get far pontificating to his children on Stone Age relics in Argyll.

At two thirty the taxi had arrived and, against doctor's orders and Frances' advice, Charles had started the journey to Edinburgh. Which was why he was sitting in the train, thanking God and asking God if He could see fit to spare a little more protection for the confrontation to come.

Stella Galpin-Lord had recommended Clachenmore. She knew Tam. By the attempt on Charles' life, she had nailed her colours to the mast, but it was a mast that only Charles Paris could see, and she thought Charles Paris was dead. His best weapon was going to be surprise.

She did look surprised to see him when he found her at the Masonic Hall. She had just given her nightly pep-talk to the cast of *A Midsummer Night's Dream* (which now only had three more revisualised performances to run; then in the third week of the Festival *Mary, Queen of Sots* took over). After Clachenmore Charles found it strange to think in terms of dates again. He reminded himself that it was now Thursday 29th August.

'Stella. I'd like to talk.'

'Certainly. I must say, this is a surprise. I thought we'd seen the last of you when you went to Clachenmore.'

'Yes,' he said grimly.

'Didn't you like it there?'

'There were ... things I didn't like.'

They went to the pub near the Hall where they had last met. She had another of her vodka and Camparis; he had a large Bell's. The pain from his patched-up wounds made concentration difficult, but he did not intend to talk for long. Stella raised her glass. 'Well, this is an unexpected pleasure.'

'I want to talk about Willy Mariello.'

The brusque statement took her completely off her guard. She blushed under her make-up, and lowered the glass as if she were afraid she might drop it. 'Willy Mariello?' she echoed stupidly. 'But he's dead.'

'Yes. As you well know, he's dead.' She mouthed at him, unable to form words. 'And, Stella, I think his death may have something to do with what he was doing in the few days before he died.'

'It was an accident,' she croaked. 'It couldn't have been anything to do with—'

'Couldn't it? Let's just suppose for a moment it could. I have become very interested in what Willy was doing over those few days. So far all I can find out is that he did a bit of rehearsing, a bit of decorating in his house ... and he slept with a woman other than his wife.'

The blush spread to the stringy parts of her neck the make-up had missed. 'So ... what are you saying?'

'That you were that woman.'

'What if I was? Who do you think you are—the bloody Edinburgh Watch Committee? If two people are attracted to each other and want to sleep together, what bloody business is it of yours?'

'None at all. So when did this little affair start?'

'We met in a pub on the Saturday night. It was obvious he was attracted to me.' Charles wondered. He had a more likely vision of Willy, furious at Anna's rejection of him, on the lookout for anything, so long as it was female. 'And I went back to his house that night.'

'I see.'

Stella saw some meaning that Charles had not intended in his remark. 'I suppose you're going to say something about our age difference.'

'No, I'm not.' His own recent behaviour would make such comment hypocritical. Anyway, it was irrelevant. 'And the affair continued for a few more nights?'

'Yes.'

'Until the Tuesday morning when he told you to get lost.' Her eyes flashed under their lash-stretched lids. 'He did not! It was my idea. I thought it unsuitable that it should continue. I believe in love on impulse; I don't think one should be tied.'

A suitable philosophy if no one's ever tried to tie you and you have to make all the running, Charles thought. But he did not say it. 'I see. Well, thank you for telling me that. I'm sure it's something the police don't know.'

She gaped and her real age showed. 'What do you mean? Surely the police think Willy's death was an accident ...? Or, if it wasn't, that that boy Martin—'

'If it wasn't, I feel we should tell them everything we know about the few days before he died.'

'I don't think it's relevant.'

'You don't. I do. Perhaps there are other things we ought to know about the period. I mean, what *was* Willy doing?'

'Willy—he was, as you said, rehearsing and decorating. The place was full of plaster dust and paint and all kinds of rubbish. Look, Mr Paris, I'd like to know why the hell you're asking me all these questions.'

'Because, Miss Galpin-Lord, I believe that, after a quarrel with Willy Mariello, in which he probably made disparaging remarks about your looks and general appeal, you arranged for him to be killed.'

Her face crumbled until it looked of pensionable age. 'What? Murder?'

'Yes.'

'And what proof do you have of this?'

'The proof comes from the fact that when you realised I was on to you you arranged to have me murdered too. Only unfortunately Tam the gamekeeper failed in his attempt, which is why you see me here now.'

'Tam?' Her voice was very weak.

'From Clachenmore. Now, come on, you set me up to go there because you knew Tam was to hand if necessary. Don't pretend you don't know him.'

'I know who you mean, but I don't know him well.'

'Well enough to know how poor he is and what he'd be prepared to do for money.'

'But how am I supposed to have arranged this?'

'Simple. You rang him at the hotel. I know he had a call this morning.'

'Don't be ridiculous. I hardly know the man.' Now she was almost shouting.

'You've known him ever since he started working at Clachenmore.'

'I've only seen him there a couple of times.'

'Then maybe you knew him before. In his previous job. It was somewhere in the same area.'

'I didn't know him then. Not at all. I've never even been to Glenloan House.'

'Where?'

'Glenloan House.'

There was only one other person Charles had ever heard use that name, someone who once owned a house in Meadow Lane.

He moved quickly and efficiently, as if the actions he had to make were long premeditated and rehearsed.

A street lamp outside the house in Meadow Lane showed it to be dark and empty. Fortunately, there was nobody about to see him enter. He moved towards the front door, thinking to break one of the glass panels and reach round to the catch, when a sudden memory stopped him. The window catch Jean Mariello had complained about had been forgotten in the rush of her leaving, and the sash slid up easily.

Inside he was glad of the light from the street lamp, which gave a pale glow to the white room.

Relevant memories came back. Again he saw Willy sitting opposite him in the Truth Game, long brown hair greyed with plaster dust. He remembered Stella's repetition of the fact that he had been decorating; Jean Mariello's words about her husband—'He'd suddenly get sick of his surroundings and want to change it all'—'Saw himself as the great landowner in his ancestral home in front of his blazing fire. The man of property.'

It was on the left. When he looked along the wall, he could see the light catch on the slight prominence of plaster where the fireplace had been filled in. There was a central heating radiator fixed to the wall across it.

The radiator swivelled on its brackets to lie nearly flat on the floor. Behind it the plaster was more uneven, as if done in haste. Even in the pale light available, it was clear that the paint over this area was newer than in the rest of the room.

He was lucky. The pile of rubble which he had noticed when he last saw Jean Mariello was still there. He found a rusty screwdriver and started to chip away at the new plaster.

Willy had made the task easier by the slapdash way in which he had replaced the bricks. As he flaked off plaster and dug into the mortar, Charles tried to visualise the scene. Willy Mariello, the spoilt child, saw things going against him. The group had split up. His new career as an actor was not going to lead to instant stardom. His marriage was in shreds and Anna had rejected him. Bored and frustrated, he suddenly decided he was sick of his house. Where was the fireplace he had dreamed of?—replaced by bloody central heating. It would be a big job to change it. But Willy was impulsive; he did not like to go the boring correct way about things. Smash the fireplace covering first, and then see if he liked it.

But something had made him decide to fill the space in again. Charles prised away one brick, but the light did not reach the void. If only he had a torch. He began to be acutely conscious of the pain in his shoulder as he drove the screwdriver into the recalcitrant mortar. He was sweating.

He had to remove six bricks before he could see anything in the space. But as the sixth was worked out of its socket, the light flowed in and he shared the revulsion that Willy Mariello must have felt at the discovery. In spite of the discoloration of dirt and time and the decay of the fabric of the trousers and sock, what he saw had once been a human leg.

Nausea rising in his throat, he made himself confirm the initial impression. But there was no doubt. He found flesh dried down on to bone. It seemed that there was a complete body in the fireplace.

Again his movements were automatic. As he rose he realised how long he had been kneeling on the floor. The pain burned in his tattered leg. He decided to use the front door.

As he opened it, a large block of stone from the portico crashed down in front of him. It was the slab carved with the date. 1797. If he had not remembered the faulty catch and broken into the house the obvious way, it would have killed him.

CHAPTER FIFTEEN

At last he shut the ponderous tome,
With a fast and fervent clasp
He strain'd the dusky covers close,
And fixed the brazen hasp:
"Oh, God! could I so close my mind,
And clasp it with a clasp!"
THE DREAM OF EUGENE ARAM

JAMES MILNE OPENED the door of his flat. 'Ah,' he said. It was not an expression of surprise, just an acknowledgement of information received. 'Won't you come in?'

'Thank you.'

'Malt?'

'Thank you.' It was exactly as before, both sitting in their comfortable chairs with their glasses of malt whisky, surrounded by books.

'I heard you had arrived in Edinburgh from one of the Derby students.'

'Yes. I know you knew I was here.'

The Laird understood. 'You've been to Meadow Lane?'

'Yes. As you see, the slab missed me. One of your little plans that didn't work.'

'Ah well.' The man did not seem emotional, just tired. 'After that, I'm surprised you came round here on your own.'

'You mean the malt could be poisoned or you could have a gun hidden somewhere?'

'It's possible.'

'No. That's not your style. The method must be indirect, done without you present. Then you can just shut your mind to the fact that it ever happened, and go back to your books.'

'You seem to understand me very well, Charles.'

'I think I do. Various things you said. Something about envying a writer his ability to live by remote control.'

'Yes. And you said writing wasn't like that.'

'It isn't.'

The Laird chuckled, as if their old conviviality had been re-established. Then he was silent for a moment. 'Right, how much do you know?'

'Just about everything. As you see from my face and hands, I've been dismantling a wall.'

An expression of pain cut across Milne's face. 'So you've seen it?'

'Just as Willy Mariello did.'

'Yes. He came and told me on the morning before he died.'

'And did he say he was going to the police?'

'No, no, that wasn't his idea at all. He suggested that I was a wealthy man and ...'

'Blackmail. That would fit everything I've heard of Willy. And sort out his mortgage arrears. He could live off you for the rest of his life.'

'I don't know. That's what he suggested. Regular payments or ...'

'He'd go to the police.' The Laird nodded. 'And that was why you had to kill him.'

There was a slight hesitation before a muttered 'Yes.'

'Who was it, James?'

The man looked flustered and pathetic. 'No one. It was ... just someone I knew ... a ... no one ...'

'Who?'

'A boy. From the school. From Kilbruce. A pupil of mine. He was called... Lockhart.' The Laird put his words together with difficulty. 'He was a good boy. I liked him. He seemed interested in my books and ... He ... used to come round for tea or ... That was all, really. In spite of what they said, that was all.

'Then one evening he came round ... he wasn't in school uniform ... and he said he was going to run away to London, and he'd left a note at school and sent one to his parents. I said I thought it was foolish, but I couldn't stop him. And that ... I'd miss him ... Just that, nothing more.

'But when I said it, he said something ... vile ... a comment on why I'd miss him. He said ... it was just like all the others ... that I ... It wasn't true!' His hands were kneading the arms of his chair rapaciously. 'I don't know what happened then. I ... he was dead. Perhaps I strangled him, I don't know. But suddenly he was dead.

'Then I knew I had to get rid of the body. The men had just finished installing the central heating. I thought of the fireplace. There were no development plans for the area. The house wouldn't be demolished, and no one was going to revert to open fires after central heating had been put in.' (No one except an impulsive fool like Willy Mariello, Charles reflected wryly.) 'It'd never be found out while I was alive, and there was nobody to mind when I was dead. So that's what I did.'

'And everyone assumed the boy had gone to London as he said, and disappeared?'

'Yes. You keep reading of cases of kids doing that.'

There was a long pause. 'And you managed to live in the house and forget it?'

'Yes. It had been so quick. Sometimes I really thought it hadn't happened, that I'd read about it in a book or ... I didn't think about it.'

'Just as you wouldn't have thought about me if Tam had drowned me or if that piece of masonry had crushed my skull.'

'Exactly,' he said with engaging honesty. 'I've always found it difficult to believe in the reality of other people. You know, I like them, but if I don't see them, it's as if they'd never existed. Except my mother, she was real.'

His eyes glazed over and Charles pulled him roughly back on to the subject. 'Right. So we know why you had to kill Willy Mariello.'

'Yes. The dagger was just a trial run, really. I never thought it would work.

But I saw them downstairs at lunch time on Tuesday and thought that'd do until I found a better way. There was a long chance it might work.' A gleam of intellectual satisfaction came into his eye. 'And it did. The perfect remote control crime.'

'Yes,' said Charles wryly. 'And then I rather played into your hands by confiding in you as my Dr Watson.'

'You did. At least it made me fairly certain that I wasn't on your list of suspects. That is, until the middle of last week.'

'Why? What happened then?'

'You started getting evasive, which seemed odd. I felt you were holding something back. But what really scared me was when you said you were going to give the case up, because it involved someone you knew well. I thought you were on to me then.'

'Good God. That wasn't what I meant at all. I was talking about Anna. You know, I told you I was having an affair with her. Well, at that stage I was suspicious of her.'

'Oh.' The Laird sounded disappointed. 'Then I needn't have planted the bomb.'

'It was you!' Charles sat bolt upright in his chair.

'Yes. I'd been building up your suspicions of Martin Warburton to keep the heat off me anyway. But I did follow him and I actually managed to break into the Nicholson Street flat. When I saw all the bomb-making equipment I knew it might be useful. Martin seemed in such a bad state that he wouldn't be able to give a coherent account of his movements. So when I thought you were on to me, I picked up the bomb and waited my chance. Once it was planted, all I had to do was stay with you until it was discovered and you'd cease to be suspicious of me. The fact that it happened at Holyrood just added drama to the situation.'

'So the break in the connection was deliberate? You knew the thing wouldn't blow up?'

The Laird nodded smugly, pleased with his own cunning. Charles began to realise just how detached the man's intellectual processes had become from his emotional reactions. For him life was an elaborate mental game, in which passion was an intruder. The Laird expanded on his plot. 'And then of course Martin Warburton played into my hands completely. I knew he was in a confused state, but suicide was more than I could have hoped for. It made the whole thing cut and dried, a complete case with a problem and an unquestionable solution. And, from my point of view, a perfect sequence of crimes, which neither I nor anyone else need ever have thought about again.

'And if you hadn't worked it all out at Clachenmore, or even if Tam (who incidentally was my mother's gamekeeper for years and would do anything for me) had made a clean job of dispatching you, it would have worked.' Charles was again amazed by the detached way in which the man could talk to someone he had twice tried to murder. The Laird went on in the same level tone. 'By the way, what was it made you sure it was me?'

'Ah, well...' Charles was damned if he was going to admit the circuitous route by which he had reached the solution. And then suddenly his mind joined two incidents whose significance he should have seen long before. '*The Dream of Eugene Aram,*' he pronounced confidently.

'What?'

'Hood's poem. When you returned my book, I asked if you had read it and you said "No", quite vehemently. But then later you quoted from the poem ...'

The Laird supplied the words as if in a trance.

' "Much study had made him very lean

And pale and leaden-eyed." '

Charles nodded, confident in his lies. 'So that made me wonder why you wanted to divert my attention from *Eugene A ram*. I looked back at the poem and there it was—the story of a schoolmaster who committed a murder and was not found out for many years until the body was discovered. Obviously you didn't want to set my mind on that track.'

The Laird agreed tonelessly. 'I didn't think you'd noticed.'

'Ah,' said Charles with what he hoped was subtle intonation. And then he quoted from *The Dream of Eugene Aram*.

' "Then down I cast me on my face,
And first began to weep,
For I knew my secret then was one
That earth refused to keep:
Or land or sea, though he should be
Ten thousand fathoms deep.

So wills the fierce avenging Sprite,
Till blood for blood atones!
Ay, though he's buried in a cave,
And trodden down with stones,
And years have rotted off his flesh,—
The world shall see his bones!" '

'I see. And that's what made you suspicious?'

Charles had not the hypocrisy to say yes; he let the silence stand. James Milne did not seem to mind. On the contrary, he looked serene, almost pleased at the literary resolution of his case.

There was a long silence, during which he refilled their glasses. Then he sat back in his chair and took a long swallow. 'The question now is, Charles, what happens next?'

'Yes.'

'I suppose you feel bound to go to the police?' There was a hint of pleading in his tone, but Charles ignored it.

'Yes, James, I'm afraid I do. Not because I hate you or anything like that.

As I said to you once, I have a stereotyped view of murderers as wicked people I dislike. You don't fit that. I like you and I'm sorry to have to do this.

'I'm not even particularly shocked by some of your crimes. I don't know about the boy, what the rights and wrongs were, but that sounds like a moment of passion, a sudden burst of insanity that could happen to any of us given the right sort of provocation. I don't even mind that much about Willy Mariello. He was a slob whom nobody seems to have mourned. And, as for your attacks on me, they were a logical consequence of your position and my actions.

'But, James, I can't ever forgive you for the crime you didn't commit—Martin Warburton's suicide. That boy was mixed up beyond belief. But he was very talented and at a difficult time in his life. He needed help. What you did by your elaborate framing of him was to put the boy under pressures that few people completely in control of their senses could manage. I know you didn't think about him as a person; he was just a counter in your game of self-concealment. And it's because you didn't think of him as a person that I regard you as a dangerous man, who should probably be put away.'

There was another silence. James Milne did not look shattered, like a man whose life had just been ruined, but piqued, like a debater who had just lost a point. He rose with a sigh. 'Perhaps we should go to the police then.'

'I think we should.'

'I'll take a book.' He turned round to the shelves and instinctively found a leather-bound copy of Oscar Wilde's *De Profundis*. 'I dare say there'll be a lot of sitting around at the police station.'

'Yes,' said Charles, 'I dare say there will.'

CHAPTER SIXTEEN

My temples throb, my pulses boil,
I'm sick of Song, and Ode, and Ballad—
So, Thyrsis, take the Midnight Oil
And pour it on a lobster salad.
TO MINERVA—FROM THE GREEK

CHARLES SPENT a lot of time with the police over the next couple of days and did not make it back to Clachenmore. Frances joined him in Edinburgh on the Sunday. They booked into the Aberdour Guest House, where Mrs Butt patently did not think they were married.

Frances wanted to get back to London to prepare for the new school term, but Charles persuaded her to stay till the Tuesday morning so that they could attend the first night of *Mary, Queen of Sots*. His stay at the Festival would not be complete without that. He also managed to fit in a visit to Lesley Petter, who was cheerful at the prospect of leaving the Infirmary in a couple of days.

On the Monday they arrived at the Masonic Hall at seven, half an hour before the show was due to start, to find Pam Northcliffe and others energetically piling up the chairs from the back part of the hall. They were watched by an unamused group of young men in track suits.

'Pam, what's going on?'

'Oh Lord, Charles, hello. There's been the most frightful cock-up, I'm afraid. This lot say they're booked in here for badminton on Monday nights. Apparently it was only cancelled for the two weeks and they aren't going to budge.'

'Whose fault is it?'

'Brian Cassells booked it.'

'Say no more. Where is he? Surely he should be flashing his dinner jacket and sorting it out.'

'Oh, he's gone.'

'Gone?'

'Yes, he got the Civil Service job he was after, so he's gone to have a holiday in Italy before it starts.'

'Tell me, which Ministry is the job in?'

'Social Services, I think. He'll be doing pensions.'

That seemed apt. There was some justice after all. Charles could visualise a glowing career for Brian withholding money from old ladies.

'So is the performance off?'

'Oh no. The show must go on. Sam says so,' Pam announced with pride.

'Why? Is Sam directing?'

'Yes. As well as playing Rizzio and Bothwell and doing the music.'

'Where's Michael Vanderzee?'

'Ah. He had an offer to go and direct Humpe's *Gangrene* at the Almost Blue Theatre.'

'And he went?'

'Oh yes. It's a chance in a lifetime.'

'Of course.'

At that moment Sam Wasserman appeared from behind the curtains, distraught in doublet and hose. 'Pam, Pam darling, my tights have laddered.'

'Don't worry, darling, I've got a needle and thread in my bag. Oh Lord, I'd better go.'

'O.K. Good luck.' Pam bustled off, blushing. Charles decided he and Frances had time for a drink. And might need one.

They did. The audience was tiny. Brian Cassells' theory about morbid publicity being good publicity had proved incorrect and the average Edinbourgeois was too affronted by the title alone to consider seeing the show. The atmosphere in the hall was not helped by the full houselights necessary for the badminton and the pounding feet and occasional curses of the players.

But ultimately it was the play that made the evening a disaster. Sam Wasserman's leaden allegories proved no more lively onstage than they had when he described them. They were presented in the metronomic blank verse that can only be produced by a Creative Writing course and were mixed with songs that provided as much contrast as a bread-filled sandwich.

Charles tensed up when Anna came on, looking very beautiful in her Tudor costume. But when she spoke, he relaxed. There was no real pang, just the impression that she was rather theatrical. She was talented, but mannered. Two years at drama school might make her quite good.

At the interval Charles and Frances snuck out to the pub, giggling like schoolchildren. And somehow they omitted to return for the second act.

On the train back to London on the Tuesday morning Charles gave Frances an edited version of the whole case. When he came to the end, she tut-tutted. 'Charles, I can't think why you've suddenly developed this very dangerous hobby. Why can't you take up golf or bowls like most middle-aged men?'

'I don't know. It's not deliberate. It's just if I get into a situation I have to find out what happened, find out the truth, I suppose.'

'Well, you did in this case.'

'Yes. Mind you, I took my time. I think I must have barked up every tree in the park before I found one with anyone in it.'

At King's Cross Underground Station they paused for a moment, slightly embarrassed. Then Charles kissed Frances goodbye. She caught the Northern Line to Highgate and he caught the Circle Line to Bayswater.

Printed in the United Kingdom
by Lightning Source UK Ltd.
130817UK00001B/162/A

9 781903 552322